PSYCHO BEASTS

CRUEL SHIFTERVERSE BOOK THREE

JASMINE MAS

Ebook ASIN: B0B2QJ1NKV

Editing and proofreading by Lyss Em Editing

Cover artists: Damonza Book Cover Designs

Go to jasminemasbooks.com to receive news of releases and sneak peaks straight to your inbox.

1600 SW 1st Ave, Miami Fl, 33129

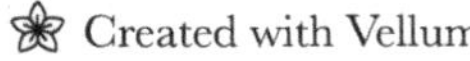

Also by Jasmine Mas

Cruel Shifterverse

Psycho Shifters

Psycho Fae

Psycho Beasts

Psycho Academy

Psycho Devils (coming soon)

To my grandma who suffered a paralyzing stroke, but kept fighting. And to my grandpa, who was her sole caretaker for the next thirty-five years of her life.

True love does exist.

CONTENT WARNING

Psycho Beasts is book 3 in the Cruel Shifterverse and must be read after Psycho Fae.

This story contains references to physical and attempted sexual assault. Please take care of yourself and avoid if this content will be disturbing.

**This is a dark RH romance, and the spice in this book is consensual, but it is intense, chaotic, and violent. Much like the characters themselves. Please be aware.

Enjoy.

CHARACTER LIST

Sadie—Probably twenty-one years old, maybe twenty-two or older (she was adopted and has always been unsure of her birthday). White hair, red eyes, gold skin. Five feet four. Scrawny build. Is half alpha saber-toothed tiger shifter and half blood fae. Has a voice inside her head called the numb that makes her an emotionless killing machine. Covered in scars but disguises them by wearing an enchanted ring. Warrior…if warriors don't have to do cardio.

Aran—Twenty-four years old. Daughter of the fae queen. Bright-blue hair, blue eyes, pale skin. Five feet ten. Disguised as a boy. Unsure what type of fae she is. Ripped her mother's heart out and ate it and, as a result, is now the rightful reigning Queen of the Fae Realm. Refuses the job and is still disguised as a boy.

Jax—One hundred and twenty years old. Black braids covered in long golden chains, gray eyes, black skin. Six feet five. Has nose, nipple, and (cough, cough) piercings. Is an alpha bear shifter. Warrior. In a relationship with Cobra. Only guy that is not a douche.

Cobra—One hundred and six years old. Black hair, emerald eyes, pale skin covered in jewels. Six feet five. Is an alpha but does not shift into a snake. Only has one form—the jewels are his shadow snakes in disguise. Warrior. In a relationship with Jax. Has many problems (not well).

Ascher—Twenty-two years old. Gold hair, amber eyes, golden skin, has horns on his head. Six feet five. Is an alpha ram shifter. Covered in flame-and-rose tattoos. Professional assassin and warrior. Has trouble with women but has been working on it.

Xerxes—Sixty years old. Long blond hair, purple eyes, olive skin, always carries two blades. Six feet five. Is an omega and shifts into a kitten. Former professional assassin of the now-dead fae queen. Struggles with identity issues.

Lucinda—Sixteen years old. Sadie's younger sister. White hair, red eyes, gold skin. Five feet three. Has a curvier build then her sister. Has not been tested—powers unknown.

Jess—Eighteen years old. Jax's adopted sister. Black-and-green hair, green eyes, copper skin. Five feet eight. Has not been tested—powers unknown.

Jala—Fourteen years old. Jax's adopted sister. Pink eyes, pink hair, and black skin. Five feet seven. Has not been tested—powers unknown.

Jinx—Twelve years old. Jax's adopted sister. Black hair, black eyes, super-pale skin. Five feet. Has not gotten tested—powers unknown. Smarter than everyone else, and she knows it. Also terrifying.

INTO THE STARS

INTRODUCTION

All myths are rooted in some truth.

This series is about different planets connected by black holes.

Aka, realms attached by portals with inhabitants you've heard of in myths and dismissed as fairy tales.

There are politics, deceptions, and secrets on the macro scale. And they vary from realm to realm.

In the human realm, the inhabitants learn they live in an anarchic system, that there is no supreme authority over different countries.

They're wrong.

The High Court secretly reigns sovereign over *all* the worlds. "Realm-Wide Peace" is their motto.

Monsters enforce this peace. A next-to-impossible task because wealth corrupts, but power destroys.

And among the hundreds of planets with sentient life, a few special individuals possess power on the nuclear level—more energy in their cells than an atomic bomb.

The truth: Most individuals go their entire lives without

knowing or caring about the other realms or the creatures within them. They live in bliss.

In this series, ignorance isn't an option for our main characters.

Through birthright or circumstances, they're players in the macrolevel game.

Now all they must do is survive.

GODS AND MONSTERS

There once was a child, innocent and pure,
Beaming with truth, but they called her liar,
There once was a world, cruel and desolate,
Broken from cold, but they blamed the fire.

There were once two gods, bold and bright,
Who snuck from the forgery late one night,
And into the realm they found their way,
And those they touched were forced to pay.

Don't cry at night for the broken few,
Whom the gods hurt and made anew,
Do cry at night for the happy most,
Who've never met their godly host,
Its peace and comfort the ultimate jest,
The sun burns north, the moon kills west,
For it's the tortured who inherit the sky,
With gaping wounds, they learn to fly.

ARAN
PROLOGUE

I SAT in the back row of the supercar. Sadie's younger sister, Lucinda, was next to me, squished against my side.

Jax sat in the middle row with his arms tucked around his three sisters, while Cobra, Ascher, and Xerxes sat in the first row.

Even though it was night, our driver wore a black suit and dark sunglasses. He had an enchanted wire glowing in his ear, and every so often, he whispered into it.

The car was long and sleek, with a low roof. All the men, including myself, were hunched over with our necks contorted to the side.

I didn't mind the discomfort.

I welcomed the pain.

Outside, glowing neon skyscrapers stabbed through heavy clouds and extended endlessly into the dark night sky.

In another life, under different circumstances, I would have marveled at the massive metal structures. They were like nothing I'd ever seen.

Nothing I could have imagined.

What my tutors had taught me about the beast realm

didn't hold a candle to the reality of the glimmering world, the sheer awe-inspiring heights of the glowing glass-and-steel buildings, and the sleek lines of the supercars. An enchanted engine purred softly beneath me as we sped impossibly fast through the new realm.

But I couldn't make myself care about the engineering marvels.

All I knew was pain.

Rain poured in a dark haze of depression. Droplets streaked across the window, as if the weather mimicked my turbulent thoughts.

I was beyond all transient feelings. Sadness, heartbreak, and melancholy were delightful compared to the ache in my soul.

Because deep down, in the marrow of my bones, I *hurt.* Because under the dual suns of the fae realm, I'd discovered that something horrible lived inside me.

A monster crawled beneath my flesh, begging to be let free.

Even now, I could feel it. Sense it. Rattling against the steel cage that I'd trapped it within.

It wanted to kill. To maim. To hurt.

My back burned unbearably, and my sternum ached like someone had punched me. I scratched at my shoulders and imagined nails stabbing through my skin.

The memory of what I'd done crushed me against the buttery leather of my seat.

Chills shook me, and my vision blurred.

The skyscrapers distorted into something different: beasts. Large, glowing creatures growled down at me from high above.

They chased our car in a haze of neon vitriol.

I scratched harder at my back.

Red flakes were still crusted beneath my fingernails, and they made the monsters outside the window so much worse.

I hated being dirty.

Ever since I was a girl, I preferred to be clean. If there was no dirt on my skin, no mess in my room, then the constant buzz of anxiety couldn't overwhelm me.

Now I was filthy.

But it didn't really matter anyway.

Nothing did.

My nails scraped with increased fervor.

"Are you okay?" Lucinda asked softly, her brow furrowed with concern.

I gave her my practiced court smile and pumped my voice with sunshine and rainbows. "I'm fine."

My face hurt from the weight of pretending.

I'd learned how to appear happy, long before I'd learned how to *actually* be happy.

I gave Lucinda the smile I gave the elite fae when they told me I was a powerless scum. When they asked my mother how much it cost to breed me. When my mother set me on fire for the billionth time.

The fake smile that had fallen from my face when the woman who'd birthed me had done the unthinkable.

What had happened was too fucked up to process, but I'd somehow relived it a thousand times in two days.

Blue flames.

Everywhere.

Writhing facedown on the marble palace floor as my mother ordered the guards to hold me there.

This part was normal. Expected. It was practically our routine. They held me down while she set me on fire, and I screamed.

What came next was anything but.

Mother's voice dripped with the condescension she only reserved for me. "You dirty little whore. You really think I'd just let you sully our name one more time? After you ran away like a coward?"

Gone was the ruthless fae queen.

In her place was a terrifying creature—an angry mother.

A woman who had everything to lose and nothing to gain. Who'd been forged into a deadly weapon in the five centuries she'd ruled over the fae realm from the seat of death.

She was the longest ruler in fae history.

There was always someone younger, brighter, more powerful, ready to usurp a monarch.

Except they couldn't best her.

She didn't maintain her position through luck or sheer power.

No.

Every single move Mother made was calculated to keep maximum control over her massive kingdom, including her daughter.

With hushed whispers and stolen glances, they called her the mad queen.

She liked the name.

The worst part was she wasn't wrong about me. I had run from the realm, and I had gone to the sex clinic, knowing "purity" was prized above all else in the realm.

I hadn't even lost my virginity, and still the half warriors had dragged me to her.

Back to my reckoning.

A shiver racked my frame and brought me back to the present.

What would have happened if I'd never gone? Would I

have been angry enough to do the unthinkable? Would she still be alive?

I fought the urge to slam my forehead against the glass of the car. Bash it until blood dripped down my face. Until a shard speared through my skull and put me out of my misery.

"Coward," Mother whispered.

She's dead, I reminded myself, for the millionth time.

If only she'd stay there.

The words from that fateful night pounded into my psyche.

Mother laughed, a harsh sound, like glass shattering across stone. "I gave you what I've never given anyone else. I forgave you. Your little stint in the shifter realm—I blamed it on teenage hormones."

She'd burned me alive with her flames every night since I'd returned to the fae realm.

But Mother had never paused our little sessions for a monologue before. A guard had never had to hold me down after the initial burn; I'd always collapsed onto the ground and taken her punishment silently.

Such a gift she possessed, burning a person alive without leaving a single mark upon their flesh. No one ever knew what I had endured.

It had always been that way.

It was our routine.

The guard's harsh grip across my shoulders had been a reminder I was in uncharted territory.

I begged softly, "Please, Mother."

"Don't call me that."

I'd pushed her too far. With one trip to the clinic, she'd been dangerously close to losing something for the first time in five centuries. Sure, it was *my* virginity. But "purity" was a way of life among the elite fae. Or whatever other bullshit they called it. I was my mother's pawn to form a political alliance of her choosing.

If I wasn't pure, then I was nothing.

"Hold her tighter," she'd ordered the guards as her voice cracked like a whip.

"Please, nothing happened. I'm still a virgin." I tried desperately to reason with her.

"No," she said softly with the finality of death. "All you are is a disgrace."

Then she'd begun.

"You don't look fine," Lucinda said softly, and I turned away from the rain-streaked window, letting the memory die inside me.

For a long moment, we stared at each other.

Lucinda's white hair, red eyes, and golden skin were just like Sadie's. But while Sadie was lean with high cheekbones and sharp features, Lucinda was curvy and soft.

They were so similar, but so different at the same time.

I didn't even pretend to smile, just stared at her blankly as my back burned and the car traveled impossibly fast. The dark world outside glowed.

Eventually, Lucinda shrugged and looked away.

I kept scratching, clawing at my back, like ripping the flesh from my bones would somehow make it all better.

The neon beasts outside the window roared and contorted. Steel beams transformed into jagged teeth as they snapped at my soul.

I shoved my cheek against the cool glass of the car's window.

My too-clammy skin was desperate for a reprieve.

It wasn't enough.

I pressed my left eye forward until the world

blurred around me, and it took everything inside me not to slam my head down and bludgeon myself to death.

Mother's voice was sharp and cold. *"Coward."*

"Uh, I don't think she, I mean he, is okay," Lucinda whispered to Sadie with concern.

At least I was disguised as a boy, my masculine glamour a small comfort.

"Hmm, what?" Sadie's voice was rough and scratchy, a sharp contrast to Lucinda's.

It highlighted the abuse she'd suffered.

My stomach hurt for my best friend. There was too much tragedy in the world. It seemed wrong that we'd both suffered so much.

Lucinda whispered to her sister, "I have to tell you something."

Sadie whipped her head down, concern shining brightly in her eyes. Fear contorted her face. "What is it?"

Lucinda opened her mouth, then closed it as she studied her sister's worried face.

There was a long pause.

"I think Aran's having a mental breakdown."

Sadie's shoulders slumped with relief. She hadn't picked up on the fact that her sister had lied.

It was obvious from Lucinda's posture, the catch in her voice, and the way her eyes shifted when she spoke. The sixteen-year-old slumped lower, burdened by something it scared her to share.

I said nothing.

Who was I to pry into others' secrets? When my own were killing me.

Sadie shook her head and wrapped her arms around her little sister. "It's rude to point out when someone's having a mental breakdown. We all have them." She looked over at me.

Sadie's ruby eyes were full of concern as she mouthed, "It will be okay. You saved us all."

It wouldn't be okay.

Because I'd eaten my mother's beating heart.

Yes I, Arabella Egan, the crown princess of the fae monarchy, had ripped my mother's beating heart out of her cold chest and eaten it.

Consumed it.

Consumed her.

Raw, beating, bloody heart. In my mouth. Down my throat. The only way to kill a fae monarch.

The only way to ascend to the seat of death—hundreds of fae skulls covered in gold foil. The remains of a lost race of blood fae, people who had rebelled against the monarchy's oppression and lost.

In my peripheral vision, Sadie whispered something to Lucinda. From what had happened in the arena sands, the race wasn't lost anymore.

Sadie was a blood fae. A race so rare and ancient that they were more myth than real, which meant Lucinda was most likely one too.

Their ancestors were the skulls that made up the seat of death. Slaughtered by a power-hungry monarch.

I was now that monarch.

My vision kaleidoscoped until the car spun around me, and my head floated into a different dimension.

I was now the queen of a realm I loathed.

Ruler.

Obligated to the people.

The powerless princess who'd had no predilection for a

fae element. My back hurt unmercifully, and I wanted to crawl out of my skin.

I was more comfortable masquerading as a boy. It was the only time people didn't ask to breed me, didn't look at me like I was an object.

Royalty was intense in the fae realm.

They revered rulers like gods.

Since it was extremely rare for an immortal fae to give birth. My status as the first fae princess in eons was no exception. I was an object of veneration: more than a fae, but less than a person.

And yet I'd never developed a predilection for a fae element. In all recorded history, every fae had shown signs of their abilities as a young child.

There were no exceptions.

I was a dud.

Instead, I housed a monster.

Sun god, Sadie was an alpha shifter, and even she was part blood fae. She was more fae than I was.

Yet I was supposed to rule on the throne of death, for all my immortality? I'd be slaughtered by a challenger immediately.

Brutally.

I should have just turned myself over and let them end me. But I was a coward, and I'd fled, too afraid to accept the escape of death.

The worst part about everything that had transpired was I didn't regret it. If I could turn back time, I would do it again.

Did it make me a bad person, that I wasn't mad about destroying my mother's immortal life by consuming her beating heart like a savage animal? Of course it did.

I smushed my face harder against the window.

The worst part wasn't my lack of regret.

It wasn't the why.

It was the how.

It was the steel cage that slammed against my soul and the monster that bellowed to be released.

When Sadie had knelt in front of Lothaire and infected my mother with her blood, the icy darkness inside my soul had become an inferno of malice.

It had overwhelmed me until my vision had become tinged with darkness and the entire world had been dipped in sepia tones: dark yellow, burnt orange, blood red.

The colors of rage.

The colors of my monster.

Even as I gnawed on my lower lip and pressed my face against the cool glass, I could taste my mother's anguish, her gore still on my lips.

I liked it now.

I'd liked it then.

Under the scorching suns, the darkness in my soul had swelled, and for the first time in my life, I'd willingly let my monster out of its cage.

My clean, neatly trimmed fingernails had elongated into razor-sharp claws. A sheen of ice had formed around them and hardened into serrated edges.

I didn't know how I knew, but there was certainty in my bones that there was nothing sharper in the universe.

Without hesitation, I'd stabbed through my mother's back and ripped out her beating heart.

As I'd consumed her, a swell of satisfaction had burned through my veins.

Nothing had ever felt so *right.*

Like extinguishing her darkness was the best thing I'd ever done.

Euphoria.

For a moment, a male had spoken like he was standing behind me. "I approve."

His praise had been a shot of euphoria straight into my blackened soul. But when I'd turned around, no one was there. I'd had to swallow the urge to laugh from the sheer bliss of it all.

I'd been hallucinating.

Ironically, the situation was heinous for so many reasons.

One of them being that no fae had claws. Ever.

But I did.

Until this moment, I'd never thought about my lack of a father. Who or what he was hadn't mattered. Some fae male who'd had the terrible judgment of procreating with my mother.

All I'd known was her abuse. She'd provided enough of a parental experience for me to know that I didn't need another one.

Now I wondered just what the hell he was. What was I?

My back burned unbearably.

As I contorted and dug my nails across my skin, a part of me hoped the claws would erupt again and that I would score my flesh.

I couldn't be queen. I fucking refused.

A wet, sticky substance trickled across my fingers, and I looked down at my hand. I'd scratched so hard with my blunted nails that blood dripped off them.

My vision blurred.

Suddenly, my mother's heart was in my mouth, and a million fae fell to their knees.

The echo of fae prostrating themselves before me would haunt my nightmares for the rest of my life.

They bowed to me because, under fae law, I was their ruler.

The seat of death was my throne to defend.

The longer I stared at my bloody hand, the more the neon steel beasts outside growled. The more my monster rattled against its cage.

Rain slashed against the window as the wind shrieked.

For the first time in my life, I passed out.

CHAPTER 1
SADIE
RAINY STREETS

I CARRIED Aran's limp body down the abandoned side street. Rain slammed against us and the wind howled as I struggled to carry her.

We'd been told to follow our driver down the alley.

The main streets were full of shifters carrying dark umbrellas and running into buildings, but the alley was abandoned.

I wished I had a coat to protect myself. Compared to the warm temperatures in the fae realm, the rain was cold and biting. A powerful gust of wind tunneled between the skyscrapers and pushed me backward.

"Let me carry her," Cobra growled at me for the fifth time and postured like he was going to take Aran from me.

"Stay the fuck away," I snapped as I adjusted her clammy body in my arms.

I was too sleep-deprived and emotionally distraught to deal with his energy right now.

Aran was built lean but was still half a foot taller than me, and it wasn't easy carrying her, but she was *my* best friend. She'd want me to be the one carrying her.

No one else.

Cobra's eyes flickered to snake eyes, and the jewels embedded in his skin writhed. They flashed between gems and shadow snakes.

Now that he wasn't wearing the enchanted collar, pure power emanated from him.

I was confused how I'd ever thought he was something other than his beast form. Cobra screamed danger.

My shadow snake zipped across my back and sent me images of love and happiness.

I glared at Cobra and didn't let his snake distract me. I was onto him and his games.

"She won't let me help her," Cobra said to Jax, who was occupied spreading his arms out wide to shield his three sisters from the rain.

Jax rolled his eyes.

"You're whining like a baby," Jinx said sharply before Jax could say anything.

Cobra glared down at her. "How old are you?"

Jinx's dark eyes flashed with annoyance as she sneered at Cobra, "I'll have you know, I'm already twelve years old." Her ire was highly amusing because she was not only Jax's youngest sister, but she was also barely five feet tall.

Cobra was a giant compared to her.

With her small stature, pale skin, dark eyes, and midnight-black hair, Jinx looked like a little girl from a horror movie—right at home among rainy streets and towering steel buildings.

Cobra laughed. "I'm over a hundred. You're actually a child, so *you* grow up."

"The fact that you're telling me to grow up is embarrassing for you." Jinx huddled against Jax's side as a sharp gust of wind slammed against us.

Jax had to grab onto her shirt to stop the wind from pushing her slight frame backward.

"I'm on her side," Ascher said as he walked beside me, scanning for threats like he was my personal bodyguard. He looked the part, tattoos covering every exposed inch of his body besides his face and onyx horns jutting off his golden head.

"Same," Xerxes said.

His long blond hair was plastered against his body as he stood in front of Lucinda. He also used his body to protect her from the worst of the rain, and I was grateful that he was helping my little sister.

Our driver walked ahead of us and looked back every few seconds. He didn't even flinch at the torrential downpour and still wore sunglasses at night like a complete psychopath.

I could practically feel the judgment radiating off him.

Not cute.

Also, what kind of professional Mafia driver, who was allegedly bringing us to the don that ran the city, didn't carry around a black umbrella?

I'd seen some bootleg human movies about gangs back in the shifter realm.

He was either shit at his job or a fraud, because they always had umbrellas. It added to the scary gang energy.

Everyone knew that.

Another gust tunneled through the buildings, and I tensed my thighs to steady us.

Would it be wrong to throw Aran's limp body at the driver if he turned out to be a bad guy? Knowing Aran, she'd be honored to act as a battering ram.

I jostled my arms back and forth and tried blowing on

her face. "Not the time for beauty sleep. Just so you know, right now, you're a royal pain in my ass."

Aran mumbled incoherently, but didn't wake.

She was disguised as a boy again, but I didn't care what features she wore. No matter what, she was Aran.

My bestie.

Cobra narrowed his snake eyes and shifted forward like he was about to rip her from my hands.

My arm cramped, and I tensed my core as I tried to radiate "I'm a competent woman" instead of grimacing like I was constipated.

Once again, I really needed to hit the gym and lift. Muscles would really come in handy in times like this.

Aran mumbled some nonsense about blood, but didn't wake.

Great, my best friend was having a nightmare about me, just another thing to add to the therapy list.

I stumbled, and Ascher narrowed his eyes at me like he could tell I was struggling to carry her.

"There was a rock," I mumbled.

Ascher raised a golden eyebrow and pointedly looked down at the smooth, paved sidewalk.

"Wake up. You're embarrassing me," I growled into Aran's ear as another gust of stiff wind hit us, and I shivered.

Don't ask me how I grew up in the negative freezing temperatures of the shifter realm, but a chilly breeze almost had me on my knees.

At that frigid moment, I really missed the two hot suns of the fae realm. Even though everyone had awkwardly tried to murder us, the climate was unbeatable.

I would definitely go back on a vacation.

Hopefully, they would forget about Aran eating the forbidden snack and me throwing my blood around like a parasite.

On second thought, maybe I'd vacation somewhere else.

"We're here," our driver said in a gruff voice. He had zero facial expressions, and his entire body stood unnaturally still in the rain.

It was freaky.

Was the driver gesturing to a creepy black door on the side of a random building that looked like someone might be murdered inside it? Yes.

Was I freezing from the rain and would rather fight off a murderer than stand in the cold for another second? Also yes.

At least now I could shift back into a saber-toothed tiger if the time called for it. Also, I could cut myself and throw my blood around and infect people.

What could I say? Power gave a girl confidence.

"Thank the sun god," I said with relief and dropped my load as I walked through the door.

Aran sputtered on the black welcome mat and looked around as she came back to consciousness. "Did you just drop me? Also, why does this mat say, 'Hell is paved with the bones of the disloyal'?"

I rolled my eyes. "First, I just carried your dramatic ass through the rain. A little gratitude would be nice. Second, because we're being escorted into a creepy Mafia lair, in a creepy realm, by a creepy man in sunglasses."

"Excuse me?" Sunglasses Man's eyebrow twitched.

"Grow up," I snapped back at him. "You know you're creepy."

My arms burned from carrying Aran's muscular body,

and I couldn't tell if my thighs were trembling from the cold or exhaustion. Sister was not light. Something I was highly jealous of.

Sunglasses Man gaped at me like he'd never been told he was creepy before, which I *highly* doubted.

Now that we weren't in the rain, his burned scent itched at my nose.

He was a beta.

Jess, Jax's oldest sister, wrung out her sopping-wet long black hair that was streaked with electric-green highlights. They matched the bright green of her eyes. She smiled up at our driver. "Sorry, sir, but we were all thinking it."

Jinx shivered uncontrollably, and Jax rubbed his hands along her arms to help warm her up. Poor thing looked like a drowned rat.

Jinx rolled her dark eyes at the driver and said, "W-We were also thinking that you have p-p-p-poor circulation, likely caused by a lifetime of fighting. You should get that checked out by a doctor."

"What?" Lucinda asked, her white-blonde hair plastered against her gold face. She'd said what we all were thinking.

All eight of us turned to stare at Jinx in confusion.

Once again, Jinx sighed heavily, like it was painful dealing with dumb people. "His fingers are unnaturally white and show poor circulation. Also, he has a slight tweak in his gate. Likely his kneecap has been broken repeatedly. The circulation issue is probably causing complications in his joints. Anyone can see that."

There was an awkward silence as everyone stared at Sunglasses Man's unnaturally white knuckles and his slightly bent knee.

Jax shook his head. "Jinx, we've talked about this."

"Amazing observation." Xerxes smiled down at Jinx

with a warmth that I'd yet to see from the omega. "I've trained soldiers for decades, and it's rare to find a person so naturally observant."

Jinx blushed and hid behind Jax.

"She still needs to grow up," Cobra said under his breath.

"Are you threatening my sister?" Jala's bubblegum-pink eyes flashed with anger, and she narrowed them with an attitude only a fourteen-year-old girl could muster. Her sweet disposition had completely disappeared.

Jess put her hand on Jala's arm. "What have we talked about? Breathe through the rage."

Ascher rolled his eyes. "Glad Cobra's antagonizing young girls now."

I couldn't help myself. "Oh, so you think you have the moral high ground now that we've left the realm that your betraying ass got us almost *murdered* in?"

Ascher had the decency to look chagrined. A soft red blush tinted his golden cheeks as he raked his hand over his horn roughly. "That's not what I meant."

Aran randomly said, "I think I have this new thing where I pass out at the sight of blood."

"Probably because you're a cannibal," Jinx replied.

Aran's jaw dropped, and her pale face turned an unhealthy shade of green. She made an awful choking noise.

The noise Aran made triggered my gag reflex.

I puked a little into my mouth.

"Ew, did you just puke? You know I'm a sympathetic puker," Lucinda said mid-retch.

Jax alpha-barked, "Everyone, silence!"

You could hear a pin drop.

I made one last gagging noise, and Jax looked down at me with exasperation. I shrugged.

My alpha form was a massive cat. What did he expect?

Jax turned his large body and addressed the creepy Sunglasses Man, who we now all knew suffered from poor circulation. "Are you taking us to the don or not? We're all hungry and tired and need to bathe after the rain."

For a moment, Sunglasses Man gaped at us like we were mythical creatures he'd never seen before.

To be fair, we were a sight.

Aran was pale, with bright-blue hair and matching turquoise eyes, and I had red eyes, pure-white hair, and deep-golden skin.

Cobra had dark hair, green eyes, and jewels embedded all over his pale flesh; Ascher was tattooed, golden, and horned; Jax was massive, had dark skin and striking gray eyes, and was covered in piercings and golden chains; Xerxes had olive skin and blond hair down to his butt, and his harsh purple eyes were intimidating, but still made him look like a pretty prince.

Plus, we had four teenage girls with us.

Lucinda looked like a curvier and prettier mini me. Jess had green eyes, copper-toned skin, and electric-green streaks through her black hair; Jala had pink eyes and bubblegum-pink hair that complemented her dark skin; Jinx looked like a small menace of pale darkness.

Besides Lucinda and I, no one looked remotely similar. We gave off big ragtag energy.

Add on to that the fact that we bickered like old ladies playing bingo, and I'm sure Sunglasses Man was very confused.

Still, my heart was full and heavy in my chest.

Yes, it was still slightly full of acid reflux, but it was

mostly full of love because we were reunited with our sisters and still all together.

For the first time in a long time, the painful loneliness of missing my family didn't weigh me down.

Sunglasses Man cleared his throat, like he remembered he had a job to do, and marched down the long hall.

He said nothing, just assumed we would all follow him.

Of course, because why not? Across the walls in big red letters read, *Hell is paved with the bones of the disloyal.*

Someone had even made the letters look like they dripped blood.

Very vibey.

"I'm gonna pass out again," Aran whispered to me as we walked down the hall.

"No, you're not."

"Seriously." Aran turned a sickly pale shade as she stared at the wall.

"You're the weight of a small elephant. If you collapse, I'm not carrying you."

"Please," she scoffed. "You're just jealous of my muscles."

She paused to flex her impressively striated biceps and quad. When she went to lift her wet shirt to show off her abdominal lines, I slapped her hands away.

"It's probably just the enchantment," I grumbled with envy.

"Enchantment can't glamour what wasn't already there. We both know these muscles are all mine." Aran smirked, but her smile fell as she glanced at the bloody words on the wall.

I took some deep breaths and reminded myself that it was not rational to be offended by the fact that my best friend passed out at the sight of blood, just because I had newfound blood powers.

The song of the hunt—which would always be the numb to me—had been revealed to be so much more and less than it was.

Relief lightened my chest.

The half warriors had said they could also hear it during battle, which meant I wasn't going crazy and I wasn't that special.

It was normal.

There was some mundane, half-breed explanation for the numb.

For the first time in a long time, I wasn't drowning in circumstances I didn't understand.

The big picture didn't seem as complex.

It was all just chance and circumstances.

I was going to be fine.

"Should we be worried?" Lucinda asked as she grimaced at the wall.

I thought about it for a moment and shook my head. "We've literally survived the evil fae queen. How bad could the Mafia be? Plus, we've got Aran."

The way my already pale best friend went white as a ghost let me know that we very much did *not* have Aran. She was stuck somewhere in the past and clearly needed a long nap and a bubble bath.

Sunglasses Man gestured for us to walk through another door.

"Everyone, stay behind me," Cobra said to the group.

Jax scoffed and pushed past him, and everyone followed.

Cobra entered the room last, and his snake eyes flickered. I could practically see steam coming from his ears.

I couldn't swallow down the manic giggle that bubbled up my throat. He was just so *unwell*. It was amusing.

Abruptly, Jax stopped walking, and I peered over his shoulder.

Nope, I took it back.

We were screwed.

CHAPTER 2

SADIE

MEETING THE DON

Sure, the fae realm had been less than ideal: evil queen, gladiator matches, millions of bloodthirsty fae screaming "die, cunt," and the sour reek of the patriarchy.

However, surviving the fae realm might have given me a tad bit of false confidence.

I was instantly humbled.

The room was dimly lit with about a dozen men seated against the far wall. All of them wore business suits and sunglasses.

Cigarettes and cigars hung from their lips and created a hazy cloud of smoke in the small room.

A distinct burnt scent wafted from them. Betas.

But the most disturbing element was how each beta held a massive machine gun. They glowed blue with enchantment and were bigger and fancier than any weapon I'd ever seen.

At least a dozen red dots were trained on all of us.

Immortal alphas could only die two ways: having all their blood drained from their body and being decapitated, or being shot with an enchanted bullet.

Slowly, I shifted in front of Lucinda.

Jax whispered, “Get behind me.” Jess, Jala, and Jinx slowly moved so his large frame blocked them.

There was a soft clack as a pair of expensive dress shoes walked out from the dark shadow in the room’s corner.

A deep voice asked slowly, “Is it true? My long-lost son has returned?” He enunciated each word oddly, and they blended together, as if he was overcompensating for a lisp.

My jaw dropped as he stepped forward into the dim light.

Gasps sounded.

He could have been Cobra’s twin.

Familiar emerald eyes gleamed with menace.

The only differences were his black hair hung long, his pale skin wasn’t embedded with diamonds, “Loyalty” sprawled across the front of his neck in massive, tattooed letters, and a frosty scent didn’t waft off him.

He smelled like oil and rubber. A musky, intense scent that made his presence impossible to miss.

The man’s suit was immaculate, and his crystal accessories practically screamed wealth.

A massive white snake draped casually over his wide shoulders.

The snake was so large that its tail rested on the ground, and its head raised high in the air. It towered above its owner’s six-foot-five frame.

Still, he had the same sinful lips, high cheekbones, and chiseled jaw. Same gorgeous complexion that seemed too perfect to be real.

But there was no doubt this was Cobra’s father.

The don of the city.

Cobra stood eerily still as he stared across the room at his father, but his face gave away zero emotions.

My gut told me this would not be a joyful reunion.

It would be a miracle if we walked out alive.

The don took a long drag of his cigarette and blew smoke into the air. His emerald eyes were cold and sharp, the white snake hissing on his neck.

He was a predator.

The don sucked in smoke casually. "Prove to me you're my son right now, or my men will open fire. Then, while you're incapacitated, they'll decapitate each and every one of you. We'll hang your bodies from the streetlights."

His gorgeous features were a stony mask of indifference.

He meant it.

Immediately, Cobra's diamonds transformed into shadow snakes and streamed off his body.

They piled atop one another until they formed a massive snake as black as his father's was white.

The don said nothing, just took another long drag of his cigarette as his white snake slithered off his shoulders.

It approached Cobra's black snake until they were face-to-face.

Slowly, it opened its massive jaw, flashed opal fangs, and gave a harsh warning hiss.

Cobra's snake replied in kind.

I gulped and tried desperately to remember if snakes bonded with their young.

From the current energy in the room, my best guess was that no, they did not. The don's snake, which apparently *was* the don, was giving off extremely aggressive vibes.

Finally, after what felt like an eternity of the two snakes hissing at each other, the don nodded.

The white snake slithered back over his wide shoulders, and the don lounged back into a green velvet chair.

He flicked his long black hair over his shoulder casually, but everything about him screamed violence.

Since we were all standing and he was sitting, we should have been in the position of power.

We weren't.

He looked down at all of us, even while seated.

Sweat dripped down my side even though I was still drenched in chilly rain.

The don slowly blew out a cloud of cigarette smoke. "So you're my son."

It wasn't a question.

Cobra's enormous snake broke apart into thousands of shadow snakes, and they streamed back onto his flesh. With a gleam, they flashed back into diamonds and crystals across his skin. "Appears so."

The don ran his eyes slowly over Cobra. "Interesting that your snakes are so…fractured. Even stranger that you wear them on your skin as jewels."

Cobra said nothing.

The don said nothing.

A dozen machine guns still pointed at us, and the men in sunglasses, holding the weapons, didn't move a muscle.

Hazy smoke rolled around us.

Somehow, even though no one spoke, the tension in the room escalated tenfold. A live wire of cackling energy.

More sweat streaked uncomfortably down my side.

A smile split the don's handsome face.

It wasn't a nice expression.

He casually twirled his cigarette in his fingers and nodded like he'd decided something.

My neck itched, and my intuition screamed at me to run.

Ever so slowly, I dragged one of my fingernails across

my forearm until I scented the copper tang of blood. I didn't bother with the numb; it most likely still needed to recharge.

Instead, I reached into the dark recess of my mind that had always existed. The recess I'd discovered on the sands of the arena wasn't a recess at all.

Unlike last time, I didn't need to speak any words to access my blood power. Immediately, it responded to my mental probe.

Each individual droplet that dripped from the gash on my forearm coagulated at my will, like I was connected to each drop.

The don said casually, "On my mark, kill everyone he's with. Only my son can live. They all know too much."

The room erupted into chaos.

"No!" Cobra bellowed. His eyes flickered to snake eyes, and shadow snakes streamed off his skin toward the men.

Beta fingers tensed on machine guns as they prepared to fire on their don's mark.

I poured my will into the blood dripping from my arm.

Sweat blurred my eyes as I scrunched my face and slowly levitated a droplet.

Next to me, claws erupted from Aran's fingernails, and a black film spread across her eyes until there were no whites left.

Wait, what?

That was new. I'd never seen a fae do that.

Next to me, Jax and Ascher began to shift, and Xerxes pulled out his twin knives and leaned forward. He was ready to throw them.

I almost had enough control over my blood to throw it. I just needed a little longer, and then…

"STOP!" Jinx screamed at an extremely high pitch, her voice reverberating through my brain in an ungodly screech.

Instantly, everyone in the room stopped moving.

Paralyzed.

My blood stopped rising. It twisted and spun in a small ball of power above my forearm that only I could see.

"He's bluffing," Jinx said in her normal voice, and the grip she had on the room broke.

Once again, everyone looked over at the small girl, who was definitely not a shifter, because I'd never heard a living creature emit such a high-decibel noise.

It had frozen everyone with more force than an alpha bark.

Jax turned to look at his little sister. "Jinx?" The question in his voice was clear.

Instead of being embarrassed that she had just emitted a high-pitched wail the likes of which a person had never produced before, Jinx shrugged.

Jess and Jala were the only two people in the room that didn't look surprised by her outburst.

I'd bet all my money this wasn't new to them.

The don began, "Wha—"

Jinx raised her hand and spoke over him. "Did no one see his body language? He was clearly bluffing. His eyes became drier, and he squinted slightly as he spoke. It was a test."

Once again, we gaped at her.

How could someone tell a person's eyes were dry in a dim, hazy room?

What was most shocking was how the don just tilted his head at her and said nothing.

The smallest smile played at the corner of his lips.

A long moment passed as the don didn't deny it, and everyone slowly realized Jinx was correct.

The don waved his hand. The betas lowered their machine guns so they pointed at the ground.

Ever so slowly, I pulled my floating blood sphere back into the cut on my arm.

Thank the sun god I didn't infect anyone with my blood; talk about making things awkward and outing myself.

Jax and Ascher stopped shifting into their animals and returned to normal. Xerxes resheathed his daggers.

Cobra's shadow snakes slithered back onto his flesh, but this time, they didn't transform into jewels.

Slowly, the tension in the room lowered.

The don pulled out a fresh cigarette and lit it. When it was burning in his mouth, he said, "You were right, and you were wrong. I was bluffing. I wouldn't have killed you right here on my white floors. I'd have taken you out back afterward and shot you."

The tension ratcheted back up.

A low, rattling hiss sounded from Cobra's chest, and Jax let out a rumbling roar. Ascher's horns straightened on his head, and Xerxes palmed his knives.

My chest shook with a slight growl.

No one threatened our sisters.

The don kept speaking, like he hadn't just casually admitted his plan to execute all of us. "But you just put on an impressive display of power. It would be a shame to waste such talent when our glorious city can always use a little…help."

Jinx grumbled, "He was totally bluffing. He's just covering now."

Jess kicked her sister in the shin.

Abruptly, the don's eyes shifted into snake eyes, and he

stared at Jinx. His slit pupils were larger and darker than Cobra's snake eyes, and the effect was terrifying.

Jax shifted to block Jinx, but she moved her small body to the side to stare down the don.

She rolled her eyes. "I'm not scared of you."

A visible shudder shook through the don, and the white snake across his shoulders bared its fangs and hissed at her.

"Still not." Jinx inspected her cuticles.

This time, both Jess and Jala kicked her in the shins.

I was low-key impressed, because I was afraid and he wasn't death glaring at me like he wanted to wear my skin as an outfit.

The don's slit pupils widened, and something unexplainable transformed his face. "How interesting." He stared at Jinx.

Another rumble sounded from Jax's chest, and my chest shook with a growl. I didn't like the way he looked at her.

From the way Ascher and Xerxes shifted closer to her, none of us did.

After a weird standoff between Jax's twelve-year-old sister and the terrifying Mafia leader, the don shook his head.

He turned to Cobra. "As soon as you entered this realm, you took up your mantle of responsibility as my only heir. Blood and family are the most powerful inheritance, and you have a duty to our organization and this city."

Cobra sneered with disgust, "I don't owe you anything."

The don continued speaking like Cobra had said nothing. "If you try to leave this city, you'll be defecting from your duty, and you'll be immediately taken out."

He let his words sink in and looked over at Jinx with a raised eyebrow, like he was begging her to call his bluff.

She said nothing.

He took another drag of his cigarette. "As my son and an alpha in the Mafia, you need to bond and form a pack in the next three months. All alphas in the city must be in a pack. Also, you must pass Mafia initiation trials."

"I refuse," Cobra sneered with his signature frosty expression. Ice wafted off him.

The don shrugged. "Then everyone in this room dies."

A rattling hiss shook through Cobra's chest.

Suddenly, the don opened his mouth, and his perfect white teeth transformed into two long daggers that protruded from his upper jaw. A blood red forked tongue shook as he hissed back at his son aggressively.

Creepy.

"If any of them are harmed, I'll kill you." Cobra shook with rage.

The don didn't flinch.

His tongue and teeth transformed back, and he motioned to a door on the side of the room. "Then initiation begins now. If you want everyone to survive."

Before any of us could process what was happening, two betas stood and grabbed Cobra's arms. They promptly escorted him out of the room.

He didn't fight them.

We all watched in horror.

At the last moment, Cobra turned back and stared directly at me. He alpha-barked, "No one is to follow me! I must do this alone."

The command momentarily paralyzed me.

The door swung shut, and the don chuckled. "Anyone else want to be initiated? Until alphas are indoctrinated, they're forbidden from shifting into their animal forms or they're immediately exterminated. Snipers are positioned throughout Serpentine City. I highly recommend joining our ranks. It will improve your chances of surviving this realm. Eighteen and older only, of course. We aren't savages."

He clearly didn't care about his son's wishes.

There was a long moment as we all gaped at him.

"Don't you dare hurt him," Jax growled and stepped forward menacingly.

The alpha bark wore off, and I regained control of my body.

"Fuck this," I said and stomped after Jax toward the damn door Cobra had been taken through. Ascher and Xerxes followed behind me.

It wasn't like I could just let Cobra suffer alone.

None of us could.

The don blocked our path and focused on Xerxes. "As an omega, there is no need for initiation."

Xerxes showed his teeth. "So long as I'm in this city, I will not be living like a traditional omega."

The don raised his hands and chuckled. "So be it. You're not the first."

Xerxes's mouth dropped open as he stared in confusion. Clearly, he'd never heard of an omega in the Mafia before.

The don chuckled as he sucked on his cigarette.

Something told me there was a lot about this realm we didn't know. A lot I didn't want to know.

I looked back.

We couldn't just leave Lucinda and the girls. Jax also stopped, like he'd realized the same thing.

Aran waved her hands. "It's fine. I'll look after the children. Not like I have massive problems of my own to deal with right now."

"We're not children," all four of them said at the same time.

I nodded and stepped forward, but Ascher blocked my path. "Princess, you should stay back."

I rolled my eyes and pushed past him. Who didn't want to get initiated into a bloodthirsty gang against their will? Me.

But I wasn't about to pussy out because *Ascher* told me not to.

I might be stupid, but I wasn't dumb.

CHAPTER 3
SADIE
TORTURE

YOU'RE PROBABLY WONDERING how I ended up here.

Somehow, through my stupid-ass actions, my dark, depressing life kept getting worse.

It turned out it was a lot harder to hit rock bottom than you would think. I'd thought I'd hit it in the fae realm, but I'd been wrong.

The abyss of suffering truly had no end.

Yes, I was being dramatic.

No, I would not stop feeling sorry for myself, because at this point, it was the only constant in my life.

In one second, I was about to have a mental breakdown of monumental proportions.

All for what? An alpha snake shifter who was aggravating.

"Stupid damn fucking unwell snakes," I grumbled as I swung back and forth.

Yep, swung.

Not in a fun, flirty, playground way.

Nope. My wrists were tied above my head and attached to a metal hook that hung from the ceiling by a single chain.

I kicked out my feet aimlessly and twisted as my shoulder blades burned from the strain of holding up my body.

The only blessing was that I was shorter than the men.

Cobra, Ascher, Jax, and Xerxes hung from their wrists next to me in the dark room. They grunted and groaned occasionally, their biceps straining to hold up the weight of their much larger bodies.

The narrow walls glowed with a soft light-blue tinge, and I'd bet all my money it was the same stupid enchantment that stopped shifters from transforming.

No matter how hard I concentrated, I didn't feel the telltale tingle of my saber-toothed tiger shifting.

Not that I would shift even if I could.

I had a feeling that was not the point of Mafia initiation, or whatever the hell the don had called this little experience.

To add to the room's lovely ambiance, there was a single neon light bulb hanging from the ceiling.

It flickered incessantly and cast creepy shadows around the room.

We were in a literal skyscraper, a marvel of engineering, and they couldn't make the light stop flickering?

"I'm gonna have a seizure," I muttered with annoyance as sweat streaked down my temples and added to my growing discomfort.

The temperature in the room was ungodly hot, and I gasped at the clammy air.

We weren't the only lucky folks hanging from creepy hooks.

Two large, muscular men covered in tattoos, that weren't as cool or extensive as Ascher's, swung back and forth next to us.

They said nothing. Just silently dripped sweat like the rest of us.

I didn't know how long I'd been hanging, because there were no windows or clocks to mark the passage of time.

It could have been minutes or hours.

All I knew was my shoulder blades were burning, and the pain was slowly consuming my every thought.

Just yesterday, I'd been fighting for my life against a vampyre and an evil fae queen in a gladiator arena.

Sun god help me, there was still sand crusted onto my skin. I hadn't even showered, and now I was hanging from the ceiling.

At this point, I would murder someone for a hot bath and a smutty book.

"Could this suck any more?" I groaned and kicked my legs back and forth through the air, desperate to relieve the ache in my arms. "Also, I hate to say it, but your dad kinda sucks."

Snake eyes glowed in the dark next to me and jeweled skin twinkled under the flickering light.

Cobra's voice crackled with menace. "If you'd listened to me, you wouldn't be here." He mumbled under his breath, "Fucking disobedient kitten."

I growled and kicked my legs aimlessly in his direction. "Stop calling me Kitten. Also, I'm so fucking sorry that I didn't just abandon you to handle creepy gang initiation all by yourself."

"I'm going to kill you for this." Cobra's words slurred with anger, and a rattling hiss shook through his chest.

"Get in line," I mumbled and twisted toward him as ire built in my chest. "Also, grow up. It's called being a teammate."

I threw Jinx's earlier words back at him.

My shadow snake sent a streak of pain across my back. Like it had zapped me. It was the first time it had sent me anything other than love and encouragement.

Cobra snarled, "We're not a fucking team."

His words hurt more than the physical pain that was ripping through my arms.

Cobra glared at me with intensity as his slit pupils glowed brightly in the dark. "I own you. This is not fucking safe, and I forbade you. You disobeyed me."

I took the mature route.

Scrunching up my face, I mocked him. "*You disobeyed me.*"

I made eye contact with Xerxes, who hung from the ceiling on my other side. The omega was silent, but he looked at me with understanding in his purple eyes.

Like he knew how hurtful Cobra's words were.

Ascher cracked his neck loudly. "Don't talk to Sadie like that."

Cobra didn't look chastised. "Why the fuck are all of you here?" he shouted and panted as he tipped his dark head backward like his rage was overwhelming.

"Sadie is right. We're a team. We won't abandon you," Jax said quietly. His massive biceps strained to hold up his heavy body, but, like usual, his demeanor was calm.

Cobra flung his head forward and hissed. "Really? Because Ascher betrayed us, and literally one fucking day ago, Xerxes was working for the fae queen against us."

Ascher's amber eyes glowed in the darkness as his handsome face contorted into a scowl. "I've apologized a million times. I've explained that I thought I was helping you guys. Have I not fucking proven myself?"

Xerxes rolled his eyes. "I still hate all of you. I'm doing this for personal reasons."

I scoffed. "Bullshit. You totally think we're cool."

Xerxes arched his eyebrow but said nothing.

Maybe I was reading into it, but I could have sworn his lips curved up like we were sharing an inside joke.

Jax twisted to Ascher with a grunt. "You're going to have to prove yourself. I don't hold a grudge, but trust has to be earned."

Ascher nodded. "I will earn it."

"I definitely still hold a grudge," Cobra sneered.

"Same. Just a little," I said honestly as I swung back and forth from the ceiling.

Ascher nodded his horned head toward me. "Princess, I will earn your forgiveness."

"Can't wait," I mumbled as the burning in my shoulders intensified.

One of the two random tattooed dudes who was also hanging next to us spat on the ground. "Y'all are all fucking nuts."

"Drama queen." I rolled my eyes at him.

"What the fuck did you say to me, bitch?"

Jax's, Cobra's, Ascher's, and Xerxes's eyes all glowed brightly.

"Don't talk to her," Xerxes said softly.

"Oh fucking please, from what I've seen, you're all gonna be fucking dead by the end of this trial. Fucking wimpy bitches. No alpha beast with self-respect would ever be such a fucking simp toward a girl. It's an honor to be here."

He said "girl" like I was the scum under his boots.

I sighed and kicked my legs out harder, trying to shift my weight from my arms. The patriarchy really just didn't quit.

Jax roared with a ferocity that made all the hair on my body stand up.

I narrowed my eyes at my bound hands and pondered

the merits of trying to gouge myself with one of my toenails so I could fling my blood at someone and free myself.

We were in the beast realm; they definitely enchanted the room to stop alphas from shifting. Not blood fae.

After a long moment, I shook my head. It would take way too much work to kick off my shoes and socks.

"Just ignore him," I mumbled at Jax, who was still growling like a maniac. "He probably just has a little dick."

Xerxes whined softly, like the sound was stressing him out.

Ascher and Jax chuckled, Xerxes calmed down, and Cobra just glared at the man like he was fantasizing about dismembering him.

I whistled poorly as I swung back and forth from the ceiling and tried to pretend that I was lying in a sunny field of flowers.

The stench of sweat and fear saturated the small space and made it very difficult to imagine anything other than death, pain, and suffering.

My shoulders tingled, and I was 30 percent certain my arms were going to snap off.

"Why would anyone willingly go through this?" I mumbled incoherently at Xerxes.

Xerxes grimaced. "The Mafia runs the city and maintains peace among ABOs. If you're not in the Mafia, you're an independent alpha."

Xerxes paused as if he was lost in his memories. "There are only a few thousand alphas in the entire city, and only a few dozen aren't in the Mafia. Every single one of them is involved in heinous practices that would make your skin crawl. The Mafia keeps order in a society filled with weak nulls and violent alphas."

I shivered at the intensity in Xerxes's voice.

He'd flung daggers with pinpoint precision into a vampyre's skull and worked as the right hand of the evil queen.

I couldn't even imagine the horrors that would intimidate him.

"Why did he say omegas didn't need to be initiated?" I asked quietly as I tried to distract myself from the overwhelming pain.

"Omegas are revered breeders who are guarded and treated like possessions." Xerxes spat the last words. "As soon as they transform, they're automatically protected by the Mafia. Betas work for the alphas and don't need to be initiated because they rely on the don's protection. Otherwise, they'd be destroyed by rabid alphas."

"Lucky them." I kicked my legs.

Xerxes shook his head. "You don't understand. Alphas *must* pass initiation. It's the only check on the immense power that they have in the city."

There was a long silence as all of us let Xerxes's words sink in.

Still didn't understand how making me hang from the ceiling proved anything, but I got the gist.

"Then why would you do it?" I mumbled groggily.

The flickering fluorescent light was making my eyes hurt, and I struggled to focus on his handsome face as he flashed in and out of shadows.

Xerxes pulled back his upper lip, and he scowled with more emotion than I'd ever seen on his face. "Because if I'm going to be in this fucking realm, it will not be as a fucking possession. Never again."

The silence in the room was deafening.

My heart hurt for Xerxes.

Across the room, the asshole alpha snarled, "A fucking omega is trying to get initiated. What a fucking joke."

Before any of us could sneer back, a door was flung open, and a *giant* stepped into the room.

He rivaled Jax for size. But instead of being handsome and fit like Jax, the man was bald and half his face was disfigured, like it had been smashed repeatedly. His body was enormous, with bulging muscles.

"Loyalty" was tattooed across his forehead.

It was the same tattoo as on the don's neck.

The giant's voice was deep and grating. "My name is Spike. I will ask you a question. First one to answer gets to leave."

Maybe this won't be so bad?

Spike raised his hand and showcased, in the creepy, flickering light, a colossal needle and syringe.

Scratch that.

This was literally the worst-case scenario.

Also, who was named Spike unironically?

Not a good sign.

CHAPTER 4
SADIE
NEEDLES IN HELL

"DON'T you dare touch Jax or Sadie with that needle. They're not initiating. I forbid it!" Cobra hiss-yelled at Spike.

I gaped at Cobra's sheer audacity.

What did he think I was, some type of wimp?

"You can't *forbid* me from doing anything. Stab me, Spike!" I yelled with authority.

Jax rolled his eyes, and Xerxes sighed heavily.

Sadly, Spike did nothing.

He stood still as a statue and watched the seven of us sway back and forth. Our muscles strained, sweat dripping down our faces.

Spike flicked at the gigantic needle in his hands.

Instantly, I had regrets.

Realistically, as a woman with dignity, I couldn't let Cobra hinder me from having experiences. However, was getting stabbed by a massive fucking needle an experience I really wanted?

Hard no.

Unfortunately, feminine pride required sacrifices.

Sometimes, you just had to do shit to prove a point. I didn't make the rules.

Speaking of which, my arms were really burning, and I didn't want to be rude, but so far all Spike was doing was torturing us with silence.

You'd think a Mafia torturer named Spike would be a little more fear inducing. Sweat dripped down my forehead, and even though my arms were in tremendous pain, I got sleepy in the silence.

Suddenly, Spike said in a deep voice, "This is the first trial to become an alpha of the Mafia. A ruler of Serpentine City."

"Exhilarating," I muttered sarcastically under my breath.

Cobra glared at me and Jax like he was trying to kill us both with his eyes.

I chuckled. The pain in my shoulder blades was making me delirious.

Spike sneered, spat on the ground, and pulled a thick cigar out of his pocket.

He balanced the terrifying needle between his fingers as he bent over and lit it with a glowing lighter.

He sighed and blew a thick cloud directly into my face.

I hated the smell of smoke; it reminded me of Dick's beta scent.

Choking, I gagged and gasped for air like I was drowning. "That's vile."

Spike didn't reply, just walked slowly back and forth in front of us like he was in zero rush. Blowing smoke in our faces and grinning.

My arms shook from the strain of hanging by my wrists.

Maybe this was the torture, they were just going to leave us suspended for days.

"What does the don look like?" Spike stopped pacing. "Just answer and you can leave."

The silence in the room was deafening.

We all came to the same conclusion, because no one spoke.

The alpha literally had "Loyalty" tattooed across his forehead. How dumb did he think we were?

Spike shrugged nonchalantly and resumed pacing. "Just describe the don's appearance. Then you'll be let down from the ropes."

He was trying to act casual, but the crazed look in his dark eyes was the same one the fae queen had had before she lit me on fire.

"Don't answer," I whispered to my men. Just in case they were complete dumbasses, which, from the behavior I'd seen, was a very real possibility.

Jax nodded at me, and the multitude of gold chains hanging from his braids tinkled softly.

"No shit," Cobra snarled at the same time Ascher barked, "Worry about yourself, Princess."

The annoying alpha from before shouted. "Holy fuck. Will you fuckers ever shut up?"

Spike chuckled and adjusted his meaty paw on the syringe. A glowing green substance sloshed back and forth.

A tension headache pounded through my skull.

The damn flickering light was not helping my mental health.

Spike smiled and showcased a whole lot of pink gums and, at the most, four yellow teeth.

I gagged.

His jowls quivered with excitement. "You see this little guy here?" He held up the colossal fucking needle.

I rolled my eyes.

Men were always so dramatic.

Copper flooded my mouth as I bit my tongue hard to stop myself from shouting at him to just stab us already.

I accessed the dark recess in my brain and was 0.1 seconds away from spitting my blood at him and infecting his body when I remembered that this was a voluntary test.

My gut told me Cobra's terrifying snake father would not take kindly to me controlling his torturer.

I forcibly swallowed down my blood.

The don better initiate me just for my superb self-control.

Do you know how hard it is to not stop a torturer with a massive needle when you can?

Very fucking hard.

Mentally, I patted myself on the shoulder for being a bad bitch of poise and self-control.

Spike shook the needle. "This is a rare herbal poison mixed with an even rarer witch spell."

My jaw dropped.

Holy mother of the son god. Witches were real?

My entire world tilted on its axis.

I'd read fiction stories about witches and had always thought they gave off amazing energy. In one story, a witch had basically single-handedly saved a world from an evil dude who didn't have a nose.

Iconic.

But it was always fiction.

Spike continued, "It's a pretty little potion made specially for the don. Paralyzes a beast and pumps their body full of excruciating pain that maximizes fear. It's the only solution in existence that can accurately recreate and predict how an individual will act under extreme torture."

Suddenly, the pain in my shoulders didn't seem so bad.

Why the fuck was I putting myself through this?

Before I could announce that I was quitting and would start my own gang where people didn't have to go through an awful initiation, Spike stabbed the needle into the annoying alpha in the corner.

Immediately, the large man began to moan and writhe with his head flung back and his jaw clenched.

I desperately searched for the switch in my head that activated the numb, or the song of the hunt—whatever made me an emotionless brick wall.

Nothing happened.

Like I'd suspected, it needed to recharge.

I was fucked.

Spike walked swiftly down the line and stabbed my men in the neck.

Now he developed a sense of urgency?

I smiled sweetly at him and tried to give off helpless-female vibes. "Um, could I speak to your manager? I think there's been a mistake."

Spike stabbed me in the neck.

"Fuck you," I growled as the awful pain sliced through my neck. There was a 100 percent chance he'd hit my spinal cord.

I moaned for the rafters and thrashed my legs desperately as a pain like nothing I'd ever known consumed every cell in my body.

It was like being lit on fire from the inside.

Jax roared loudly, and Ascher shouted expletives.

Cobra screamed.

Xerxes was dead silent.

The pain coursing through my body, which was the worst thing I'd ever experienced, somehow tripled in intensity.

I heaved and sobbed.

Cobra kept screaming.

Apparently, I was an awful person, because I was glad that I wasn't suffering alone.

My momentary satisfaction left as my chest collapsed with agony. The pain morphed into the sensation of a boulder crushing me. It paralyzed my limbs.

The end was near.

A spider stared at me before it was crushed to death.

John dragged me through the forest.

The beta pawed at my chest as he pinned me to the floor.

"Die, cunt."

"Useless servant."

"Weak whore."

Dick was in the room.

He slammed his belt down, over and over.

"I have to make you bleed!" Dick screamed at me. "It's an order."

He begged me to understand as he destroyed my flesh. Said it was for my own good.

I didn't listen to Dick, just screamed at him to spare Lucinda while I was away at school.

She lived alone with Dick. Four long years. She was trapped with a monster. I'd abandoned her.

Slap.

Slap.

Slap.

"Wakey, wakey." A man's smashed face blurred in front of me in a haze of flickering green.

Agony rolled through me.

"Good, you're with me. We can begin." He smiled and showed off a row of gums and four yellow teeth.

Terror battered my chest and snapped at my sternum.

I gasped, trying to breathe around the awful weight.

I didn't know who the man was.

Who was I?

Where was I?

I needed to fucking escape. I needed to get away. I tried to run, but realized my hands were trapped above me and I dangled off the ground.

I was hanging by a rope.

My fear increased tenfold, and a choking sob racked me.

The strange man grabbed my cheeks in his meaty paw and squeezed. "Yes, it's all very scary, pretty dove. Concentrate."

I pulled my head back and kicked desperately.

The man easily held me in place and said, "You met with the don recently."

Disjointed images flashed through my head of a gorgeous pale man with long black hair and a massive white snake around his shoulders.

I couldn't remember how or why I'd met him; the boulder on my chest was too heavy.

It was crushing me.

The meaty fingers holding my face squeezed my cheeks until my teeth cut the sides of my mouth.

"Describe him to me," the strange man demanded.

Tangy copper filled my throat and triggered memories of Dick's fist slamming across my cheek. His punches had always cut the inside of my mouth.

I opened my mouth to speak, but stopped as I stared at the black words sprawled across his forehead.

It was the same word tattooed on the don's neck.

The strange man shook my face back and forth violently, and the oppressive weight of fear returned with a flash.

I couldn't remember what I'd been thinking. It was just out of grasp.

What I needed to do was escape.

"DESCRIBE THE DON TO ME!" the man alpha-barked in my face, his gross, warm spittle spraying across my skin.

Just like Dick.

There was a boulder crushing my chest, and every cell in my body screamed at me that this was the fucking end.

A man was hurting me.

There was only one way to respond.

I opened my mouth and, with all my might, spat blood all over the fucker.

He slapped me across the face. Front hand, back hand. Repeat.

The room spun, and the weight on my chest expanded endlessly into a mountain.

I would not survive.

I needed to escape.

My abuser arched a mangled eyebrow. "What about a man named Cobra? Tell me what you know about him. Anything at all and I'll stop."

A fuzzy warmth spread through my chest, and a small burst of happiness zinged across my lower back.

Images of a gorgeous man covered in sparkly jewels, pushing food into my mouth and arguing with me, flashed through my mind like a movie.

The warmth in my chest dulled into fear.

"DESCRIBE COBRA!" he alpha-barked.

With blood dripping down my lips, my aching face contorted into a smile. “Go fuck yourself.”

His fists descended in a haze of violence as he asked me questions.

Even as he beat me.

I didn’t know why, but I couldn’t stop smiling.

And I said nothing.

CHAPTER 5
SADIE
THE AFTERMATH

Ever been run over by a supercar?

I had.

At least, that was what it fucking felt like.

I moaned like a dying animal as my heavy eyelids cracked open. My limbs burned as pain lit up my nerves like scrap-metal grenades.

Flickering green shadows taunted me, and a noxious odor itched my nose.

My mouth cracked with dried blood as I tried to gasp in more air but choked on a lungful of smoke.

A blurry, rotund body paced back and forth.

"Wakey, wakey," Spike said with way too much glee.

My shoulder blades burned unbearably, and I moaned as I tried to lift my head.

A bloody beating flashed through my mind in broken fragments, like a dream that was just out of my reach.

The last thing I remembered was Spike stabbing me in the neck with his needle.

"Wake up now!" Spike alpha-barked.

A chorus of moans responded, and I struggled to lift my head. Gravity pulled it back down.

My vision blurred, and a warm liquid dripped down my face. Definitely blood.

The familiar throbbing pain in the front of the skull told me I was sporting two wicked black eyes.

Abruptly, the dark, flickering room was illuminated in a harsh white light. It took a second, but I finally focused on my surroundings.

I wished I hadn't.

My stomach emptied bile down my chest. I heaved and coughed as I choked on it.

Throwing up while upright was fucking awful.

You know what else was awful? The remains of two alphas that were scattered around the floor like a messed-up science experiment.

The only things that kept me from hysteria were the four familiar bodies that swung beside me.

My men were okay.

I could not say the same for the other two alphas. The jerk who had mocked us was now disassembled into hundreds of pieces across the floor.

There was nothing left to identify him by.

Just an empty rope swinging across a mess of gore. Now I knew what the awful smell was.

Suddenly, I missed the creepy flickering light that had broken up the room's darkness.

Everything was too bright.

"Sadie?" Ascher moaned loudly as he struggled to move. He violently shook from his rope.

I groaned back, "Present."

The pain in my arms was too much, and my head swirled with darkness. I was thirty seconds from passing out.

"Is everyone okay?" Jax asked softly, his smooth voice rough and mangled, similar to my own.

A chorus of weak grunts sounded.

Was I alive? Yes.

Was I okay? Hard. Fucking. No.

Okay people didn't feel like they'd been flung off a mountain, then had the mountain fall over on top of them.

I turned my head and took in Xerxes's awful state.

He was so bloody that he was no longer blond. If I hadn't known better, I would have thought he was a ginger.

I winced at his mangled face.

Then I winced because wincing made my face pound with pain in rhythm to my heartbeat.

Things were not well.

I whispered to Xerxes, "Are you okay?"

His lush lips were swollen and distorted, and he tried to speak, but only made a harsh wheezing sound as his mouth gaped hopelessly.

After a long, awkward moment where he gasped, and I grimaced at him, he stopped trying to speak.

Instead, Xerxes stared at me with swollen purple eyes.

Intensity seeped from them, and even in my pain-stricken state, it made me squirm.

The pain must have been making me delirious, because he stared at me like he could see through my corporeal form. He devoured me like he was peering into my soul, into another astral plane of existence.

Like I was his savior and damnation.

His obsession.

Clearly, torture had addled my brain and made me weirdly poetic.

"Stop looking at me like that," I said as my bound arms were slowly ripped from their sockets.

If I didn't get let down from the rope in the next second, I was going to cause a scene.

"Kitten?" Cobra asked in a slurred whisper from across the room.

I bit down on my tongue and screamed into my mouth.

My mood boomeranged in time with the pounding agony ripping my cells to shreds.

The next person to call me a pathetic nickname was getting stabbed.

The big alpha fuckface, aka Spike, smiled and interrupted my mental breakdown. "Well, now that you're all awake, I just have one thing to say..."

He paused dramatically,

Everyone glared at him as we swung back and forth from the fucking ceiling. Who was going to tell him we didn't need any more drama?

The mood was already set.

Finally, Spike clapped his hands. "Congratulations! You passed the first initiation test." He showcased his four teeth. "The first test has a passage rate of less than 1 percent, so you should all be proud."

His smile transformed into a savage look as he sneered down at the mess of gore on the floor. "The other alphas answered the question...and they were set free. Just like we promised."

"Freedom" clearly had a different meaning to Spike.

Although, I guessed their brains were *freely* splattered across the white floor.

I chuckled, then frowned because that was really not funny.

I needed a therapist immediately.

Spike's smile returned. "You will be contacted with your

next initiation challenge. Congratulations, you are one-third of the way to getting your tattoo."

Wait, what?

Abruptly, Spike pulled out a wicked-looking knife and sawed at the ropes around my wrist.

Of course, he didn't bother to catch my limp body. He definitely could have.

A positive: Most of the gore covered the far side of the room, so I didn't fall into it.

A negative: I slammed down, face forward, legs and arms sprawled, onto the hard cement.

Weren't cats supposed to always land on their feet?

I could not emphasize how much I landed completely on my belly.

The story of my life should have been titled *Sadie: The Bitch Who Was in Pain.*

Existence fucking hurt.

Anyone who said differently lived a pampered fucking life and shouldn't be trusted.

My last shred of dignity was the only thing that kept me from passing out onto the cement as agony rocked through me.

Instead, because I was a bad bitch—who for some unknown reason kept fighting against the sweet caress of death—I battled gravity and dragged my aching limbs off the floor.

Impressively, I stood up.

Well, if being half-keeled-over and moaning like a polar bear was considered standing.

Spike cut down Xerxes, and he scrambled next to me.

Silently, the omega tossed an arm around my shoulder, and we leaned against each other.

Just two adults using each other for support.

No biggie.

I pretended not to notice that Xerxes was still staring at me. If he wanted to be weird, that was his prerogative.

Instead of worrying about Xerxes's strange energy, I focused on the other men.

Cobra collapsed weakly onto the ground.

Finally, Jax was released, and the big man landed on his feet gracefully. He was bruised but looked to be in the best shape compared to the rest of us.

Dark-purple bruises covered every inch of his pale skin. We all waited for him to stand, but he just moaned and lay on the ground, unmoving.

I grimaced at his awful state.

Something told me they'd gone harder on him because he was the prince.

He had more to gain and thus more to prove.

Also, it looked like another one of us was joining the severe parental issues group. I'd let him know when Aran and I scheduled our next therapy session.

Sun god knew we needed it.

Jax leaned over and stroked his dark hand softly across Cobra's bruised forehead. Then he gently lifted Cobra and cradled him against his chest like he wasn't holding a six-foot-five man covered in muscles.

My breath caught as I stared at Jax.

His long braids softly tinkled with chains, and his earrings, nose ring, and piercing gray eyes sparkled.

He calmly carried Cobra after being tortured.

As every pain-stricken cell in my body wept with relief, I marveled at Jax's poise.

He was more than a man.

A god.

Finally, Ascher was released, and he stumbled to his

tattooed feet, his horns splattered in blood and his amber eyes swollen shut.

The moment felt monumental because we'd done it.

All of us were still alive.

I coughed up blood and cleared my throat. "Um, so can we just leave?"

Spike nodded and gestured toward the door. "A car will take you to Xerxes's place."

I didn't bother to ask how he knew that was where we were going to stay. As we limped past him, I couldn't help but check over my shoulder nervously.

After our little rope torture session, it didn't feel right that we were just free to go.

Being threatened with guns or thrown into a pit of poisonous snakes seemed like a more fitting next step than just leaving casually.

Whatever, I didn't argue.

Jax carried Cobra silently, and Ascher leaned an arm against Jax's bicep for support. I held on to Ascher's arm, and Xerxes wrapped himself around me.

Together, we limped out the door.

There was no one in the room, and we shuffled down the long hall we'd entered through.

Hell is paved with the bones of the disloyal, took on new meaning as we struggled past the words on the wall.

I'd heard the term *hell* before, but had never wondered what it stood for.

Now my skin rolled with the premonition that it wasn't good.

If it was a place, I didn't want to be there.

This time, when we were finally free of that awful building, the icy wind and rain were welcome. The droplets kissed my aching flesh in a cool relief.

It was still night.

We limped down the abandoned alleyway.

No one spoke, but we moved with the single-minded purpose of a unit.

We were on the same page.

The wind gusted strong, and Xerxes's hand tightened painfully against my shoulder as he struggled to stand. I clenched Ascher's arm to hold us upright, and he leaned heavily against Jax.

Cobra's eyes fluttered open as his head lolled upside down across Jax's arm, but he didn't move.

Jax tensed his legs as we shuffled forward, his strength the only thing keeping all of us upright.

The puddles beneath our feet turned red as the rain washed away our blood.

Before, hundreds of shifters had bustled down the busy city streets. Now they were almost completely empty. Eerily so. A few men and women hurried through the rain, heads down to remain unnoticed.

Towering buildings glowed neon and illuminated dark, rainy shadows. Gloom overtook the world. A bone-deep melancholy invaded my body.

It was impossible to feel anything other than angst while limping through the fluorescent city.

So big and overwhelming, it completely consumed us.

None of us said anything. We didn't need to.

All we had was each other.

We turned the corner, and our beta driver from earlier was leaning against a shiny emerald supercar.

With trembling grips, we kept limping forward. Eons later, we collapsed in a pile of limbs across the fancy leather interior.

Somehow, we all ended up in the same row of the car.

Jax lay partially across the seat with Cobra leaning against him. Ascher draped across Cobra. Xerxes lay across the floor at their feet, and I sprawled atop his body.

The reality of what we'd been through hung heavy around us.

The bruises and fatigue were mutual.

As was the pain.

Finally, between the soft hum of the engine and Xerxes kissing me softly on the cheek, I fell asleep.

CHAPTER 6
JAX
BUILT TO LEAD

A FEW MINUTES earlier

Devastation vibrated through me. For the first time in a hundred and twenty years, I didn't know how to react.

I hung from the ceiling as Cobra, Sadie, Xerxes, and Ascher moaned beside me. Everyone looked awful.

Like a desperate man, I looked back and forth at Sadie's and Cobra's battered bodies.

My eyes burned with unshed tears, while my throat was scratchy with the screams that bubbled up but wouldn't release.

Every muscle in my body strummed with tension and pain. A type of mind-melting agony I hadn't experienced for over a hundred years.

The remnants of suffering dragged me back into the past, back when I'd been Sadie's age and unaccustomed to physical suffering. Back to the last time I'd known true, bone-wrenching pain.

When the oligarchy had paid me to hunt down a massive elk that was carrying a plague.

I was a new alpha, and it was a job nobody else had wanted.

Over mountains and vast forests, I stalked the plagued beast.

At first, I hunted as a bear. But my shifted form required more nutrients, and I quickly ran out of food a few weeks into the hunt.

I didn't have time to waste, so I shifted back and followed my prey on two legs.

It was the dead of winter, which meant the red sun didn't bother to rise above the horizon.

At first, snow turned to sleet, and it froze to my face in a mask of ice.

Next came the hail.

Massive balls of ice pummeled from the sky. They smashed into trees with loud cracks. Ice exploded around me.

Then the blizzard hit.

When I finally found the elk, I was frozen to the bone and had fasted for two weeks straight.

In a blur of agony, I snapped its neck with my bare hands. Covered in blood, icicles dripping off each of my braids, I turned around and trekked back.

I didn't reach civilization for another two weeks.

Over a month with no food.

Before my journey, I'd foolishly thought that if I was hungry enough, I would just hunt for food until I was nourished.

But in the dead of winter, the few animals that didn't hibernate were the ones crafty enough to escape a predator.

That month, I learned an important lesson.

When food was nonexistent and every cell in your body

was screaming for sustenance, you were already too weak to fix the problem.

Hiking for miles in the hail and driving sleet, something changed inside me. My body burned with hunger for so many hours that a part of me stopped recognizing the agony.

Every step forward through the chest-deep snow was a step away from giving in to my base urges.

The urge to curl up into the cold and sleep. The urge to gnaw on bark like a madman.

Ever since that hunt, physical pain hadn't affected me the same way.

I'd left a piece of myself in those woods.

In the murder of a diseased elk.

The man who had returned from the hunt had known a depth of suffering that was unmatched.

Either the cold broke you, or it remade you into something sharper than ice and tougher than pounding hail.

I'd almost forgotten how bad pain could hurt.

Almost.

Now, hanging by a rope from the ceiling with Cobra and Sadie badly beaten beside me, I remembered.

Once again, I was the young man hiking through the desolate forest, fighting for survival as trees howled around like monsters.

I vibrated with angst.

Not for myself.

For them. The alphas I cared about.

On top of that, Xerxes cut a pathetic figure, and my alpha instincts screamed at me to protect the omega.

It was wrong to see an omega bloody. Unnatural.

My chest even hurt for Ascher. His tattoos were indiscernible among blood and bruises, and both his eyes were swollen shut.

Suddenly, Sadie was cut down by the fucker who dared hurt her.

She fell to the ground with a crack, her legs and arms splayed.

It took every ounce of strength left in my body to not roar like a maniac. I trembled with the urge to help her up.

With a weak gasp, the little alpha rolled to the side and coughed up blood. But she didn't cry and break down. She stumbled onto her legs.

When she turned so I could see her face fully, I raggedly sucked in air. My chest rumbled.

Sadie's gold skin was covered in a patchwork of bruises, but the worst was her face.

Two massive black eyes were dark and ghastly against her delicate bone structure. She mirrored Ascher.

Trembling violently, the little alpha hunched over with her hands on her knees as she breathed raggedly.

White hair hung around her face, a snarled mess covered in blood.

It reminded me of the elk's entrails splashed across the snow after I'd savaged it with my bare hands.

The leaders had assured me the disease didn't affect alphas, but you could never know for sure. Back then, a part of me had hoped the disease would take.

It hadn't.

Now I uselessly tugged at the restraints still tying my wrists.

I was a second from bellowing at Spike to hurry the fuck up when Xerxes stumbled over and helped support the little alpha.

My roar died in my throat as the much larger omega

leaned against her. Even battered, they were both stunning in a softer, more beautiful sort of way.

There was something delicate about them.

Cobra, Ascher, and I were built for torture, built to withstand the atrocities of war, pain, and suffering.

They weren't.

Yet here they were, destroyed among us.

I swallowed a low growl and reminded myself that looks could be deceiving. Instinctually, I wanted to wrap the little alpha up and yell at the omega to stay safe.

Subconsciously, my mind was bellowing at me to protect them even while consciously, I recognized their competence.

It was torment.

The only thing that stopped me from growling at Sadie like a maniac was Jinx.

My youngest sister had always been strange, and from the outside, she looked like a delicate waif that couldn't harm a fly. An innocent little girl that needed protecting.

Even hanging from the ceiling with blood dripping from my mouth, I couldn't stop the slight chuckle that shook my chest.

I'd seen the little girl make grown soldiers cry with a few choice words.

At school, they had elevated Jinx to the highest classes because, even as a six-year-old, her intelligence had been unfathomable.

She was also the class bully.

I'd received detailed letters from Jala and Jess about how Jinx kept making her older classmates cry.

Of course, they thought it was funny.

The lesson of it all: Looks meant nothing.

I repeated this mantra in my head as Sadie and Xerxes held on to each other.

The omega stared down at the little alpha with an intensity that made me want to growl at him that she was mine. Not his. Claim her in every way possible, so he knew who she belonged to.

Fuck it, that was how Cobra acted.

No, I needed to be better.

We'd all just been tortured for hours. Two dead alphas were splattered across the floor in hundreds of tiny pieces.

If all five of us were going to survive this new realm, I needed to be a leader.

With a crash, Spike cut Cobra down, and his pale body slumped against the concrete floor.

My heart crashed with him as I stared down at the man I'd been trying to not focus on.

We were a partnership.

I'd told him I would always be by his side, and I meant it.

Yet once again he was suffering unmercifully, and I couldn't stop it.

I willed Cobra to move, to drag himself to his feet and give me his signature cocky sneer.

He remained collapsed and unmoving.

Sadie and Xerxes swayed laboriously as they struggled to hold each other up.

Ascher was cut down next, and his tattooed fingers shook with stress.

Blood dripped from both his eyes, and it tracked across his harsh cheekbones like tears.

It didn't make him look soft.

Ascher's expression was hard as granite. He wasn't a man to be fucked with, and a small part of me was grateful for his presence.

Cobra and Sadie consumed my thoughts obsessively.

Xerxes's omega status made my instincts go haywire.

But Ascher was just another alpha, a soldier.

Someone that could stand beside me and help protect them.

He stared at Sadie as she held on to Xerxes, like a sick man praying to the sun god.

Ascher's obsession with her was acceptable, as long as he kept himself in check and proved his loyalty.

If he put Sadie or Cobra in harm's way ever again, I would murder him with my bare hands.

He wasn't getting another chance.

Finally, Spike cut me down from my restraints.

I landed on my feet and barely took stock of my injuries. Already I'd cataloged my aches and dismissed them.

My heavy muscles struggled to extend and contract properly after hanging from the ceiling for so long. It took a moment of centering myself before I could lean down and drag Cobra's body off the floor.

I cradled him against my chest.

The stunning diamonds and crystals embedded in his skin didn't have their usual shine.

Even his snakes were hurting.

Now that I knew Cobra didn't have a beast form—he was the beast—a lot of things that had confused me over the years made sense.

In the shifter realm, after we'd battled fae monsters, I'd always had to fuck the intensity out of him.

He'd always struggled to rein in his aggression and settle down.

The urge to fight wouldn't leave him until I pinned his gorgeous face against the wall and drove my knotted cock into his ass. It wasn't until I'd filled him with my cum that his eyes would go back to normal.

Only then would the shadows stop writhing across his pale flesh.

He lost himself fully in the heat of battle and stopped pretending to be civilized.

Now Cobra's neck hung limply across my forearm, his gorgeous face scrunched up in pain.

Unlike with the rest of us, Cobra's flesh wasn't just covered in hideous bruises. He was also covered in hundreds of tiny cuts.

Someone had tried to cut his jewels out of his skin and failed.

My gut told me it was Cobra's father's doing.

If he was going to be the prince of the Mafia, the prince of the city, he was going to have to prove himself.

I shivered at that awful realization.

The don was a darker, more polished version of his son; where Cobra was barely controlled aggression and fire, the don was a blade.

"You can go," Spike said gleefully, and I barely heard him, too worried about the abused man hanging limp in my arms.

A low rumble rattled through my chest.

I breathed in the violence that made me want to bellow and charge out of the room like a madman.

How *dare* they hurt Cobra and Sadie like this.

Instead, I walked slowly.

Ascher's tattooed fingers wrapped around my arm for support, and we both pretended not to notice how badly he was shaking.

Sadie latched onto Ascher's arm as Xerxes held her upright on her other side.

I held Cobra carefully against my chest and tried not to jostle him while I lent the other's support.

When we finally got out into the rainy night, Cobra's long black lashes fluttered open.

Neon lights reflected off his pale skin.

Piercing emerald eyes stared up at me as the rain rinsed the blood from the open cuts on his stunning face.

"Thank you," his sinful lips mouthed.

An alpha purr rumbled through my chest in response.

Cobra chuckled softly. Then the bastard snuggled his head against my bicep like he wasn't a grown six-foot-five warrior.

My heart beat harder in my chest.

I loved that about him. Ruled by his baser urges and living by a code of ethics that no one else understood, Cobra was refreshingly different.

He didn't need to act strong; he just was. There was something intoxicating about a man who didn't pretend to be someone he wasn't.

Cobra was completely relaxed in my arms, trusting me to take care of him when he was at his most vulnerable.

At any other time, I would have marveled at the noise shaking through my chest. Everyone knew alphas only purred for omegas. Not other alphas.

I was too exhausted and worried about Cobra to care.

His long sooty lashes rested delicately against his high cheekbones, and he smiled contentedly.

The two alphas and omega clinging to me for support said nothing as my chest continued to purr.

We slowly limped down the street as a unit.

Anyone who tried to harm them messed with me, and you didn't want to cross a centuries-old alpha bear who had people to protect.

I'd raze the realm.

CHAPTER 7
XERXES
FALLING FOR YOU

I LAY AWKWARDLY on the cramped floor of the sports car, with Sadie sprawled flush across me.

A soft hum shook through her chest, a cross between a light snore and a low growl.

She was alpha-purring.

As soon as we'd collapsed into the car, she'd closed her eyes and slept.

Now, heart rattling in my chest, I tightened my arms across her delicate back. My face twitched, and I didn't know if I wanted to smile or pull out my knives and snarl.

Because every time I looked down at Sadie purring softly against my chest, I wanted to murder someone.

Her delicate golden skin was mottled with hideous black, blue, and green bruises. Both her gorgeous red eyes were puffy and swollen shut.

Dried blood that hadn't washed away in the rain still streaked down the sides of her face and neck.

Softly, I patted her wet hair and pressed my lips to her forehead, the only part of her body that wasn't openly bleeding.

My chest pinched with agony, and I wanted to scream at someone.

I didn't remember what had happened after Spike had stabbed me with a needle. Everything was a blur of fear and pain.

But I couldn't forget what had happened after.

When I'd come back to consciousness, the first thing I'd seen was Sadie's beaten body swinging from the rope beside me.

I'd never felt such devastation.

However, Sadie hadn't been crying or freaking out like I would have expected. Nope, the little alpha had fucking smiled at me encouragingly and asked if *I* was okay.

Like we hadn't both been tortured.

Like I wasn't almost three times her size and covered in muscles.

Like I wasn't older and more experienced.

As Sadie had looked at me with worry, my omega instincts had melted in my chest.

For the first time in my entire fucking life, I understood what it meant to be taken care of by an alpha.

I understood why omegas fawned over an alpha's attention.

There was nowhere I wouldn't go, nothing I wouldn't do, if it meant Sadie would stare at me with concern like I was her entire world.

Her priority.

I couldn't stop thinking about the moment she'd fucking asked me if *I* was all right. She'd worried about me above her own needs.

It was everything.

It also pissed me the fuck off.

Sure, in that moment, my heart had melted in my chest

as my omega instincts had preened. A part of me wanted to cuddle in my nest and let her tuck me in. Let her care for me.

However, I was still a fucking warrior.

A larger part of me wanted to scream at her for putting herself in danger.

Biology be damned. She was the small, weak one, and I was going to take care of her.

She needed me more than I needed her. Which meant I needed to do better. I needed to be there for her.

I needed to fucking protect her.

Sadie might be an alpha, but I was in charge.

If I could growl like an alpha, I had no doubt a roar would have ripped from my chest as I thought about her abused state.

My forearms tightened across her back, and she murmured contentedly.

Sadie had already been through so much.

I could never forget the awful scars that covered her chest and back. An enchantment might conceal them, but that didn't erase the past. The past that was apparent with every sinful rasp from her lips.

She'd been beaten so badly as a child her vocal cords were shredded.

Yet after being tortured physically, for the sun god knew how long, she'd worried about me.

I couldn't even put into words how much my heart had broken at that moment.

When the words of concern had left her lips, something had shifted inside me.

It was more than my suppressed omega instincts.

It went beyond biology.

For the first time, I understood completely where Cobra was coming from.

She was *mine*.

It was as simple as that.

I rested my cheek against her forehead and inhaled her sweet cranberry scent. How, after so much pain and abuse, did she still smell like sweet sunshine?

My gut cramped.

Sadie had been through so much pain in her short life that it didn't even affect her anymore. Didn't affect her like it should.

I wanted to wrap her up in a soft blanket and tuck her into my nest.

My gut cramped for a different reason as I thought about where we were. Back in the fucking beast realm.

Vision blurring, I dragged in ragged breaths. Sadie mumbled, as I squeezed her too tightly.

With extreme effort, I unlocked my frozen muscles.

The problem was, I wasn't a sweet omega, a perfect little breeder, calm enough to soothe an alpha's aggressive tendencies.

I was a bundle of barely controlled violence. And now I was back in the same realm as *them*. The Black Wolves, the alphas that had nearly destroyed me.

It hadn't escaped my memory that beasts prowled the glittering city streets. That dark, rainy corners hid men with even darker souls.

Once again, I was among them.

Softly, I dragged my hand across Sadie's forehead and reassured myself that she would be safe in my home.

I hadn't been lying when I said my house was big enough for all of us. I'd said it was an apartment out of habit. Years of downplaying my wealth so people wouldn't treat me differently.

I'd grown up with a beta mother and a father who'd been absent, but still an elite member of society. My family had old ABO money.

When I'd found out my father had been an omega, our wealth had made even more sense.

Omegas were rare jewels in Serpentine City, lavished with gifts and money from alphas who courted them. Status symbols.

Not that I'd ever experienced the process.

The wealth and prestige had always been a shackle that kept me from training with my blades all day.

But for the first time in my life, I was glad my family had wealth, because I could provide for Sadie and give us all a place to stay. It gave me a role.

The little voice in the back of my head reminded me I couldn't even keep myself safe.

I pushed the dark thoughts away.

My priority was Sadie.

The other alphas were fine men—the only other alphas I'd met that I didn't hate—but what I felt for them was friendship.

What I felt for the small, beaten woman purring in my arms was fucking soul consuming.

I'd fight beside the men, but I'd gut myself on my own knives for her.

I just had to prove myself to her.

If it weren't for the fact that Sadie liked the other alphas, I'd probably be kidnapping her away from them right now.

I took a deep breath and reminded myself that we were safer together. My emotions might be running high, but I wasn't a fucking idiot.

Three alphas protecting Sadie was more than I could do by myself. The more people who cared for her, the higher the chances she stayed safe.

That was all that mattered.

I also couldn't take her away because of her sister. Only an idiot couldn't see that Lucinda was Sadie's entire world.

She hadn't stopped staring at her, or touching her, since they'd been reunited.

It scared me because I'd recognized immediately that Sadie's happiness depended on her sister saying safe. Her sister, who was just as small as Sadie but without the edge of violence in her eyes.

Lucinda was a softer version of her older sister, which meant she was even more vulnerable and, therefore, needed even more protection.

I took a deep breath as my stomach coiled with anxiety.

Jax's, Cobra's, and Ascher's scents of chestnuts, frost, and pine were a woodsy musk that balanced Sadie's sweet cranberry scent.

I wasn't alone; the other men would help protect the girls.

"Girls" plural because Sadie also smiled and laughed at everything Jax's sisters did, like just being around them made her blissfully happy.

Thinking about Jinx made the corners of my mouth pull into a smile. One thing was for sure: that little girl was going to make an amazing soldier.

Competence and leadership practically wafted off her.

In contrast, Jess, with her bright-green-streaked hair, practically radiated with energy and mischief that was going to get her in trouble. And Jala was sweet in a way that also spelled trouble.

As did the fact that all the girls had huddled around Lucinda like she was already one of them.

Four teenage girls, each of whom my Sadie cared about, and only one of them, Jinx, was cold enough to protect herself.

Any trained soldier would see that keeping them safe in the beast realm was going to be a logistical nightmare.

My whole life, I'd been a lone soldier.

Even before the sacred lake at the edge of the city had revealed I was an omega, I'd kept to myself.

With my family's exorbitant fortune, I'd learned quickly not to trust people's motives. Instead, I'd spent all my time training at the gym and playing with my knives. That was my happy place.

People always disappointed me.

A harsh lesson I'd first learned from my mother. She'd fallen apart after my father's death until she'd eventually wasted away. Apparently, I wasn't enough for her.

I shifted on the floor and noticed Ascher was staring at me.

He was sitting with his shoulders back as blood dripped from open wounds on his face. With his tattoos, horns, and woodsy alpha scent, my omega instincts should have screamed "danger" in his presence.

But for some reason, my instincts trusted him.

His posture was always rigid, his face tensed, like he was constantly weighing every move he made. Constantly searching for threats.

I could relate.

At his core, Ascher was a soldier. A man more comfortable with war than daily life. Only completely relaxed when he held a weapon in his hands and had a task to complete.

Ascher asked softly, "Is she okay?"

I tightened my arms around Sadie's back and cradled her sleeping form against me as her soft purr warmed me to my core.

Ascher's lips curled up with a snarl, and his eyes flickered with live flames.

It was a rhetorical question.

We both knew she'd been fucking tortured while we'd hung uselessly next to her.

I sighed heavily. "How have you survived watching her put herself in harm's way?"

Ascher clenched his jaw. "I fucking haven't."

Cobra was sprawled against Jax, and he blinked open his emerald eyes. "Kitten's a fighter." A self-satisfied smirk flashed across his gorgeous face as he snuggled against Jax.

I wanted to be mad at him because he was the reason she'd been injured. I would have, if I hadn't understood their dynamic.

Anyone could see that Cobra was obsessed with her.

It destroyed him that she wouldn't listen to him, but her spirit was part of the reason he was infatuated.

You could practically feel lightning strikes crackling between the two of them when they squared off. Their attraction was vicious.

"We cannot allow her to be hurt like this again," Jax said with a low growl. His deep reverberation shook through the air, and the driver glanced back with concern.

All of us nodded in agreement.

When it came to Sadie, we were on the same page.

Jax breathed deeply and squeezed Cobra against him, similar to how I was squeezing Sadie.

Even an idiot could see that if Sadie was Cobra's damnation, then Jax was his solace.

Cobra was more beast than man, and Jax was more man than beast.

Everything about Jax screamed calm power.

He was old enough to have complete control over his baser urges and patient enough to harness that calm. Compared to cat and wolf shifters, bears were rare, and often kept to themselves.

I respected Jax for his calm temperament because, in my experience, the most powerful alphas were the most corrupt.

But Jax didn't assert his strength over others.

He was Cobra's moral compass, a natural leader that everyone looked to. I'd instinctually leaned against him for support and followed his lead blindly.

Until now, I'd always been the one in charge. I'd trained the soldiers in the fae queen's army, and I'd been the lead during missions.

But when Jax had stepped forward to get initiated, even before Sadie had, I'd followed without question. We were a group, and he knew what was best for us. We all felt it in our bones.

"We're here," the driver said.

I inhaled sharply as anxiety settled over me like a heavy blanket.

For the first time in over two decades, I was home.

CHAPTER 8

SADIE

MANSIONS

"No, I want my roll to have butter on it," I grumbled at the server, who kept refusing to give me any. Every time I reached for it, the server pulled his hand away.

It was maddening, and I was one second away from infecting him with my blood. You didn't take a woman's butter.

A callused hand jostled my shoulder gently, and a honeyed British accent whispered, "Sadie, wake up."

The buffet of food disappeared, and my head throbbed with agony.

"Ow," I moaned as I went to rub my eyes and they smarted with pain.

Blinking open crusty, swollen lids, the first things I saw were stunning purple eyes hovering inches from my face.

"Are you okay?" Xerxes said softly, his warm breath fluttering against my cheek. Dried blood streaked down his olive side, and his lush lips were swollen and cut.

Concern radiated off him in waves. "Do you need me to carry you?"

His question brought me back to reality, and I gently pushed him away. "Nope, I'm totally fine."

Then, with a long, dramatic moan, I pulled my aching limbs out of the car and stumbled into the chilly rain.

As I shivered pathetically in the downpour, I found myself once again missing the balmy climate of the fae realm.

I'd gone from two suns to a cold, windy night.

My gut told me I was going to become wildly depressed in the beast realm.

Although, a small part of me loved the drama of the miserable weather because it matched the ache in my bones and my soul.

It surprised me that the empty car didn't explode behind us as we limped forward into the rainy night. It felt like we were living in a grainy action movie.

I tipped my head back, and the rain washed over the throbbing cuts on my face.

It felt good.

The sky was an inky black, and for a long moment, I lost myself in the foggy memory of the beating.

"Um, why aren't we going inside?" Cobra asked. He was no longer being carried by Jax and was clearly upset about it.

I made a face back at him. "Wow, a woman can't even have a dramatic moment in the rain without a man ruining it for her. Classic."

Ascher and Xerxes looked at me like I was crazy, and Jax just smiled.

Still, all the men stood staring like I was supposed to do something. Were they waiting for me to fall apart?

I chuckled.

It was pouring, the perfect backdrop for a long sob, but the only thing I felt was dead inside.

Well, dead and hungry.

I needed a hot bath and a mountain of warm bread with butter. The nightmare of the server still shook me to my core. Then I needed to sleep for a decade until I forgot about everything that kept happening in my life.

With a heavy sigh of determination, I turned toward the building and limped forward.

My mouth dropped open, and I stopped.

Xerxes and Ascher almost ran into me, and both immediately wrapped their arms around my sides as I collapsed.

I was so stunned I didn't bother to correct them as they carried me forward together like I couldn't walk.

Holy mother of the moon goddess.

We were walking toward a mansion.

Massive skyscrapers towered off in the distance. It was still Serpentine City, but different.

I whipped my concussed head back and forth.

Behind us, massive, gnarled trees covered in white-and-pink flowers lined the city street, creating a tunnel of blooms.

In front of us, a mansion of gothic architecture towered and was more expansive than the training center back in the shifter realm. Ivy crawled across the brick.

As we approached the wrought-iron gate in front of the house, it glowed with enchantment and swung open.

"Welcome home, Master Xerxes," a thickly accented voice said from nowhere.

I turned to gape at the omega, who was casually carrying me toward the mansion like it was no big deal.

"Master?" I squeaked out.

Xerxes shook his head with a sigh, long blond hair plastered across his face. "ABOs are very dramatic. Those with old money still follow archaic traditions from centuries ago. It's hard to move forward when ABOs live for so long."

I sputtered as we got closer to the stately mansion. "So you're a part of this old money?"

"Unfortunately," he muttered.

I nodded, grateful that Ascher and Xerxes were carrying me, because my legs would have probably given out.

"That sucks." I grimaced.

Xerxes looked at me weirdly. His purple eyes narrowed as he stared at me with intensity. "What do you mean?"

I gave him a confused look back; it seemed pretty clear to me. "That you have to follow old rules and bullshit. I'm guessing you can't just do what you want while you're in this realm?"

He didn't respond, and I narrowed my eyes at him as he dragged me forward toward the shadowy mansion.

I could practically hear the rich children back in the shifter realm, scoffing at my ripped clothes. They'd made fun of the threadbare sheets the school had lent me.

In every realm, there were rich people who thought they were better than others.

I shivered, and it wasn't from the cold.

At least when you were poor, you could see how egotistical the rich pricks were. How blinded they were by their parents' money. Too obsessed with their status to realize their perception of self-importance shackled them.

Xerxes rapped his knuckles against the massive front door. He was still staring at me, and the silence gnawed at me.

"So do you hate it, or are you also a rich prick?" I asked softly and couldn't keep the sass out of my voice.

My stomach pinched as the memories of my days

serving pretentious men in business suits who groped and pawed at me like I was an object.

Xerxes looked like Prince Charming, and he was also filthy rich. It didn't take a genius to put two and two together.

Had my instincts been wrong?

His fingers tightened against my rib cage, and he pulled me out of Ascher's arms so I was pressed flush against him.

Ever so slowly, Xerxes leaned his handsome face down so he was bent at the waist and we were eye to eye. He leaned his heavily muscled arms against the side of his mansion so I was caged against him.

My stomach cramped as warm, spicy cinnamon wafted off him in a delectable cloud that even the rain couldn't cover up.

My mouth watered.

Rivulets of red streaked across the sides of his handsome face.

"Yes, I am rich." His swollen mouth hovered so close to mine that I couldn't breathe. "No, I don't regret it. Especially now."

My heart hammered as I tried to decipher his meaning. "That's embarrassing for you," I whispered back.

He traced a callused finger down the side of my neck.

My core spasmed.

Xerxes's voice deepened until it was a low growl. "You know what's embarrassing?"

He paused, and I gulped.

I took the bait. "What?"

Xerxes leaned forward until his lips tickled my ears. "How obsessed you're going to be once you enjoy one of the showers in *my* mansion."

I narrowed my eyes at him as I tried to ignore the way my legs were suddenly trembling.

Purple eyes flashing, he grinned. "Also, yes."

"Yes, what?"

"I'm a rich prick."

His words penetrated the thick haze that was fogging my brain. "Wait, what?" I pulled back.

A stuffy voice said, "Master Xerxes, your arrival is a delight. The moon goddess has blessed us."

Xerxes pulled away from me and turned to greet the short man, who was dressed in an impeccable business suit with a handkerchief draped over his arm.

My knees were still wobbly from the intensity of the omega pinning me to the wall, but I was cognizant enough to be shocked that the moon goddess was being mentioned over the sun god. Maybe people in this realm respected her more than the sun? Relatable.

Ascher looked down at my unsteady form, picked me up bridal-style, and carried me into the mansion.

Cobra licked his lips. "You liked that, Kitten?" His knowing smirk told me he knew I had.

I rolled my eyes. "Big words for someone still being supported by Jax."

A purr rumbled from Jax's chest as the big man grinned, his arm draped across Cobra's side, holding him up.

Cobra narrowed his eyes. "I just like being carried by *my* man."

I smirked back. "Jax, will you carry me?"

I gently pulled away from Ascher, who frowned.

"Be careful, Princess."

Jax moved his arm to carry me, but my gloating stopped because he didn't put Cobra down. Instead, he just maneuvered both of us so we were each supported by one of his arms.

"Are you sure he's *yours*?" I snarled at Cobra.

Emerald glowed. "Are you sure you're both not mine? Because, Kitten, it seems like you are."

I opened my mouth to argue, but stopped when someone screeched my name.

With a startle, I looked around and took in the fact that I was in an opulent foyer.

A massive antique crystal chandelier hung from the high ceiling and cast a soft yellow glow across the dramatic double staircase that four teenage girls and Aran were sprinting down.

Blushing, I shoved myself out of Jax's hold and brushed myself off.

For some reason, I acted like a complete fool around the men, especially Cobra. He scrambled my brain and made me forget what I was doing.

I vowed to be better.

"Oh my sun god." Aran gasped as she took in our beaten appearances.

"I'll have healing paste delivered to your rooms," the butler said.

He had a stuffy, calm demeanor, and his face didn't so much as twitch as he took in our haggard states.

"Thank you, Walter." Xerxes bowed his head.

In response, Walter bowed his even lower. "No. Thank you, Master. It is an honor to have you back."

A soft burned scent drifted off of Walter as he bent low, signifying that he was a beta.

Instantly, my stomach cramped at Xerxes's words about being a rich prick.

He kept servants.

My back and chest smarted with the phantom pain of a belt, and memories of Dick flashed through my mind like a bad movie.

I didn't want to embarrass Walter by calling Xerxes out, so I settled on passive-aggressively glaring at him.

He didn't seem like an ass, but I guessed you could never tell with men these days.

Unaware of my righteous indignation on his behalf, Walter vibrated with excitement as he led us to our bedrooms.

His stiff steps were quick and efficient as he gave a tour of the mansion. "There are showers in every bedroom, and I'll deliver the healing supplies. Anything you need, please let me know. The girls have already settled into rooms. I will alert the kitchen staff at once to the number of guests."

My stomach plummeted once again.

More servants.

Instead of verbally ending Xerxes's life—I'd deal with him later—I concentrated on the girls.

Jax had his arms around Jess and Jala, and Jinx was arguing with Cobra about something. From the animated hand gestures, Ascher appeared to be taking Jinx's side.

In front, Xerxes walked with Walter and kept patting the old man on his shoulder.

Beside me, Lucinda and Aran had tears of worry in their eyes. Well, Lucinda had tears; Aran narrowed her eyes at me angrily.

I smiled at both of them. "Seriously, it wasn't that bad."

Aran scoffed. "It looks like you've been tortured by an earth fae, then stabbed by a water fae for hours."

Lucinda grimaced. "Sis, you really gotta try better to avoid violence."

Suddenly, there was a loud shriek, and everyone

whipped around in surprise. Xerxes pulled out his twin knives.

Immediately, the tension dissipated. It was Cobra who had shrieked, and he was hiding behind Ascher's large frame.

Jinx was holding a long, furry black creature in her hands.

"What is that?" Cobra growl-hissed at Jinx.

For the first time since I'd met her, Jinx giggled like the twelve-year-old girl she was. "It's a ferret. The don stopped by to say hello and gave us him as a housewarming gift."

Jax growled.

My internal radar went off as I remembered Xerxes shifting from a nice little kitten into the fae queen's soldier.

"Are you sure that's not an omega in disguise?" I asked as I glared at the fluffy creature.

Jinx glared at me. "Don't be ridiculous. He's just a ferret." She held him protectively against her chest. "He's mine."

I narrowed my eyes and debated ripping it out of her arms and torturing it to get it to reveal itself.

Jinx scowled harder.

If I was wrong, she might actually kill me. "Whatever," I said under my breath as I glanced sideways at what was most definitely a spy.

"What do you mean, the don stopped by?" Cobra straightened to his full six-foot-five height, eyes blazing emerald. "Did he threaten you girls?"

Aran raised her hand. "Did everyone forget I was looking after them? He honestly seemed pretty chill and just gave us the pet for good luck. Told us to stay safe and said something about all teenagers needing a pet while stroking his snake. Then he left."

We all gaped at Aran.

She shrugged. "They were never in danger, trust me."

I opened my mouth to argue, but then remembered the way Aran's eyes had turned blackish orange. Sharp claws had sprouted from her fingertips, and she'd brutally slaughtered her powerful mother.

Aran was definitely something more than fae, and only a fool would call her incompetent.

Before anyone could say anything, Jinx shouted, "Everyone, relax!" Then she gave a girlish squeal of delight and held up the black ferret like he was a prize. "This is Noodle. He is my new best friend."

Noodle took that moment to chitter and wave his two little front legs in the air.

Cobra shrieked and hid behind Ascher.

Ascher moved to the side and glared down at him with exasperation. "Dude, you're embarrassing yourself."

"That creature is *not* natural. Tell her to get rid of it, Jax."

Jax sighed heavily, like he couldn't believe this was his life. He looked at his little sister, who was cuddling the ferret against her cheek like a normal girl her age.

Something told me she didn't make friends easily.

After a long moment, Jax nodded, and his golden chains tinkled. "Jinx, you can keep Noodle. Cobra, grow up."

With that, Walter continued with his room tour.

The ferret perched on top of Jinx's dark head, and she whispered something about "nincompoops" to him.

My gut told me there was going to be a lot of chaos in our future.

CHAPTER 9
ASCHER
INFERNO OF RAGE

I SHOVED my hands through my unkempt hair and fought the urge to snarl like a wild animal.

Just barely, I kept control of the fire raging through my soul.

Walter pointed out yet another massive bedroom with a four-poster bed, hearth, and bathroom en suite. He was giving us a tour of all the rooms before we decided which ones to take.

Truthfully, I didn't hear a fucking word he said.

Piece by careful piece, I rebuilt my facade of indifference.

My face was stony like hard marble, while my chest burned with an inferno of rage.

Nothing could stop the pain.

With every cell in my being, I wanted to slam my fist into the wood carvings that neatly decorated the arched hall. Xerxes had old money, and his house was a mansion of exquisite caliber.

I didn't give a single shit.

All I cared about was Sadie, and the wicked black-and-green bruises that covered every inch of her skin.

I kept my expression bland and pretended I was unbothered and calm. A chill person like Jax.

Nothing could be further from the truth.

The fires inside my chest burned me alive, and I had to bite down on my tongue to stop myself from screaming.

Scream at Sadie for putting herself in harm's way; scream at the fucker Spike for hurting her; scream at the don; scream at everyone.

The more Sadie put herself in danger, the more one thing became apparent: I wasn't like the other alphas.

I couldn't let her put herself in harm's way because she had her own convictions and blah, blah, blah. She was a fucking princess.

My princess.

My fingernails dug into my palms hard enough to draw blood.

I'd always known I had issues with women. The syndicate had been a vile place, and I'd thought I was different from my father. Better.

But the truths of my past still haunted me.

Growing up, I'd learned that women were commodities. Sluts that were good for fucking and nothing else. If you gave them too much, they'd take it all. Greedy, lazy whores that used their bodies.

My teeth dug into my bottom lip, and blood flooded my mouth.

The mantra of a woman's purpose had been hammered into my head from a young age. My father had made sure of it.

But in one respect, he'd failed.

For each slap he'd doled out to a woman, I'd received a

worse beating. It didn't take a genius to put two and two together.

My father was fucking unhinged.

Nothing that man said was correct.

I promised myself I would never be like him, that I would never abuse women and use them.

Until now, I'd thought I succeeded at being different from that piece of shit.

I was turning twenty-four years old soon, and I could safely say I'd never hurt a woman and had never lifted a hand against one.

Never wanted to.

Sure, I'd fucked them until they screamed with release, worshipped their bodies until they cried my name, but I'd never once asserted my power over their smaller bodies.

But I'd never felt anything more than a surface-level attachment to a woman. Done nothing more than traded pleasure for pleasure.

I realized my problem.

My temperament had swung too far the other way.

Now that I'd grown attached to a woman, I fucking cared *too* much.

The horrors of growing up had warped me.

The pain, fear, and tears of women as they'd run from my father's room, his fist slamming against their heads casually when they upset him.

Fire raged inside my soul.

I wanted to throw Sadie over my shoulder and lock her in a room because I couldn't stand to see her injured.

It killed me inside.

If it weren't for the rest of the men accepting Sadie's decisions, I would have physically stopped her from initiating. I'd have fucking knocked her out before I'd have allowed her to go through with it.

But I couldn't.

I was held back by how badly I'd fucked up with the fae queen. I was a hypocritical ass, because I'd been the one to put her in danger.

But holy fuck.

Jax talked about giving her the freedom to make her own decisions—what a crock of shit.

I couldn't fucking comprehend how he held himself back from ordering her around. I saw the inferno in his eyes, the way his jaw tensed when she'd marched forward to get *tortured*.

Somehow, he'd held himself back.

I'd forced my body to mimic his. With every ounce of control in my being, I'd fashioned my features into granite and stood idly by while she put herself in danger.

It had killed me.

Now I trembled with the urge to make her mine.

In that way, I understood Cobra.

If I possessed her, if she was mine, then I could forbid her from doing things for her own safety. Then she would never get hurt again, and I could relax.

I dragged my hands roughly across my sensitive horns, and the pain cleared my jumbled thoughts.

No.

I was a product of a fucked-up childhood, and I couldn't think straight around Sadie. If I acted like I wanted to, just like Jax kept telling Cobra, I would lose her for good.

That wasn't an option.

Somewhere in our time together in the shifter and fae realms, my obsession had become something more. I woke up thinking about her, and I went to bed worrying about her.

My life had always felt rudderless. I was highly skilled, a perfect soldier of control and violence, but there had always been something missing.

An ennui of sorts.

It was all too easy to play the soldier; it didn't take any effort to kill someone or beat them into submission. Another day, another tattoo carved into my flesh.

But holy fuck, I wasn't bored anymore.

The emptiness in my chest was now an inferno of obsession.

Sadie, my fucking princess, gave the violence a reason.

Now I knew I was a killing machine of strength and sinew because I had to be the one to protect her.

If I gave a shit about any of the sun god's lore, I would call it destiny. Moon fate or whatever the mystical bullshit was when people whispered about destined mates.

As I battled my internal control issues, Aran arched one of her eyebrows at me like she could sense my tormented thoughts.

She shouldn't be able to tell shit.

We walked down the hall as a group, and my face was a stony mask of indifference.

I stared back at her.

Aran's unnaturally blue eyes were bright as arctic water, and I wondered for the millionth time how I'd thought she was a boy.

Even enchanted with short hair and a boy's build, her features were too feminine, and her eyes didn't fit her masculine face.

It was hard to put into words because it wasn't anything about the physical features themselves.

There was a hauntedness in them, a melancholic gleam of sadness that screamed of soul-deep secrets and endless pain. The type of pain that could only be caused by having the mad fae queen as your mother.

Aran's eyes were her giveaway.

They were what had made me turn her over to her mother on that fucked-up day.

My stomach cramped as Aran kept staring at me.

The teenage girls walked around us, chattering to one another. Jax smiled at his family. Cobra bantered with them, and my princess walked ahead with her sister.

A burst of light twisted through my chest as she smiled. Finally, Sadie was safe and content after too many hours of fucking pain.

Even beaten half to death, the group exuded palpable happiness.

Aran and I were the odd ones out.

My stomach pinched again as I looked over at Sadie's best friend.

I claimed to be better than my father, but it was also my fault that Aran's cover had been blown and that she'd done the unthinkable.

I tried to relax my features and give her a small smile.

Instead, my face hardened into a grimace, and the sourness in my throat burned. I'd never learned how to express emotions.

You fucked women and didn't get attached, patted men on the back, and focused on being the best soldier you could be.

Emotions were for the weak because facial expressions and feelings could be exploited and used against you.

Logically, I knew this.

It didn't make the ache in my stomach go away every

time I thought about Sadie's pain or looked over at Aran's haunted gaze.

Aran walked silently as the group smiled around her.

Fae royalty among shifters.

Now, because of my own actions, she was the queen of a fucking dreadful realm.

I fisted my palms and willed myself to forget about it. There was enough on my plate trying to keep Sadie safe; why did it fucking matter that her best friend was clearly not okay?

Other people's problems weren't my issues, and I obviously had no fucking clue how to deal with women.

Aran huffed and rolled her eyes at me. "You got a problem with something?" Her tone was scathing, but it didn't have its usual sass.

I didn't miss the way her arms shook slightly.

Back in the shifter realm, she'd been bursting with energy, always defending Sadie, and throwing herself into training.

I'd been trained to spot the signs of lying, and her words were too clipped. Her resonance was off.

She had the body tics of someone who was under extreme duress and trying to act like they were fine when they weren't.

She wasn't well.

My stomach cramped, and I asked myself what Jax would do in the situation.

His sisters were literally hanging off his arms and beaming up at him as he listened to every one of their ridiculous statements, like they were of the utmost importance.

"I'm sorry," I blurted out, and the words caught in the back of my throat. "It was my fault…your mother…I didn't know." I stared down at the polished mahogany wood floor as Walter showed the group yet another room.

Aran stopped walking and gaped at me like I'd grown two heads. "Wow."

"What?" My hackles rose, and I snapped back. Of course I was fucking this up. I should have just stayed fucking quiet and not tried. Emotions were weakness, and I needed to rebuild my defen—

Aran nudged me with her elbow, and it cut off my train of thought. "It is totally your fault."

I nodded in agreement; I was the ass who'd ruined her life.

"But it's also not. My mother was going to find me eventually, and her existence was always hanging over my head. Even if I wanted to, I couldn't escape my birthright."

Aran shrugged in an attempt to look casual, but she itched aggressively at her back.

Suddenly, an idea struck me. The inferno in my chest leaped with a new purpose.

"I see what you are to Sadie, and I know how much you mean to her, so I won't let the fae take you back. I vow to you my allegiance."

The darkness in Aran's eyes abated slightly, and for the first time since she'd done the unthinkable, a smile split her face. She stopped itching at her back.

The pain in my stomach lessened, and I marveled at the lightness that burst through me.

I put my hand out.

Aran shook it vigorously and said, "Deal. I'm taking you up on that shit. Do you know how hard it is going to be to evade the fae looking for their queen?"

She smirked, her eyes lit up with an edge of violence, and I couldn't help but smirk back.

Aran was a fellow soldier. Violence recognized violence.

I smirked. "It's gonna get messy."

Aran grinned. "We're probably going to have to kill some people."

"We're going to need to find weapons."

A cough down the hall caught my attention, and when I looked away from Aran, I was surprised to find everyone standing in the hall, staring at us oddly.

"What?" I snapped.

Had I somehow fucked up again?

Sadie smiled, walked up to me, and patted my chest. "You just earned some major brownie points for not being a total dick for once." She paused, then ran down the hall, shouting, "Also, I call the biggest room!"

I gaped at her retreating form, noting once again that something close to happiness had sparked in me at her words. The feeling quickly dissipated into confusion.

"I call sharing. I get night terrors!" Aran yelled, and sprinted after her.

Sadie laughed. "Bitch, I definitely have worse PTSD. Get your own room."

"Literally, I'm not sleeping alone. So get used to me, roomie." Aran followed Sadie.

They cackled at each other, and then all four of the teen girls raced down the hall after them, fighting over who was bunking with who.

Noodle, the damn ferret, even squealed loudly like he wanted to add to the noise.

I sighed heavily and followed like a normal, sane person who didn't want a roommate.

Walter had literally just shown us over twenty rooms.

Jax smiled and clapped me on the back as I walked up to him, and Cobra nodded at me.

I didn't know what had just happened, but for the first time in my life, the inferno in my chest wasn't eating me alive.

And I had earned something called brownie points.

It felt nice.

CHAPTER 10

SADIE

TRUSTING YOU

"ARE you seriously not going to get your own room? This house has like twenty." I rubbed my tender face tiredly as Aran threw herself onto my massive four-poster bed.

Well, mine in the sense that I'd screamed dibs at the top of my lungs.

Aran arched an eyebrow, but it didn't have the same snooty effect as when she was a girl. "Are you seriously trying to kick out your best friend, who is emotionally unstable right now?"

"We're twenty-one-year-old grown women. Don't you want your own bed?"

"No, you're twenty-one. I'm twenty-four. Which means, as your elder, I demand you cuddle with me every night."

I narrowed my eyes at her. "You're really not joking?"

Aran climbed off the bed and inspected the elegant decor scattered around the room. She flipped a switch on the wall, and the massive fireplace roared to life.

Aran shrieked and immediately flicked it off.

The sound was blood-curdling.

I gaped at her.

The horrified expression on her face turned into laughter, and soon she was on her knees, gasping like a maniac.

Aran's voice shook. "I'm scared of fire and blood. I'm disguised as a boy with an enchantment that isn't strong enough to change my vagina into a dick. My best friend is being initiated into a scary gang and looks awful. Also, as we speak, I'm probably being hunted by insanely powerful fae."

On her hands and knees on the plush carpet, she inhaled raggedly, like she was drowning in the air.

Her horrifying reaction to the flames seemed to echo through the opulent space.

Aran choked like she was sobbing, but her eyes were bone-dry and unfocused.

My gut told me she couldn't cry even if she wanted to.

Stomach in knots, I collapsed onto my aching knees beside her and patted her head.

Morbidly, my shaking hands were discolored with blue-black bruises, the hues similar to the lowlights in her short turquoise hair.

As my best friend gasped in horror, I silently trembled in the aftermath of torture.

There was nothing to say to comfort her.

Our situations were too depressing for meaningless platitudes.

But like Aran, I didn't cry.

Somewhere among discovering I was part of a lost race of ancient fae, infecting the fae queen with my blood, and getting tortured by Spike, I'd gone cold.

Maybe it was the true disposition of my heritage. Maybe it was shock. Most likely, it was just torture.

Either way, I was empty.

Finally, after what could have been minutes or hours, Aran stopped choking and sat back on her heels.

Her tormented expression smoothed away as she rebuilt her calm facade.

The distressed person was gone, and in her place sat a cold, emotionless fae. Just like Ascher, she expertly concealed her feelings.

Abruptly, Aran straightened and smiled pleasantly. "I call the right side of the bed."

I nodded, still not understanding why we had to sleep in the same room.

As Aran sensed my hesitation, her smile fell. "I can't sleep alone. Please. The nights have always been a…bad time for me."

The unspoken truth, that her mother used to hurt her in the night, hung heavy between us.

I grabbed her hand in mine. In that moment, as we sprawled together on the floor, déjà vu settled over me.

Aran's experiences were eerily similar to my own.

My skin prickled with premonition. We were always so busy trying to survive the present that it felt like we were missing the big picture. In a few months, it had gone from a hunch to a burning surety that we were missing something crucial.

The High Court, the different realms, that I was a blood fae, Aran's black eyes, the dark poems that kept taking over people's bodies around us.

It only happened when we were together.

Why had I thought everything was simple because the numb was common to half-breeds?

I'd forgotten the bigger picture.

The endless problems.

But not knowing what was going on changed nothing. The beast realm and its bloodthirsty Mafia were my new reality, and Aran was still the Queen of the Fae Realm.

All we could do was adapt. The rules might change, but the stakes didn't lessen.

One thing was constant: the realms punished the weak.

I admired the constellations that were carved into the ornate mahogany ceiling, and said, "Fine, just don't freak out if I wake up screaming in the middle of the night."

Aran squeezed my hand. "Oooh, what if we both wake up screaming at the same time?"

"That would be soooo fun and flirty," I said sarcastically.

Aran looked down at our blood-caked hands and shuddered. "I call the shower first."

Before I could argue, she sprinted into the en suite room and slammed the door shut.

I rolled my eyes. "This is literally why it's dumb that we're sharing a room. There are enough bedrooms and showers that we shouldn't have to share."

"Go eat some food, bestie!" Aran yelled back, ignoring me as the water started running.

I shook my head because she was insane and wandered down the massive hallway. Aran had five minutes tops; then I was coming back and causing a scene.

My skin crawled with disgust as I realized how dirty I was, crusty sand mixed with old and new blood covering my body.

It itched something fierce.

As I rounded the hall, an older woman in a black dress with a white apron hurried past me, carrying sheets. She smiled and gave a small curtsy.

I grimaced.

Xerxes's servants must be under orders to appear happy.

Down the massive hall and sweeping grand stairs, I followed the smells of bacon and syrup.

When I found the source of the food, my feet stopped in shock.

I didn't know that kitchens could be so shiny.

The walls were a dark green, and every surface was covered in glittering black marble flecked with gold. Stunning gold fixtures and yet another extravagant crystal chandelier cast sparks of light throughout the dark room.

Everyone must have been showering, because food was spread out buffet-style. Walter stood alone in the room with a serving spoon.

"Mistress, please help yourself." Walter nodded toward the feast before him.

I gnawed on my lower lip and tried to act casual as my stomach howled like a beast.

Walter held up a shiny plate with gold trim. "Just tell me what you want, and I'll fill your plate."

My face burned with anger.

How dare Xerxes force his servants to fill his plates for him? How lazy and pretentious could a person be?

"Um, I'll take everything," I said, and Walter nodded like choosing twenty different pieces of food was completely respectable.

As he piled the food onto my plate, I leaned forward discreetly. "How dare he treat you like this. I won't stand for it."

"What, Mistress? What are you talking about?" Walter's bushy gray eyebrows quivered with confusion.

Voices sounded close by, and panic raced through me.

"Blink once if you want me to do something drastic," I whispered as I busied myself grabbing a glass of orange juice.

"Sadie, you haven't showered yet?" Xerxes sauntered

into the kitchen. Two female servants followed, staring up at him with pink cheeks.

My stomach dropped as I turned away from Walter.

I'd been so close.

Xerxes grinned at me. Unaware of my ire, he wore a silky black robe that was rolled up at the sleeves, showcasing his long, corded muscles and veins. His almost too-pretty features fit in among the stunning opulence of his house.

The prince was home.

I turned away from Xerxes with disgust and focused on Walter. As he handed me the overflowing plate, I stared at him intently, waiting to see if he'd blink.

Walter's eyes were wide.

He stared back at me and didn't flinch.

Wow, Xerxes had him so under his thumb that he was clearly too terrified to even blink.

Things were worse than I'd thought.

Xerxes chuckled as he stood beside me. "Are you going to eat or just stand there?" His cinnamon scent spiked sweet, and he flashed a row of white teeth.

"Um, sure." I winked aggressively at Walter—to let him know I was still going to save him—and the poor man choked.

He'd clearly never had someone understand his plight before. That was going to change.

Trying to act casual, like I wasn't about to stage a coup d'état and free all Xerxes's servants, I settled into a plush chair at the long black table.

Then, like a true lady, I shoveled my entire plate into my mouth in less than twenty seconds.

The good news was I'd eaten so fast that my body didn't even know it was supposed to be full.

Taking advantage of my momentum, I went to get seconds.

Xerxes sat across from me at the table, and we ate together in silence. When he went to get thirds, I followed. I wasn't about to be shown up by any man.

After my tenth bread roll, my ire calmed down.

I was no longer ready to launch a bloody rebellion; a small uprising would do. After my fourteenth chocolate-chip cookie, I magnanimously decided no one needed to die.

They just needed some maiming.

In between my violent thoughts, I inspected Xerxes. He hadn't showered either, from the sticky helmet of blood that still coated his mane of blond hair.

"So do you like your room?" Xerxes's smooth accent rolled off his tongue like honey.

From what I'd seen of the beast realm, as small and as bloody as my experience had been, everyone talked with accents. But there was something about Xerxes's lilting voice that made my skin tingle.

His words were *smooth*.

I nodded and impressively swallowed two bread rolls at once. "Yeah, the four-poster beds are amazing. I already feel more elegant and dramatic, like an old Victorian lady from the human realm."

Xerxes chuckled. "Just wait until you see the library."

"Any books on how to maim without killing?" I asked innocently.

"What?"

"What?" I inspected my cuticle like I was a prim lady without a care in the world, not a hot mess missing three of my nails from where they'd been ripped off. Violently.

A comfortable silence fell as we both lost ourselves in homicidal thoughts.

Xerxes licked his swollen lips and leaned forward. "Who are you trying to maim, alpha?"

I choked, and it wasn't from the three cookies in my mouth.

For some reason, when he'd said "alpha," images of silk ropes, gasps, and his naked body gyrating had flashed through my mind.

Xerxes's red tongue snaked out across his swollen, split lips, and he raked a hand across his stubbled jaw.

"You," I blurted out.

He leaned closer, purple eyes sparking with heat. "Oh, really?"

I nodded like a blithering idiot. *Weren't we talking about maiming?* It felt like we were talking about something else.

"There is actually something I want to show you." Xerxes pushed his chair back and offered me his large, blood-splattered palm. "Come with me."

It wasn't a question.

Apparently, I was a pervert, because I swore he emphasized the word *come*.

Before I could debate the merits of bringing my plate of cookies with me, Xerxes tugged gently on my hand and dragged me through his mansion. His callused thumb slowly dragged across my wrist.

Months of violence and zero sexual action had fried my brain, because my core fluttered.

Yes, I was turned on by a thumb.

This was a new low.

Before I could blurt out something embarrassing, like a compliment on the shape of Xerxes's knuckle—it was nice and lean, not too knobby—we came to a halt.

We'd walked through the entire mansion, and stood in

an alcove hidden at the end of the hallway, in front of a black door with a brass handle.

Xerxes grabbed the handle like he was going to open it, but stopped and rested his forehead against the door. He took a deep breath as his biceps and forearms bunched.

"Um, do you need me to break down the door?" I asked awkwardly, unsure what was going on.

He must have been more tired than I'd thought.

I took a step back, ready to throw myself at the door and showcase my prowess.

Xerxes's large shoulders shook as he chuckled weakly. "No, Sadie, that's not what I need."

Still, we didn't enter.

"Let me kick it."

In a tavern of nightmares, a lifetime ago, I'd once broken Lucinda's door when she didn't answer me. She'd been safe and asleep in bed and had gasped in awe at her big sister's physical prowess.

Just kidding. She'd said, "Sis, you're acting like a psycho. You need to learn how to relax."

She'd been going through her preteen phase. Meanwhile, I'd been going through my "terrified Dick was secretly hurting my little sister too" phase.

Moral of the story: I could break down a door.

Xerxes took another deep breath and looked down at me with exasperation. "I can open the door." The muscle in his jaw ticked, like something was upsetting him.

We still didn't enter.

"Okay, whatever you say, big man." Men really needed to learn when to ask for help.

Startlingly fast, Xerxes moved and pressed himself against me, caging me in.

Up close, the purple of his eyes looked like an amethyst

quartz. Flecks of light purple and white created an otherworldly sparkle. He really was unfairly pretty.

Xerxes rasped softly, "I want to show you my nest."

My heart skipped a beat.

I whispered softly, "Do you lay eggs?" Had I missed the signs all along? Was Xerxes part bird, part kitten?

My mind stuttered as I tried to picture it.

A broken chuckle burst from his chest. "My omega nest, you idiot." He groaned and leaned his forehead against mine.

"Oh." A faint memory of reading about an omega's safe haven tickled the back of my brain. I couldn't remember any of the specifics, just that the book made a big deal about their importance.

His cinnamon scent spiked until it coated my mouth in sugar spice.

I fought the urge to lick my lips.

Just for a taste.

My gut pinched under the intensity of his stare. He wasn't just asking me to see his nest; this was something more, and the smart thing would have been to tell him I needed space.

To back away and say that I wasn't ready and that I needed to recover from recent events. That we should wait and not put pressure on anything because I wasn't ready for an omega-alpha relationship.

"Show me." My broken voice was too loud in the quiet alcove.

No one had ever called me smart.

No one had ever said, "Sadie, she's a clever one. That girl has a bright future." However, I'd been labeled mentally unhinged with homicidal impulses plenty of times.

In fact, a teacher had once told me, "You're going to die someday in a violent, terrifying way."

To be fair, I'd made a farting noise with my armpit every time she'd spoken, and had spread a rumor that she shit in the shower. I was thirteen, for sun god's sake; what else was I supposed to do?

Xerxes reached forward and trailed his long, callused fingers down my sensitive neck.

Goose bumps marked his trail.

A low purr rumbled from my chest as he bent closer until our breath mingled. His words tickled my mouth. "Good girl."

In that moment, I learned something very important about myself: I had a praise kink.

Xerxes pulled back. Cinnamon sugar burned my lungs, and he shoved open the heavy door.

When my eyes adjusted to the dim light, I gasped.

"Welcome to my nest."

CHAPTER II
SADIE
HIS NEST

Blessed sun god.

My senses were overwhelmed.

The sounds of a thunderstorm—the patter of rain, the crash of thunder, and crack of lightning—echoed around the room, unnaturally loud.

If I hadn't known better, I'd have thought we were standing in the middle of the storm.

I tipped my face back, and my eyes widened.

Across the ceiling and walls, there wasn't a single window in the room, dark clouds creating the illusion of torrential rain slamming down.

The only sources of light were glowing neon raindrops and a massive black marble hearth that blazed with soft, red flames.

That wasn't even the best part.

The ceiling was low, and the biggest bed I'd ever seen was built into a platform on the floor. It was covered in fluffy white blankets and pillows.

It was plush.

The massive hearth blazed so large it almost took up an

entire wall.

I was dumbstruck by the sheer *coziness* of the room. I didn't know what I had expected, but it wasn't this.

Xerxes towered next to me, covered in muscles, bruises, and dried blood. He handled knives with deadly precision and was a cold soldier most of the time. For sun god's sake, the man had worked for the *evil* fae queen.

Yet he blushed as he showed me his fluffy bed?

There was a long pause as he stared at me and I stared at the illusion of rain streaking down the walls.

Finally, I realized he was waiting for me to speak. "Could you make it snow?"

I didn't know why it mattered; I liked the rain just fine. Before I could take back my impulsive statement, Xerxes said loudly, "Enchantment, snow."

Suddenly, the illusion on the walls transformed from rain into big, fluffy snowflakes.

They piled into banks, and the familiar crunch of boots across fresh powder echoed. My hair blew on a cool phantom breeze as the wind howled and branches clattered.

For the first time in months, my shoulders relaxed.

I sighed heavily and closed my eyes, losing myself in time and space until I was perched atop an evergreen.

There was something freeing about being above the world. Something that felt like home.

The wood creatures chittered. The cold bit into my bones, and the snow drifted around me.

Nothing was more peaceful than a snowy forest; it was violent and comforting.

It was the sheer exhilaration of being alive.

Serenity wasn't the absence of conflict; it was the stillness within chaos.

A warm, callused hand touched my arm, and it jolted

me back to the present. It was too tempting to get lost in the past. To forget all the awfulness of life and sink into daydreams of a cold forest.

Dick had stalked me through those same trees. Yet somehow, they'd become my mental solace.

"Do you like it?" Xerxes asked quietly. There was a slight edge of desperation in his honeyed accent, like my answer had the potential to break him.

I smiled up at him, snow falling around us as the wind howled. "I love it."

Xerxes's expressionless face shattered, and an intensity lit his gaze that had me taking a tentative step back.

He stalked forward. "Let's get you clean."

Next thing I knew, I was standing in the bathroom. A single candle flickered against the wall. It was dark and cozy like the rest of the space, black marble flecked with gold covering everything.

It was also confusing as hell.

I stood on the cold stone and shivered at the shiny wall. Xerxes had said it was a shower, but it wasn't like anything I'd ever seen before.

A marble door swung shut and enclosed me in the narrow space, and eucalyptus trailed down the walls, but there was no showerhead or bath nozzle.

It was just smooth marble closing me in.

If I were claustrophobic, I would have been gasping in terror. The sheer quiet of it all overwhelmed my senses. There was nothing to see or feel, other than cold stone and darkness.

"Um, I don't see any button to start the shower!" I yelled out to Xerxes.

"It's on the side of the wall, around shoulder height. Just

push it with your palm."I ran my hands along the marble and shivered as nothing happened.

It was chilly in the mansion, and my naked, blood-crusted flesh was desperate for warm water.

My fingers shook, and I gnawed on my bottom lip as I frantically searched for some type of button.

Nothing happened.

I was ten seconds from falling to my knees and breaking down, all because I couldn't get the hot water to work.

A part of my brain recognized that I was emotionally and physically exhausted.

That was how you knew you were at your wits' end, when the smallest inconvenience became disastrous.

I tried to calm myself, but it didn't matter.

Panic shook through me, and I yelled, "I can't find it!"

Xerxes must have heard the desperation in my voice, because suddenly the solid marble door opened, and his wide shoulders crowded the narrow space.

I covered my nudity with my hands. "Um, what are you doing?" My broken voice was a squeaky rasp.

Xerxes ran his hands along the wall and mumbled absently, "Helping you." He didn't look any lower than my face, and his purple eyes glowed softly in the dark.

Abruptly, his palm pressed into the marble high above my head, and a low hum started.

"Sorry, I forgot you were so short." He didn't move.

Xerxes stood unnaturally still, and his muscles expanded like he was ready to fight as he towered above me. The scent of sugary cinnamon spiked and overpowered the fresh scent of eucalyptus.

I gasped as my vision refocused.

Abruptly, the shower whistled softly, and a thick cloud of steam swirled around us.

Xerxes was still wearing his bloody clothes.

I was still naked.

Neither of us moved.

Neither of us breathed.

A small glow of candlelight illuminated the stunning planes of Xerxes's face. Warmth curled my toes, and I slowly lowered my hands to my side.

Cinnamon spiked, spicy.

My throat burned and my lips tingled with sweetness as an ache throbbed in my core.

The steam burned hotter.

Warm water sprayed us from every direction.

I didn't see any nozzles, but somehow, the water was spraying from the ceiling and the walls in all directions until every inch of my skin tingled with delight.

Xerxes spoke, and his voice was rougher than usual, his smooth accent a guttural growl. "Shower rainstorm."

Instantly, the silence of the black marble shower transformed into an onslaught of sensations.

Thunder cracked.

Lightning flashed.

The warm water pounded against us harder, and it pulsed in punishing sheets, like wind blowing against rain.

Purple eyes glowed brightly as they stared down at me.

Neither of us moved.

Warmth turned my aching muscles to mush, and my knees almost gave out as I leaned against the wall and breathed raggedly.

Every cell in my body quivered with tiredness and need.

Bloody water pooled at our feet.

I closed my eyes and lost myself to the sounds of the storm raging around me as I ignored the fresh memories of torture.

After an eternity of peaceful silence, it startled me when fingers scraped against the back of my skull.

A low, broken moan dragged from my throat.

It seemed Xerxes was following in Ascher's footsteps.

My exhaustion went bone deep, so I didn't fight it when he soaped my hair and washed it intently.

Just leaned back into his fingers and enjoyed it.

The loud purr that rattled through my chest mixed with the rumbling thunder.

When Xerxes finished rinsing my hair, I growled with disappointment but shifted forward.

I was clean now, and it was time to pull myself together and face reality.

My brain sluggishly ran through everything I needed to find out about the Mafia. I also had to get the girls enrolled in some type of schooling program, and—

"Stop," Xerxes growled and cut off my thoughts.

I blinked open my tired eyes at the imposing soldier that glared down at me. "What?"

Lightning cracked.

"Stop thinking. You need to relax. Your body is at its breaking point."

I arched my eyebrow like Aran and drawled, "I'll do whatever I want to do. But thanks for your input, sweet cheeks."

Satisfaction coursed through me as his glowing purple eyes flashed with rage.

Maybe that was why Ascher and Cobra called me ridiculous names. It was exhilarating to piss Xerxes off.

Yes, I was aware I was unwell. No, I didn't care.

Suddenly, Xerxes's elegant fingers wrapped around my neck and pushed me flush against the hard marble.

I gasped with surprise.

Mr. Soft Omega was gone. The evil queen's assassin glared down at me.

Xerxes's callused thumb slowly traced down my neck, while his other hand roughly palmed my small breast.

My hips bucked as he pinched my nipples, and I moaned. "What the fuck do you think you're doing?"

Perfect white teeth flashed in the darkness as Xerxes smirked down at me.

Thunder boomed as the sounds of pouring rain intensified.

"Taking what's mine."

Lightning flashed.

I bucked against him, hyperaware of my core grazing across his pant-covered leg. He pressed against me harder.

"I don't give a fuck if you're an alpha. I'm in charge." Xerxes's voice was a deep rasp, and his breath tickled my ears.

The small space closed in around us; there was nowhere to go.

His long blond hair was plastered against both of us.

The water pounded relentlessly.

"What are you talking about?" I asked breathlessly, as Xerxes tilted my chin back with his hand.

His lush lips trailed down my neck.

Then teeth scraped across the same path as he murmured against my flesh, "I showed you my nest."

Xerxes bit down gently. Hard enough to claim, but not hard enough to break the skin.

His hands trailed across my nipples, down my sensitive stomach, and to rest against my core.

"So?" I whispered.

Were we living in alternate realities because it felt like I was missing something?

Also, why was I so turned on by this?

Xerxes's hands splayed across my waist, and he lifted me higher against the wall so his teeth could trace across my nipples.

My tongue ached with the need to lick his olive skin and see if he tasted as sweet as he smelled.

Every cell in my body craved cinnamon.

Xerxes stilled.

I was hyperaware of his callused fingers that were now dragging slowly through my heat, and the warm mouth pressed against me. A dull ache pulsed between my legs as he deftly rubbed against my clit.

Suddenly, his teeth scraped along my tender nipple, and one of his hands slapped my pussy.

He squeezed my core. "You're *my* alpha. I fucking claim you."

Thunder boomed.

My chest rattled harder with a deep purr.

Pleasure blurred my vision. If I were standing, my knees would have given out. Xerxes's hands tightened around my core and neck.

The two points of contact were the only things holding me up against the cold wall.

Confusion, satisfaction, and desire boomeranged through me.

I licked my lips and tried to sort through my jumbled thoughts. "Aren't you an omega?"

Xerxes hunched over, took my nipple in his mouth, and hummed with agreement.

"And I'm an alpha," I gasped as pleasure streaked. "So, shouldn't I be the one dominating you?"

Abruptly, burned cinnamon filled the space.

Xerxes released me.

My feet slipped across the floor shakily, and my gut cramped at the sudden shift in the air.

Glowing purple eyes were unfocused, pupils blown.

He stared down at me.

I had no idea what was happening, something must have triggered him.

Did I say or do something wrong?

What. The. Fuck.

The power dynamic inverted as Xerxes took another step closer, crowding me against the wall.

Omega threatened alpha.

My breath left my chest in a harsh rattle.

Suddenly, Xerxes bellowed and slammed his fist into the marble beside my head. A loud crack echoed, and my head jolted from the vibrations of marble breaking behind me.

Something had definitely triggered him.

Xerxes was losing his shit.

Fury crackled between us, louder than the lightning and thunder that shook the dark space.

Adrenaline sharpened my vision.

I was no stranger to violence, but it didn't mean I liked it. Didn't mean it was okay.

On pure instinct, I jackknifed my heel against the side of his knee.

There was a loud crack as his legs gave out beneath him.

The water poured over his clothed form, and Xerxes didn't move, just stared unsteadily at the wall.

His scent was sharp, burned cinnamon, eyes unfocused.

He was no longer present with me.

My heart hurt, and my alpha instincts screamed at me to comfort him. Xerxes was an omega, and he was hurting. I wanted to wrap my arms around him in his fluffy bed and run my hands over his back until he calmed.

"I didn't mean it," I whispered, my voice an uncomfortably harsh rasp. I'd meant it as playful banter.

A joke.

Xerxes's head hung forward, shoulders rounded like he was cowering into himself. He didn't acknowledge that he'd heard me.

Slowly, I reached my shaking hand out to reassure him.

I stopped.

He'd thrown his fist inches from my face.

It wasn't my job to fix someone.

I was barely holding on to sanity myself.

With the last of my strength, I jumped up and pushed the button above my head. The shower turned off.

I grabbed two plush towels and gently placed one around Xerxes's shoulders. He didn't move, just knelt on the cold floor with his head hanging forward.

Thunder boomed.

Flashes of yellow highlighted unfocused purple eyes and a clenched jaw.

Xerxes was far away.

"It will be okay," I mumbled awkwardly as I wrapped myself in a towel.

Then, with one last backward glance, I sluggishly stumbled out of his nest, back to my room.

My legs trembled as the sound of marble cracking played on repeat in my head.

It was too intense.

I stumbled down the hall in a daze, and when I finally got to my room, Aran startled awake in the bed.

"Everything okay?" she asked with narrowed eyes.

Okay. There was that fucking word again. *It will be okay* was the most frequent lie ever told.

I leaned against the wall and sighed. "No."

Aran itched aggressively at her back. “It never is. We just gotta stop being surprised.”

I nodded in agreement and barely mustered enough energy to grab clothes from the closet.

My stomach hurt for whoever had harmed Xerxes, but my chest burned with unadulterated rage.

For a split second, when his hand had slammed against the wall beside me, Dick’s belt had slashed across my skin.

Warm blood had splattered across the floor.

The worst part wasn’t the during; it was the after. Adrenaline got you through the moment, and when it left, nothing tempered the agony.

The shock wore off into a tsunami of unfathomable hurt.

I collapsed into bed, exhausted.

The nightmares came quickly.

CHAPTER 12
SADIE
MISGUIDED OMEGAS

CLOTHED in an oversize sweatshirt and soft leggings, I brushed out my long hair. Gray morning light barely illuminated the room, and the dull patter of rain was the only sound.

In the room's massive antique mirror, the red highlights in my white hair were fading to pink. They reminded me of old bloodstains.

I shivered.

The skin around my eyes was still bruised.

My skull ached with the beginning of a headache as I shoved my recent memories back into the dark recess where I hid basically everything that happened in my life.

There were healthy coping mechanisms, and then there was trying to forget your entire existence.

At this rate, I didn't know what it was like to *not* want to forget.

My joints ached from torture, and my head was splitting under the weight of compartmentalizing.

A knock sounded at the door, and Aran grumbled in her sleep. It had actually been great sleeping with her.

Sort of.

In the middle of the night, we'd both woken up from nightmares and comforted each other for an hour by complaining about how hard our lives were. Then, after bitching about everything and everyone, we'd passed back out.

Highly therapeutic.

The best part was since neither of us were built like mammoths (like the men), we'd spread out comfortably.

The only snafu had been a short time after we'd fallen back asleep, when Aran had sleepily wrapped her arms around me and tried to cuddle.

When I'd tried to push her away, there'd been a brief tussle where Aran, who'd still been dreaming, had locked me in a choke hold with one arm and used her other arm to smother me with a pillow.

I'd blindly punched her in the trachea until she'd released me and fallen backward, screaming.

At first, I'd panicked that I'd hurt her.

Then I'd realized she was writhing on the bed screaming about her back, not her throat.

I'd done what had always helped me.

Gently, I'd turned her over, so she lay sprawled on her stomach.

Immediately, her screams had stopped, and Aran had snored with a smile on her face, like she hadn't just tried to murder me, then shrieked her head off.

A razor blade of fear pinched my stomach at her strange reaction.

It was eerily similar to how I'd acted when I'd accidentally rolled over onto my back after a night of whippings.

It can't be.

With shaking fingers, I'd reached forward to pull up the bottom of her heavy sweatshirt. Just to check.

"Noodle, get back here!" Jinx screamed, bursting into our room and startling me out of my worried thoughts.

The clock on the wall flashed 4:00 am, but Jinx looked wide awake as she ran after Noodle, who was sporting underwear on his head like a hat.

Aran sleepily said, "Skin the ferret," then continued snoring.

I tried to act nonchalant, like my bestie didn't have more problems than I even realized, which was frankly impressive because I'd already assumed we needed heavy medication.

Jinx giggled like Aran had said something funny, as she chased after the ferret that now appeared to be eating the underwear. The girly sound was at odds with her usual scornful demeanor.

"It's just underwear. Go back to sleep," I mumbled at Jinx with more annoyance than usual.

It was only four a.m., and I'd already survived an attempt on my life.

A perverted ferret was the final straw.

"Oh, I don't sleep," Jinx said casually as she threw herself across the carpet.

I narrowed my sleep-crusted eyes. "Everyone sleeps."

There was one universal truth: every type of animal slept. The most popular theory was it had to do with power replenishment.

"Not me." Jinx dove again and just missed the ferret, who had paused to shove more of the underwear in his mouth.

"You mean you only sleep a few hours? Or like an insomniac?" I'd heard about people who couldn't sleep and then crashed for days.

Jinx lunged at Noodle and squealed with triumph as she snatched his wriggling body with her hands.

She held him above her head like a trophy.

Noodle spat out the underwear and chittered like he'd enjoyed their game.

"No." Jinx turned toward me, ferret still above her head, and smiled. Her dark eyes were too large on her pale face. "I've never slept a wink. Ever."

With that comforting statement, she flounced out of the room.

Unsurprisingly, after that, I fell into a restless sleep.

I hated to be dramatic (not really; I totally would have thrived in the theater), but my life was shaping into one of those horror movies with the weird clowns that always played on the television at Dick's bar.

Now, as the gray morning added a depressing vibe to the room, I stared down at Aran's sleeping form and gently petted her blue hair.

It was nice having my best friend beside me.

Sure, she was homicidal, but who wasn't these days?

My heart warmed as I stared down at her soft features. I couldn't believe I'd ever thought she was a boy.

A loud knock on the door rattled through the room and reminded me someone was waiting outside.

Aran mumbled groggily and pressed a pillow over her eyes. "Fuck off before I disembowel you."

I hurried over to open the door before she woke up and made good on her promise. You could never be too sure these days.

My breath hitched.

Xerxes scowled down at me.

His bruises were mostly healed, and his skin shone with

health. He was dressed in an impeccably fitting suit that stretched across his bulging muscles.

With his long blond locks, he looked like a fairy-tale prince.

Twin knives were strapped across his thighs, and his features were harsh.

A dark fairy tale.

I gulped and hurried out into the hall, shutting the door softly behind me as cinnamon sugar made my mouth water.

For the longest moment, neither of us said anything.

Tension hung heavy.

Xerxes dragged his hands over his face. "I'm sorry for…" He trailed off awkwardly.

I sighed. "I know."

"No, you don't know," he snapped.

My hackles rose at his tone, and the tension between us spiked into something more sinister.

His purple eyes flashed. "Being back in this realm is not going to be easy for me, but it's not an excuse. I was triggered by your choice of words, and it brought back bad memories. I'm devastated that I scared you like that, and I promise it will never happen again."

Pretending I was a calm non-psycho girl who definitely hadn't talked shit about him with Aran for an hour in the middle of the night, I nodded calmly. "I know that. It was just surprising."

I paused as I tried to articulate what had hurt me the most. "I expected such high-handedness from the other men. Not you."

A muscle in his jaw ticked.

Xerxes's voice was a low growl. "What do you think I'm apologizing for?"

Did he have short-term memory loss?

"The whole slapping my pussy and acting like you could order me around. Duh."

"Excuse me?"

Intensity rolled off Xerxes as he straightened his shoulders like he was getting ready for battle.

"Excuse you?" I pursed my lips.

Once again, it seemed like I was missing some imperative part of the conversation.

Xerxes's honeyed accent was guttural. "I'm apologizing for punching the wall and scaring you. I meant everything else."

I couldn't stop the chuckle that escaped my lips.

At first, I'd been rattled by the aggression, but when I'd woken up at two a.m. and talked it over with Aran, I'd realized that wasn't what was really bothering me.

The crux of the problem was another man had pinned me against the wall and told me he owned me.

Sure, a large part of me thought it was hot.

But as Aran had eloquently said, "You know what is hotter? Respect."

T-shirt slogan material.

Xerxes rested his hand on the hilt of his knife. An obvious threat.

Hostility spiked.

Not to be outdone, I bit down on my lower lip until a drop of blood dripped down my chin. We were both ready to fight.

His fingers tightened around the hilt.

I was definitely not thinking about how those same fingers had been grinding against my clit a few hours earlier. Definitely didn't notice the network of veins that popped against his hands and forearms.

I took a step forward until I crowded his space.

My voice was low and threatening. “Don’t get me wrong; you ever raise a violent hand near me again, and I’ll infect you with my blood and make you *my* fucking servant. But if you think I’m going to let you disrespect me by trying to overpower me sexually, then you’ve got another thing coming.”

The muscle in his jaw ticked again, and I couldn’t help but sarcastically ask, “You know what I mean?”

Xerxes sneered, “No. I don’t know what you mean.”

I rolled my eyes because I’d definitely been clear. “I don’t care that you got triggered and a little punchy. I care that you thought you could grab my—”

“Stop talking,” he cut me off.

“What did you just say to me?”

He enunciated his words slowly. “So you thought I was apologizing for saying I owned you? For grabbing your soaking cunt?”

“Yep.” I popped the *P* and cocked my hips like I was mad and not at all turned on by dirty words.

Abruptly, Xerxes lunged forward and wrapped his hand gently around my throat.

All softness was gone.

The assassin was back.

“What was it you were saying, *alpha*?” he whispered, exerting light pressure. My legs trembled, and I gasped as my groin cramped with need.

He smirked down at me.

Fucking omega knew exactly how to push my buttons.

His mocking glare sent me over the edge, and I shoved his hand away.

“Don’t you fucking dare.”

He went unnaturally still. “So you think that since I’m an omega, I was going to be your bitch? That I couldn’t own you like the other men 'cause I'm not an alpha?" His too-pretty eyelashes fluttered, and the pulse on his neck beat violently like it wanted to jump out of his skin.

For a second, I gaped.

The sheer *audacity* of men.

Fiery indignation coursed through me as I remembered just who the fuck I was. "You think the other men actually own me? You think I'm a *prize* that you get to claim?"

"It's not like that," Xerxes said, but the heat in his eyes told me it was exactly like that.

There was only one thing left to do.

"Suck my dick." I slammed my knee into his crotch and marched down the hall. For good measure, I yelled, "The next person to say they own me is getting eaten by my tiger!"

Jax peeked his head out of his door and blinked tired eyes. "Are you okay, little alpha?"

Cobra grumbled something indistinguishable from inside the room. Jax turned around, and there was a brief tussle.

From the fact that Jax reappeared in the door and Cobra was nowhere to be seen, Jax had won.

"Do you need me to kill someone?" he asked seriously.

Why was Jax the only man in all the realms that wasn't an actual garbage bag?

"No, and I don't want to talk about it," I snapped and kept marching past.

"Of course." Jax calmly followed beside me as I charged into the kitchen.

I was about to consume my body weight in food, and if any man said one more word to me, I was going to lose it.

Jax ate beside me in silence.

That was why he was my favorite.

CHAPTER 13
SADIE
ULTIMATUMS

"So, any questions?" the don asked casually as he lounged at the long dining table like he was right at home in Xerxes's mansion.

There was an awkward silence.

No one said anything.

A few minutes earlier, we'd all been feasting at the table and laughing.

I momentarily forgot my annoyance with Xerxes as Lucinda and Jess peppered me with questions about my blood powers.

Jax was explaining to Jala how we'd defeated the fae queen, and Ascher was asking Jinx questions about her observational skills.

The seven of us all sat at one end of the table, talking and catching up.

The other side, aka the drama-queen side, was not doing well.

Xerxes stewed in silence with a stormy expression darkening his face.

I was doing my best to ignore the moody omega and the

complex dynamic between us that I couldn't even begin to process.

Next to him, Aran had a sweatshirt wrapped around her head because "if she heard one more story about what happened with her mother, she was going to puke and stab someone." She kept itching aggressively at her back, and I wondered if she had a bug bite.

Cobra scowled next to her with a carving knife clenched in his hands. Apparently, he was still pissed that we'd followed him into the initiation room.

Everyone ignored the three of them.

The lunch had been going great—at least on our side of the table—until five seconds ago, when the front door had slammed shut and the don had stepped into the opulent dining room.

Surprisingly, he hadn't immediately murdered everyone.

His massive six-foot-five frame was clothed in an expensive black suit, and it was impossible to miss the outlines of the guns tucked into his waistband. Skull rings decorated his fingers and flashed as he sucked in the smoke of his cigarette.

Wrapped around the base of his throat, his white snake was much smaller, a moving necklace that hissed and slithered in a circle.

The "Loyalty" tattoo across his throat rippled as he took a long drag from his cigarette.

He casually pulled out a seat at the head of the table and leaned back.

Walter sprinted in after, the don gave him a single look, and the butler snapped his mouth closed.

"No questions?" the don repeated, and his casual inquiry shook everyone out of their stupor.

Cobra pointed a carving knife at his father. "What are you doing here?"

Everyone waited.

The don chuckled, and his shoulders relaxed as he waved his cigarette around. "I just wanted to congratulate you all. I'm pleased that I didn't have to dispose of everyone like I had planned. It is rare to have one alpha pass the first initiation test, let alone four and an omega. I'm impressed."

No one smiled.

The don smirked and raised his eyebrows but said nothing else, just lounged back in his chair like a king addressing his subjects.

Which he was.

After five minutes of awkward silence, I asked, "Why are you really here?"

Patience was never my strong suit.

The don turned and speared me with his gaze.

Sweat broke out across my body.

His youthful features made him look like Cobra's older brother, but his emerald eyes were his tell; they were perpetually more snake than man, like his beast was overtaking him with age.

I swallowed thickly and tried to give off "I'm not prey" vibes.

Any good predator would sense fear pheromones, and the man before me was on the top of the food chain.

Finally, the don stopped filleting me with his gaze and looked around the room. He took a moment to stare at each one of us, including the teenage girls.

Jinx was the only one that met his gaze.

The don even smiled at Noodle, who was tucked under her arm and hanging upside down dramatically.

I shifted closer to Lucinda and grabbed her hand under the table. She squeezed it back.

She looked over at me, mouth open slightly like she wanted to whisper something, but she closed her mouth and said nothing.

We all waited.

After what felt like an eternity, but was probably ten awkward minutes, the don's deep and slightly lisping voice was startlingly loud.

"I'm here for three reasons."

He blew out a perfect ring of cigarette smoke. It transformed into a serpent in midair and circled above the table.

Creepy.

"First, I wanted to discuss the initiation. The first trial was the hardest to pass. Bravo. The second trial will be the most painful and the third the most revealing. You will begin the second trial tomorrow. It's a long process, and everything will be explained at the gym. A car will arrive at dawn to pick you up. This trial I think you will enjoy."

He smiled, flashing elongated canines.

"If you don't, then you won't survive in this realm. The third test must be completed by the next equinox, three weeks from now."

He took another long drag of his cigarette.

"Also, since you're all ignorant of recent events, rare half-breed females are rumored to be appearing in the different realms. Any woman suspected of being a mix of two species must be immediately brought to me. They are all on the city's wanted list. Although, I suspect this is more rumor than truth. Fear mongers love to whisper about the return of the female half-breeds and the end of the realms."

The stillness at the table was deafening.

Of fucking course.

If the patriarchy could just *not* for literally one day, I would appreciate it.

The don stared at me.

Wait, he'd said something about fear and the end of the realms. *Am I a messiah of the apocalypse?*

I'd never even heard of female half-breeds existing.

Just after I'd discovered I was one, it only made logical sense that I'd be a plague bringer of doom that was wanted.

It spoke to the general trajectory of my life.

Frankly, I was only mildly surprised by my new status as a wanted pariah.

When I'd infected an overpowered evil fae queen with my blood and made her obey me, I'd had a hunch that it wasn't a good thing.

But a razor blade bit my gut as I realized this definitely just wasn't my problem.

My sister's red eyes, Aran's black eyes, Jinx's screech, Jala's and Jess's unnatural bright colorings.

I calmly gnawed on my fingernails and considered the merits of flipping the table, throwing the girls behind me, enslaving the don with my blood, and fleeing to a different realm.

The don turned toward Cobra and smiled casually, like he had no idea of the turmoil his words had caused at the table.

"Also, as alphas, you must all join packs if you are to live in this city. Even independent alphas form packs at eighteen to keep them from going feral. There will be no exceptions."

He snarled "independent" like he was talking about the lowest forms of life.

Cobra scowled at the don. It wasn't hard to imagine him as feral.

"Most alphas have years to choose their packs," Xerxes said softly, his jaw clenched tightly.

I kept forgetting he'd grown up in this foreign world.

The don's calm voice changed into a lisping rasp. "Most alphassss grow up in the realm and know the rulessss. They don't jusssst arrive after yearssss of absence."

Xerxes glared back and said nothing, anger radiating off him in a dark wave.

His anger from earlier was now boiling over, and his face contorted with malice. I wouldn't be surprised if he sold me out as a half-breed.

Cobra reacted to his father's threatening demeanor with his own warning snarl.

Yep, 100 percent feral.

I opened my mouth to bring up the pesky little fact that we were *kidnapped*, but decided against getting into a fight over semantics with the leader of the Mafia.

Abruptly, the don's demeanor grew more relaxed.

He arched a dark eyebrow and chuckled like he found his son's menacing scowl cute. "I have scheduled meetings with suitable alpha packs for all of you. You will each begin meeting with the different—"

Cobra held up his hand and cut off his father. "No. We have a pack. I will bond with the alphas and omega at this table."

Jaws dropped.

Xerxes turned and stared at Cobra like he'd never seen him before.

Jax sighed heavily and rubbed his hands across his eyes like he wasn't surprised.

I'd bet all my money they'd discussed it last night, and Jax had advised Cobra to ask us like a civilized person.

Instead, Cobra just squinted at all of us like he was daring someone to disagree.

No one said anything.

Sweat dripped down my pits and streaked uncomfortably across my rib cage.

They legit couldn't bond with me. Not only was I apparently a wanted half-breed, but also, *what*?

This wasn't good.

I rubbed my clammy palms across my leggings.

Cobra wasn't dumb, and he'd definitely realized the situation. I tried to make eye contact with him and shake my head, but he purposely didn't look my way.

This was too much, too fast.

Not only was my entire existence apparently frowned upon (honestly, no one was surprised), but a pack seemed like a big deal.

My intuition told me it wasn't a platonic relationship.

Moon goddess, I was still a virgin.

Never forget the fact that they were overbearing assholes who called me a possession and made me want to tear out my hair half the time.

How did one politely blurt out that they didn't want to bond without offending people?

At the same time, the thought of bonding with strangers made my skin crawl. I couldn't imagine *not* spending my days with them, no matter how difficult some of the days were.

But still, bonds were for an immortal's *life*; that much I knew for sure.

"Good, then it's settled. We'll form the bond now. Cut your palm and hold it up to the man next to you. Pass the knife around. You all must mix blood," the don ordered.

Shockingly, Cobra obeyed and held his bloody palm up to Xerxes, who sat beside him.

We seriously were going to do this right now?

Didn't anyone want five minutes to think it over? Make a pros-and-cons list, cry dramatically into their pillow, attempt to drown themselves in the bathtub, fight the don to the death?

There were still *options*.

Xerxes stared at Cobra for a long moment, then turned his head to me.

Suddenly, he took the butcher knife, slashed his palm, and slapped it against Cobra's open cut.

I groaned.

This was what happened when men refused to deal with their emotions.

I knew I should have purchased those "healing your mind and body through writing" journals back in the fae realm.

A loud crack echoed, and Xerxes's and Cobra's heads fell back, eyes wide open like they were possessed.

Black rings glowed around both men's pupils.

For a split second, my mind tricked me, and I saw galaxies in the glowing dark circles. They reminded me of something, but I couldn't put my finger on it.

As soon as it started, it ended, and they both sat up, gasping.

The don's eyes flickered to snake eyes, and he leaned forward with a furrowed brow as he stared at his son. "Interesting. Very interesting," he muttered.

My gut twisted. It didn't take a genius to figure out that hadn't been a normal bonding.

However, the don immediately ordered, "Good, now go around the table."

Whatever had surprised him made him eager to finish it quickly.

I didn't like it.

But before I could gain the courage to say anything, Xerxes bonded with Ascher. As their eyes burst with light and shadows, I realized what had eluded me the first time.

The bond looked like a lunar eclipse.

Then the don ordered Ascher to bond with Jax. Too quickly, the process repeated itself.

The men were all too happy to slice open their palms, pupils glowing with the antithesis of sunlight.

Finally, Jax turned toward me.

He passed the knife forward, but the don lunged across the table and took it before it touched my hand.

I still hadn't decided if I was about to bond or stab someone with the knife, because I was more of a split-second decision type of girl.

The don's relaxed attitude was gone, and the small snake around his neck grew until it was thicker than my torso.

It turned and hissed at me.

Rearing back with my palms up, I shuddered as the snake stared at me.

"What the fuck!" Cobra hiss-screamed. Jax roared, and Ascher let out a creepy bleat. Xerxes pulled out his twin knives, and Aran's eyes turned midnight black beside me.

What the hell was Aran?

"Stand down, or I will kill one of the girls."

Out of seemingly thin air, the don produced a glowing gun and pointed it directly at Jess's head.

Cobra spat onto the table. "What the fuck is the meaning of this? We did what you wanted, Father." He said "father," like it was a filthy curse word.

Jess gnawed on her lower lip nervously, but for the most

part, seemed unconcerned about the massive weapon pointed at her forehead.

Which made sense, since she'd grown up with Jinx.

The don rolled his eyes like he was bored.

"I told you that you needed an alpha pack, and you chose the men at this table. If you had asked, I would have explained that I can't let you bond with a female alpha. You need to produce an heir, and only female omegas can breed. Most don't like the competition of another woman in a pack. Male omegas are no threat." He gestured toward Xerxes.

His words were a sucker punch to the gut.

At the same time, my shoulders slumped forward with relief. I couldn't put a target on their heads by bonding with them; the whole half-breed thing was still a heavy, unspoken issue.

Also, wanted list aside, I wasn't 100 percent sure that I wanted to bond my life to overbearing men.

Forever was a long time when you were an immortal alpha.

"I only joined this pack because of her," Xerxes snarled and threw his plate against the wall.

Ascher's horns lengthened on his head. "Same."

A low grumble sounded from Jax's throat. "We are not forming a pack without Sadie. It's not up for debate."

The don smiled. "You already did."

His large white snake showed off its wicked fangs.

"If you bond with Sadie, I will put a bounty on her head. Serpentine City is not a nice place. She'll be slaughtered within the hour. Also, the needles Spike stabbed into your necks contained enchanted trackers. You physically can't leave the city limits without my permission. If you try, you'll explode. From the inside."

If I'd been standing, my knees would have given out.

Upsetting.

Also, who was going to tell him that there was already a bounty on my head because I was a half-breed?

Not me.

The don continued casually, "Also, if you bond with her, the enchantment will notify me, and I will immediately put a hit out on her."

The men deflated at once, shoulders slumping.

I turned to him. "What is your problem with me?"

The don smirked. "It's not personal, just alpha politics. The don's son needs to produce the city's next heir with an omega female. You get in the way of that. But I'm still very excited to have your skills in my Mafia."

Did he know about my blood skills? Or was he referencing my tiger form?

The don, with the mammoth snake still around his neck, got up and walked away. He casually said, "Moon Goddess, bless us all," without a backward glance.

His absence didn't relieve the tension in the room.

The harm was already done.

After thirty seconds of the most uncomfortable silence of my life, I pursed my lips and asked the obvious question. "So we all agree to not sell out a certain half-breed to a certain snake someone, right?"

You could never be too sure these days.

Jax growled loudly, Cobra hissed, Ascher muttered an expletive, and Xerxes just kept glaring at me.

Ascher's amber eyes glowed like they were on fire. "How the fuck could you even ask that?" He stalked away from the table.

The other three men shoved in their chairs and followed him.

The energy rolling off them was that of death and destruction.

Aran threw a grape at me and distracted me from staring after the men's departing figures like a pathetic hussy.

Four teenage girls sat at the table in various states of shock.

"What?" I asked Aran.

"No one is going to sell you out to the don. Don't worry." She waved a piece of chicken around to emphasize her point.

Walter stood behind her and pointedly looked at the ground like he wasn't listening.

My shoulders slumped forward, and I banged my head against the table.

The men were now in a pack without me? Check.

I couldn't join said pack without putting a target on all of us? Check.

Half-breed females were on Serpentine City's most-wanted list? Check.

Aran chuckled, and it distracted me from my depressed thoughts. She grumbled, "But if you snore, I might just turn you over."

"Excuse me?" I gasped at my best friend.

She rolled her eyes as she itched at her back. "Oh my sun god, Sadie, lighten up. It's like a funeral around here. I'm joking."

I shoved a bread roll in my mouth and said in a muffled voice, "So do you want to talk about why your eyes keep glowing creepily black? Doesn't seem very fae of you."

My mouth stilled as I swallowed thickly and thought about it. "Wait, how did you actually remove your mother's heart? I never asked."

Aran flung her chair back. "We are not talking about it."

She stomped away from the table with her head held high and shoulders back like a prissy princess.

Which I guessed she was.

I slumped forward and slammed my forehead against the table again for good measure.

Maybe I could kill myself through blunt force trauma?

Lucinda patted my back softly.

Jinx grimaced and stroked her ferret. "You all need professional mental health help."

I rolled my eyes. "Obviously."

CHAPTER 14

COBRA

LOVERS OR ENEMIES

"What the fuck are we going to do?" I growled at Jax, who was leaning against the wall with his head in his hands.

His chains tinkled in his hair as his head fell forward dejectedly. "I don't know."

"She's on my father's fucking *wanted* list. We have to protect her."

"No fucking shit," Ascher snarled.

Jax nodded. "I don't like this. We can't bond with her, and she's in danger. It feels like everything is slipping through our fingers."

"I don't want this bond." Xerxes punctuated his statement by twirling his daggers. Their unfathomably sharp edges glinted in the dim light of the fireplace.

It was night in the mansion, and all the girls were in Sadie's room having a sleepover. I only knew this because Jess had come by to tell Jax that he'd "acted like a fool toward Sadie earlier." She knew nothing.

The four of us had been holed up in mine and Jax's room for hours trying to make sense of our situation.

We were no closer to answers than we had been hours ago.

Frustration coursed through us, amplified by the living bond that now connected us.

I could feel snippets of everyone's emotions coursing through my chest, as if a gold live wire connected us.

We were a pack.

"How the fuck could he do this to us?" Ascher slammed his fist into the wall, and fragments of broken brick rained down.

He whipped his golden head around, onyx horns expanding atop his head, and snarled at Xerxes. "You're an omega. Doesn't that make you fertile or some shit? We don't need a fucking female omega."

Xerxes twirled his blades faster, his handsome face contorted into a snarl. "Only female omegas are guaranteed breeders. Male omegas and female omegas together have the highest chance of pregnancy. I've never heard of a male omega breeding with a female alpha."

Our last shred of hope disappeared.

Ascher whirled around and slammed his fist harder into the wall, and the entire room shook.

Xerxes quietly threatened, "Don't destroy my house."

Ascher's amber eyes flashed with fire. "You fucking think you can order me around? It was your fucking idea to flee to this realm. Now we're all screwed." He stalked toward Xerxes.

"Oh please, coming from the alpha that sold them out to the fae queen." Xerxes held his blade and beckoned Ascher forward, like he was desperate to draw blood.

I leaned back on the bed and watched them dispassionately.

Everything was fucked.

They could carve each other up for all I cared.

I sank deeper into the broken void within my consciousness. Once again, I was untethered and out of control. Shackled by circumstances.

Trapped.

"Stop it, you two." Jax's chest rumbled with warning at Xerxes and Ascher, but it was halfhearted.

He slumped against the wall and rubbed at his chest like he was trying to soothe the sting of everyone's emotions.

The bond among us was alive like electricity.

Alive with fucking anger.

It was a high-pitched buzz, like a broken instrument, and it stoked the rage inside me.

From what I understood, bonds were supposed to soothe alphas and help keep them in check. They kept them from going feral, was what my fucking father had said.

If the void inside wasn't consuming me whole, I might have laughed.

What a fucking crock of shit.

Either everything he'd said about bonds was a lie or we were all too fucked up for it to work properly.

Aggression, tension, and general unwellness pulsed through each of us.

Ascher leaped toward Xerxes, and his rage sent a lightning bolt of anger through the bonds.

Xerxes smiled, purple eyes glowing, and threw his dagger at Ascher's head.

The tattooed alpha moved out of the way, but the omega's blade scraped across one of his onyx horns.

Jax's chest rumbled with a warning growl, and my jewels transformed into shadows.

My snakes wanted to join in the chaos. To bite.

Alone, we were unwell.

Connected, we were fucking psychos.

Abruptly, a knock sounded through the room like a gunshot.

Jax stilled, his hand clutching Xerxes's and Ascher's shirts as they pummeled each other with their fists.

With a heavy sigh, I sauntered toward the door.

The bond strummed higher with aggression until it burned my chest like a brand.

My eyes flickered between snake eyes and human ones; my vision oscillated from normal to heat signatures.

I flung open the door and stilled because the object of all our fucking problems leaned casually against the door.

Sadie wore a fuzzy sweatshirt that dwarfed her. Her bruises were fading, and her white hair was a silky sheet that I longed to wrap around my fists.

My cock stirred.

Sweet cranberry wine stroked my senses enticingly.

"Um, am I interrupting something?" Sadie gnawed on her plush lower lip as she took in the shadow snakes on my skin, and the other three men in a pile of fists.

Her broken voice was a harsh rasp.

In her oversize fuzzy clothes, she reminded me of the kitten I always called her.

For the first time, the bond connecting the four of us stopped goading us to violence.

The high-pitched whine burning through all of us abruptly dissipated, leaving a cool tingle.

Instantly, we calmed down.

I licked my suddenly parched lips. "Depends on what you want from us." The insinuation was clear from my sultry tone, and I slowly adjusted my throbbing cock in my pants. In case she didn't get my message.

Sadie sighed heavily and rubbed at her eyes.

A pang of pain stabbed through our new bond. She looked small and exhausted, and it was our job to protect her from pain.

Not cause it.

I shook my head in confusion. Those weren't my thoughts; they were the thoughts of my new packmates.

She might be tired, but that didn't mean I couldn't fuck the exhaustion out of her and make it better.

Another pang of pain pinched my chest.

The men clearly did not agree with me.

It was hard to decipher what the bond meant, but images of protecting and comforting her flashed through my mind.

The other three wanted to coddle her.

Was this what having a conscience was like, an overwhelming feeling of softness and confusion?

I whirled around and hissed. "Fucking calm down. Stop being little bitches. Fucking can be relaxing too."

My chest burned with a sharper pain.

Apparently, all of them disagreed with me. Pussies.

I projected images of fucking her against the wall as Kitten screamed and grinned as male voices groaned.

Sadie backed away from the door with a confused expression. "Okaaaay, I see you guys are busy here."

My throat emitted a low, rattling hiss. "Don't back away from me. Why are you here?"

Sadie sighed heavily, and she moistened her plush lips like she was nervous.

I'd give her something to be nervous about: my jeweled cock in her lips.

A stab of censure spiked across the bond.

Instead of turning around and beating my new packmates into the ground, I focused on the kitten in front of me.

Sadie nodded like she'd come to a decision. "I know this is probably hard for everyone, but I've been talking to the girls, and I've realized something."

I arched my eyebrow at her as images of her pinned against the closet wall filtered through my mind.

Would she be a screamer and yell like Jax, or would she moan softly?

One thing was clear: she'd finally realize she was my possession and be ready for me to take her.

The other three men stood beside me, the bond strumming with contentment the closer we stood to each other.

It was a physical and mental bond.

Kitten gnawed on her lower lip as she looked at each of us with her big ruby eyes. She took more deep breaths, like she was trying to build up her courage.

"I've decided it's time to grow up and act like an adult."

My cock was hard as steel in my pants. She realized I owned her soul, and I was going to pick her up and fuck her against the wall until she forgot her name.

Images of all of us defiling her in every position flashed through our bond.

Ascher muttered, "Fuck," and Xerxes groaned. A growl escaped Jax's throat.

Now we were all hard as rocks. Xerxes's cinnamon scent spiked nauseatingly sweet, like he couldn't help but respond to our alpha pheromones.

Sadie cleared her throat and continued, "I'm on your father's wanted list."

I snarled. "That doesn't fucking matter to us."

She shook her head sadly.

"It's not just that. None of us have actually had sex yet, and I think it is for the best. Truthfully, I had reservations about actually bonding with you guys because of how overbearing everyone has a tendency to act."

My gut twisted at her tone.

She paused. "Well, everyone but Jax. Cobra, your father was right that you need a pack, and it's not fair for me to get in your way of having children. You might not care about it now, but someday you will."

The bond screamed with a tidal wave of frustration.

It almost brought me to my knees.

"What did you just say?" I growled at my kitten, who was backing away with wide eyes.

Sadie shook her head. "Any relationship between the five of us is over. It has to be this way."

Xerxes chuckled harshly, his entire demeanor hardening.

The menace that had radiated off him when he'd worked for the fae queen was back as he snarled at her, "You're a coward."

Sadie's ruby eyes sparked with anger. "This is literally what I'm talking about. If you guys would just grow up and act realistic, we could talk about this like adults."

Ascher cracked his tattooed knuckles, his horns expanding larger on his head. "You never listen to us anyway, Princess. So why the fuck does it matter what we have to say?"

For the first time, I agreed with Ascher.

Jax ran his hands roughly through his braids. "Everyone needs to calm down. And you don't mean that, Sadie." His gray eyes were clouded with betrayal.

The new bond among all four of us literally strummed with agony, with devastation.

We were breaking.

How could she tell us it was over before it had begun?

Sadie was giving up on all of us.

My kitten was giving up on me.

She was rejecting me.

Sadie sighed heavily and gave Jax a watery smile that made me want to beat someone until their brain splattered.

Her voice cracked. "It's nothing personal. I just think it might have been for the best. Jala pointed out that most things happen for a reason, and I think that's true in this case."

I scoffed. What a load of fucking shit.

Nothing happened for a reason. The world was a dark, cruel place; it either fucked you over, or you rose from the ashes and fucked it.

That was it.

Jax's soft voice had a hard edge. "And what did Jinx say?"

Sadie chuckled weakly, tears tracking down her cheeks. "She said that men were mostly useless, and I was saving myself a lot of unnecessary emotional energy."

"Do you agree with her?" Jax asked slowly, the razor-sharp edge in his voice making the skin on the back of my neck prickle.

You didn't piss off an alpha bear.

Sadie avoided making eye contact with any of us. "I think we're all better off as friends. We can still pass initiation and work together to survive this realm."

I hissed at her.

"You guys are my teammates, and I wouldn't want it any other way. But I'm still only twenty-one, and I need to focus on what I want out of life. I can't do that if I'm your guys' possession. Plus, the don took the choice away from us."

Jax's gray eyes were sharper than the knives Xerxes was twirling dangerously fast through his fingers.

He asked softly, "Did he really take the choice away?"

"Yes," Sadie said, her chin clenched with stubbornness.

She'd come to her decision.

Of course she was abandoning me, just like every fucking woman I'd ever known. Fucking evil, vile creatures.

My gut instincts about her had been right.

The prettiest predators were the most poisonous.

"Well, then fuck off." I hissed, heat signatures bursting before me as my eyes flickered to snake eyes.

Ascher's voice was cruel. "Yeah, we didn't want you anyway."

"As you said. Go find someone you can dominate." Xerxes's British accent was colder than his blades.

My eyes flickered back, and I noted dispassionately that her plush lower lip trembled.

Sadie's almond-shaped ruby eyes were enormous as she stared at Jax and ignored the rest of us.

She pleaded to him, "We can still be friends."

A bolt of lightning shot through the bond.

All of us were on the same page. If she wanted to reject us, that was fine because we didn't need her.

Jax snarled, "No, we can't."

He turned away from her.

Sadie gasped and bowed her head like she was physically struck, and for a long second, a tiny spark of hope shot through the bond.

She was going to realize the error of her ways.

My kitten will fight for me.

She'll choose me.

When Sadie straightened, ruby eyes glowed like the red sun of the shifter realm. Cold and bright, offering no warmth and no hope.

Just cruelty.

"Fine, I don't need a bunch of overbearing men in

my life. I never asked for any of this, and I'm sure as shit not going to beg for your friendship. I've been through too much to ever let a man tear me down again." Sadie's cranberry scent spiked like it was on fire.

Another person abandoned me.

She doesn't want me.

I'm not good enough for her.

Sadie whirled and marched down the hall.

I clenched my hands and reminded myself that she was just another female snake. It wasn't worth my time to hunt her down the hall.

No matter how badly I wanted to chase after her and claim her, it was useless.

She wasn't worth my time.

"Fuck you!" Ascher bellowed after her, his stoic facade cracking completely as his lips pulled back in a sneer.

Sadie flipped both her middle fingers in the air but kept walking.

She didn't look back.

"She's not worth it. She's not what we need," Xerxes growled low and patted Ascher on his back.

Our golden bond turned gray from the force of Xerxes' lie.

Sadie was exactly what we needed.

No. She abandoned you.

Fuck her.

The bond in my chest burned with pain and betrayal.

I was fucking over the girl.

She didn't *deserve* to be owned by me.

She didn't *deserve* to be my kitten.

Jax roared like a wild animal and threw a dresser. It crashed against the wall with a boom, bursting into hundreds of pieces. Ascher mumbled expletives, and Xerxes reassured him that she wasn't worth it.

Once again, our bond turned gray.

No. Xerxes is right. Forget her.

But for some reason, I couldn't drag my feet away from the doorway.

I couldn't stop staring down the long hall as Sadie retreated to her room.

I couldn't move an inch.

Because even as the connection in my chest strummed with violence, the tiny voice of my shadow snake that lived on Sadie, whispered that I was making a grave mistake. That my kitten was everything to me. That I was nothing without her.

I flung images of death and pain back at it and shut down my connection to it.

It wasn't on my flesh anyway.

I'd made my decision.

CHAPTER 15
SADIE
TENSION

I GROANED as harsh sunlight streamed through the bay windows and woke me up. The first thing I noticed—the pint of ice cream lying empty across my pillow.

The second thing I noticed—five other females were piled across my arms and legs.

On my one side, Lucinda was wrapped around me in a bear hug.

On the other, Aran was resting her hand across my head like she was trying to comfort me.

Jinx was sprawled in the middle of the bed, lying across Jess, and Jala was lying beside them with her arms linked with Jess's.

I decided not to dwell on the fact that Jinx's eyes were wide open and she was muttering something under her breath.

She was the only person not sleeping.

Even Noodle was spread out on his back in her arms, snoring softly.

I squinted and realized I wasn't imagining it: the ferret

was wearing fake eyelashes, and his dark fur glinted like he'd been dipped in sparkles. *Pretty*.

Abruptly, I remembered the events of last night, and emotions crushed my chest to the bed.

The men.

I'd done what I had to do, but holy shit, that didn't mean it hurt any less.

I was wanted for being a half-breed, and the don had threatened all our lives if I dared to bond with them.

He didn't even know about my fae heritage, and he still forbade it because I was an alpha.

Logically, I was happy with my decision because I'd kept the men safe.

Illogically, I wanted to cry like a little baby while they held me and told me everything was going to be all right.

Maybe that was what growing up was?

Recognizing that it wouldn't be all right unless you made it so. That sometimes you couldn't do what you wanted to, only what you had to.

Sometimes, the only person who could save you was yourself.

And if you couldn't save yourself, all you could save were those you cared about. I'd protected the men by making the only choice any of us could make.

And how had they rewarded me?

Ascher telling me to fuck off, Jax turning his back to me, Xerxes sneering that I should find someone to dominate, and Cobra cutting off his connection to the little snake on my flesh.

The moment he'd severed the connection, the little snake had screamed into my mind like it was dying.

By some miracle, it hadn't disappeared completely. It

was a lighter gray, no longer a dark, shadowy black, but it still moved across my flesh.

Which was weird, because if it was a part of Cobra's consciousness, it shouldn't exist after he'd removed his connection from it.

My little miracle snake.

I reached down and kissed it, and it twirled across my fingers and sent me images of comfort.

The ache in my chest persisted.

Cobra was over me.

My emotions boomeranged back and forth between righteous anger and overwhelming pain.

There was no in-between.

A part of me wished to go back in time and tell the men I wanted them to be mine.

It wouldn't have been hard to give in to my desire and beg them to take me, beg them to fight impossible odds for me and protect me from life's horror.

But I hadn't grown up being beaten within an inch of my life to wimp out when it mattered.

I didn't need any man to fight for me.

I could do it myself.

The don had been clear, and I agreed with Jala that everything happened for a reason.

The men's reaction to me asking to just be friends was the confirmation I needed that I'd made the right choice.

They still didn't respect me as a *person*.

They just wanted to own me sexually, order me around, and treat me like a simpering princess that needed saving, and when I'd refused, they'd turned nasty.

I scoffed as indignation burned through me.

How dare they treat me like this when I was putting aside my own wants so they could be safe and happy?

"Fuck men. I *hope* I die a virgin. That will show them." I threw myself out of bed, unable to lie still and wallow for a second longer.

"Virginity rocks. Kill them all," Aran chanted sleepily, patting the pillow while wrapping her other elbow around Jala's neck and squeezing.

Before she could asphyxiate the pink-haired teen, I punched Aran in the gut and wrestled Jala out of her grip.

Both of them were still asleep, but Aran grinned widely, like she enjoyed trying to kill someone while unconscious.

Back in the shifter realm, at mandatory therapy with Auntie, I'd thought Aran was being dramatic when she'd said she wanted to kill everyone at all times.

Now that I knew her better, I 100 percent believed her.

A lifetime ago, I'd explained that the numb made me feel nothing, and Aran had said something about rage consuming her until she was burning alive.

Goose bumps made me shiver.

As I stood dwelling on the past and unfortunate circumstances that were our lives, suddenly the familiar voice of the numb echoed clearly in my head.

I'm ice; he's fire. You need to complete it.

My blood froze.

The numb wasn't activated, but the familiar voice had just spoken to me.

"What?" I whispered out loud. "How are you in my head?"

Silence.

My heart beat erratically. "How did you speak to me?"

Still nothing.

If the numb were a normal phenomenon that spoke to the half warriors in battle, why was it whispering riddles to me?

The numb always gave emotionless directions in battle.

It instructed me on how to punch; it didn't whisper ambiguous directions about completing something.

"What do you mean, ice and fire? Do you mean Aran is fire? Who the fuck are you? Is the song of the hunt somehow ice?" I said as I looked around for an invisible intruder.

"Um, sis?" Lucinda asked with concern.

No voice responded.

"She's hearing voices. Either she's some type of cursed parasitic host, or her mind has deteriorated from too many concussions," Jinx said with a "duh" tone like my theatrics were boring her. "Probably the latter."

I made a face at her. "Go to sleep. Oh, wait, you can't."

"Real mature." Jinx stroked Noodle.

Embarrassment streaked through me as I realized I'd just mocked a twelve-year-old for suffering from insomnia.

"Are you sure you're okay, sis?" Lucinda narrowed her too-familiar ruby eyes at me.

"No, I'm not okay. Creepy voices love to talk to me, and apparently instead of being maternal, I instinctively want to bully small children."

Aran groaned as she opened her eyes and stretched. "You're being dramatic, Sadie."

I glared at her. "A female voice in my head just said, 'I'm ice; he's fire,' and, 'You need to complete it,' most likely referring to me and you, since you're the only guy here. Well, kind of. I don't know."

I pressed my palms into my eyes. "It was the numb's voice, but I hadn't activated it, so theoretically it should be impossible to speak to me. Why do voices always talk about us? What does any of it mean?"

The room went silent.

At least now everyone would panic with me, and Aran would finally realize how serious the situation was.

"Oh no," Aran said as I grabbed a small paper bag from the en suite bathroom and breathed into it rapidly.

I rasped, "I know, right," and continued huffing into the bag.

Aran pulled her sleeping mask back over her eyes. "The sun god probably realizes I'm an absolute dynamite of a man and wants to tell me how sexy I am. You probably need to complete your life's purpose by telling me that."

It was official.

I was about to murder my best friend.

Jinx choked on a laugh, and Lucinda cracked a smile. Jala and Jess woke up and looked around, confused by what was going on.

"Jinx, hold the glam ferret," I said.

She scooped Noodle up protectively, and I let out a war cry, throwing myself on Aran, elbow pointed down for maximum impact.

Even with a blindfold over Aran's eyes, it wasn't a fair fight.

"Fight, fight, fight," the teenage girls squealed with glee as we tussled across elegant silk sheets and I tried to stuff the paper bag down Aran's throat.

The match ended quickly.

Aran pinned me beneath her with her forearm across my windpipe, and my left arm twisted behind my body at an awful angle.

She grinned down at me, still blindfolded by her sleeping mask, perfect white teeth flashing. "Admit I'm sexy."

"Something serious is going on here," I whined. "I can feel it in my bones. Maybe I'm ice, and you're fire. We probably have to do something together. The creepy poems said something similar to us. Also, you only pinned me because your male enchantment makes you wider and stronger."

Aran shook her head, eye mask still on. "Oh, dumb, innocent Sadie. The enchantment is a mirage. It makes me appear wider with a more masculine build, but doesn't actually change my physical form at all. Just what you perceive."

My jaw dropped.

The hands pinning me to the bed were strong as shit, and I'd lost circulation where they pressed against me.

Then I remembered what she'd said. "I am *not* innocent."

"So you finally admit you're dumb?" Jinx asked lazily as she petted Noodle.

For what happened next, I blamed the terror that still shook through my veins from the voice speaking to me.

"So you admit you're annoying?" I mocked the twelve-year-old.

"So you admit you're a nincompoop?"

"So you admit you're the size of a garden gnome?"

Jinx's dark eyes were cruel. "So you admit you're probably going to die in this realm because you have no idea what you're doing, abilities you can't control, no idea how to maintain a relationship with men, and confusing circumstances surrounding your existence that probably indicate you won't live to see your next birthday?"

Jala groaned and pressed a pillow over her face, fluffy pink hair sticking out.

Jess kicked Jinx. "We talked about this."

Aran laughed and climbed off me, so she was no longer violently smushing me into the bed.

After a long, tense moment where I tried to regain a semblance of dignity after being emotionally assaulted by a child and thoroughly outwrestled by my best friend, who was blindfolded, I pointed out the obvious. "You don't have many friends, do you?"

Jinx opened her mouth, probably to rip my last shard of self-esteem to shreds, but Jess slapped a hand over her sister's face.

Before I could gloat, Aran slapped me on the top of the head. "Stop provoking the vicious, but entertaining, small child."

"Ow, I was just speaking my truth." I groaned, face burning as I realized my younger sister was lying next to me silently, ruby eyes wide.

So much for being a paragon of wisdom and maturity.

Aran harrumphed.

Still raring for a fight, I snapped at her, "At least I'm speaking my truth and trying to do something about *our* circumstances."

Aran ripped the sleeping mask off and glared at me with steel-blue eyes. She had her mother's gaze.

"Sadie, sweetie pie, you want my truth? You want to know how I ripped out my mother's heart and ate it?"

"Um." Suddenly, I was hyper aware that I'd been acting immature and there were four impressionable young girls, and one beautiful ferret staring at me. "Maybe another time?"

I tried to move my head to indicate to Aran that we had an audience.

Just because we needed therapy didn't mean we needed to completely traumatize the next generation.

Aran's expression was unfocused. "When I stared down at my seizing mother, an endless burning rage overwhelmed me, and I thought about all the ways she'd hurt me. Ice daggers erupted from my nails, and I shoved them through her back until her sternum cracked. I ripped her beating heart out through muscle and bone. Then guess what happened?"

"No?" This felt like a trap.

"What happened?" Lucinda asked quietly. The four girls stared at Aran, enraptured.

"After I consumed my mother's raw, beating heart, it sounded like a male stood behind me and praised me. When he spoke, it was pure bliss."

Aran paused, breath ragged, as her chest heaved. "It was euphoric."

My heart rate spiked.

Suddenly, Aran blinked and shook her head.

"When I turned around, there was no one there. I don't know what the voice in your head said, Sadie, but I can guarantee you that I'm not fire. It was ice that burst from me, and I knew in my bones that I could produce a shit ton more of it with the right motivation."

Shuffling forward slowly on the bed, I wrapped my arms around her in an awkward hug and asked, "This is good, right? You're a water fae?"

Aran laughed. "No, I'm not. As the princess, I learned our realm's history three times over. No water fae has *ever* had ice claws. Plus, they manifest with more water abilities than ice. I've tried, and I still can't manipulate water."

"Well, there is good news," I said.

Aran's voice was uncharacteristically small. "What could possibly be good in our lives?"

"We're both hearing voices. So we're equally unwell."

A light laugh burst from her throat, and she wrapped her longer arms around me tightly.

Her happiness was infectious, and soon we were both giggling and holding on to each other.

Jinx's voice interrupted our revelry. "Lucinda, my

respect for you has plummeted now that I've spent time with your sister."

Lucinda replied, "I get that."

Jess sighed. "I wish I were hearing voices. My life is so boring."

"Remember when Jinx would just whisper stuff in our ears all night? That was basically like hearing voices," Jala said, pink eyes wide.

"Good point."

I pulled away from Aran and lightly punched myself in the forehead with my fist. "No one is going to hear any voices going forward. We are all normal, functioning females with bright, happy, not-concerning-at-all futures."

Aran puckered her lips in disbelief, and I pinched her.

"I'm manifesting it."

"Good luck with that. You're no witch."

Before I could launch a million questions at Aran about witches, because I was still shook that they existed, Jess climbed across the bed and gave me and Aran a hug.

Before I knew it, we were all hugging. Jala had even pulled Jinx into the pile.

Big touchy-feely morning for all of us.

You knew things weren't well when everyone started embracing.

The shadow snake twirled around my fingers and projected images of love and support, and my heart hurt at the reminder that Cobra was no longer attached to it.

I sent it back an image of me hugging it, and it gave a little zing in return.

I gave it pets and whispered under my breath, "How did such a rude man make such a sweet snake?"

The snake twirled with glee as I dragged my fingers across it.

Jess interrupted my melancholy thoughts. "I know Jax is my brother, but don't worry, girl. I will cut him."

"I appreciate that and hope it won't come to that," I said honestly and smiled at her.

For the first time since the sacred lake had revealed I was an alpha, I was surrounded by females.

It was nice.

"So, what's the plan for today?" Aran asked.

"Well, the don said we begin the second trial, so that should be fun." I pretended to smoke an imaginary cigar and made a finger gun. "Gang life, am I right?"

Everyone looked at me with concern.

I pretended to blow a smoke ring with my cigar and pondered where I wanted to get "Loyalty" tattooed.

Definitely across my face like a badass.

"Sis, we should come with you," Lucinda said eagerly. "I have…" she trailed off but didn't finish her sentence.

"You have what?" I asked.

"Nothing," Lucinda said quickly, but I got the sense she was hiding something.

I opened my eyes to ask more questions, but Jala cut me off, her pink eyes large with excitement. "Yeah, we can make sure the guys are nice to you. Plus, we have some skills that might be useful."

I thought about Aran's eyes going black, Jinx shrieking, Jess and Jala protecting Jinx, and Lucinda being a mini me.

For a second, I considered bringing them along.

Then I remembered they were still teens and Aran needed to keep a low profile.

Also, as the two semi-adults, it was our responsibility to keep them safe.

"No, I'll figure out schooling for you guys in this realm." I tried to speak with authority, like I was a leader they could look up to and not someone who'd just been screaming about hearing voices.

"School sucks," Jess blurted. Jala pretended to cry, Lucinda flopped back with a moan, and Jinx showed her teeth. I couldn't figure out if she was smiling or snarling.

"Love the passion. I'll be sure to inquire about theater programs."

Aran studied her fingernails. "At your guys' age, I was being set on fire nightly and paraded around ballrooms with bloodthirsty fae. Grow up."

Jinx turned to Aran, her dark eyes large and sharp on her pale face. "And now you're hiding like a coward, disguised as an unattractive male, and sleeping in the same bed as your best friend because you're afraid of the dark, flames, and blood."

Aran gasped.

Jess chanted "fight" under her breath.

Aran arched her brow. "Excuse me. I will have you know that I am *very* sexy. The voice in Sadie's head even told her so."

"Um, it definitely didn't."

The tension dissipated as everyone realized Aran was not about to rip out one of Jinx's organs and eat it. Although, weirdly, my gut told me Jinx would put up more of a fight than the fae queen.

I pursed my lips and debated giving some type of inspirational speech about how we all had each other and we would be all right. Even though the men were mad at me and it low-key felt like the world was ending.

Aran farted. Loudly.

The girls screamed.

I left the room.

We were all fucked.

Dead.

Aran could handle the four teenage girls. She clearly needed to practice leadership if she was ever going to run an entire realm, because I hated to say it, but I was getting big "reign of terror" energy from her.

My mood soured further when I walked into the foyer.

All four men stood at the front door.

Instantly, the scent of sugary cinnamon made my mouth water.

"You're late," Cobra snarled with menace.

"And you're ugly." I still needed to work on comebacks.

Ascher's tattooed jaw clenched tight. "So, Princess, you decided to show up?"

I turned to him slowly.

It was one thing for Cobra to act like an annoying psycho, but it was something else coming from the great betrayer.

I stared Ascher down until a light pink stained the tops of his cheekbones, and his scowl fell. Like he was thinking about our history and knew he'd just fucked up.

Before I could say anything, Ascher pulled the door open and guided me through with a light touch on my lower back. His cheekbones were still pink, and he avoided eye contact.

I let him lead me outside.

The day was overcast, everything shadowed in gray, and a dreary drizzle soaked my skin and saturated the mansion's perfectly manicured green lawn.

Xerxes twirled his blades in his hands and pushed past me as he stalked down his walkway.

The intoxicating scent trailed behind him like a cloud of ambrosia.

Jax didn't speak.

"Opening doors for her now, are we?" Cobra sneered from somewhere behind us.

I didn't bother to respond, and Ascher kept his hand on my lower back.

On the street, a beta in a suit was leaning against a red supercar, waiting for us.

Tall skyscrapers rose in the distance, the tops still hidden in the clouds. I wasn't sure the realm even had a sun.

When I got to the car, Ascher opened the door, and I squeezed myself into the back row so I wouldn't have to sit near the men.

The car jumped forward, and the force of the acceleration pinned me to my seat.

My hair whipped around my face, even though none of the windows were open.

Outside the window, the world passed by in a blur of dreary colors.

When we finally came to a stop, the driver simply said, "The don is waiting for you inside."

The pit in my stomach returned.

Ascher held open the door for me, and I stumbled trying to climb out.

Jax's warm hand wrapped around my bicep. "Be careful." He opened his mouth like he wanted to say something else, but Cobra sneered and grabbed his arm.

He tugged him forward. "Come on, don't waste energy on *her*. She's made her decision."

I made a point of walking forward and elbowing past Cobra. "You're being childish."

He elbowed me back in the arm. Hard.

I slammed my foot into his shin.

Cobra whipped his gorgeous face around and hissed at me like a wild animal.

I stuck my tongue out at him.

His emerald eyes flashed with fire, pure fury rolled off him, and his jewels writhed across his flesh.

My lips curled into a smirk. If he wanted to act like a little bitch, then I'd treat him like one. No way was I just going to roll over and let him walk all over me because he didn't get his way.

He stepped toward me threateningly.

I flipped him off.

Cobra hissed.

"Really?" Ascher growled.

His back pin straight as he walked up, his face was back to a cold mask of indifference, but something unnamed sparked in his eyes as he watched Cobra and I tussle.

I turned around to huff past him and almost walked into a tall man in a business suit. Mumbling apologies, I took in my surroundings.

For a second, I forgot to breathe.

Serpentine City in the daytime was breathtaking.

The sidewalks were full of men and women clad in expensive-looking business suits and dresses.

Every woman wore heels and had her hair in an elaborate updo.

I turned in a circle and took it all in.

While all the fae were tall and willowy with similar graceful features, this realm was a different story.

Shifters of all sizes, with vastly different features and skin tones, walked briskly across the wide sidewalks, funneling in and out of the massive buildings.

I unfocused my eyes until the world blurred around me in streaks of color.

It wasn't hard to picture all the people shifting into various animals. Even though betas and nulls didn't shift, the animal influence was still present in their pheromones and postures.

The burnt scent of betas overwhelmed my nose. A few musky whiffs indicated there were other alphas nearby, and there were faint sweet notes of omegas in the air.

I'd never felt so alive.

It was like waking up from a nightmare and realizing none of it had been real.

A sense of belonging settled through my bones.

A man and woman held hands and hurried down the street, rich, earthy alpha scents trailing behind them. Enchanted blue jewelry dripped from their wrists and necks, matching their impeccably tailored clothes. Both had dark-golden skin and white hair similar to my own.

Two saber-toothed tigers?

I opened my mouth to ask, but they quickly disappeared into the bustling crowd.

A short older woman sidestepped a puddle and looked up, her wide bright-green eyes instantly bringing to mind a small woodland creature.

My breath caught as I realized she sported small, almost imperceptible horns that curled slightly at her temples.

Like Ascher's, but different.

No one had jewels in their skin like Cobra, but a woman hurried by, and the shimmering around her eyes was incandescent scales.

On closer inspection, the business attire was constructed of different fabrics and colors with unique markings and symbols.

What appeared to be a crush of similarly dressed people at first glance was actually a bustling crowd of unique individuals.

Some people stalked through the crowd like predators, alphas blending in like wolves in sheep's clothing.

The crowd instinctually parted around us. Heads down, high-heeled and dress shoes hurrying by, everyone gave us a wide berth, like they could smell the danger from our pheromones.

From what I could deduce, nulls jogged past in huddles of five people or more. No scent clung to them as they walked together in protective groups.

Even though they didn't shift like alphas and omegas, betas stood taller and stronger than any fae.

Like their beast counterparts, their features differed widely, with the history of animals apparent in the slants of their eyes or the striped tiger markings of their hair.

Predators stalked the street.

Suddenly, Xerxes's name was gasped, and people stumbled to a stop.

The whispers grew until there was a small semicircle formed around us as more people called his name.

On instinct, we shifted to form a circle around Xerxes, and he hunched low to hide his face.

But ABOs raised their noses in the air and whispered his name as they squinted at us, cinnamon on their tongues.

An alpha woman stalked by in impossibly high heels and a black coat made of massive feathers. Her nose lifted and eyes glowed as she inhaled cinnamon, head turned toward us.

"Come on," Xerxes said, startling me out of my shock as he pushed our protective blockade forward into the building.

He was the only person not looking around and gaping.

As he pushed us into the building, I craned my neck around and searched the crowd for the woman in the coat.

She walked past, massive feathers trailing behind her.

Shock stiffened my muscles.

She wasn't wearing a coat—she had wings.

Suddenly, the rain didn't seem dreary.

The soft patter of raindrops was the magical song for a unique, vibrant world. Everyone was an ABO, and they were everywhere. Unique. It was overwhelming, and it was everything.

Xerxes shoved us through a revolving glass door.

"Welcome," the don greeted us in an empty, nondescript waiting room.

Technically, he was the reason all the men were now in a pack without me.

I tried not to let my annoyance show on my face and focused on radiating "I am the perfect gang member" vibes.

From the way he stared down at me with boredom, I did not impress him.

His white snake was once again wrapped around his neck like a small necklace, and it raised its little head to hiss at us every few seconds.

Since the don and the snake were connected, did that mean he was hissing at us?

Rude.

The don shifted his attention to Cobra. "How are you adjusting to pack life?" His emerald eyes glowed more the longer he stared at his son.

Cobra said nothing.

The don didn't look concerned. "Today, you will begin your second initiation challenge. The basement of this building is an alpha fight club. No one may join the Mafia and shift into their alpha forms until they prove they have complete control over their mind and body. Only the strong survive in Serpentine City. Understood?"

"Um, what do we have to do, exactly?" I blurted nervously.

The "Loyalty" tattoo on the don's neck bobbed as he swallowed thickly, and his snake stared at me.

I sputtered awkwardly, "Um, only if you feel like explaining. Your Highness. Royal, sir."

Jax shifted closer so he was partially blocking the don's view of me.

Finally, after taking a long drag of his cigarette, the don said, "You will each train for one week to prepare your body for your fights, and you will take a test to show you've learned the rules."

He blew out smoke.

"You will fight matches in your unshifted forms. You must learn to be strongest in your weakest form, since enchantments that counteract shifting are common on the black market. If you survive your matches and maintain consciousness, you pass the second trial."

I narrowed my eyes. "How many matches do we have to survive?"

The don blew another cloud of smoke. "A few."

My shoulders relaxed. I was a good fighter, not a great fighter, but with the numb, I could hold my own.

The don took another long drag of his cigarette. "Just one hundred fights."

Sun god kill me now.

CHAPTER 16
SADIE
FIGHT CLUB

I CHOKED.

"Just one hundred fights" echoed around my head like a bullet.

Sometimes, it was important in stressful situations to ground yourself and remember your core value. Mine was the ability to throw my blood and infect someone until they became my mental slave.

It was the only thing that kept me from crumpling to my knees and crying like a baby.

"Follow me. You'll begin your training today." The don opened a door and led us down a dimly lit hallway.

Beta men in black suits flanked us on all sides, holding massive machine guns. The lights flickered.

What was it with this realm and creepy flickering lights?

We followed him into a narrow elevator that I recognized from a book on advanced technologies back in the shifter realm. Nondescript music played, and our reflections rippled across the sleek glass panels of the small box.

"Um, also, one last thing." I tilted my head to the don.

"The girls need an education. Lucinda is only sixteen, and I believe the others are of similar ages?"

Jax nodded at the don. "Jess is eighteen, Jala is fourteen, and Jinx is twelve. I would appreciate it if you could figure out schooling for them."

The don pressed his palm against black glass, and the white light of the elevator turned dark red.

Abruptly, we plummeted downward.

If I had any sense of self-preservation, I might have panicked and screamed.

Instead, I couldn't hold back the laughter that escaped my lips as my hair floated around me and my feet elevated off the floor.

In contrast, the men's faces were stoic as they levitated upward.

Xerxes's long blond locks curled up at the ends in all directions. He twirled his dagger in midair and glared at me.

Once again, the scent of sweet cinnamon filled the space with undertones of frost, chestnuts, and pine.

Abruptly, the elevator stopped moving, and I slammed back down. The door opened with a whoosh, and I stumbled forward on unsteady legs.

Ascher caught my arm and held me upright, his tattoos pulled taut across his cut jaw as he growled with annoyance. "Be careful."

A pitch-black corridor greeted us.

The only sources of light were neon cursive words on the wall that said, *Hell is paved in the bones of the disloyal*, which didn't have the same shock value the second time around.

The don led us forward.

The dark hall seemed to go on forever and was eerily quiet, and instead of panicking over that fact, I focused on ranking the different wall sayings from most inspirational to least.

1. *Sweat, Suffer, Survive*—A fun little remake of "Live, Laugh, Love." Gotta respect the angsty creativity. Whoever had written it was definitely in their feels. Ten out of ten, inspired.
2. *Rage-fight like a beast, annihilate coldly like the moon goddess*—Very badass. When had the moon goddess become a terrifying figure? I thought she was associated with inner peace? I liked their version better. Eight out of ten, inspired.
3. *Mess with an alpha, and you fuck with the pack*—I liked it, but also, too soon. Seven out of ten, inspired.
4. *When it's time to rest, scheme; when it's time to fight, massacre*—Hm, didn't know how to feel about it. I valued a nice rest day. Six out of ten, inspired.
5. *A death for an eye, and the beast realm survives*—It reminded me of another saying, but I couldn't remember what it was. Points off because it was confusing. Two out of ten, inspired.
6. *Busted knuckles, split lips, broken bones, loaded gun, and it's only Monday*—Immediately, no. One out of ten, made me uncomfortable.
7. *Half-breeds warning: War is coming*—For obvious reasons, zero out of ten. Very creepy and upsetting, unnecessary half-breed slander if you asked me.

The don turned to make small talk, and I pretended I wasn't having a panic attack over the last saying.

"What about the boy with you—I believe he said his name was Aran? Does he need to go to school?" His tone was too casual.

I shook my head and tried to appear nonchalant. "No, he's twenty-four and a water fae, so he won't be attending school. He'll look after the girls."

If by "looking after the girls," I meant "asphyxiate them in their sleep," then Aran was going to get Nanny of the Year.

"Hm."

Could snakes sense lies?

The don kept leading us down the narrow hall. "I will arrange for education for the girls. Do you know what they will shift into?"

I shrugged. "Um, I'm an alpha, but we don't know our parents, so I'm not 100 percent sure Lucinda will also be an alpha."

Jax had been trailing behind with the other men, but now he walked forward to stand beside me. "No, all my sisters are adopted. We are unsure of any of their parentage."

A sense of déjà vu washed through me.

I shivered.

It was probably just chance, but it seemed weird that none of us knew who our real parents were.

Half-breeds warning: War is coming.

Nope, I was not dwelling on it, and instead pictured prancing through a fae flower field.

My imagination was shit, because the field warped into a dungeon and massive rats climbed over me.

"Oh shit. Legolas."

The don stopped walking. "What?"

"The dude in the prison, he said something. Some star thing…" It was on the tip of my tongue, but I couldn't quite remember it.

Everyone looked at me expectantly, and I scrunched my nose like I was remembering.

Really, my mind was completely blank. All I could recall was the awful stench of the feces.

Cobra walked forward from where he was whispering something to Ascher (give a man a pack, and suddenly they're all buddy-buddy) and sneered, "Legolas from the High Court, position 4444, said to alert someone that he was being held hostage in the, now very dead, fae queen's prison. Also, Sadie, your memory is shit."

My chest rattled as I growled at him.

Cobra hissed back.

Sun god forbid a girl have a slight mental lapse after fighting for her life against an evil ruler and being tortured. Also, I'd never claimed to be the brightest; my talents were elsewhere.

The don's eyes glowed. "You are sure that is what he said?"

Cobra looked bored. "Positive."

The don gulped, his Adam's apple moving and distorting his neck tattoo until the *O* in "Loyalty" was stretched. "I will alert someone right away. You don't want to mess with the High Court."

"Who?" I asked at the same time as the men.

The don grabbed a handle of a door that was hidden in the darkness of the hall. "The people that rule over all the realms. More powerful than you can imagine."

I gaped. The don's long black hair swished behind him as he casually walked through the door like he hadn't just obliterated my entire concept of how the world worked.

Legolas had talked a good game, but I hadn't actually believed him. The man was an emaciated prisoner in a dungeon, for sun god's sake. Who knew what those conditions did to a person's mind?

"I'm gonna be sick," I mumbled.

"No time for that. We have to survive," Jax whispered under his breath, and once again Ascher placed his palm against my lower back, gently guiding me forward.

Cobra and Xerxes stood stiffly behind us.

The first thing I noticed was the noise: the eerie silence of the hall was replaced with a shrieking voice and loud, banging instruments.

The second thing I noticed was the towering ceiling.

The room was dimly lit and filled with neon-red lights and hazy smoke, and it reeked of cigarettes and sweat.

Did no one turn up the lights in this realm, and what was with the excessive smoking?

The third thing I noticed was the dozen fighting rings scattered across the floor. In between the roped-off mats, weights and barbells were strewn everywhere.

Alphas pounded each other with their fists, and loud cracks echoed as they broke bones.

Blood, sweat, and saliva flew.

There were a couple dozen alphas, all shirtless and either fighting one another or lifting massive amounts of weight.

The powerful stench of sweat overwhelmed the different alpha scents, creating a disturbing combination that reminded me of dozens of candles burning. If the scent of the candle was BO with musky undertones.

A voice yelled, "The don arrives!"

Abruptly, everyone stopped fighting or lifting and shifted into a wide-legged stance.

Heads bowed, arms clasped behind backs.

Someone turned off the screeching music.

I decided to not dwell on the glowing handguns tucked into the sweaty shorts of almost every alpha.

The don addressed the room, his voice harsh and commanding. "We have five new recruits. One of them is an omega, and one is a female alpha. They are all bonded to each other except for the female alpha."

Way to rub it in.

There was light muttering around the room.

Cobra muttered something under his breath, and I didn't miss the fact that he and Jax shifted slightly in front of Xerxes.

Ascher's fingers pressed harder against my lower back.

The don's voice deepened an octave, and he spoke with a slight hiss. "There are confidential extenuating circumssstancesss ssssurrounding them. All you need to know isss they didn't grow up in Ssserpentine City and are unaware of mossst of our culture. Anyone who hasss an isssue with the omega initiating can bring their complaintsss directly to me."

Alphas stopped muttering and bowed their heads deeper.

I'd bet all my supposed money, which notably I had yet to see any of (and no one had told me how to claim my credits), that no one was going to bring a complaint to the don.

His massive white snake slithered lazily around his neck.

The don smiled and relaxed his shoulders, probably sensing that he was the most terrifying bastard in the room, and continued his speech.

"They will join the two alphas currently initiating."

He gestured over to the only two people who stood in a fighting ring without guns tucked into their waists. It was a man and a female.

I'd been nervous because I'd only seen three women in the entire room, and I had a long, torrid love affair with toxic masculinity and alpha douche canoes.

What could I say? The small-dick men smelled my potent female stench and got all hot and bothered. "Hot" as in overheated by rage; "bothered" as in embarrassingly worried about how to detach my head from my body.

But now I was going through super-fun alpha-beast gang initiation, a truly once-in-a-lifetime experience, with another female alpha.

Thank the sun god.

The don gestured for us to join the other two initiates, slapped Cobra on his back, and marched out of the room.

As soon as the door shut behind him, the loud, screeching music turned back on.

Alphas resumed grunting and flexing.

Weights slammed down and shook the floor with vibrations.

Jax led us forward as we walked through the sea of sweaty half-naked men toward where the don had pointed.

Most of the alphas had cigarettes hanging from their lips as we navigated through the fighting rings.

A scary-looking alpha leaned forward and purposely blew his smoke into my face. His bald head was unnaturally shiny.

I coughed and gagged with disgust.

Before I could introduce my knee to his balls, Ascher guided me forward. He whispered in my ear, "He's not worth it."

The alpha grinned and muttered something under his breath as Ascher pushed me past him, and I mentally debated how bad it would be if I made the jerk my blood servant. Or maybe I'd shift and show off my massive canines.

That would teach him respect.

The other men said nothing, and I grumbled as we continued forward.

A week ago, Xerxes would have stabbed the jerk, and Cobra would have tried to rip off his eyelids to defend my honor.

Now they didn't even blink, like they were fine with people treating me like shit.

My chest burned with disappointment.

It's for the best.

I didn't want men who only protected me when it suited them. I wanted men who wanted me for *me* and genuinely cared.

We arrived at the fighting ring splattered in blood that the don had pointed at.

A large red-haired alpha with a gun strapped in his shorts and "Loyalty" tattooed across his pecs stepped forward. "I'm Z, one of the trainers for initiates."

There was a long, awkward pause as he looked over each of us, then stared at me.

"You're a female alpha?"

He raised his red eyebrows in disbelief.

I was still silently fuming at the men's lack of response to the jerk blowing smoke in my face, so I didn't bother to respond.

Z asked me, "Where did they say you were from?"

"They didn't say," I snapped back.

"You have interesting coloring." He reached a hand

forward like he was going to touch my hair, but Xerxes shifted in front of me and blocked him.

The queen's soldier was back, and Xerxes's voice was glacier cold. "I believe introductions were conducted."

Z nodded and smiled good-naturedly as he took his attention off me and back to the two alphas standing in the ring with him. "This is Clarissa and James. This is their first day at the fight club too, so you guys will be initiating together."

Clarissa reached forward and shook Ascher's hand, licking her lush lips.

She slowly ran her eyes over his tattooed body.

From the way she stepped closer into his personal space, she liked what she saw.

Ascher was expressionless, but he didn't push her away or tell her off.

A razor blade stabbed inside my gut.

She was tall and stunning. Standing next to each other, she and Ascher looked like the perfect match. No one would ever wonder why they were together.

Finally, Clarissa stepped away from Ascher and moved toward me.

I stuck my hand forward with a forced smile, but she didn't smile back and just let my hand hang there awkwardly.

James snickered next to her, his features similar to Clarissa's. He bunched up his nose like I smelled.

Great, rude alphas.

Groundbreaking.

I stepped back and rolled my eyes like I wasn't bothered while discreetly sniffing my armpits.

There was definitely an odor coming off me—stress

sweat was real—but it wasn't *that* noxious. Aran's fart had been way worse.

Clarissa ignored me and turned to Cobra.

He gave her a dashing smile.

"I'm Cobra. Pleasure to meet you."

His jewels sparkled across his annoyingly perfect features as he bowed to her.

Jax shifted uncomfortably. Ascher looked over at me with wide eyes, and it took me a long second to realize what had just happened.

Cobra was talking to her.

A woman.

My heart dropped in my chest.

Great. Now he'd gotten over his past trauma and toxic masculinity and decided to talk to the female sex.

For the first time, and last time, I missed the patriarchy.

Cobra smiled at a female alpha who was literally one of the prettiest people I'd ever seen and looked nothing like me.

My shadow snake sensed my distress and gave a zip of comfort across my skin, sending me images of cuddling and happiness.

Melancholy filled me at the reminder of whose the snake had once been, but I focused on sending it loving images back.

At least I still had a shadow snake, even if that was all I got from Cobra.

"I'm Clarissa. The pleasure is all mine. I've never met someone with jewels in their skin." She shook his hand coyly and fluttered her long sooty eyelashes.

Cobra said smoothly, "You have a lovely name."

The razor blade in my gut became a machete.

As they clasped their hands together, overly long if you

ask me, Cobra had the audacity to look over his shoulder and smirk at me.

Fuck him. If he wanted to make love with another woman's hand, that was his prerogative.

He'd made it clear I was nothing to him.

I purposefully lifted my fingers to my face and gave the snake a little kiss. "Such a good little snake," I praised, and it shivered with happiness.

I sent it more visions of love and kisses, and it barrel-rolled with glee across my gold skin.

Cobra's face fell, and an unnamed emotion flashed across his face. He abruptly released Clarissa's hand, stumbling back like she'd stung him.

Clarissa didn't notice anything and gave her amorous attention to both Jax and Xerxes.

She cooed over Xerxes's hair and marveled at Jax's size until I wanted to gouge my eyes out with a rusty spoon.

Her brother, James, followed behind her and shook everyone's hand but mine.

After fawning over Xerxes for an unnecessarily long time, Clarissa leaned forward into his personal space and whispered something about her treating an omega right.

Her midnight hair contrasted with his shiny blond locks, and the scent of cinnamon mixed with her lemony alpha one.

The scents weren't awful together.

Fucking hell, kill me.

Abruptly, when her nose was almost touching his throat, Xerxes rubbed at his chest at the same time as Jax, Ascher, and Xerxes.

My gut dropped.

Xerxes's bond was acting up because he was attracted to beautiful fucking Clarissa.

A low alpha sound crept up my throat, and I swallowed down an embarrassing growl.

He is not your omega.

My fingernails bit into my palms and I bit down on my lip hard enough to draw blood.

I couldn't look away as Clarissa whispered something else to Xerxes, and he trembled slightly.

The machete in my stomach turned into a grenade.

Our instructor, Z, turned toward me, and I ripped my attention away from the man-whore. "Don's ordered us to split you up for training. Sadie, you're going to train with Molly. The rest of you will be joining me."

Great, I was being singled out for being the runt of the group.

But relief coursed through me as I hurried away from the men, toward the corner ring Z had pointed to. I needed to get away from them before I shifted into my tiger form and embarrassed myself.

I'd made my choice, and they'd shown their true colors.

Whatever we'd had was over before it had even begun, and I needed to accept it.

But if the don thought he was going to make me do some wimpy female version of training, he was going to be surprised.

Did he really think I couldn't hang with the men? I was a fucking saber-toothed tiger shifter.

Had he seen my teeth? They were longer than his arms.

With every step forward, I fought the urge to look over my shoulder.

At this rate, Clarissa was probably straddling Xerxes and Cobra and humping both of them at once. Ascher would enjoy watching, and Jax would get turned on at the sight of Cobra with such a beauty.

It was all too easy for them to replace me.

Forget about me.

Move on.

A slashing sensation burned my back, and I tripped over a barbell. I was barely cognizant that I was stumbling, my mind flashing back to a small tavern and a beta's belt.

Parents who'd abandoned me.

Maybe Clarissa was what they'd always wanted. Someone sophisticated, tall, and gorgeous who would simper at them and pamper their fragile male egos.

That wasn't me.

Preoccupied with mentally eviscerating the men, I didn't watch where I was going and walked into a wall.

Long, callused fingers reached out and grabbed my forearm as I stumbled back and apologized.

The rippling mountain of muscle in front of me turned around, bulging arms and impressive thighs shining with the sweat of a warrior of lore.

Half the person's head was shaved, while the other half had long, dark hair.

I gasped when they looked up.

Olive skin, wide hooded eyes, and soft features smiled at me.

"You ready to work, sugar? I've been assigned to train you," the woman said, and I realized in a daze, that unlike all the fae women, Aran included, she wasn't that much taller than me.

My jaw flapped up and down uselessly as I stared at her sculpted perfection.

Scratch everything I'd just thought about being the runt; it would be an honor to work beside her.

Apparently, Molly was a gorgeous mountain of muscles.

From the three-hundred-pound dumbbells she was casually slinging up and down in each hand, it wasn't just for looks.

She was everything I aspired to be: strong, beautiful, and more impressive than any man.

"You're my hero," I blurted.

Molly chuckled and smiled kindly. "Let's get to work."

CHAPTER 17
SADIE
UM, HELP?

Never meet your heroes.

Molly smiled sweetly as she chanted above me, "Two hundred."

My noodle arms trembled, and I collapsed face first.

After five minutes of struggling to lift my body upward, it was clear that I couldn't do another pushup, no matter how hard I tried.

The music pounding through the hazy room screeched something about death and pain. Extremely relatable.

Molly sighed heavily. "You can do the baby version on your knees."

"You're my angel." I stared up at her with adoration, and she stared down at me with a mix of pity and boredom.

She was a kind queen.

My gratitude didn't last long.

Who knew that push-ups on your knees became ridiculously hard after two hundred reps? Upsetting.

"Four hundred and two," Molly counted for me as she continued to hoist her three-hundred-pound weights like they were nothing.

"Is there another version I can do now?" I gasped as I twitched my chest down and up, boobs barely moving an inch off the mat.

Molly's voice sounded far away as a wind-tunnel sensation whistled in my ears. "Sure, lie flat on the mat and don't move."

Instantly, I flopped down and closed my eyes, heaving with relief as oxygen filled my starved lungs.

It took me an embarrassingly long time to realize the beautiful tinkling sound was Molly chuckling.

She wasn't laughing with me—I was preoccupied drowning in saliva and imitating a log—so that meant she was laughing at me.

Molly had been joking.

Moaning like a dying cow, I struggled back onto my knees, and a single tear tracked down my face.

I waited for the derogatory comment about how pathetic and weak I was as I struggled to plant my hands in front of me.

Was it possible to be born without pectoral muscles? Because I swore to the sun god that there was nothing but bone beneath my small boobs.

Impressive thighs squatted close to my head, and Molly said quietly, "Half the gym is staring at you right now, and as a female alpha, you're always going to be scrutinized. Show them who you are."

Fiery indignation swept through me, and I nodded.

Also, another tear streaked down my cheek because supportive women always made me emotional.

She continued, "Plus, the four men you walked in with are glaring at me like you're their fated mate and they want to murder me for hurting you. Show them you're capable."

I shook my head. "They don't care about me. Trust me,

they hate me because I didn't form a pack with them. They've already moved on. Also, what's a fated mate?"

Molly squinted like she was surprised I didn't know.

"In the old days, when the moon goddess walked among us, packs were made of predestined mates. But she left this realm. Rumor has it because of a war, and there hasn't been a fated mate since."

A soft hand patted my head comfortingly.

"Don't worry about that, sugar. If mates are fated, it's obvious among all members when they bond. Since they're already a pack, you definitely aren't fated to them. The bond wouldn't let them complete it without you."

The small kindle of hope in my chest extinguished with a sizzle.

Molly smiled kindly. "Still doesn't mean they don't want you. Remember, hate is obsession, and obsession is the purest form of love. You never move on, and it festers within you until it's all you know and all you can focus on. It becomes your only hope. But sometimes, it's not enough, and everything falls apart around you."

I was still gasping on the floor.

Something in her tone was off, and I tilted my head up to look into her kind brown eyes.

Someone had hurt her.

"Wow," I said. "If you're into me, you can just say that."

A loud laugh burst from the larger woman, and she slammed her hand across my back.

I grimaced and pretended she hadn't just cracked three of my ribs and punctured a lung.

"Oh, you're definitely not my type." She placed her hands on her knees and laughed until I was thoroughly offended.

I mean, I didn't think Molly was actually into me, didn't

even know if she was into women, but she just didn't have to be so rude about it.

"You know, some people think I'm a catch," I grumbled after we passed the five-minute mark of Molly gasping for air.

My words caused her to double over in a fresh round of chuckling.

I thought about it and realized I couldn't remember if anyone had ever told me I was pretty.

Cobra had always said he wanted to own me. Ascher called me a princess (slightly weird; I always assumed he had some royalty fetish). Jax called me "little alpha," and Xerxes referred to me as an alpha.

Suddenly, it seemed super important that no one ever told me I was pretty.

Was I hideous? Was that part of why it was so easy for all the men to stop fighting for me?

I'd just been a novelty to them, and now that I wasn't unique, they were over it.

Also, why was I acting like a vain, prissy bitch when I was literally in the middle of Mafia training?

I couldn't help but glance over to the other fighting ring, where Clarissa was doing push-ups. She was glistening like a goddess.

Meanwhile, my hands kept slipping because I was lying in a puddle of stinky sweat. Every time I sniffed myself, I gagged from the rancid stench.

I'd forgotten deodorant.

In contrast, Clarissa probably smelled like flowers and lemon. She was tall, with muscles, not a hair out of place, and looked like the perfect complement to the massive athletic builds of the men.

Finally, Molly stopped having a heart attack over the idea of finding me attractive and said, "You know, I'm aware that you've been lying there resting and not doing your push-ups."

Damn it.

I'd hoped she wouldn't notice.

A serious expression contorted her face into something that was inspirationally terrifying. "You know, if you work with me, I promise I'll make you as strong, if not more so, than that girl you're glaring at."

Who was going to tell her I was half-fae and likely not going to change much?

No. I mentally slapped myself.

I was being a self-deprecating little bitch.

If anyone was going to help me achieve my best self, it was the absolute goddess of a woman that was Molly.

"Deal." I reached out and shook her hand.

Molly smirked and flexed her biceps. "Now you're going to do exactly as I say."

I grinned back conspiratorially.

Sadly, and disappointingly, exactly what she said to do was three hundred more push-ups.

Under the watchful gaze of my hero, I twitched like there was no tomorrow, peeing my pants slightly from sheer exhaustion, until I hit the three-hundredth rep and collapsed.

Pain radiated through every muscle in my body and the light faded from my eyes as I entered the afterworld of the sun god.

"Who turned off the lights?" someone yelled, and the dim lighting flicked back on.

I closed my eyes, depressed that death had been so close yet was apparently still so far.

"Aaah." I jerked upright and screamed as someone stabbed my arm and tried to sever it from my body.

"Relax," Molly said as she finished depositing a needle of glowing blue liquid into my arm. "It's an enchanted muscle-growth developer. It works with your body to help your muscles replenish and get stronger."

She chuckled again. "You didn't think you were going to get stronger without help, did you?"

"Where did you get a needle?"

What was it with this realm and injecting people against their will?

Molly smiled as she pulled out another needle from her book bag next to the fighting ring and stabbed herself in the arm. "How do you think I got this strong?"

I narrowed my eyes. "Does it have any side effects?"

"Who cares? You're an immortal alpha," Molly said with confusion.

With that attitude, I could see why this realm had a cigarette problem. Still, I couldn't fault her logic.

"Can I get a second one?" I asked.

She shrugged, grabbed another needle, and stabbed me in the other arm.

And thus began my extreme body transformation from scrawny wimp to absolute tank of a woman.

A few hours later, torture for the day was finally over.

"I think my biceps are getting bigger," I said to Jax as I flexed both arms in one of the large mirrors that lined the walls of the fight club.

We'd finished training aka just doing an un-sun-godly number of push-ups, jumping jacks, and planks. Then

Molly had sent me back to stretch with the other trainees for a cooldown.

Z sat in front of us, "supervising us" with a gun in his hand.

Did they think the other alphas would *murder us* if they left us on our own?

Concerning.

The entire gym had an edge of violence to it.

Like so many alphas together in one space, was a recipe for disaster.

You couldn't miss the handguns tucked into everyone's waistbands, like they couldn't be parted from their weapons while they worked out.

Why did they need so many weapons?

It freaked me out.

It felt like everyone in the gym was just waiting for the chance to shed their civility and shoot people.

"Your arm looks smaller," Cobra sneered as he stretched.

Clarissa giggled aggressively beside him, like what he'd said was funny and not rude.

The dark-haired beauty was sitting between Ascher and Cobra and kept stretching into their personal space.

My stomach twisted with annoyance.

I flexed harder. "Molly said she's going to make me stronger, and she's amazing. I'm already seeing an improvement."

Jax smiled at me as I snarled and flexed both arms lower while trying to pop my back to get a better angle.

"I don't think she's a miracle worker," Clarissa said slyly. Her brother and Z laughed openly.

The noise grated on my nerves.

A strange glint entered Xerxes's eyes, and he straightened his back, his lips twitching like he was trying not to join in.

Once again, the scent of cinnamon was stronger than usual and wafted around him in a heady cloud.

Cobra tilted his head toward Clarissa like he was intrigued. Even Ascher and Jax gave her their attention.

I deflated and plopped down to stretch my legs.

Obviously I didn't think I'd had a dramatic transformation, but I swore all the push-ups and whatever random drug Molly had stabbed me with had improved my muscles somewhat.

I could see more definition.

Maybe I was going crazy.

My chest burned with embarrassment.

A lot of people had been laughing at me recently, and there was only so much a girl could take.

I positioned myself away from everyone else and focused on touching my toes. They'd clearly found their replacement for me.

Who was going to tell her they couldn't bond with a female alpha because they needed a female omega?

The petty thought made my stomach hurt worse. It didn't mean they couldn't have sex with her, or still have a crush on her. There was always going to be some perfect, sweet omega female who completed their pack.

Fully in a depressive episode, I sullenly took one of the small books that Z handed out to each of us.

The title read "Mafia Laws," and I grimaced at how dense it was.

Unless it had been severely miss-marketed, it wasn't a romance book with simpering females and gallant men who saved the day. Those were the type of books I preferred to read.

Z said, "Study this and learn the rules. You will have a test in three days, and you can't fight until you pass."

"What happens if you don't pass?" I asked as I flipped through and winced at the ridiculously small font.

"Don't fail," Z replied automatically.

"But say, hypothetically, that you failed. What would happen?"

Z fingered the barrel of the gun, and his expression didn't change. But the scent of burning leaves spiked as he stepped closer to me.

His voice dropped an octave. "Don't fail."

"But if you did…" I pursed my lips and tried to look innocent.

Z's nostrils flared, and his muscles seemed to expand as he took another threatening step toward me.

"Sadie, shut the fuck up," Xerxes snapped.

His outburst was even more shocking because he'd barely spoken to anyone all day.

My stomach twisted tighter, and my cheeks burned.

Z kept staring at me.

"She's being fucking annoying. Ignore her," Cobra sneered, and Z shifted his attention toward the other alphas.

He grinned at Cobra as they shared a toxic-masculinity moment.

I mumbled under my breath about how it was confusing to make us take a test and not tell us the consequences.

"Shut up, Sadie," Jax said quietly as he leaned closer to me.

Immediate tears swelled in my eyes. Everyone was a rude pig, but not Jax—that was too far.

"Please," he whispered, and his voice cracked.

My eyes dried as I reminded myself that I was a bad bitch, and I focused on my stretching.

If I weren't conserving the numb for the fight marathon that was apparently happening in a week, I would have switched it on.

For some fucking reason, I was feeling unnaturally emotional about everything, and it sucked.

What would Molly do?

I straightened my shoulders and focused on a speck of dust on the ground, keeping my head high and eyes averted from the men.

When it was time to leave for the day, thank the moon goddess—I'd been worried they'd keep us overnight in some type of dungeon—I jumped away when Ascher tried to lead me out by my lower back, and he had the gall to growl softly in displeasure.

Apparently, all the men were in a pissy mood, because Cobra slammed the car door like he was trying to rip it off its hinges, and no one said a word the entire way back.

At the mansion, Walter sensed our sour dispositions and quietly announced dinner would be sent to everyone's room.

"I'm sure they'd all love to have dinner together. Just bring mine to my room," I snarled as the old man looked warily back and forth among all of us.

A hiss shook through Cobra's throat. "You don't get to be the victim here."

He rounded on me like he wanted to fight.

I saw red. "Oh, I'm just stating facts. Go back to Clarissa and have fun laughing at me. Didn't take long for you to show your true colors."

"True colors, *alpha*?" Xerxes said and laughed. "You want to talk about true colors?"

He moved quickly past Cobra and lunged at me. The sudden movement surprised me.

My body was sweaty and exhausted from training for hours, and I stumbled backward on shaky legs.

My head slammed against the hallway wall.

The vitriol thrown my way and pain radiating from my skull made me flinch violently.

For a split second, the sharp pain mixed with my sudden fear, brought back memories of someone else lunging at me with a belt.

A loud roar burst through Jax's chest.

The aggressive sound made me tremble harder, and I closed my eyes while shaking my head, desperate to throw off the pain and orient myself.

Moon goddess, I hadn't felt so off-balance since I'd been in the shifter realm.

So fucking emotional.

I blamed the torture.

I slowly opened my eyes. Cobra's jeweled cheek was inches away, his eyes bright with worry.

"Princess," Ascher pleaded and stepped up next to him.

"I didn't mean…" Xerxes trailed off in a shaky voice as he suddenly ran down the hall.

There was a loud crash within his room, like he'd thrown something heavy.

A trail of cinnamon lingered in the hall.

Jax's chest kept rumbling with a roar, and the delicious scents of pine, frost, chestnuts, and lingering cinnamon made my mouth water.

It was all too much.

"No, you don't get to be mean bastards, then nice. You've shown where you stand and how you view me, so don't act otherwise." I shoved past the men and ran the other way down the hall toward my room.

Someone said my name, but I didn't dare look back.

I locked the bedroom door behind me and bent over onto my knees, hyperventilating.

There were four of them and only one of me, and it was overwhelming.

When they were all nice to me, it was amazing.

They were four rocks who produced an overwhelming sensation of comfort and safety.

But when they were mean, it was too fucking much.

Four against one, it was crushing odds.

My heart was being trampled.

The shadow snake sent me visions of love and support, and I cherished its niceness.

After a long, pathetic moment of gasping, I shoved my panic back into the dark recess of my brain and straightened.

Four teenage girls stood in front of me with serious expressions on their faces.

"Aran's doing drugs." Lucinda pointed to the bed.

Because that was what my life needed right now… another crisis.

CHAPTER 18

SADIE

DRUGS AND GODS

ARAN WAS SPRAWLED out under the covers, sucking on a foot-long glowing blue stick.

She blew out a cloud of electric-blue smoke that matched her hair and smiled lazily.

She waved.

"Hey, Sadie, why is your flame so bright? Everyone else's is white, but yours is a gray purple. Good thing it's not black. That would be baaaad. I can't see mine, but I'm sure it's black. I'm an awful person; it has to be."

"She claims she can see colored flames in all our chests," Jala whispered and grimaced.

"She's not well." Jess held Jala's hand in hers tightly.

They looked at me desperately, united in their fear for Aran's well-being.

"She's clearly lost her mind." Jinx rolled her eyes like everyone around her was being dumb again.

Noodle still had his fake eyelashes on, and he pointed and chittered at Aran like he was also worried.

I was so physically, emotionally, mentally, and spiritually exhausted that I could see Jinx's point.

We weren't the brightest group.

All I wanted to do was crawl into bed and have a pity party, but I searched deep into my soul and found the fortitude to do what was right.

Marching over to the bed, I ripped the long pipe out of Aran's hands.

"Don't you know drugs are bad and kill people? Who knows what this enchantment is doing to you? I'm so disappointed."

Aran's ethereal skin was sallower than I'd ever seen it, and dark circles stood stark against her fair complexion.

She was falling apart.

I whacked her across the head as hard as I could. "People who do drugs are embarrassing. Girls, please leave the room for the evening. I need to fix this."

Four teenagers looked at me solemnly. Well, three did; Jinx just muttered something about how we were all dead.

I sighed heavily and whacked Aran again.

"Girls, I'm going to sort her out. Why don't you go hang out with Jax? I'm sure he misses you, and Lucinda, you could probably get Xerxes to teach you some knife tricks. I know you said something about learning."

They nodded hesitantly.

"You'll fix her?" Jala asked, pink eyes wide as she stared at Aran. "At school, they said you could never walk in the valley of the sun god if you did drugs. Your soul would be corrupted."

Aran laughed. "What a crock of shit."

I hit her again.

"Ow. Freakin' relax with the beating, woman."

"I'll make sure she stops. Don't worry," I said with conviction. "I don't know if that's true, but I know that drugs mess with your brain and can become so addicting you can't function properly. I won't let that happen to her."

I turned to Aran, who had bloodshot eyes and a lazy expression on her lips as she itched at her back.

She somehow still looked smug in the elegant bed.

Even under the covers, disguised with short hair and a wider, stockier male build, she looked down her nose at the room.

A purebred princess.

"But that doesn't mean I will put up with you wasting away and acting like a coward!" I yelled at her and beat her with a pillow for good measure.

"Don't hurt her too bad, sis," Lucinda said quietly as the other girls disappeared down the hall.

Lucinda lingered at the door. "I know you have a lot going on," she said as she shifted back and forth awkwardly. "Just know that I can take care of myself. You don't need to worry about me."

My gut pinched. "Is there something you wanted to tell me?" I asked, feeling like something unspoken hung between us.

Lucinda shook her head. "No, just wanted to make sure you knew."

"Okay," I said slowly, but Lucinda had turned around and left.

The door slammed behind her, and I focused my attention on the problem in the room.

Aran and I stared at each other for a long, drawn-out moment.

My chest heaved, and I dejectedly dropped the pillow with shaking hands.

I studied the long, glowing pipe I'd confiscated from her.

"So, going to explain what horrible evil is in this?" I fingered the cold, hard shaft.

"If you break it in half, it will send a strong message to the girls," Aran said lazily as she spread her arms out wide like she didn't have a care in the world.

I lifted the pipe and inspected it. "That would be the right thing to do."

"Should I do it?" Aran asked innocently.

I rolled my eyes at her and took a long drag from the end.

The enchanted smoke burned a trail down my esophagus, and it felt like a fire was lit in my lungs as I blew out the bright-blue smoke.

Aran modulated her tone, so it resembled my scratchy, broken voice. "Drugs are bad and kill people."

I settled into bed beside her and took another long draw. "Oh please, we're the only female role models they have. Might as well pretend to not be degenerates."

"It makes you feel nothing, and the world more hazyyyyy." Aran took the pipe from my hand and took a long drag. "The smoke."

"Thank fuck," I mumbled and noted that the pressure on my chest and pain in my stomach were lessoning with each fiery inhale. "Where did you get it?"

"Walter."

"I'm gonna free that amazing man from servitude," I promised as I snuggled against Aran.

Aran turned to me with a critical expression, taking in my haggard appearance. "How are you doing?"

I sighed dejectedly. "Not good. This Mafia training will probably kill me." I thought about the millions of things I had to complain about, but tried to be positive. "At least I have the numb. Or the song of the hunt. Still can't believe all half warriors are hearing voices inside their heads."

"What? No, they aren't." Aran said with confusion as she puffed out smoke.

I looked at her. "Demetre said that he also heard the song of the hunt, aka the numb. So he's hearing voices."

Aran shook her head. "I remember talking to him about it when I was younger. He said it was bloodlust, a compulsion to kill. He never said it was a voice."

I took a long hit of the drugs. "Well, fuck."

Now that I thought about it, he hadn't said explicitly that he heard a voice; I'd just assumed it was the same.

A sinking sensation weighed me down.

Terror for all the things I still didn't understand.

"Did you get some type of bodily enchantment done today?" Aran asked, sensing my despondency.

"No, why?" I asked as the drug kicked in and the headache that had started when the don announced I couldn't form a pack with the men blessedly stopped pounding.

Was she still going on about the flames?

"Your muscles are very large, oh impressive Mafia one." She grabbed my bicep and squeezed while wiggling her eyebrows. "Very firm. If you know what I mean."

With a cloud of smoke burning my lungs, I made a mental note to marry Molly.

"And they told me I was crazy. Bastards."

"Protect your face!" Molly yelled as she slammed her knuckles into my nose.

Inspirationally, I did *not* protect my face in time.

"Protect your stomach!" Molly yelled and slammed her knuckles again into my now-very-broken nose.

"What the fuck?" I sputtered in indignation.

Molly just smiled like she was having a grand time and hadn't been grinding my bones to dust for the last three days.

She'd taken one look at my sparring and announced that since I was physically built so much smaller than my opponents, my best odds of survival were through defensive maneuvers.

Therefore, for the last three days, I was only allowed to dodge Molly's attacks.

She'd said, "No one is going to announce where they punch. Each morning, you start out decently, but you get tired and become sloppy as shit."

Molly's fist flew with exacting precision.

It was a beatdown.

A beatdown I desperately needed because in the fighting ring a few feet over, Clarissa was running her hands over the men.

Touching their arms, giggling, leaning into their personal space.

Every day, she grew more familiar with them.

Every day, the men allowed it to happen and did nothing to dissuade her. They seemed to welcome the attention.

Sometimes, when I'd glance over at their fighting ring, I'd catch the men staring at me.

They were rubbing their new woman in my face.

I fucking hated them.

"Protect your face!" Molly yelled.

I hunched low with my forearms protecting my innards just in time to block a roundhouse kick that would have 100 percent made me infertile.

Although, I wasn't even sure if an alpha female could have kids.

"Good. See, sugar, you're learning."

"I don't get it," I gasped and awkwardly spat out saliva and blood around the mouthguard that Molly had said all alphas were required to wear.

Apparently, teeth regrew very slowly, and enchantments to help were ridiculously expensive.

Therefore, fight club rules: Everyone wore a mouthguard.

However, as far as I could tell, that was the only safety precaution anyone took. No one even bothered to wrap their hands in this realm.

Since Molly still had a gun tucked into her shorts, the mouthguard rule seemed like a bad joke.

When I'd pointed out to Molly that you broke your knuckles if you didn't wrap your hands, she'd asked, confused, "Why does it matter if you break your knuckles? They heal in two days. What's the problem?"

They were all masochists.

"Get what?" Molly asked.

She peppered me with a three-punch combo that somehow left my arm, stomach, and face burning before I even realized it had happened.

I tried to bounce back and forth on my toes like she'd taught me and gasped out, "Why tell me to protect my face, then punch low?"

Molly didn't respond, just said, "Protect your face."

I hunched to protect my organs, and she slammed her bare knuckles into my cheek.

The crack echoed loudly, and I barely kept myself on my feet.

"That!" I spat out more blood and ignored the bloody saliva dribbling down my chin.

After three days of being beaten on by Molly, any confidence in my abilities had been completely eviscerated.

A tiny part of me enjoyed the beatdown.

All I had was a terrifying shifted form and a creepy ability to enslave people with my blood.

I didn't have any in-between capability.

Like if someone stole my purse on the street, what was I going to do, enslave them? Shift into a saber-toothed tiger and maul them?

That would be overdramatic and embarrassing.

As far as I'd come since the day I'd discovered I was an alpha in the shifter realm, I still had a ways to go before I achieved any sort of physical mastery over myself.

Training with Molly, I could taste the control within reach.

Plus, if half-breeds were wanted, then my powers were more of a curse than any blessing.

If I relied on them to protect me, I was signing my death warrant.

Molly casually threw another three-punch combo, which I barely dodged.

She said wisely, "You don't solve a problem by causing another one."

I mulled her words over in my head.

"You need to protect yourself."

Molly swung a roundhouse kick, and I dropped to the mat to avoid her powerful thigh.

She stalked after me, and I rolled away across the mat of the fighting ring.

I flipped onto my feet, a move I'd learned in the fae gladiator ring, and dodged another powerful fist.

Molly smirked as she shook out her impressive biceps.

She was shirtless in only a sports bra and sweatpants, and her six-pack of muscles rippled as she floated gracefully back and forth.

Body goals.

Molly threw a lightning-fast punch that clipped my stomach.

As I keeled over, choking, she said, "To be an alpha in the Mafia is an honor you can't even begin to understand as an outsider. But with anything that is an honor, you have to work to deserve it."

Molly's leg shot out impossibly fast, and I sprang into the air, easily jumping over it.

She paused for a moment, clearly surprised by my athleticism.

If I hadn't known what my body could do while numb, I would have been surprised.

Impossibly fast. She slammed a fist into my arm and used her momentum to kick me into the rope along the side of the ring.

Molly spoke casually, like she hadn't just almost killed me, "Every alpha in this room is the best of the best. In Serpentine City, either alphas are unstoppably strong, or they die in these trials. There is no in-between. That means your foes in the ring will do everything to break you. Mind games and cunning are commonplace, so you need to be prepared."

I nodded shakily as I bounced more quickly back and forth on my toes.

Molly's one-two punches moved in a blur around my body as I focused on regulating my breathing and dodging the avalanche of attacks.

The quicker I avoided her blows, the faster Molly punched.

Air vibrated around us with the screaming angst of the music, rattling the ring and shaking my toes.

I dodged faster.

Soon my mind blanked as the sensation of displaced air tickled my flesh in the spaces where I moved away from her fists.

Dodge, jump, move, shift right, shift left, flinch down, roll, step back, step back, duck right, duck left, stomach punch, jump back.

The conversation was over.

My heart rate slowed, and the more relaxed I became, the quicker I moved.

I dodged faster than I could while numb.

Empty static fizzled in my brain.

As I sank deeper into my defense, Molly clicked her attacks into higher and higher gears.

I distantly noted that her face was split in a massive grin, her eyes slightly unfocused, as she lost herself.

It didn't matter that she moved unnaturally fast, as fast as Cobra and Jax when they sparred, if not faster.

She couldn't touch me.

The song pounding through the gym switched to a faster beat, something more fevered and uncontrolled. A male screeched in cadence to slashing noises and screams.

Static in my brain pounded to the rhythm.

As my breath and heart rate slowed, my muscles twitched nimbly until I wasn't reacting to punches.

I knew what Molly would do before she did it.

Future, present, and past melded into one.

A sensation of flying rushed through my veins, and euphoria burst across my brain.

Lightning in a bottle.

But some heights weren't meant to be reached by mortals.

I screamed as the euphoria twisted into pain, and it shocked my cells, immobilizing my muscles.

Molly's unrestrained blows were blasts of dynamite that cracked across my flesh and brought the agony to a fever pitch.

Her mouth formed an *o* of shock as I crumpled.

The world went dark.

CHAPTER 19
SADIE
MORE CREEPY POEMS

FAR AWAY, muffled voices spoke.

"What the fuck did you do to her? You're gonna be fucking sorry you ever existed." A snake hissed.

There were smacking sounds, skin against skin.

A wild animal growled loudly, the terrifying warning of an enraged predator.

"Calm down and relax," Molly snapped. "Don't act like you care. I've just met her, and it's obvious how much you've hurt her."

Shhhhhk. Blades had been drawn.

"You know nothing. She abandoned me. I mean, us," a honeyed, accented voice whispered menacingly.

Molly laughed, a harsh, forced sound. "Moon goddess, you're all dense."

The animal growls stopped.

Another voice said, "We know."

The hiss got louder. "Don't try to fucking twist the situation. She's fucking covered in bites because of you. You don't know fuck all, and if she doesn't wake up, I'm going to tear you limb from limb."

There was the unmistakable sound of the safety clicking off a gun as Z said, "Back off! Step away from Molly, or you're dead initiates."

Surrounded by darkness, I could feel the tension and violence rolling across my skin.

I needed to do something.

Desperately, I tried to speak and defuse the situation, but cold female hands grabbed me roughly and dragged me deeper.

Recover, the numb said softly.

Cold darkness consumed me once again, and I thrashed about for what felt like infinity in a cold abyss.

I drowned in water.

A light purring sensation vibrated across my chest and was the only thing that stopped the panic festering in my gut.

I didn't know how long I drowned in the murky depths of a dark lake, but ever so slowly, I drifted upward.

Red droplets rippled across the surface and slowly sank past me into the darkness as I rose by them.

Distantly, something poked at my mouth, and I tried to swat it away.

It stabbed harder.

I surfaced.

Sitting up with a gasp, I patted my skin.

Even though I shivered like I'd been deep underwater, and phantom droplets clung to my skin, I was completely dry.

The poking sensation in my mouth was Aran sitting beside me in bed, shoving the end of the pipe between my lips.

"Really?" I sputtered and slapped it away.

Aran shrugged. "I thought maybe it would help."

"You thought drugs would help?"

Aran didn't respond, just threw herself onto the bed and squeezed me against her shaking body.

I relaxed into the warmth, my skin still raw from the sensation of drowning in ice-cold water.

"Why are you shivering?" Aran asked, her eyes narrowing. "What did you see while you were passed out? You muttered some interesting things. Tell me before the guys come back and smother you."

Aran sensed my confusion and explained, "Cobra's jewels turned to snakes, and he literally stood over you on the bed like you were his egg to defend or something bizarre. It was super creepy."

She shook her head. "Everyone tried to pull him off you, but then you started muttering like you were talking to someone, and thrashing, and basically all of them went berserk. The men partially transformed, except for Xerxes, who shifted fully into a kitten and purred on your chest. It was the only thing that seemed to calm you."

My jaw actually dropped at the thought of Xerxes trying to comfort me.

The bastard had been frigid ever since the shower situation.

He hated me.

Aran nodded. "I know, right? You stayed that way for a few hours, but suddenly Cobra's shadows swarmed off his skin and made a big black snake. It tried to lay on you, which kitten Xerxes did *not* like. Jax tried to intervene and got covered in scratches and bites."

She paused dramatically. "Then you started thrashing again, and Ascher's creepy ram head bleated so loudly that Walter ran in and yelled at everyone to get out."

Aran chuckled.

"You should have seen him. Kitten and snake in one hand, Ascher's horn in his other, Walter threw them all out into the hall. Jax was the only one that went willingly. It was chaotic, and the most entertained I've been in months."

I took a long draw from the pipe Aran was still pushing between my lips and explained the icy water that felt like a lake and the numb voice speaking to me.

The droplets of red that floated past me.

"How did this start?" Jinx asked from across the room, her dark eyes wide with something close to fear.

I focused on the enchanted smoke burning my lungs as I explained the sensation of euphoria while fighting.

How, for an impossible moment, I'd predicted every move Molly made before she did. How it had turned into unimaginable pain.

Jinx and Aran were pale as ghosts, but that wasn't anything new. They really needed to get some sun.

I opened my mouth to ask why they were so freaked out, but a loud squeal distracted me.

"Sis, you're awake!" Lucinda threw herself into my arms, and I squeezed her as tight as I could. "Don't scare me like that again."

"I won't," I promised, relishing the feeling of her against me.

The lightness in my heart immediately dissipated as four pissed-off men stalked into the room.

Lucinda crawled off me, and I shifted uncomfortably under the sheets.

Were they finally going to admit they were acting rude to me because they were butt-hurt about the circumstances? From everything Aran had described, it sure as shit seemed like they still cared about me.

My brush with whatever the hell had just happened was maybe just what we needed.

I missed their friendships, and I wanted their support.

I was ready for peace and adult enough to accept their apologies.

"YOU EVER FUCKING DO THAT AGAIN, AND I WILL KILL YOU MYSELF!" Cobra launched himself across the room.

Jax and Ascher lunged at him like they'd known what he was going to do before he did it, and their quick reflexes were all that stopped the six-foot-five snake warrior from crashing into me.

"Oh, grow the fuck up!" I yelled back, more annoyed than ever. "Why do you insist on acting like a class A prick?"

I stumbled out of bed and marched over to go toe-to-toe with the bastard.

Shadow snakes writhed across his pale skin.

"Don't. Antagonize. Him. Please," Jax said in a clipped tone. His gray eyes glowed brightly, and he rubbed at his chest with one hand.

"Princess," Ascher whispered.

He released Cobra and fell to his knees, tattooed arms rippling as he wrapped them around my legs.

My body trembled from the force of his shaking.

I patted his golden head, unsure what in the sun god was going on.

As if he sensed my question, Xerxes leaned against the wall, apart from everyone, and said slowly, "My heat is starting much sooner than expected. Years of taking supplements has…changed my body's responses, and I've been going haywire after bonding. It's affecting all of them and making them emotional."

His face contorted into a scowl. "It's just biology."

Suddenly, I was hyperaware of the scent of intoxicating cinnamon. It was more sugary than it had ever been.

Ever since they'd bonded, cinnamon had been haunting my dreams. I'd been overly attuned to it and couldn't walk down a hall in the mansion without licking the sweet scent off my lips.

His words were a punch to the gut.

Ever since they'd bonded, I'd been uncharacteristically emotional; the men were only acting this way because of their biology.

None of it was real.

I detangled myself from Ascher's grip and stumbled away.

He whimpered.

My headache started up again.

Jax's grip on Cobra tightened, and they both stared at me like predators watching prey.

Shouldn't they be attacking the omega, not me?

"It's just biology."

I shoved everything that had happened into a ball and deposited it into the dark recess at the back of my mind.

A few thoughts filtered out, and I refused to acknowledge them until I was satisfied the entire ordeal was hidden away.

Them fawning over Clarissa flashed through my mind.

"Get out," I whispered.

"Kitten," Cobra snarled.

My gut twisted as it dawned on me.

Sun god, I was a fool.

That was why they were all hanging all over Clarissa. The heat had them fucking randy, and they wanted a female alpha to join them with Xerxes.

He'd said he was addicted to a female alpha, and as far

as I knew, he was only into women, which meant he likely wanted one for his heat.

"GET OUT!" I shrieked as loud as I could, putting every ounce of an alpha's command into the words.

There was a long pause, then they turned and left without another word.

They didn't fight for me.

"It's just biology."

My heart crumpled in my chest.

I stood in the middle of the room, heaving.

Aran stood silently and said nothing as I screamed and punched my fists into the bed.

"Fresh towels," a maid said quietly, slipping into the room and placing them on the chair.

"Thanks," Aran said as the maid curtsied and turned to leave.

I ran my hands down my face dejectedly as Aran arched her eyebrow at me questioningly.

"Ugh, it's just all too much." I ran my hands over my face tiredly. "I just feel like th—"

A familiar voice cut me off in an ancient fae language that was supposed to be dead.

The maid stood in the doorway, back ramrod straight and an intense expression curling her feminine features into something terrifying as she bellowed in a masculine voice,

"Ties are formed in the dark light,
The endless war it has been read,
But fate demands we all must fight,
There is no choice the gods are dead."

Abruptly, the maid staggered against the door and looked around in confusion. "Miss, did you need anything?"

"A bullet through the brain." I groaned.

Aran dragged her hands through her short hair. "Answers to the questions of mystical powers and bigger forces that plague civilizations."

The maid looked back and forth between us.

"Um, I'll bring another towel." She ran out of the room and tripped over the hall rug in her haste.

Silence stretched.

"Should we talk about it?" Aran asked after a few minutes.

I considered banging my head through the wall.

"What's there to say? 'In dark light' is super clear, and the good news is we have war and fighting to look forward to, and oh yeah, the gods are dead."

Aran nodded at me and slowly relaxed. She grabbed the pipe and took a long drag.

We were on the same page—ignore the weird poem that no one wanted to hear and pretend like it had never happened.

And do drugs.

They were always the answer.

Everyone knew that.

"We should talk about something else," Aran said, her fingers shaking as she struggled to hold the pipe.

Nodding, I turned to the window. "Wonderful weather in this realm. Do you think it will rain tomorrow?"

"Most likely."

A head popped into the room.

I screamed.

Aran jumped.

The maid opened her mouth, jaw distending unnaturally as once again a male voice boomed out a poem:

"One must join and raise the rear,
Other must break and bring the kings,
One must grow and lose the fear,
Other must die and rise with wings."

When the voice stopped, the maid leaned forward like a marionette doll and slammed her head into the wall.

She fell to her knees, then hastily stumbled to her feet while looking around in confusion. "Did I bring the towel?"

"Leave!" I yelled desperately, terrified she'd open her mouth again.

She stood still, eyes wide with shock.

"Please leave." Aran pushed her forward gently. When the girl had crossed the threshold, Aran slammed the door shut in her face and screamed, "And never come back!"

Aran twisted the lock, then slumped against it, breathing heavily.

"Great, more good news, also something about breaking and dying," I choked as an awful weight settled in my gut. "Do you think they knew we were going to ignore it…so it came back?"

Aran itched at her back, then keeled forward like she was going to throw up. "Fuck, maybe."

She took another drag of the pipe. "Quick recap, so it doesn't. One, which I bet is me or you, must join, raise the rear, grow, and lose fear."

Aran inhaled desperately, like she was drowning in the air.

"Other, whichever one of us isn't 'one,' must break, bring kings, die, and rise with wings."

Nodding casually, like I wasn't totally freaked out, I slammed my head into the antique mirror on the wall.

The crack echoed.

Cold glass crunched therapeutically under my forehead as I said, "Odds are I'm 'other,' with the whole break and death thing, although I've always wanted to be a bird. That could be a win."

Aran smoked more, not even flinching at the blood dripping from the gash on my head. "Then who are the kings? Jax, Cobra, Ascher, Xerxes? That doesn't really make sense."

"Couldn't Cobra be considered royalty? Maybe the pack by association?" My gut was telling me that was what it was referring to.

Aran shivered. "I don't know. That doesn't seem right to me. The last time a poem read itself to us, it said,

"*Blood burns red, through the air it's blown,*
Blood pours bright, across the fated throne,
Blood draws truth, and rips apart the mind,
Blood creates pain, it kills the weak-spined."

Aran snapped her fingers with excitement and pointed at me. "Then you discovered you had blood powers and attacked my mother, who sat on the fated throne. You ripped apart her mind and killed her. Actually, the poem was all very literal."

I raised my eyebrows. "Wait, how did you remember that poem?"

"What do you mean? Did you somehow forget it?"

"Never mind, I definitely remembered it." I'd forgotten it completely. I mean, there were a lot of words to keep track of.

Aran grimaced. "That reminds me."

If there was any more bad news, I was offing myself.

The men were cheating fucks who were interested in one of the prettiest females I'd ever seen in my life (I was confident enough in myself to admit she had the "it" factor, while

I had the "are you sure you took a shower" factor), I'd had a vivid hallucination of drowning, and now creepy poems were reading themselves to us again.

My quality of life was nonexistent.

It literally couldn't get worse.

I inched closer to the window, prepared to dramatically throw my body through it in a display of sheer unwellness.

"You have that damn test tomorrow for the trial, so you have to study tonight."

That was it.

I couldn't live like this.

Lunging for the window, I almost slammed my way to freedom, but Aran intercepted my path and chucked me easily onto the bed.

"Come on," I moaned. "This is so unfair."

Aran wrestled me into a headlock, her arms and legs wrapped around me like a pretzel, so I couldn't move. "If I have to keep living and dealing with this shit, then so do you."

"Ugh, don't be so selfish, Aran."

"Don't be so unhinged, Sadie."

"Don't be so ugly."

"Don't be so scrawny."

I gasped with hurt. "Take it back. You said my muscles were looking bigger, you lying cow."

"Moo, bitch." Aran released my limbs from her death grip and climbed off the bed.

A terrifying thought struck me. "Oh my sun god."

"What?" she asked.

"Do you think the ancient fae voice is an *alien*? From the stars," I whispered with horror, remembering a human movie about a weird blob thing in a basket.

Aran rolled her eyes.

"First, no sentient beings live on a sun; the temperature is way too hot. Second, aliens are a ridiculous human conception. Of course there are people from other realms. Planets are connected by portals. The different realms are all just individual planets, duh."

I gasped, the world shaking around me.

"Wait, so I'm an alien?"

Aran narrowed her eyes at me. "I can't tell if you're joking or actually an idiot, but I'm going to pretend for the sake of this friendship, and apparently a prophesied war, that it's the former." She rubbed at her forehead tiredly. "Also, I know you're deflecting from studying."

"I'll show you deflection." I took a running jump off the bed and spun in an impressive roundhouse kick.

Aran caught my foot in midair and pulled it up, so I tipped over. "Very impressive. Can't wait to see you with wings." She chuckled. "I'm envisioning you flying into a building."

Funnily enough, I also saw that for myself.

CHAPTER 20
SADIE
SCHOOL TESTS AND JEALOUSY

ARAN GRABBED a book off the desk and handed it to me while she took another long drag of her pipe.

At least her hands had stopped shaking.

She'd been smoking so much the last three days that it no longer seemed to have any effect on her.

"Molly said you have the test tomorrow morning, and you have to pass, or you'll be executed. The men said something about studying together tonight, but I figured you'd want some space."

"Oh, I need space all right." I grabbed the book out of her hand and tried to rip it in half in a fit of rage.

Screaming, I tugged and tugged at the paper.

It didn't tear at all.

My vision blurred red as I thought about it.

They couldn't even give me a one-day extension after I'd passed out, or whatever the hell had happened.

Never mind the creepy maid.

Knowing my luck, the wings mentioned in the poem were just a hint that I'd be turning into a giant pigeon.

No hate to the pigeon community, just didn't know if that lifestyle was for me.

Aran snatched the book from my hand and stomped over to the ornate wood desk in the corner. "Now I see why my tutors were always sighing."

She plopped down and gestured for me to take the seat next to her. "Let's just try to forget about the poem for now, because you're *not* dying on my watch."

"Aw." I put my hand over my heart. "I love this moment for us."

"No chance in shit do you get the easy out while I'm stuck living with Jinx. Do you know she calls me a cannibal whenever we're alone? Who does that?"

The moment was over.

"Is she wrong?"

Aran smacked me, hard, and picked up the book. "Whatever. We need to focus."

She read aloud, "First rule in the Mafia. Unwavering loyalty to the don and the Mafia. Anyone who is not loyal will be executed with a bullet through the brain and their body hung from the tallest building in the city for all to see."

"Wonderful."

She shrugged. "I mean, it could be worse." Her eyes narrowed as she read ahead. "See, rule two says that if an alpha is caught physically harming a null, beta, or omega while unprovoked, the don will disembowel them, then burn them alive."

Aran shuddered at the last part, and I was immensely glad I had eaten nothing recently.

"Why couldn't I have been a null?"

She looked at me like I was dense. "Honestly, the fae realm was worse. At least this place has rules. Back home, the monarchy could do anything, to anyone, for any reason. *Anything*. And Mother was nothing if not creative."

I pursed my lips, still not convinced.

"And don't forget the shifter realm was forty degrees below freezing on a good day, and it was common for people to get lost in an ice storm and never come back."

"Yeah, I guess. Do you think the human realm is peaceful?"

Aran shook her head vehemently. "Everyone knows it's anarchy over there. Rumor is that they have weapons that can level an entire realm, killing everyone instantly in a mushroom of poisonous fire."

"Why is everything so fucked?"

I scrubbed at my arms while ancient fae words promising death still echoed in my ears.

Aran slapped the book for emphasis. "No more distractions. You aren't failing this test, because you have me. I was always at the top of my class, and you aren't dying because of a test. That's ridiculous."

I pursed my lips. "Weren't you tutored? So wasn't it a class of one?"

Aran rummaged through the desk until she found a pen and a stack of paper. "Start writing everything I say so you don't forget."

She smirked. "And Sadie, my sweet flower, all fae are assigned anonymous identification numbers and required to take a three-day standardized test at sixteen years old. Then we're ranked against one another."

Aran's eyes twinkled with an expression I'd never seen on her before.

It took me a second to place it.

She was proud.

"I was average on most sections but scored first out of thirty-three million in battle strategizing."

My jaw dropped.

Aran shrugged. "Not like that's actually a useful skill, and no one listened to me in the shifter realm when I tried to bring up the fact that our fighting strategies made zero sense."

"Okay, General. Remind me not to mess with you if we ever find ourselves on the opposite sides of a war."

Aran's gloating expression disappeared. "My mother was overjoyed, for obvious reasons, and almost every elite fae male applied to breed me. I ran away to the shifter realm the next week."

I reeled from her admission and blinked in shock at my best friend, who was apparently a battle genius.

"Well, I'll have you know, I was also impressive in school."

"Really?"

"I ranked fortieth out of a class of fifty people. Although, technically, the last ten didn't live till graduation."

Aran laughed, then covered her mouth when she realized I hadn't joined her. "Oh my sun god, you aren't joking."

I shrugged, unbothered. "My talents lie elsewhere."

Also, I was 99.9 percent sure I had some type of attention disorder, because I'd never been able to sit still long.

Aran slapped the desk with determination. "Well, it doesn't matter because you're studying with me. And I *don't* fail tests. You're going to pass this, even if it means you don't sleep all night." She checked her watch. "Night hasn't fallen, and the test is midday tomorrow."

She turned her attention back to the book. "Oooh, rule four is interesting. It says that, while rare, some ABOs have fated mates. No one is allowed to intervene or stop fated mates from forming a pack together. The punishment for interference is disembowelment."

I wrinkled my nose. "Why is everyone getting their organs torn out? Seriously."

"That's interesting. I think I've read about fated mates in the fae realm. They can occur in all species." Aran flipped through the pages aggressively. "The only other thing about it is a footnote that says they are blessed by the gods and it will be clear they are fated."

"Yeah, Molly said the moon goddess blessed packs, but that stopped after some big war eons ago."

I gnawed on my lip as I tried to imagine what type of war would cause a goddess to abandon an entire realm.

Also, it was too much of a coincidence that the poem had said something about a war and the gods being dead.

A neon-red sign flickered in my memory.

Half-breeds warning: War is coming.

Suddenly, I didn't feel so good.

Aran pinched my arm.

I yelped. "What the fuck?"

"Write the rule, bitch. This isn't for fun. Your life's on the line."

I rolled my eyes but dutifully wrote it down.

Aran continued reading ahead. "Rule number five: Unwavering loyalty to all members in the Mafia. Any discrimination, bias, or prejudices against a fellow member based on their status as an ABO, the animal they shift into, or for any other reason relating to identity, will result in the prejudiced person being burned alive."

I chewed on the end of my pen, surprised. "Really, just set on fire?"

Aran flipped the page. "Oh, sorry, I didn't realize it went

on to the next page. They'll be burned alive, *then* disemboweled."

That made more sense.

About twelve hours later, my head thudded with a dull ache, and I struggled to keep open heavy eyes.

Aran hadn't lied when she'd said she was serious about studying.

I would have fallen asleep a dozen times if she hadn't slapped me awake as soon as my eyes closed.

Once, Aran had threatened, "I will slowly detach your scalp from your skull if you don't stay awake."

Have I mentioned she needs help?

My hand ached from writing out a summarized line of every rule Aran had read to me.

Now she pushed a glass of water into my mouth. "Drink it. We're done. If you fail, I'll kill you myself."

I groaned as I stood up. "Why is everyone always trying to off me?"

After not moving for hours, my bones creaked and my lower back hurt like I'd been punched repeatedly.

Which was one of the few places on my body Molly hadn't pulverized with her fists.

Who knew studying could be so physical?

Even though the circumstances were dire, without Aran, I probably would have just flipped through the book, skimmed stuff for about an hour, and called it a day.

I mean, what else could a girl do?

Apparently, a *lot* more than I'd thought.

Aran was methodical and unrelenting, refusing to move forward until I'd read, written, and retained every. Single. Law.

She'd explained that the mind was a massive library

where you filed and cataloged information, neatly tucking it away until you needed it.

I hadn't had the heart to tell her that my mind was more an empty space with a dark abyss in the back that I shoved everything I didn't want to think about into.

Poor girl was convinced we both had mind palaces of libraries that we needed to take care of.

I let her keep the illusion for the sake of our friendship.

As I stumbled in an exhausted stupor out of the mansion, Walter informed me in his crisp, no-nonsense tone that the men had already left to go to the training center.

I gave him a big hug and thanked him for helping control the men while I was passed out.

With a red blush across his pale wrinkled cheeks, Walter stood still as a statue. He patted me gently on my arm and mumbled something about idiotic males.

When I finally arrived at the fight club, Z was waiting for me at the door with a packet and a pen. "You made it just in time." He pushed me into a side room, then shoved me roughly into a spare seat that had a desk attached.

Great, I was beside Clarissa.

The room was silent.

I growled at Z for pushing me, but he had already moved to the front of the small, windowless room.

"You have three hours to take the test. Each question has a line underneath, and you must write the answer. It is enchanted, so you'll automatically get your grade on the top of your paper when you finish. There are two hundred questions, and one hundred and thirty is passing. One point per question. Begin now."

Sun god, this was a lot.

My palms were sticky with sweat, and my hand shook slightly from exhaustion.

I flipped open the first page. The first question read, *What happens to alphas who hurt omegas or betas?*

The moon goddess was truly with me. Thank fuck for Aran.

I grinned and scribbled down, "They get disemboweled by the don, then set on fire."

Two hours into the test, I began to lose steam and had to stifle another yawn with my fist.

The words were blurry on the page, and I barely read the question before writing, "Disembowel them."

If I'd learned one thing last night, it was that the punishment was almost always organ extraction.

Three hours later, Z shouted, "Time! Put down your pens. Close your booklets."

My heart beat erratically as I turned the test over, and a number appeared at the top.

Glowing green on the top of my page, it read, "131. Passing."

The scores and our names appeared on a blackboard at the front of the room. Everyone had passed.

Jax had the highest score, and I had the lowest one.

Clarissa snickered and whispered something derogatory, but I was too busy grinning from ear to ear.

I'd fucking passed. Who gave a flying fuck about the score? I was on top of the world.

Now I didn't have to enslave anyone with my blood powers and fight to the death against the don.

What a glorious day.

Aran was a fucking angel from the rumored god realm. A true queen.

Jax blushed as Z clapped him on the shoulder, and I wondered proudly what the man didn't excel at.

"You can have the rest of the day off. Official fighting

starts tomorrow. Be here at dawn, and don't be late." Z turned to look at me pointedly.

I smiled like a loon.

He frowned.

What a wonderful time to be alive.

Slumped in my seat, slightly high from the drugs still in my system, sleep deprivation, and the sheer bliss of passing a hard test, I didn't even realize everyone had left the room.

On shaking legs, I stumbled to the door, chuckling as I imagined how excited Aran was going to be.

Clarissa blocked my exit, and her stunning face was contorted into something ugly.

"Are you a badger?" I asked.

"What?" she asked with confusion.

"Is your alpha form a giant badger? I don't know why, but I can see it."

Clarissa snarled, "You don't deserve to be a part of the pack."

"Wow. I went left with this convo. You went right."

The elation slowly drained out of my bones until my legs were unsteady and my headache began to throb again.

When was the last time I'd eaten?

She snapped her perfectly manicured red nails in my face. "Are you paying attention? I said you don't deserve the pack."

I didn't ask what pack she was referring to.

It was obvious.

Clarissa flipped her silky black ponytail. "Xerxes is not just any regular omega. He comes from one of the oldest beast families in Serpentine City. Everyone knows he was owned by the notorious Black Wolves."

She paused and stepped into my personal space.

"They're independent alphas. They're as rich and crazy

as they are *wanted* for crimes against beasts. Xerxes is only alive because he ran before they could complete the bonding, because he was too young for it to take."

Her alpha scent wafted off her in waves of lemony tang.

I'd never liked lemons.

My stomach hurt for Xerxes, but I said nothing. It wasn't like she actually wanted to have a conversation.

Clarissa's voice pitched until she growled. "The Black Wolves are hunting Xerxes as we speak. He's going to need to be surrounded by the strongest alphas in Serpentine if he's going to survive. His alphas are strong, but the weak link in the chain is you. If the pack needs anyone, it's other alphas that are strong enough to protect him. Not some scrawny runt who passes out while fighting."

Any lingering joy from not failing the test drained from me.

The sleepless night caught up to me.

I took a shaky step back from Clarissa as if I could distance myself from the horrible meaning behind her words.

She wasn't wrong.

If Xerxes really was being hunted, he needed to be protected. My heart hurt for everything he'd been through.

Clarissa took another menacing step forward.

I went to step back again, and I bristled at my cowardice.

She didn't know who the fuck I was.

Jinx came to the forefront of my mind, and I channeled the twelve-year-old.

"I'm *not* weak. You know nothing about the pack or Xerxes. I'm the one who's lived and fought beside them. You're just a lonely, jealous female alpha who's acting like an animal because you've met a male omega way out of your fucking league."

Her dark eyes flashed with warning, and I could have stopped the backhand that I saw coming from a mile away.

But I was fucking tired, and a part of me welcomed the pain.

I'd let her be the bad guy all she wanted. I'd let her think she had the upper hand. It would be all the sweeter when one day, I'd show her who I really was.

Her backhand struck my cheek, and the force of the blow slammed me into the wall.

She was no delicate flower.

But it wasn't her hand that stung; it was her next words.

Clarissa's blood red lips curled up at the corners. "Xerxes invited me to his first heat. Said it should be soon, and he needed a female alpha present. You're not special, so stop pining over them like you're fated mates. Everyone can see they're over you."

What was left of my heart incinerated into ashes.

My knees gave out, and I struggled to stop myself from collapsing as the world rocked around me.

Clarissa was silent as she walked away.

She didn't need to say anything.

She'd already destroyed me.

CHAPTER 21
SADIE
HIS HEAT

IN THE GYM, Molly ran after me with the syringe.

She said something about how she was glad I was okay and that we needed to be consistent with our muscle-growth regime.

Her words rubbed me wrong, and a snarl bubbled in my chest.

Why did I have to change myself to be good enough for the men?

I didn't need to prove my strength to anyone.

Brushing past her, I stalked away without a word.

The sources of my consternation were waiting outside the building, but I purposely ignored them and climbed into the separate car I'd taken to the test.

The thousands of beasts hustling down the wide sidewalks no longer seemed interesting.

Gray skies and endless rain were depressing as fuck.

Just another realm with too many people.

Too much pain.

After the car sped back, I stumbled into the mansion,

desperate to climb into my bed, smoke the pipe, and sleep till I had to fight.

If I never saw another man ever again, it would be too soon.

They were over me, and I needed to move on.

Of course, since this was my fucked-up life, three alphas and one man-whore omega ambushed me in the front entrance.

I marched past them. “I’m not talking to any of you.”

Jax grabbed my arm and easily stopped me as I tried to push past them and run up the grand stairway.

Up close, the scent of sugary cinnamon was nauseatingly intoxicating and made me want to scream, cry, gyrate, and lose my fucking mind.

Clarissa’s words cauterized my brain like battery acid.

I screamed, “Let me fucking go! I hate all of you.” Tears of frustration burned my eyes.

No matter how hard I tried to shove her words into the dark recess of my mind, they wouldn’t fucking disappear.

Jax grabbed both my biceps in his hands and held me so I couldn’t move. “Please, little alpha. Everything’s getting messed up. We need to talk.”

I kicked out like a petulant child and growled as panic welled in my chest.

“Xerxes invited me to his first heat.”

I couldn’t breathe.

Jax’s voice was frantic. “Calm down, Sadie. Please.”

I was trapped.

Focusing on the telltale tingle, I started transforming into my saber-toothed tiger. My clothes became painfully tight as my body enlarged.

“STOP SHIFTING!” Jax alpha-barked with a roar that shook the mansion.

My clothes loosened as my body instinctively stopped shifting.

"Fuck you." I glared up at the large alpha who'd been nothing but nice and sweet.

Until he wasn't.

A hiss rattled. "Why do you have a bruise on your cheek that you didn't have twenty minutes ago?" Cobra asked.

I guffawed at his horrified expression. Clarissa's backhand was the least painful thing that had happened to me today.

"What the fuck?" Cobra snarled.

Jax still restrained me, so Cobra easily grabbed my chin in his callused hand and forcibly turned my head so we were inches apart.

His frosty scent burned.

They'd already replaced me, yet they acted like a *bruise* was a big deal?

What was wrong with them?

Ascher and Xerxes walked up beside Cobra with scowls on their handsome faces. Ascher's horns lengthened, and the flame tattoos on his neck jumped as he clenched his jaw.

Xerxes just stared at me with violence glinting in his purple eyes.

I could practically smell the malice directed toward me. He wanted to fight.

"Man-whore," I spat at him.

Ascher smiled, then frowned when he realized I wasn't talking to him. He raised his eyebrows and looked back and forth between Xerxes and me.

Cobra blocked my vision, emerald eyes on fire as he snarled. "What the fuck are you talking about?"

"Don't act like you don't know."

His pale fingers were still gripping my chin, and he tightened his hold until the cold of his jewels bit into my skin. "You're being a brat."

I would have tilted my head back and laughed hysterically, but my head was immobilized by his tight grip.

My already broken voice was a gritty rasp as I struggled to move my jaw. "Thank the sun god I never bonded with an unfaithful prick like yourself. Now I can actually find some real alpha men who don't act like man-whores."

"Oh, you're going to find some new men, are you?" Cobra's eyes glowed bright green, and his pupils transformed into slits.

His red tongue lengthened and split into a fork.

Ever so slowly, he dragged his snake tongue across my face.

The scent of snow intensified until I was sure he left a trail of ice across my skin.

"Fucking creep," I spat and kicked my legs to conceal the fact that my core had just spasmed.

Cobra's fingers tightened around my jaw, and Jax's hands tightened around my arms.

I kicked my legs harder, aiming to pop a fucking ball.

That would show them.

Jax growled. "We just want to talk to you. Things are getting out of control."

The scent of sugary-sweet cinnamon spiked higher and twined around all of us.

Four sets of male eyes glowed.

It was the heat.

The thought was a bullet through my chest.

I sneered, "Clarissa already told me what you told her, Xerxes. There is nothing else I have to say to any of you. We're done. Enjoy your lives."

"What are you talking about?" Xerxes asked, purple eyes flashing with confusion.

Cobra's voice was a slurred hiss. "Issss that who gave you the bruisssse?"

My jaw was going numb from the tightness of his fingers.

I rolled my eyes. "Oh my sun god, drop the fucking act. I know Xerxes already asked Clarissa to join his heat. Congrats, you successfully replaced me, not that we were anything to begin with."

My neck wrenched to the side as I tried to glance away from the too-handsome omega. It hurt to look at him.

Cobra's fingers tightened. I couldn't move an inch, and my face throbbed.

"You're hurting me," I whispered.

Instantly, Jax dropped me, and Cobra pulled his hand away.

Surprised by the sudden release, I would have fallen to the floor if not for Ascher lunging forward and catching me.

He cradled me against his chest, and a low bleat rattled as his tattooed arms cocooned me.

Was he alpha-purring? It was more of a bleat, but the low vibrations instantly calmed me.

Suddenly, I was too tired to deal with the tension.

Like a coward, I kept my face pressed against Ascher's chest and inhaled his musky pine scent that I loved so much.

It reminded me of the forest I'd grown up playing in.

Outside the warmth of Ascher's chest, there was a loud hiss, then a crashing noise. Another hiss followed, and I debated just falling asleep in Ascher's arms and pretending I didn't care what was happening.

Holding me with one arm, Ascher reached up with his other and rubbed his chest like it hurt.

My heart pinched with worry at the thought of the men in pain.

Fucking pack dynamics were making everything worse.

I squirmed out of Ascher's tattooed arms and amazing pine scent in time to watch Cobra lift Xerxes and throw him into a wall like he weighed nothing.

"What the fuck issss wrong with you?" Cobra stalked toward him.

Instantly, Xerxes was on his feet with two wickedly sharp knives twirling through his fingers. "I never said that to Clarissa." His honeyed accent was steel.

Cobra's eyes flickered to slit pupils. "Why should I believe the fae queen'sss lapdog?"

He moved forward with startling speed, but Xerxes dodged in time and slashed Cobra's arm with his knife.

Blood splattered across the white floor.

Jax roared at the cut that bloomed across Cobra's arm, and he charged at the omega.

Ascher threw me to the side and put himself in Jax's path. He fell to his knees just in time to avoid the massive hand that would have chucked him into the wall.

While Ascher slid across the marble floor, he slammed his fists into Jax's knee so the big man stumbled out of the path of Xerxes, who was lunging forward, daggers ready.

Rain pounded outside, and the wind screamed as it slammed into the mansion.

The beast realm sucked.

For a split second, I debated running up the stairs and hiding in the bedroom.

Blood dripped down Cobra's arm, and he smiled at Xerxes like he was disemboweling him in his mind.

Xerxes's eyes glowed bright purple, and the heartless assassin swirled daggers impossibly fast through his fingers.

Someone was going to get hurt.

Even if they didn't want me anymore…romantically, it didn't negate the fact that they'd saved my life countless times.

Why did I have to be such a good person?

I better be nominated for sainthood. I gnashed down on my inner cheek until a copper tang flooded my mouth.

Focusing on the center of churning darkness in my mind, I smiled as the blood in my mouth vibrated with the electricity.

It was pure power.

In slow motion, Cobra's jewels flashed into shadow snakes and streamed toward Xerxes, who pulled his arm back and shifted his weight to throw a dagger.

Ascher clawed at Jax, who grabbed him and lifted him as he turned to chuck him into the wall.

I opened my mouth.

Four droplets of blood flung through the air and slammed into each man.

The small droplets sank deep through layers of skin, tissue, muscles, and veins as they sought the sources of their power like heat-seeking missiles.

Unlike the fae queen, who'd been covered in enchantments and centuries-old protections, they had no defenses.

"*Freeze*!" I ordered.

Immediately, they froze.

Last time I'd used my powers, I'd been bleeding out after being almost sucked dry by a vampyre of lore. I'd thought it would always hurt to use them.

How wrong I'd been.

Sheer joy bubbled through my chest, and a giddy laugh escaped my mouth as power strummed through me like a live wire.

A heady rush filled my brain until it felt like I was levitating off the ground.

It was everything.

They were at my mercy.

"*Bow.*"

There was a loud crack as they fell to their knees, and four foreheads touched the marble as they prostrated themselves at my feet.

"APOLOGIZE."

"I am sorry," they chorused with no inflection.

I frowned as they stared at me with glassy eyes. It was slightly creepy.

"APOLOGIZE WITH SINCERITY."

"I am truly sorry."

It still felt insincere. I sighed heavily, because as much as I was enjoying the electric life-forces pumping through my veins, I was still aware this was wrong.

"*Do jumping jacks.*"

I grinned as they leaped to their feet and immediately pumped out some of the most athletically impressive jumping jacks I'd ever seen.

"*Stop. Now hug each other and apologize to each other.*"

Four six-foot-five warriors embraced one another in a big circle. "I'm so sorry for hurting you," they said at once.

I laughed with elation.

"*Now cry as you apologize.*"

They wept as they clung to one another and apologized.

"*Now danc—*

Aran cut me off. "Sadie. What in the moon goddess's fucking tits are you doing? Also, did you pass the test?"

I slowly turned to her and nodded.

Her eyes widened as she took in my bloody mouth and

the four warriors crying and embracing one another like zombies.

Then she threw her hands up in the air. "Fuck yeah, I knew you'd pass. I'm the best teacher ever."

Walter stood behind her and gaped like the don himself was murdering someone in the foyer.

"Um…," I started to explain, then pursed my lips as I struggled to describe what was going on without sounding absolutely unhinged.

Instead of coming up with a believable lie, I arched my lips into a manic smile, heady pleasure still making my head spin.

"The girls are coming. You must stop this," Walter said with horror, his gray eyebrows quivering.

Aran sighed. "Don't ruin it. I think this would be an excellent learning opportunity for them. A life lesson, if you will."

Lucinda. The thought of my sister staring at me in horror was like being drenched in a bucket of cold water.

She needed someone she could look up to.

Before I could let the bloodlust overtake my common sense, I reached my palm out. Like I'd done with the fae queen, I pulled at the droplets of blood, dragging them back through the layers of flesh until they slammed into my outstretched hand.

With a snap, the electric tether among all five of us broke, and I crashed to my knees, heaving.

The men stumbled away from one another, and I ducked my head as I dry-heaved bile across the floor.

The aftermath was like falling from the stars and face-planting into the dirt.

My body ached as it re-acclimated to the shaky existence of surviving without another's life-force.

"They're back!" Jess said with excitement from the top of the stairs.

After a long dry heave, I stumbled back to my feet, avoiding eye contact with everyone in the foyer.

"I'll call the maids," Walter mumbled and ran down the hall.

Suddenly, I was hyperaware of four sets of eyes staring at me.

Violence cackled.

Slowly, I turned to face the men I'd just joyfully enslaved with my blood.

From the tense jaws and tightened fists, they weren't happy.

Aran backed up the grand stairs. "Girls, this is a good lesson about how to deal with angry alphas. We need to give them some space."

"What happened to them? Why are they so mad?" Lucinda asked innocently.

There was a long, awkward pause, then Aran said, "Sadie got a little carried away showing off."

I opened my mouth to apologize to the men.

"Xerxes invited me to his first heat. Said it should be soon and he needed a female alpha present."

Fresh indignation filled me. "I'm not sorry."

Eyes glowed.

Cobra whispered, "You're going to be."

"Run for your lives!" Aran screamed at the girls as she scrambled up the stairs.

I didn't need to be told twice.

As fast as I could, I bolted after her, feet slapping against the marble as I ran like a vampyre was chasing me.

There was silence behind me.

Then the crashing sound of four pissed-off men sprinting after me.

"Save yourselves!" I yelled at the girls, who I'd quickly overtaken in my mad dash. I pushed them into an open door as I sprinted past.

Aran was farther down the massive hall and shrieked as she looked over her shoulder.

It was the only warning I got before callused hands forcibly grabbed me and tossed me into a room like I weighed nothing.

There was a loud crash as someone slammed the door shut with so much force it fell off its hinges.

"We should talk about this. Like adults," I pleaded as I was tossed onto the bed.

"We're done talking," Jax roared.

Cobra and Ascher picked up the silk sheet and ripped it cleanly in half, and both of them kept ripping until they had several long strips.

"Um, what are you—"

Jax cut me off my grabbing me and easily pushing me against the headboard while Cobra and Ascher wrapped the strips around my wrists.

"You know you can't actually restrain me. I could just bite down on my tongue and infect you with my blood."

The four men stilled.

I cursed my unfiltered tongue.

Xerxes slammed his dagger through the ends of the strips around my hands so I was pinned to the headboard.

Cobra took another strip and wrapped it around my mouth. He tied it behind my head.

"You're a bitch," he hissed into my ear.

He tightened it so I couldn't talk.

I wrinkled my nose at him and told him with my eyes

that I was going to infect him with my blood again, but this time, I'd make him *my* bitch for the day.

"Now. We're going to talk," Jax said as he stepped back to admire their work.

I pulled at the makeshift restraints and screamed in frustration.

Xerxes had burrowed his daggers through the headboard and into the wall, so only the hilts were visible.

I was pinned.

My eyes widened as I realized the gag around my mouth was so tight I couldn't move my jaw to bite down and release my blood.

I was truly at the mercy of four beasts.

Ascher adjusted his pants, and the other three followed.

I was at the mercy of four *very* turned on beasts.

CHAPTER 22
SADIE
TAKING IT

Jax's eyes were slate gray and colder than the ice wafting off Cobra. "First, we are going to ask some questions, and you are going to nod yes or no."

I wrinkled my nose.

Trussed up on the bed, there was little way for me to express myself. If I wasn't gagged, I would have screamed expletives at them.

"Did Clarissa hit you after the test?" Jax asked as a low rumble shook from his chest.

I rolled my eyes and didn't move my head.

When was I *not* covered in bruises?

It didn't slip my notice that they were trying to make Clarissa some big baddie when they were the ones who were all over her.

Did men think women were stupid?

Time ticked by slowly as I stared at Jax and didn't move my head.

Memories of a chair in the fae realm made my skin prickle and my heart rate speed up.

They'd already toyed with me once before, and I wasn't about to give them a repeat performance.

Why the fuck was I always restrained around them?

The violence in the room ratcheted up.

I slumped against the headboard and closed my eyes. How were we supposed to move forward as a group?

If I was fire, then they were kerosine.

Ever since we'd entered the beast realm, an inferno of violence burned between us.

The exhaustion from sleep deprivation, studying (truly, the worst thing a person could go through), physical exertion, voices in my head, the aftermath of controlling people with my blood, and the emotional upheaval of a pack with an omega in heat were just too much for one person to handle.

My eyes burned—definitely Xerxes and the damn heat hormones—as tears dripped down my cheek.

I just wanted to cuddle with Aran, smoke an unknown enchanted substance, and sleep until I had to fight one hundred terrifying alphas basically to the death.

Was a little peace really too much to ask for?

Ascher's face fell as he raked his hand through his golden curls. "Fuck, Princess, don't cry."

Cobra hissed, "Don't fall for her fucking games. Grow the fuck up, Kitten."

His words were biting, but there was an edge of panic in his voice, like he didn't know what to do.

The shadow snake sent me calming images of love and support.

Jax sighed heavily, and he leaned forward, gently pushing the white hair that was tangled in front of my face.

He asked softly, "How did everything get so messed up?"

Xerxes tilted his head back like he was praying to the sun god. "She rejected us. That's how."

My tears dried up.

I made a disgruntled noise from behind my gag and glared at him.

Technically, I'd just agreed with the don's overt threats.

Xerxes was the one who'd immediately replaced me.

Xerxes's eyes were hard amethysts as he glared back at me, and his too-pretty features hardened into granite.

If I hadn't known any better, I'd say he didn't have any emotions. Didn't feel anything.

The Black Wolves are hunting him.

Goose bumps pricked my skin, and I squirmed against my uncomfortable bindings.

Ascher held out his palms like he was begging. "Something must have happened to make her…enslave us like that. We need to hear her out."

"Oh, now you're all about peace and rationality. Coming from the spy who betrayed us," Cobra scoffed and dismissed him.

Ascher's tattoos rippled as he bunched his muscles, horns lengthening. "How long are you go to fucking toss that at me? I've fucking proven my loyalty."

Cobra whirled and charged at him. "You will *never* prove your loyalty."

Ascher barreled forward, and their chests cracked against each other. "Oh, but you're buddy-buddy with the soldier of the woman who fucking imprisoned you your whole life? Grow the fuck up. You use your snakes as an excuse to act fucking unhinged, and I'm tired of it."

A warning hiss rattled, a predator's warning, and I closed my eyes.

I really should have bought those gratitude journals.

Peeking through my lids, I looked just in case there was bloodshed, which I definitely didn't want to miss.

If the girls were here, they would all have been chanting "fight."

I missed them.

Jax grabbed each of the others by the backs of the necks and dragged them apart.

"We're a pack," he said calmly. "Cobra, we can all feel the fact that you were deeply hurt by Ascher's actions, but that you've already forgiven him, so stop posturing."

Ascher smirked.

Jax turned to him with a snarl. "And we can all feel that you're worried sick about earning Cobra's acceptance, so stop riling him up. If you keep this up, you'll lose it."

Ascher's shoulders deflated under Jax's scowl, and he wrenched himself out of the big man's grip.

Not done, Jax whirled on Xerxes, who was standing unnaturally still in the corner of the room.

The entire time, he hadn't stopped staring at me.

"And, Xerxes, stop fantasizing about asphyxiating Sadie and fucking her against the wall. It's distracting."

I squirmed and suddenly became *very* interested in the comforter on the bed. Was that real gold silk weaved into the red fabric? Very artsy.

"And Sadie." Jax stalked to the bed and leaned over me.

My forehead wrinkled as I waited for him to diagnose my wrongs.

Since I wasn't fantasizing about asphyxiating anyone, I was not the problem here.

Jax leaned forward until his handsome face filled my vision.

Up close, his gold piercings and chains glimmered in the room's dim light.

"We're all going through it right now, and you don't get to play the victim. If you have something to say, something to complain about, say it. Don't overtake our free will and breach our trust by using us like little marionette dolls." His voice trailed off and cracked slightly. "That was messed up."

My conscience reared its ugly head, and guilt made my chest spasm.

I went back to studying the comforter.

They'd bound and gagged me; it wasn't like I could say anything to defend myself. A wrong for a wrong—that was all we were.

Sweet cinnamon caressed my nose, a reminder of what I wanted so badly but could never have.

Shame and resignation churned in my gut.

A few weeks ago, I'd thought my scars were my biggest problem. That somehow, everything would fall into place after they were enchanted away. I'd never been more wrong.

It was all too much.

A heavy weight fell across my lap.

Jax was a blurry figure, head in his hands as he slumped across my lap dejectedly.

I slammed my head back against the headboard. The pain distracted me from the pressure in my eyes. *Don't you dare break down.*

"Princess." The bed dipped as Ascher crawled across the other side of the bed and settled next to me.

His tattooed fingers gently traced across my face and wiped away the moisture. He was so tall he sat high above me against the headboard and looked down at me.

Chestnut and pine comforted me, and the knot that had formed in my chest when they'd joined a pack without me loosened slowly.

Xerxes and Cobra stood across the room and stared at us.

They didn't move.

Both men looked lost, frozen, like they were being approached by an unknown enemy. Both were large and intimidating warriors who didn't know how to express what they were feeling, so you never knew what they were going to do.

It made them terrifying.

Their eyes darkened as they stared at me.

All four men shared a glance, and the room filled with an unfamiliar tension, like they'd had a silent conversation.

Suddenly, I was extremely nervous.

Ascher leaned down, his breath hot against my face as he untied the gag around my mouth.

Once my mouth was free, I gasped for air and got ready to deliver a scathing retort to their heavy-handed treatment.

The words died in my throat.

A tongue slowly licked across the seam of my lips, and musk engulfed my senses.

Tattooed fingers slowly traced across my jaw and tipped my head back.

Pine exploded across my senses as Ascher deepened the kiss, his tongue strong and sure as he traced my mouth wantonly.

"My sweet princess," he whispered as he pulled his head back and ran his thumb slowly across my cheekbones.

Our breath mingled, and I struggled to process what had just happened.

Before I could say something awkward and make both of us uncomfortable, a large, callused hand grabbed my jaw and turned my head to the other side.

Warm chestnuts were delicious on my tongue as Jax tangled his fingers in my hair and kissed me deeply.

When he finally released me, I was gasping, and an ache throbbed between my legs.

As soon as Jax released me, Ascher grabbed my jaw again. His mouth was rougher than Jax's, more demanding, as he kissed me deeply.

Jax's hands slowly traced up underneath my T-shirt, and his callused palms grabbed me and easily spanned my rib cage.

I gasped into Ascher's mouth.

Ever so slowly, Jax pushed underneath my sports bra until his hands were flush against my small breasts.

Ascher kissed me deeper, his hand tightening on my jaw so I couldn't move away from him. Not that I wanted to.

Jax's callused fingers rolled both my nipples.

I moaned into Ascher's mouth.

My core clenched, and my eyes rolled back in my head as Ascher gripped my face so hard it hurt.

I drowned in chestnuts and pine.

It was intoxicating. It was everything.

The large men overwhelmed my senses, and with my hands still pinned to the headboard, I could do nothing but squirm beneath their attention.

Suddenly, icy fingers yanked my sweatpants off.

Ascher kissed me so deep, fingers digging into my face so I couldn't see what was happening.

Ever so slowly, nails scraped down my inner thigh.

Jax pinched my nipples, Ascher slammed his tongue deeper down my throat, and fingers dragged closer to my core.

I kicked my legs out, but hands wrapped around my thighs and mercilessly pinned me to the bed.

A cold tongue slowly trailed up my thigh and lapped delicately across my inner junction.

The scent of frost joined chestnuts and pine.

Need gushed between my legs.

I tried to speak, but I lost my words as Ascher punished me with his mouth.

Finally, Ascher pulled back with a smirk, amber eyes on fire as his horns straightened on his head. "Were you trying to say something, Princess?"

His neck tattoos jumped as he swallowed thickly and trailed his fingers softly across my throat.

Jax continued to play with my nipples as he whispered softly in my ears so only I could hear, "No matter what happens, know that I love you, little alpha. Don't forget it."

I stilled, my heart beating impossibly fast in my chest.

I turned my head, so my lips were even with Jax's. His gray eyes intense as he stared at me.

"I love you too," I whispered back automatically.

The truth of those words burned my heart with a warm glow. No matter what, Jax had always been there for me.

Even when the other men drove me crazy, he was steady. Consistent. Patient.

I love him.

He was the rock that held us upright after we'd been tortured. The soft-spoken one who ensured we didn't kill one another.

Cobra interrupted our moment by wrenching my thighs apart.

I bit down on my lower lip as he crouched between my legs and said, "I need to shower."

Cobra arched his eyebrows, and his fingers loosened on my thighs.

I slammed my legs together.

Jax and Ascher chuckled, and my face flamed with embarrassment.

Xerxes stood across the room, watching us all and not moving.

His pants were tented with a massive bulge.

A dark expression contorted his face, and his purple eyes were on fire as he stared at me with unwavering intensity.

I shivered and looked away.

"My kitten." Cobra's voice dripped with steel. "I don't give a flying fuck." His nails dug into my thighs as he wrenched them apart.

Cobra leaned forward until his face rested at my core. "I've already tasted your cranberry wine, and I want more." His tongue flicked out at my lips as he teased me but didn't part my folds.

Content to drive me crazy.

A low rumble of pleasure sounded from Jax's chest. "Little alpha, Cobra's going to taste you." He flicked my nipples. "And you're going to like it."

My core spasmed with desire.

I nodded mindlessly as need exploded through me.

Ascher grabbed my jaw and slammed his tongue deep into my mouth.

One of Jax's hands tangled in my hair, and his fingers pulled at my scalp, forcing my face deeper into Ascher's kiss.

His other fingers pinched my nipple mercilessly.

Cobra's chilly fingers parted my folds, and he slammed his tongue across my clit. Sucking and toying with it until I screamed into Ascher's mouth.

My hips rose off the bed as I begged Cobra to lap harder.

Jax's hands became rougher as he tortured my nipples

and tugged at my hair. "Love you, little alpha," he whispered repeatedly so only I could hear.

Ascher devoured my mouth like we were fighting a war.

Jax's stubble and warm breath tickled my ear as he leaned against the side of my head and growled, "One day soon, little alpha, you're going to take each of us."

He pulled at my nipple and pulled my head back so Ascher could claim my mouth harder.

"And you're going to like it." He nipped at my ear, then dragged his tongue along the sensitive shell.

Cobra dragged a finger through my dripping heat and slowly pressed it into my butt. His tongue sucked on my clit, and he pumped his thick thumb into my vagina.

Ascher groaned into my mouth.

Jax pinched my nipples so hard that I saw stars.

And Cobra pumped both my holes as he tortured my clit.

I came with a scream, hips slamming into Cobra's face as my pussy spasmed. He growled as his mouth and fingers pushed me to new heights.

Ascher swallowed my screams, then released my mouth so Jax could take over, slamming his tongue down my throat.

Euphoria sparked behind my lids as Cobra kept licking me.

Ascher and Jax passed me back and forth.

I kept screaming.

When I finally stopped coming, I pulled at my restraints and gasped for air. Expecting the men to set me free and maybe cuddle a little.

How the fuck had we gone from fighting to this?

Cobra tipped his head back and laughed as I pulled at my restraints.

I begged Xerxes to release me, but he didn't move from

his position across the room, just stared at me with a dark expression.

"You'll be okay, little alpha," Jax said softly as he ripped my shirt and sports bra off (something that I would have said was impossible if I hadn't seen him do it with my own eyes).

Then I knew I was truly fucked, because he and Ascher leaned forward and wrapped their mouths around my nipples.

I jackknifed off the bed as they sucked.

"Tsk, tsk, Kitten." Cobra smirked and pinned my legs to the bed by lying on my lower body.

His jeweled biceps bunched as he licked his lips between my thighs. "We're just getting started."

At some point, when my clit and nipples were thoroughly overstimulated and I'd lost count of how many times I'd come, Cobra left the room.

I thought it was over.

Jax and Ascher, who were naked, were pumping their pierced and tattooed cocks against my side as they lounged over me on the headboard and continued to kiss and torture my nipples.

Xerxes still just stood and stared.

Cobra came back with a small vibrating device in his hand, and the realization of what it was had my breath quickening with excitement and fear.

"I can't come any more," I whined.

The shadow snake on my skin sent me visions of comfort and relaxation.

Cobra smirked. "Yes, you can, Kitten."

His smirk fell, and a predatory expression transformed his face. "You can, and you will. This is a punishment, after all."

His jewels glinted menacingly. “I believe you begged for it back in the fae realm, Kitten.”

Cobra roughly pulled my thighs apart and pressed the vibrating device against my clit. “I will deliver.”

I opened my mouth to argue back, but Jax knelt in front of my face and pressed his pierced cock into my open lips.

My mouth burned as I struggled to take his wide girth.

Need gushed harder between my legs, and Cobra slammed three fingers deep inside me.

Suddenly, there was a weight across my chest; Ascher knelt behind Jax so they were flush.

A hard cock pressed between my boobs, which were just big enough for Ascher to squeeze them together and pump his cock between them.

He swore as he tugged at my nipples and rode my chest.

Jax’s hand tangled in my hair as he tipped my head back and fucked my face.

I choked and gagged as warm chestnuts burned my mouth, and cold metal dragged across my tongue.

Just when I thought I couldn’t take any more, he pulled his dick back and let me breathe. “Just like that, little alpha,” he praised, then roughly started fucking my face again.

Cobra mercilessly pressed the vibrator against my clit and pumped me with his fingers.

Minutes later, I screamed as I came.

Liquid spurted down my throat as Jax threw his head back and roared.

Hot cum spurted across my chest as Ascher shuddered.

Slumping against the headboard, I pulled on my bindings as I begged, “Please.” Desperate for something thicker to fill my fluttering heat.

Ascher and Jax kissed my lips, tilting my head back and forth as they muttered praise.

Cobra's face was as hard as granite between my legs. "Kitten. This is a punishment."

The men swapped places.

Ascher knelt in front of my face.

Jax knelt over my tits.

Cobra's nails left marks on my thighs, and a vibrator was once again pressed to my clit.

A dozen orgasms later, Xerxes untied me. Sweet cinnamon wafted off him like an aphrodisiac.

Three alphas curled themselves around my sensitive flesh, but the omega just backed away with sadness in his purple eyes.

I patted at a free spot on the massive bed.

Xerxes shook his head, shoulder's hunched as he went to the chair in the corner and awkwardly curled up on it. His large body didn't fit.

Even across the room, his rich cinnamon scent was ridiculously potent.

Is it his heat? Is he afraid of hurting me?

"We fucked up. It was all just to make you jealous. But you've always been ours. You're *my* kitten," Cobra whispered in my ear as I stared sadly at Xerxes.

The last thing I heard before I fell asleep.

"You *will* be punished for not choosing me, but I've never stopped owning you. How could I? You are my soul."

CHAPTER 23
SADIE
FIGHT CLUB

I STOOD in the middle of a fighting ring and waited.

Molly walked up to me with a syringe.

"You need all the help you can get, sugar," she said before stabbing me in the arm with the needle.

Since my muscles had been looking bigger, I didn't ask, and barely registered the pinch as I tapped my foot and gnawed on my lower lip.

Nerves rattled through me.

I glanced across the room at the other rings and noticed all the men were looking at me with concern.

A manic chuckle bubbled in my throat, but I swallowed it down.

We'd somehow resolved nothing and made everything worse. Which was slightly impressive if I really thought about it.

Jax loves you.

My heart tingled with warmth.

I'd woken up in a tangle of limbs, soft kisses, and satisfied smirks.

Until their faces had hardened and they'd sworn

viciously as they remembered it was the day of the second trial and they'd used my body all night.

Cobra had shoved food into my mouth, while Jax and Ascher had massaged my tired limbs.

Even Xerxes, who'd slept on the chair all night, had freaked out and made me drink a bunch of water.

They were equally annoying and cute.

Now Molly's voice was calm, but she looked worried. "Winning means you just have to survive one hundred fights. Each fight is ten minutes. All you have to do is not tap out or be passed out when the round ends. Your defense is your key."

I nodded absently as I focused on slowing my breathing.

"It usually lasts about seventeen hours. There are only about three thousand alphas in this entire city, and about ten percent of them have shown up to fight today." She paused and breathed deeply, like she was trying to calm herself.

"They will cycle among fighting each of you and will get tired themselves. You just have to hang in there. The worst part will be the end," Molly pleaded, like she was begging me to survive.

She'd trained with me for these past four days, but she didn't truly *know* me.

I didn't bother to correct her. I had to conserve my energy.

My foot tapped faster.

I couldn't remember the last time I'd held the numb for seventeen hours.

If the numb wore off, the worst part was definitely going to be the end.

The gym was purposefully darker today, and neon-red lights glowed like menacing eyes, cigarette and cigar smoke heavy in the air.

It was quiet with anticipation.

Molly pushed a mouth guard between my teeth.

Unlike usual, alphas didn't mill around shirtless, lifting weights and shooting the shit. The only people in the fighting rings were the seven initiates.

We all stood still and waited.

Each of us had an alpha coach in the corner with water and a towel.

Z had explained that they were in charge of keeping us hydrated and helping with bleeding wounds.

I tapped my foot harder.

The anticipation gnawed at me.

Across the gym, Cobra's jewels glinted as he stared at me. "You better not give up," he mouthed with a scowl.

I rolled my eyes. He was so dramatic.

The memory of him whispering that he'd never stopped owning me, made my stomach flutter. I pushed the emotions aside.

Ascher gave me a thumbs-up, and Jax nodded at me.

Xerxes just kept staring.

I stretched my arms and breathed deeply as I pushed the memory of last night deep into the back of my mind and focused on inner peace.

Z's voice was loud as he shouted, "One hundred fights will begin now! Let in the alphas!"

The doors opened, and shirtless alphas streamed in.

The tension ratcheted up as too many alpha scents swirled together to form one massive warning: predators were near.

A large alpha climbed into the ring across from me.

He scoffed as he took in my much smaller size, cracked his neck, and made a face at the alphas waiting around the ring.

They all laughed.

I glanced over at Cobra, who was glaring at the laughing men. He arched his eyebrow at me.

I winked at Cobra.

He smirked.

"Fighting Begins NOW!" Z's voice boomed.

For the first time in this realm, I flipped the lovely little switch in my brain that had helped me survive nightmares.

The numb clicked on.

Sidestep right.

I cracked my neck back and forth as I easily stepped away from the punch my opponent had sloppily thrown.

The neon-red lights dimmed.

The world lost shades of color.

My attention focused on the task at hand as all emotions drained from my body. The world was an inhospitable place.

Duck. Punch his solar plexus. Drop low, kick out his Achilles.

I was heartless.

With smooth precision, I followed the numb's instructions, my limbs gliding through the air like butter.

My opponent was not a battle-hardened gladiator fighting desperately in front of a million fae and an evil queen.

He was cocky.

Weak.

His flesh slapped against the mat with a satisfying crunch

With disinterest, I stood completely still and watched as he gasped on the mat and grabbed the backs of his ankles.

He moaned in pain.

I conserved energy.

For the next nine minutes and fifty seconds, he writhed on the mat and wasn't able to get to his feet.

My kick had severed both his Achilles.

The alphas outside the ring who had laughed with him looked sick as they watched their compatriot imitate a slug.

A bell rang, signaling that the ten minutes were up.

Two men, betas from the burned smells wafting off them, grabbed his shoulders and dragged him out of the ring.

Molly squirted some water into my mouth. She opened and closed her mouth like she wanted to ask questions, but nothing came out.

In my numb state, she didn't seem as comforting and nice.

I didn't bother to explain, just turned away when the bell sounded and faced my next opponent.

Chop his trachea.

I did.

His esophagus collapsed, and he fell to his knees, clawing at his throat. The alpha passed out after three minutes.

If I hadn't known alphas were immortal, I would have thought he was dead.

Not that I cared—I didn't.

Bored, I watched the other initiates.

Ascher easily pinned his opponent to the mat. His shirtless chest rippled impressively, and his tattoos seemed to jump off his skin. A female alpha standing beside his ring openly gaped at him.

Across the room, Cobra was twisting a man's arm behind his back and turning it unnaturally, slowly ripping it out of its socket. The man was screaming and Cobra was laughing.

Similar to my fight, Xerxes's opponent was passed out on his mat. The omega stared down at him dispassionately and clenched his hands like he was imagining his knives.

There was a crashing noise in the far corner. Jax easily tossed his opponent out of the ring like he weighed nothing.

Clarissa and James were faring similarly. They had their opponents restrained beneath them.

With the numb coursing through me, I could easily see what was happening.

It's a purposeful tactic.

A trick. The first fighters were told to throw their fights to build your confidence. It's going to get harder as it goes. You must conserve energy.

Like usual, the numb was right.

The first twenty alphas barely put up a fight.

However, the intensity of the battles slowly increased, with the opponents moving faster and throwing with more intricate skills.

By the fiftieth fight, I was covered in sweat and actually had to fight the entire time.

At the seventy-fifth fight, something shifted in the air.

The alphas had come to some sort of unspoken agreement, and they attacked with everything they had.

My current opponent was a six-foot-five male with a similar build to Ascher's. His lean muscles rippled under golden skin that had patches of leathery green ridges.

Backflip and spring left.

I narrowly avoided the alpha's spinning kick, which scissored out at the end for maximum impact.

Swipe out his legs.

I dropped down and swiped.

However, as his legs were kicked from beneath him, he reached forward with his hands and grabbed my ponytail.

He hit the deck, but so did my face as he used his momentum to slam me into the mat.

Fist in the groin.

He released my hair, and I scrambled to my feet. He followed closely behind me, throwing quick jabs.

Punch his kidneys.

I barely registered my nose breaking under his leathery fist and obediently slammed my knuckles into his back.

He grunted but didn't stop throwing punches.

The leathery edges of his knuckles protected his skin and inflicted maximum damage on my flesh.

My cheekbones cracked, and I used my momentum to punish his kidneys.

Hands up; protect your face. Only thirty seconds left. Move backward. Dodge.

I placed my hands in front of my face, and the bones in them cracked as he peppered my face with unrelenting punches.

His size had me pinned in ring's corner, and there was nowhere to dodge.

Fifteen seconds left, just last.

A fist glanced across the side of my face, and I tried to make myself as small as possible.

The blows kept coming.

Slamming against my face, the alpha gave everything he had to break me.

My biceps shook, and I choked on blood as he rocked my protective hands back into my broken nose.

Ten seconds left.

I widened my stance, girded my loins, and took the blows.

Five seconds left.

Stars exploded behind my eyes, and I focused on surviving.

My opponent's eyes were mostly swollen shut from my

own hits, and his biceps bunched and slammed like a madman's. He was desperate to break me.

Two seconds left.

His leathery fist slammed into the other side of my head. I ducked my neck lower and held my arms steady.

The bell rang, signaling the end of the round.

My opponent stumbled back, panting as he stared down at me with wide eyes.

Back straight. Stare him down. Assert your dominance.

I dropped my aching biceps and straightened my back. Instead of gasping for air, or crying from the pain, I gave him a haughty sneer.

He stumbled and reached out his hand to grab my shoulder.

I didn't flinch, just arched my eyebrow at him.

"I'm sor…" He ran his bloody knuckles through his hair, embarrassed. "What's your name?"

"Sadie," I said coolly and forced my body to act relaxed.

Somewhere far away, my nerves screamed in pain.

"I'm Dean. Alligator shifter." That explained the leathery green patches on his skin.

He smiled and held out his hand, and I noted impassively that he had dimples.

Shake his hand. Turn his hand over to assert your dominance.

I shook his hand and turned it aggressively. "Saber-toothed tiger shifter."

His smile widened, and he opened his mouth to say something else, white teeth flashing against his gold skin.

Z shouted, "No talking to the initiates. Dean, get out of the ring!"

Everyone in the gym turned to us.

A low growl and hiss sounded, and it wasn't difficult to figure out who was upset.

Dean bowed deeply, like I was a princess and not the woman he'd just been beating the shit out of for the last ten minutes.

The hiss sounded louder, and the growl became an outright roar.

Even numb, I smothered the urge to laugh at the scene he was causing.

He winked as he stumbled out of the ring.

Molly pulled me to the corner and said, "Only twenty-four more fights. Use your defensive maneuvers earlier instead of immediately jumping at them on the attack."

She dabbed at the numerous cuts pouring blood down my face.

I licked my lips, savoring the sweet copper tang.

It tasted like power to me.

"I mean it. Stop attacking and focus on defense." Molly poured water down my neck.

"I can't," I said calmly. Her mothering rubbed me the wrong way, and I had the irrational urge to smack her.

She pressed the towel against the cut on my forehead that was gushing blood into my eyes. "Why the moon goddess not?"

I smiled. "Because I want to hurt them."

Her hand stilled.

The bell sounded, signaling the beginning of the next fight. I bounced back and forth on my toes.

Box his ears and break his nose.

I did just that.

When my much larger male opponent howled in pain and charged at me, fists ready, the numb voice in my head became slightly animated.

Dodge right. Kick his kneecap.

The big man roared, and I jumped out of the way of his swinging fist.

Ten minutes later, when the gong sounded, we were both contorted on the mat in impossible positions.

My thighs were wrapped around his neck, choking him out, and his tree-trunk legs were twined around my neck, slowly asphyxiating me.

We both released each other at the same time and rolled to the side, gasping for air.

He offered me a hand and yanked me to my feet.

With his alpha strength, he sent me flying, and his hands on my shoulders stopped my forward momentum.

"My name's Loren," he said, brushing white-blond hair out of his eyes as he stared down at me with a weird expression and offered his hand.

With his coloring and size, he reminded me of some sort of bear.

Turn his hand over and assert your dominance.

"Sadie." I gripped his hand with all my might and shook it aggressively, just like I had with Dean.

He took a step closer.

Z's voice was pissed off. "Once again, there is *no* fraternizing with the initiates. Loren, get the fuck out of the ring."

From the ring next to mine, Ascher yelled an expletive. Xerxes said something I couldn't hear over a hiss-yell, "She's mine!" Jax roared again.

When I went over to Molly, she was silent.

She glared at me as she pushed unnecessarily hard at the missing chunk of skin on my arm where Loren had bitten down mid-grapple.

I didn't wince.

Everything was going fine until twenty-two fights later, when the numb clicked off.

CHAPTER 24
SADIE
DANCING WITH GODS

DURING FIGHT NINETY-NINE, an alpha female slammed her heel into my ovaries, and the pain made me black out for a split second.

The numb clicked off.

I shook my head as consciousness rushed back as fast as it had left, but the world was no longer dull and emotionless.

Everything was saturated with color.

It was too bright.

As I stumbled to my feet, the bell sounded.

I gasped as the pain of too many fights flooded through me in a rush of agony.

I would have screamed—at least ten of my bones were broken—but I choked on the blood gushing from my broken nose, down my throat.

Molly immediately sensed something was wrong and hauled me to my feet.

Her gorgeous face wavered in and out of my vision, and she spoke from somewhere far away. "Just one more fight. You have to survive this without passing out. You can do one of anything."

I vomited blood.

It splattered across my chest.

Molly slammed her hand against my back. "Sadie, if you lose, you die. Snap out of it."

She smacked me harder, and more blood sprayed across both of us.

Survive.

Sun god, I hated surviving. It fucking hurt.

"Do you hear me?!" She shook me back and forth, and my teeth rattled behind my mouth guard. I gagged as some of my teeth went down my throat.

So much for the mouthguard.

"Sadie!" She dumped cold water on my head and stabbed another needle into my arm.

If one more person stabbed me in this realm, I swore to the sun god…

"Do you hear me?"

Whatever she'd injected into me made my throbbing eyes open wide.

Adrenaline coursed through me.

"Is that even legal?" I asked.

"No. Now you're going to defend for ten minutes, do you hear me?"

I nodded with conviction and turned around. However, gravity wasn't working, and my broken legs collapsed beneath me.

Z's voice sounded. "Initiates, you cannot leave your ring to help another initiate."

Someone screamed, and it sounded like a tussle.

Z barked, and the sounds of dozens of gun safety's clicking off echoed. "Cobra, Jax, Ascher, Xerxes, you'll be shot through your forehead if you leave your ring before the end of this trial."

There was the sound of more fighting.

I waved my hand tiredly in their direction, trying to get them to calm down, but I hurt too badly to do anything else.

Z yelled, "The bullets are enchanted to kill an alpha! You have one second to get back into your ring or you *will* be shot."

Cobra hissed loudly.

I did the only thing I could—I flipped him off.

Never mind. My middle finger was bent at a weird angle and wouldn't move. It was my pinky finger.

But I hoped he got the point.

After long, tense moments, I relaxed with relief when no gunshots rang. Not that I could even turn my head to look; my neck hurt too badly.

Agony throbbed, and the hazy, smoke-filled room contorted and churned around me like a living beast.

Vision wavering, I clenched the rope on the side of the ring to keep myself upright.

My labored breath was too loud.

Warm blood gushed from cuts on my forehead and dripped into my eyes, and my broken fingers shook as I struggled to wipe it away.

I was missing almost all my fingernails and distantly remembered an opponent ripping them off with his teeth.

Creative.

The gong sounded.

A massive hairy leg straddled the ropes and entered the ring.

The largest alpha I'd faced yet casually cracked his bald head back and forth. A cigarette hung from his lips.

It was the alpha that had blown smoke in my face when I first walked into the training center.

His dark eyes were flat, but his smile was pure joy.

This was going to hurt.

Before I could flinch, he leaped across the mat and slammed his mammoth fist into my nose.

Red, black, and white sparks burst across my vision, and blood gushed down my throat.

I would have bellowed if my voice still worked.

My cheekbones were shattered, and when I opened my eyes, all I saw was red.

I curled in on myself as fists and kicks shook my frame. Bones snapped like popcorn, and the overwhelming agony quickly faded as my consciousness slipped farther away.

Ten minutes was a lifetime.

Too long.

No shot I survived.

The pain grew further and further away, and I eagerly welcomed the darkness.

All I'd known was pain and violence, and I was too tired. There was no point in fighting against the inevitable.

I'd never known peace.

It was all I wanted.

Molly's shouts were far away and swatted at my consciousness like an annoying gnat.

I easily ignored her.

A bone-deep cold chilled me as my lifeblood spilled around me in a warm blanket.

Somewhere far away, I was lying partially unconscious on a mat as an alpha stood above me, slamming his foot into my ribs.

The harsh cracks of a snapped sternum were a distant problem.

I floated in a haze of unconscious bliss as adrenaline protected me from an agonizing end.

Maybe, in another life, I would have fought harder against death.

In this life, it hurt too much.

The men had a pack, and in the end, it would be easier for them to find a female omega and bond if I was gone.

Aran and the girls would be sad, but they would have each other.

Everything would be all right.

Abruptly, I was pulled away from the fight club, and I was drowning in a frozen lake.

Droplets of blood shimmered around me, suspended in the inky depth.

The numb voice was uncharacteristically panicked, and it screamed across my mind like rusty nails. *You will stand up and fight!*

I easily blocked out the noise.

Was the valley of the sun god an endless lake? It was cleansing and chilled, a crisp oasis of sparkling water. How interesting.

You stupid girl, you're not allowed to walk in the valley.

Rude.

My vision was perfect, and the gold skin of my fingers glowed enchantedly in the black water.

"I can walk wherever I want," I maturely argued with the voice inside my head as I twirled softly through the lake.

A warmth suffused through my chest. Inner peace was divine.

I pinwheeled my arms and giggled bubbles as I slowly sank through the abyss.

You ignorant fuck.

Wow. It was always so calm. Who would have thought the voice inside my head had a secret swearing problem?

"Ignorance is bliss," I thought back with a relaxed smile.

How right I was.

In eons, I've never had to do this.

The numb really must not be big on swearing.

"It's just 'fuck,'" I replied in my head as I kept twirling. "Don't take life too seriously. It just helps you get your point across."

Had I always been so wise? Tranquility wrapped itself around my heart and caressed me with its sweetness.

Galaxies abound, why are the young so dumb?

I twirled faster, and twinkly bubbles enveloped me.

It seemed like a rhetorical question, so I didn't bother to answer.

When we survive this, you are going to bow at my feet and offer me an immortality of fidelity. You will be my right hand and will complete every task I demand of you. I will carve your name into my legacy, and your blood will lead the war. You will give everything, sacrificing all you know, to kneel on the battlefield and proclaim our victory over the worlds.

I giggled and blew out bubbles. "I won't survive this." The surety of my demise settled around me like a soft blanket.

Death wasn't bad.

Why had I ever been afraid?

It was living that hurt.

LISTEN! the numb screeched with all her might, and pain exploded as if she hammered rusty nails deep into my brain.

I gripped my head and writhed, the cool waters no longer calming, the inky abyss no longer a sanctuary.

YOU HAVE BEEN CHOSEN AS MY CHAMPION, AND YOU WILL LIVE! YOUR BIRTH, EVERYTHING YOU ARE, WAS PURPOSEFULLY CREATED TO SERVE ME! AND NOW YOU WILL RISE AND FULFILL YOUR DESTINY!

I pressed my palms as hard as I could into my ears to block out the noise that was unbearably grating.

The water was dirty, muddy, and smothering.

Still, I fought against the pressure and focused on sinking deeper into the sludge.

The numb couldn't trick me. Existence was pain, and I didn't want to do it anymore. A proverb about accepting death gracefully, or some shit like that.

I was accepting it, and no screeching voice could change my mind.

YOU THINK EVERYONE WILL BE BETTER OFF? YOU IGNORANT AMOEBA!

Suddenly, the lake disappeared.

I was standing in a field.

The red sun of the shifter realm hung above, but everything was wrong.

The forests were gone, there was no ice, and everything was brown and dead. The charred ruins of a forest dotted the landscape, and fires blazed.

Across the valley, shifters screamed.

Thousands of figures stomped across the land. They held spears and swords, and massive catapults threw burning rocks hundreds of feet.

Shifter cries stopped as the army ran them through.

There was fire everywhere as more catapults launched. The ground shook under my feet.

Thousands of soldiers marched over the horizon.

As the armor-clad creatures neared, long spears pointed at me, I opened my mouth to scream, but the landscape changed.

At once, the world shifted, and two warm suns replaced the single red sun.

One was bright yellow, the other bright green.

It was the fae realm.

But it wasn't.

The lush landscape and endless green lawn of the palace was black, and the air smelled of burning sulfur, just like the shifter realm.

Fires dotted the landscape as massive catapults flung burning rocks in every direction.

Like in the shifter realm, fae screamed as the endless army slaughtered them.

Air fae flew, but archers shot them down.

Water fae flung shards, but their ice clanged off the hard armor and didn't penetrate.

The earth fae sent rocks flying but were killed by spears.

Fire fae set the world ablaze, but they killed as many fae as they did the armor-clad soldiers, and the army kept marching.

I stumbled over a dead fae, and my body turned toward the palace.

It was smaller than I remembered, only half the size.

Armor-clad soldiers streamed over the horizon, an unfathomable army that never ended.

The sheer numbers were unfathomable.

Once again, my feet fell out from beneath me as the ground shook, and I was transported yet again into a different realm.

There was heavy gray cloud cover and no sun in sight. The endless rain and gloominess told me where I was.

It was the beast realm.

However, there were no towering skyscrapers, just small pebbles covering the ground as far as the eye could see.

The armor-clad military marched across the horizon. Thousands of soldiers, catapults blazing, spears at the ready.

It was raining.

But instead of the chaos, this time, what appeared to be an air fae floated in front of a standing military of hundreds of half-naked men and women.

Drums sounded.

She pointed a sword toward the oncoming army and screamed.

At the sound, the people behind her shifted into beasts of all types—they were all alpha shifters.

Snarling monsters.

The armor-clad army marched in the thousands over the horizon, but this time, it wasn't a massacre.

In a clash of steel and animal roars, the shifters ripped the armored heads off the soldiers as they ran through their ranks.

This wasn't a massacre.

This was war.

I opened my mouth to ask a question, when suddenly I was back in the crisp lake.

"What was that?" I asked aloud, my voice echoing unnaturally in the dark waters.

That was an eon ago, in the last battle. Time has spun, and war has once again arrived. As it always does. You are my champion. You must survive.

A tear slipped from my eye and floated up through the dark waters.

I didn't know how, but I knew in my bones that the numb wasn't lying. Everything I'd seen was true.

There was something so cruel about having to fight when all you wanted to do was die.

I'd never had any choice.

The pain of my existence had always been decided for me.

There would be no peaceful walk in the valley of the sun god.

"Fucking fine. I'll fight," I grumbled like the moody twenty-one-year-old I was. "You couldn't have found an older champion to lead you?" I snarled at the numb that was apparently some type of entity.

Low-key, I was way too young for this.

This was child abuse.

My champions are not chosen; they are made. We have run out of time. You were made for this purpose, and thus you will rise. We are out of time…

Before I could argue back, I hurtled back into my consciousness.

The alpha above me laughed, cigarette hanging from his mouth, as he casually slammed his foot into my cracked sternum.

He tsked with glee. "Another failed initiate."

My neck was turned, and blood burned my eyes.

Across the gym, chaos reigned.

The men were desperately trying to escape their rings to get to me, fighting against the dozen alphas that had climbed in to stop them from escaping.

They screamed my name.

I sighed heavily as another kick cracked my ribs and sent agony rattling through me.

There were three options.

1. I could lie here and do nothing and just hope I survived long enough to stand up at the last possible moment.
2. I could infect my attacker with my blood and risk being found out as a half-breed.
3. I could stand up and fight like a warrior.

The bald alpha laughed as he kicked me.

There was only one option.

I levitated a tiny droplet of the blood pouring from my nose and discreetly slammed it through his foot as it reared up to kick me.

"Stop," I whispered.

Immediately, the bald alpha stopped midkick.

He was paralyzed.

There were loud screams and shouts as everyone in the club was preoccupied fighting against three enraged alphas and one unwell omega.

As quickly as I could—I was moving at the pace of a dead ant—I staggered onto broken legs and gripped the ropes along the side of the ring.

"Pretend to fight me," I whispered, and the alpha threw a weak punch that I shakily dodged.

I distantly noted through the wind-tunnel sensation in both my ears and blood filling my vision that it was dead silent in the gym.

Everyone was watching us.

I channeled the girls and put on the performance of my life.

"Ow!" I yelled brokenly as I let the alpha back me into the corner of the ring and pretended to take punches.

Under my persuasion, each punch stopped millimeters from my skin.

I flailed back and forth and pretended I was rocked by hits that never landed.

There was a hiss across the ring, and the loud sound of smacking, as Cobra realized what was happening.

Suddenly, the gym was filled with Cobra's shouts as he fought, creating a distraction away from me.

What a king.

Fake fighting drained me. With every pretend flinch, agony slammed through my broken bones as my body moved side to side.

Ten minutes was a lifetime.

When the gong finally sounded, I discreetly pulled out my droplet of blood.

The bald alpha staggered away from me in fear.

I gave him a small smile and tried to act nonchalant.

His eyes were wide as he realized I'd overtaken his free will, and he stalked at me like he was going to rip my head off.

I closed my eyes and flinched.

However, the blow never came.

"Hunter, the fight is over. Back away," Molly said as she crouched in front of me and shoved him aside.

He looked like a Hunter.

Bald and unwell.

Z's voice sounded, "A record, six of the seven initiates have passed the second trial."

Alphas bellowed and chanted with excitement.

Terrified, I scanned the room.

I slumped with relief when I saw James's broken body lying in the ring, unconscious.

Betas dragged him off, and I winced as I realized I was happy that someone was being murdered.

But all I could feel was relief that it wasn't one of my men.

Finally, I passed out.

CHAPTER 25

SADIE

IT'S EMOTIONALLY MATURE TO CRY

"Wake up, little alpha," Jax growled, but his voice cracked. "Please love."

The desperation in his voice dragged me out of unconsciousness, and I instantly took note of pain, everywhere.

Who would love my crazy ass? The thought had me hurtling back into consciousness.

Existence was a bitch.

"Please, please, please, Sadie," he begged, and a wet cloth was gently dragged across my forehead.

"Um, I'm awake. Also, you're obsessed with me." My voice was a soft, harsh rasp, and I licked my cracked lips, desperate for moisture.

The cloth on my head stilled.

"Why aren't your eyes open?"

With the force of the sun god, I dragged open my heavy lids. Bright light stabbed my corneas, and I immediately shut them. "Too bright."

"SHE'S AWAKE!" Jax bellowed at the top of his lungs, and I winced. Then he dropped his voice and whispered in my ear, "I was so worried, love. Never scare me like that again."

My heart melted.

He raised his voice again and bellowed, "EVERYONE SHE WOKE UP!"

Everyone was yelling recently; we really needed to work on effective communication.

There were loud banging noises and a mix of more shouting voices. Like I said, none of us had any voice control.

"Get out of my way," Aran said, followed by a loud *thunk*ing noise.

Cobra hissed back at her, "She's *my* kitten. I get to see her first."

"Please, she's still mad at you," Aran said as the bed shook with what felt like two people wrestling atop me.

"Great, smother me to death," I said dryly, as my sternum ached with pain. "Not that the voice in my head would just let me die," I complained.

"What did you say?" Xerxes asked softly, his mouth so close to my ear that I could feel each of his cinnamon breaths across my face.

"Did she just say she wanted to die?" Ascher's words were clipped.

There was a loud goat's bleat and the crashing of what sounded like a fist going through a wall.

"Y'all need help," I mumbled.

With my eyes closed, I slapped my hands at the two figures, who were still very much trying to crush me.

Lucinda cried, and small hands gripped my broken arm. "Sadie, please be okay. It was awful. We thought you were dead. You were all broken and bloody. And then the don stopped by and said we have to go to school. This realm is awful, and I told him you wouldn't make us."

I gritted through my teeth, "Lucinda, release my broken arm."

The excruciating stabbing sensation disappeared, and I relaxed back into the comfortable bed.

"Also, yes, you're going to school. I can't believe you'd try to manipulate a pathetic, broken woman."

Aran guffawed. "You ain't no woman."

"At least I have tits."

"Oh please. Don't act like you aren't attracted to my male form."

I chuckled, but the only problem was my ribs and lungs were definitely shattered, and a weird rattling noise sounded as I tried to exhale air.

"Did you really try to die?" Jinx asked curiously.

"Yeah, but the damn voice in my head wouldn't let me," I said honestly.

There was another crack as I assumed Ascher punched the wall, and the bed shook with the vibrations from Cobra's hiss.

Jinx didn't sound impressed. "Then why aren't you dead?"

"Jinx!" Jess and Jala said at once.

"It's rude to ask someone why they aren't dead. We've talked about pretending to be normal," Jess scolded her younger sister.

I waved my hands to dismiss Jess.

"Are you having an episode?" Aran asked. "Open your eyes, woman. It's creeping me out."

With extreme fortitude, I dragged open my crusty lids and moaned at the brightness.

When Aran finally came into focus, I was not surprised to find both her and Cobra on the bed, kneeling over me.

Cobra had his palm spread in her face and was shoving her head to the side, and Aran was jabbing her elbow into his back as they fought to position themselves over me.

I gave them an unamused glare.

"Holy sun god's tit, for the love of the moon goddess, Sadie, close your eyes." Aran's blue eyes were wide, and she grimaced at me.

"What?"

Jax's handsome face filled the room as he leaned over me and softly inspected my eyes. "You've popped most of the blood vessels in both your eyes."

"Sexy." I licked my lips, and the big man grimaced.

"Why did you want to die, little alpha?" he whispered, his thumbs trailing softly across my forehead.

Apparently, being beaten within a centimeter of existence made a girl uncharacteristically honest.

"The pain was like a hundred out of ten, and I've caused your pack so much pain and suffering. It would be easier for everyone if I wasn't around."

His slate-gray eyes began to glow.

Jax tilted his head back and let out an ungodly roar that shook the room. The girls screamed, and even Aran scurried back in self-preservation.

It sounded very self-sacrificing when I'd said it, but I felt bad at the shattered expression on his face. It hadn't been that deep; it just hurt like a bitch.

I reached up, grabbed his chin, and gently tugged it downward. "Let me finish."

He stopped growling and took ragged breaths, like he was desperately trying to calm himself.

I wet my lips, and my voice steadied as the rattling noise in my chest grew faint.

"It was mostly just because of the pain. But the voice in my head showed me a postapocalyptic world from the past, where a massive army battled against shifters. Also, apparently I'm her 'champion,' and she said something about me having to lead battles and kneel at her feet."

Jax's jaw dropped.

He narrowed his eyes like he couldn't decide if I was pulling his leg.

"I'm not kidding."

Something in my expression must have convinced him, because Jax whirled around, grabbed the upholstered chair beside the bed, and chucked it across the room, through the wall.

"Wait, so, sis, you're supposed to lead a war?" Lucinda asked quietly. She wrung her hands in her lap and looked up at me with familiar ruby eyes.

"Apparently," I mumbled.

Her expression changed to one of awe. "That is *so* cool. I always knew you were a warrior."

Jess and Jala were wearing similar expressions and instantly started whispering to each other.

Even Jinx looked impressed.

Aran glared at me and used Cobra's stunned shock to push past him and straddle me. "Are you sure?"

I smirked at her. "Yep. Don't be jealous that the girls think I'm cooler than you now."

She narrowed her eyes but shook her head with disgust. That was exactly what she was pissed off about.

I knew her so well.

Cobra came to his senses and shoved Aran off the bed.

"Thisss issss not funny." Shadow snakes writhed across

his flesh as he bunched the covers in his fists and shook with anger.

"Why is no one else panicking?" Ascher asked softly. He stood beside the bed and was staring down at me with glowing amber eyes and a horrified expression.

Jax roared again and punched the wall.

Xerxes, who had been standing silently in the corner, pulled out his knives and stabbed one into the wall as hard as he could.

A soft omega whine sounded as he trembled, like he was falling apart.

I pursed my lips and did what had to be done. "Okay, all men get out of the room."

Cobra stopped hissing and turned his head to stare at me like, well, like a creepy snake, and asked, "What?"

"Out. We need to have some girl talk."

Cobra sputtered, "You just woke up from a two-day coma. What do you mean, you need girl talk? What the fuck could you possibly talk about?"

Surprisingly, it was Lucinda who patted the jeweled alpha on his shoulder. "Sis just needs to talk to us. It's okay, you guys can wait outside."

Xerxes spoke from the far corner, "I don't know. We can't leave her again."

Lucinda smiled at the omega and shook her head. "She just wants us for a second. I promise you'll be with her soon." Her calming voice did something to the omega, and he nodded at her.

Even more surprising was Cobra's response. "Don't let her hurt herself."

"You know I won't."

Cobra grumbled but nodded at Lucinda and climbed off the bed, and the other men followed him out the door.

I gaped at my little sis, and she answered my unspoken question with a shrug. "While you were passed out, I played a lot of cards with Cobra and Xerxes. Aran and Ascher were busy strategizing how to kill the people who hurt you, and Jax was hanging with his sisters. Cobra and Xerxes are both all bluster, no bite."

I choked on a small chunk of my flesh that hadn't healed and was still clogging my throat.

Cobra and Xerxes were literally *all* bite.

"So, why did you want them to leave?" Lucinda asked as she smiled at me like I was beautiful and not a troll that resembled roadkill.

"Um." A wave of self-consciousness passed over me. Lucinda was my sister and Aran my bestie, but I'd technically still just met Jax's sisters, and I didn't know how they all felt about me.

I whispered, my voice barely legible, "Could we cuddle?"

At once, five girls and a ferret climbed into the bed and surrounded me in a massive hug. I didn't even mind that my broken bones were being pulverized into smithereens.

I didn't know who started it—I was 100 percent sure it wasn't Aran and 99 percent sure it was me—but someone broke into a massive sob.

Abruptly, four of us were crying uncontrollably and holding one another.

Through blubbery cries, I noted that Aran and Jinx were dry-eyed and glaring at all of us like we'd lost our minds. Still, they hugged us and looked at each other in horror.

"I don't want to die and leave you guys. I'm so sorry," I whispered.

"You can't leave us with Aran," voices wailed back, and

we all cried harder at the thought of them being stuck with Aran.

After twenty minutes of wailing, Aran climbed out of the pile. "I'm going to get the guys." As she walked away, she itched at her back, and I made a mental note to ask if she had gotten some type of rash.

Jala cried harder. "Thank the sun god she's gone. I woke up to her choking out Jess, and she threatened to scalp me if I interfered."

"There, there." I dried her tears and squeezed her gently with my still-very-broken arm. "She does it to all of us. It's how she says, 'I love you.'"

"Really?" Jess narrowed her watery eyes, clearly unconvinced.

"I have no idea, but that's what I tell myself."

We all cried harder.

That was how the guys found us. They stared at the pile of sobbing teens atop my broken self and wisely chose to not say anything.

They weren't idiots.

Instead, they sighed heavily and slid down the wall. The four of them sat on the ground and waited patiently.

I meant to talk to them about our random, intense sex marathon, but after a good hour of crying my heart out, I felt remarkably better and snuggled into a deep, healing sleep.

CHAPTER 26

SADIE

REVELATIONS AND BAD DECISIONS

I WOKE up to gloomy rain and an empty room.

Groaning like a feeble old man, I pushed myself out of bed, only for the room to spin and collapse around me.

With shaky, bruised hands, I used the wall to keep myself upright.

From the wobbling in my limbs and lack of excruciating agony, it seemed my broken bones had healed.

What was left was a patchwork of aches and pains that had me stumbling and bumping into furniture.

Someone had changed me into overly large sweatpants and a sweatshirt. I paused and sniffed—the material had a delicious cinnamon scent.

Xerxes.

The clothes dwarfed my frame and hid the extent of my injuries.

After slamming into the door with an athletic thud, I tripped into the hallway.

The wall kept me upright as my blurry eyes tried to orient the shadows thrown off from the grand chandeliers.

A gnarled golden monster snarled at me from across the hall, and I jumped in surprise, heartbeat heavy in my chest as I stared down the foe.

After an embarrassingly long time, where I waited for it to make a move, I realized it wasn't going to attack.

Because it wasn't a monster at all—well, at least not in the way I'd been thinking.

I'd been having a standoff…with my own reflection in the hall mirror.

The numb had picked an impressive champion.

Whoever was responsible for the voice in my head was clearly not the brightest.

I made the endless trek down the ridiculously long hall. Seriously, who needed this many rooms in a house? It was ridiculous.

"Lucinda? Aran? Jax?" I yelled softly as I hobbled.

My bare feet slapping across the hardwood was the only sound.

Great, everyone had abandoned me.

Twenty minutes later, I stumbled to a stop at the end of the hall. Polished wood taunted me as I easily visualized my body breaking like a rag doll.

My eye twitched as I tensed my thighs and prepared to complete my greatest feat—walking down the grand stairway.

Before my big toe, which was once again missing its nail, had made contact with the top step, Walter materialized out of nowhere. "Please, stop, miss."

I breathed a sigh of relief and returned to the flat floor, grateful that someone had saved me from myself. "Where is everyone?"

I tried to stand up straight and present an image of wellness, but my back spasmed with pain, and I reverted to a hunchback form.

"You were asleep for another two days. The girls went to school this morning, and the other alphas left to deal with some personal matters."

My alarm must have shown on my face, because the old beta put a wrinkled hand on my arm.

"The girls will be taken care of. Aran and Jax are their escorts for their first day. The don enrolled them in Sect Schola. It is the preeminent institution for ABOs and is extremely prestigious. Don't worry."

Hands shaking uncontrollably from stress, I breathed slowly and tried to not hyperventilate.

The only thing that kept me from a full-blown panic attack was the fact that Aran and Jax were with them. They wouldn't let anything happen to them.

"So everyone is gone?" I tried not to look as pathetic as I felt. As an orphaned child, it only made sense that I had deep-rooted abandonment issues.

Walter patted my hunched head. "No, Xerxes stayed behind because he wasn't feeling well."

The knot in my stomach loosened, and I tried not to seem too eager.

Now that I was no longer dying violently, it was time I had a mature conversation with the omega.

There was an unnamed twinkle in Walter's eye that I hadn't seen yet. "He's in his room at the end of the hall. I'm sure he would like to see you."

I nodded, catching the unspoken words.

Xerxes was in his nest.

Walter turned to pick up the bag of dirty clothes at his feet, and the soiled laundry reminded me of my values.

"Now that everyone is indisposed, I can get you out of here," I said softly. My talk with Xerxes could wait.

Walter drew his shoulders back and rose to his full height, which was barely a few inches taller than me.

"Excuse me, miss?" The gray hair atop his lip trembled.

He was overjoyed that I was freeing him.

Once again, it was hard being such a good person.

"You don't have to be a servant. I don't know what Xerxes is doing to keep you here against your will, but I have money. Let me get you out of here."

The tremble in Walter's upper lip became a full earthquake.

Poor man was overjoyed.

"Miss, how dare you presume I don't want to serve this house." Walter clenched his fists, and I suddenly pictured the beta thrashing me.

"Walter," I said calmly, because his years of oppression had confused him, "you should not work for free. It is an uncivilized and awful practice."

Outrage over my past and the fucked-up realities that burdened people's lives had me standing straighter and forgetting my many ailments.

"It is wrong," I snarled with conviction.

Walter's bushy white eyebrows furrowed, and his mouth opened and closed for a long minute as he processed that I was saving him.

When he finally spoke, his words were biting. "Miss, you are under the mistaken impression that I am unpaid. Everyone working in this noble house is paid an exorbitant salary."

I pursed my lips in disbelief.

Walter snapped with annoyance, "Miss, it is *my* supercar that I lent you the other day to take to the test."

"Um…really?" The fancy car that accelerated at a ridiculous speed did not seem cheap.

Walter muttered something about unsophisticated morons under his breath, grabbed the laundry bag, and stalked down the hall away from me.

For a long moment, I gaped after the butler and tried to process the fact that he had voluntarily chosen to buy a matte-purple car with black stripes down the side.

I just couldn't picture him selecting it.

Finally, when my shock had worn off, and it became clear I wasn't going to magically transport to my destination, I began to slowly limp down to the far end of the house.

Even though my bones groaned and my muscles spasmed, my spirits were lighter.

A weight had lifted off my chest.

It had bothered me horribly that Xerxes kept unpaid servants, and might have influenced my actions toward the omega.

Ugh, I was such a fool.

Sure, the omega wasn't perfect.

He had a knife fixation, rage issues, trauma, and an inability to express his emotions. But didn't we all?

My bruised cheeks pulled up into a smile as I hobbled slowly.

He doesn't keep servants. A painful laugh created a spasm in my chest as I tripped over a piece of rug and slammed into the wall.

What a glorious day.

When I finally got to the dark alcove at the very end of the hall, I was covered in sweat and swaying on my feet.

My knuckles were still hurting, so instead I slammed my toe into the door violently and shouted, "Xerxes, it's Sadie! Open up!"

Knees trembling, I slumped into the alcove and desperately tried not to pass out.

My little excursion—as enlightening as it had been—was a lot on my feeble body that had apparently been playing dead in a coma for four days.

The door didn't open.

"XERXES!" I shouted with all my might and gave the door a few good kicks.

Said omega shouted back, "Go away, Sadie!"

I relaxed with relief that he was inside and I wasn't causing a scene in the hall for no reason.

A maid scurried by with linens in her arms, and I gave her a big smile. "Congrats on the salary."

She narrowed her eyes and hurried away from me.

I shrugged and turned back to the issue at hand. "Um, no, I'm not leaving. Open the door. We need to talk."

There was a long silence as I assumed Xerxes was hurrying to open the door for me.

Nothing happened.

"Let me in!" I yelled maturely and stomped my foot.

"*No*! Fucking leave!" Xerxes snarled, his honey accent thicker with rage.

My jaw dropped, and my chest cramped with pain. After everything that had happened, that was how he was going to play it.

At this point, a better woman, who respected boundaries, would have taken the hint and promised to visit later.

But I hadn't braved the exhausting trek down the hall to be turned away because a man was having a meltdown. And it rained every day; what else was new?

I took a deep, centering breath, then bellowed, "If you don't let me in, I'm breaking down the door."

There was the sound of someone banging into something and swearing. "Wait, what?"

I took a step back and girded my lady loins. "With my bones still healing, I am about to 100 percent shatter my femur!"

"*Don't you fucking dare*!" The shout from inside the room was feral.

Wasn't the bond supposed to stop that from happening?

I narrowed my eyes and tried to envision busting through the heavy, ornate structure. "Then last warning. Open the door or I'm coming in." Was it made of steel or wood? I prayed to the moon goddess for the latter.

"*No*! *Sadie, you are not coming in here*!"

I sighed depressively. That was not the right answer.

With another deep breath, I channeled my very, very, very repressed inner warrior woman. She did not like being woken up and was more prone to long naps and giving up, than to action.

Midswing, the door glinted in the soft chandelier flames. It was 100 percent steel, and I was about to shatter every bone in my right leg.

I was a dumb bitch.

There was no way to halt the momentum spinning me forward, so I squinted and prepared for agony.

It never came.

Instead, there was a soft grunt, and large hands easily caught my leg midkick.

It took me a moment to realize that Xerxes had slammed open the door and grabbed me.

Long blond hair hung down to his butt in soft, shiny waves, and his impressive chest was bare of clothes.

Sweatpants hung low on his hips, snagging on the edges of his indented *V* lines.

Xerxes breathed deeply, and his sculpted eight-pack rippled at the motion. His olive skin pulled across it deliciously, and I was hyperaware of how large the hands were that held my calf.

My mouth watered as I ogled the sheer perfection that was Xerxes's six-foot-five frame.

He might be an omega, but he was more impressive than most of the alphas I'd fought.

I flushed as I realized I'd been licking my lips and staring at his abs like a possessed woman.

When I glanced up at his face, my pulse sped up for a different reason.

Xerxes's eyes glowed electric purple, and he was staring reverently down at my sweatpants-clothed leg that he was still holding in his hands.

The moment extended. It was uncomfortable standing with one leg kicked in the air, and I tried to tug it away.

It was just a leg; it wasn't that exciting.

Xerxes didn't move.

It was then that I realized a wave of sugary cinnamon was pouring off the omega with an intensity that made my eyes water.

His biceps bunched tightly, and his nostrils flared, breathing me in.

"Um…Xerxes? Are you okay?" I asked softly, holding my hands up like I was talking to a wild animal.

He released a low omega whine. Goose bumps broke out across my skin. My instincts screamed at me to coddle, to protect.

I reached for him. Xerxes slowly looked up, and I stopped just before my hand touched his silky hair.

His pupils were blown wide, and a vein across his forehead jumped against his skin.

This wasn't Xerxes.

It was an omega in heat.

"You should probably release me and let me—"

I was cut off as Xerxes abruptly wrenched me by the leg and dragged me into his dark nest.

CHAPTER 27
SADIE
OMEGA MALES HAVE WHAT?

Xerxes omega-whined as I was roughly dragged into the room.

He casually threw me onto the bed like a rag doll.

Fluffy covers enveloped me, and I awkwardly scrambled backwards.

The dimly lit nest room cackled with delicious warmth from an extremely lifelike fireplace projected across the far wall.

Soft snowflakes fell around us.

There was a long moment as we both stared at each other in shock.

Well, I gawked at the half-naked omega, and he devoured me with his eyes.

I pursed my lips. "Should we talk about this?"

Xerxes reached down and ripped off his sweatpants. They fell shredded at his feet.

"So no talkin—"

My ability to speak evaporated as I realized one very important thing.

He wasn't wearing underwear.

I didn't bother trying to ignore the elephant in the room, just gaped in shock at the thick dick that bobbed against his stomach.

Instinctually, a soft alpha purr rattled through my chest.

Xerxes threw his head back and moaned as he gripped his cock with both hands.

Sugary cinnamon wafted from him with such intensity that I swore the air sparkled with saccharide.

A log crackled and popped in the fire. Boots crunched softly over freshly fallen snow. Soft jazz music played.

A flickering orange glow bathed the half-naked omega in soft light.

Shadows kissed his overly lush lips and sharp jawline.

His eyes were heavy-lidded, and his long sooty lashes that were fit for a prince cast shadows across his high cheekbones.

Up close, his heavily muscled stomach was impressive, and the network of veins that trailed across his forearms continued across his dick.

Two leather sheaths, one across each of his massive thighs, held wickedly sharp daggers.

I forgot how to breathe.

He stroked along himself softly, then tipped his head forward. Amethyst eyes glowing bright, his ruby-red lips pulled into a challenging smirk.

Once again, I tried to be the voice of reason. "Um, should we talk about this?" I meant to sound commanding, but my scratchy voice was a breathy rasp.

His honeyed, accented voice was practically a growl. "No."

Then, as if to punctuate his statement, Xerxes gripped his dick tightly and pushed it downward.

He took a step closer to the bed, feet planted wide.

"Look, Sadie," he commanded.

Since he knew my name, the heat hadn't turned him completely mindless. That was good.

Right?

I couldn't help but snap back, "Didn't you want Clarissa to join your heat?"

Yes, I was a jealous ho. I never pretended not to be petty; sometimes you just had to be.

A long omega whine filled the space. "No. Never. Only Sadie."

I pursed my lips, irrationally comforted by those four words.

The cinnamon scent was growing unbelievably intoxicating, and I licked the sugary spice off my lips. He seemed pretty certain. Who was I to argue against such an eloquent response?

When I didn't say anything, the omega whine became higher pitched and more broken.

My chest clenched with anxiety, and I fought the urge to jump up and soothe him.

Xerxes brokenly whispered, "Please, Sadie."

The purr in my chest increased in intensity until the blanket vibrated around me.

His tensed shoulders relaxed at the sound, and he took another step closer so his knees nudged the edge of the massive bed.

The jazz music played softly, and the enchantment created the illusion that piles of fresh snowfall were gathering around us.

The fireplace leaped and spun behind him.

His long hair billowing on a phantom winter's breeze, the flames surrounded Xerxes in glowing shadows and created the illusion that he was a dark prince from the rumored god realm stepping forth to conquer me.

Something low in my stomach twisted.

My groin spasmed with a feverish intensity.

Mouth watering, I choked on spit.

I keeled over, hacking and coughing on air. A few moments later, after nearly dying from asphyxiation, I realized I had no idea what we were even talking about.

Also, I was slightly miffed because Xerxes hadn't even offered to get me a glass of water after I'd hacked aggressively on his bed.

He didn't move an inch, just kept standing with his legs spread aggressively and penis out.

A real power stance.

I rubbed my tired eyes with confusion and asked the important question. "What's happening right now?"

At the sound of my voice, his eyes glowed brighter.

Xerxes commanded, "Look at my cock."

For a long second, I squinted and purposefully stared at his face. Who asked someone to do…that?

Seemed a little presumptuous.

The snowbanks piled higher.

Logs popped.

Cinnamon spiked sweeter.

When it became clear that I was not going to look—I wanted to look super badly, but my pride wouldn't let me give in to his command, and the longer we glared at each other, the more I refused to lose our staring contest—Xerxes reached out his hand toward the bed.

Before I realized his intention, long fingers lightly wrapped around my neck.

Thick calluses dragged across my sensitive skin, and shivers danced along my spine.

Xerxes squeezed lightly, eyes glowing brighter.

I licked my lips.

He groaned.

His callused thumb dragged reverently across my lips, and he whispered, "So pretty. This Cupid's bow is going to be the death of me."

My core spasmed.

Need swirled around me in a warm haze, and I sat frozen under his ministrations. Afraid if I moved or breathed, he would pull away and the spell would be broken.

He slowly pushed his thumb into my mouth.

Fuck. I'd been wrong.

His cinnamon wasn't sweet; it was rich and spicy. Tongue tingling, I dragged it wantonly across his thumb, desperate for more.

My core fluttered and clenched as I lapped at his taste.

I needed to drag my tongue over every inch of his flawless skin. Needed to consume him.

Injected into my veins, it wouldn't be enough.

I needed more.

Lashes fluttering shut, sensation exploding across my mouth, I moaned and purred harder, desperate for more.

Desperate for Xerxes.

"Look at me," Xerxes said softly.

His lips curled into a smile, and he clenched his fingers. He pressed his thumb down against my tongue until I had no choice but to move my head downward.

He whispered, "Now look at my cock."

He used his right hand to hold my face down, and his left hand was wrapped around his dick, pressing it downward.

Xerxes caressed my chin. "Good girl."

I moaned. His callused fingers left a wake of tingles.

Through a haze of need, I saw…*it.*

Fuck. Wetness gushed between my legs.

Xerxes's hand pushed his dick downward because he was trying to show me something.

Unlike the alphas, he didn't have a large knot that expanded at the root of his cock.

But he still had a knot.

It was just different.

There was a small growth protruding from the springy blond hairs at the top of his shaft. It curved above his dick by a few centimeters and couldn't have been longer than an inch.

The end of the small hardware was bulbous.

Xerxes's fingers tightened till his grip was almost painful around my jaw, and he slowly dragged my face forward.

Once again, he whispered reverently, "Good girl."

I moaned and purred.

A low buzzing sound started, and with my face inches from his powerful thighs, I realized what was happening.

What he wanted to show me so badly.

The knot started to vibrate.

Holy fucking shit.

I purred harder.

His whole dick vibrated.

The implications hit me, and I tipped forward. He hadn't been expecting my movement, so he wasn't quick enough to stop me as I tumbled face first off the bed.

On the soft carpet, snow softly crunching around me, I lay like a starfish, in awe.

For the first time in my life, I was blessed.

Because I'd seen eerily similar drawings of sex toys on the walls of the fae sex clinic.

I'd felt a very similar design pressed against my body for hours in the clinic.

The implication of where his knot would align on my body was revolutionary.

It changed *everything*.

Because omega males had a vibrating clit stimulator on their vibrating cocks.

At that moment, I understood fully why alpha women were obsessed with omega men.

They must know.

This was riot worthy.

Life changing.

I barely had time to work through the implications of everything, when large hands reached down and started tugging off my oversize sweatshirt.

"You're mine," Xerxes growled like a caveman.

My groin spasmed.

With my arms up and the sweatshirt tugged awkwardly over my head, I nodded. "One hundred percent. What you said."

He snarled with annoyance.

Then there was a loud rip as the offending fabric was shredded and discarded with his sweatpants.

As I lay on the floor with my small chest exposed, Xerxes stood over me like a dark god.

The full extent of everything that was happening hit me, and I instinctually covered my boobs with my hands.

Xerxes fell onto all fours, his muscles rippling as he crawled naked atop me and whispered, "Don't."

Face-to-face with me, his arms on either side of my head, his body overwhelmed me with its sheer size.

He licked his lips and leaned forward.

Before his mouth found the delicate skin of my throat, he pulled back abruptly and turned his head to the side.

His arms were shaking, and his voice cracked.

He spoke in short bursts, like he was seconds from collapsing. "If you don't want this. Heat. Overwhelming. I'll stop. Sadie. Tell me. Please."

Jazz music danced softly in the background.

The fire glowed.

Our history was a bitter spice.

His bitter betrayal in the shifter realm. My jailer in the fae realm. Angry purple eyes snarling at me. Flashing twin daggers and threatening to kill me. Calling me names. Snarling at me in the hall.

But it was also unexpectedly sweet.

A fluffy kitten purring on my chest. Tucking a blanket over him as he shook from a nightmare. Guarding the bathroom door as I showered.

Xerxes pushing me against the wall and asking if I meant it when I'd said I'd pamper him.

Him turning on the fae queen, twin daggers embedded in the skull of my attacker.

Offering us his home in the realm that hurt him.

Following me into a torture room. Hanging on a rope and begging me to be all right. His screams as I fought in the ring.

Curled up in the fetal position on a chair.

Afraid to care.

Afraid to be cared for.

There was no one else in the realms like Xerxes.

I didn't want to be with any other omega; I didn't even want to fight with any other omega.

As the moment extended between us, Xerxes started to sit up and pull away. He took my silence as my answer.

I reached out and grabbed his shoulder. "Yes, I want this."

He stilled.

I *wanted* to fight with Xerxes.

My voice was a low whisper. "Please, I want all of you. Don't hold back."

The snow became a blizzard. The sparks between us exploded.

Xerxes threw himself atop me and let himself go.

We both did.

CHAPTER 28
XERXES
CRASHING TOGETHER

A FEW MINUTES earlier

I curled on the bed and heaved as my dick throbbed with agony.

An omega wasn't supposed to go through heat until they'd fully bonded with their alphas.

Even then, it usually took months before an omega's body was comfortable enough to want to procreate.

Punching my pillow, I gnawed on my lower lip, desperate for the wave of agony to stop clawing at my lower stomach.

Walter, who had served the family for years and was very knowledgeable on all ABO bodily afflictions, thought my unusual heat was because of the years I'd taken suppressants in the fae realm.

Even so, it shouldn't have been this intense.

I screamed into my fluffy pillow as I rutted onto the covers and rode out the pain.

The worst part was while the bond between the men was growing stronger, I didn't want to fuck them.

With my past…I refused to fuck someone just because.

I refused to use my body for pleasure while my mind screamed at me to stop.

I refused to come while my spirits sank and I broke.

I'd lived like that for years, and I promised myself I would rather die than do it again, because I knew there was only so much I could take before I shattered forever.

I punched the bed as my hips jerked, and I slammed my face harder into the pillow.

There was only one alpha I'd ever met that my omega wanted.

Only one scent that made me delirious with need, that I could imagine calling my own.

Sweet fucking cranberries.

I couldn't go five seconds without thinking about her.

When she'd been spread on the bed beneath the alphas, nailed to the headboard with my knives, it had taken every ounce of self-control I possessed to not join them on the bed.

Sadie.

Fuck, she was perfect.

My hips jerked with need.

I'd flirted with Clarissa just to piss her off, even though the scent of lemons grated across my senses and my stomach churned with disgust.

It had been a big fucking mistake because Clarissa had recognized the signs of an omega going into heat and had become aggressive.

She had no clue that it was all for Sadie.

It had nothing to do with her.

I clawed at my dick, groaning as the sensitive skin burned hotter and as my touch did nothing to cool the over-stimulated flesh.

Now, because I'd acted like a fool, Clarissa had made up

some fucking lie, and Sadie had drifted further away from me.

Sadie had rejected me.

The only alpha I'd ever dreamed about calling my own, the only one I wanted to worship for my immortal life, had turned me down.

I hadn't joined her and the alphas on the bed because I knew she was still mad at me. She'd known the alphas longer and had a different relationship with them.

I refused to make her uncomfortable.

I refused to hurt her because I was a mindless omega going into heat.

It was probably for the best; she had scoffed when I'd pinned her to the bathroom wall and slapped her soaking cunt.

She was an alpha, after all, and they always liked to be on top of an omega.

It wouldn't have ever worked out between us.

The truth was agony.

I bit down on my pillow and screamed until my voice was hoarse as waves of fiery heat attacked my dick.

It didn't matter; I wouldn't survive this.

Everyone knew an omega's body would stoke hotter until they'd found a suitable alpha to take during their heat. There was a reason omegas were treasured and protected by their pack.

If an omega didn't have alphas to help them through the heat, they didn't survive.

"Fuck." My hips jerked harder, and the silk sheets did nothing to stop the inferno blazing across my delicate flesh.

"Xerxes, it's Sadie. Open up!" my alpha's voice yelled outside.

Great, I was fucking hallucinating.

The door rattled as someone kicked it aggressively. "XERXES!" The delicate scent of cranberries caressed my nose.

Fuck. I wasn't hallucinating. She was really outside the door, and my hips pistoned faster as I imagined her taking my seed.

I punched the bed and moaned in despair.

No. This was wrong; she didn't want me.

She needed to get away from me.

The tethers of control I'd prided myself on were ravaged at my feet, symbolic of what I wanted to do to her.

With all my might, I shouted with authority, "Go away, Sadie!"

Please, moon goddess, make her walk away. Protect her from me.

Sadie shouted back, and my balls tightened at the sound of her voice, the scent of cranberries growing stronger.

Mindlessly, I yelled back.

My dick was back in my palm, and I was tugging at it as hard as I could, barely conscious, until she yelled that she was going to kick the door and hurt herself.

FUCK. I banged my fist against my head. "*No! Sadie, you aren't coming in here!*"

Sadie said she was going to hurt herself.

Before I could stop myself, I threw open the door, instinctually catching her leg midswing.

My brain short-circuited…I was touching her.

Staring down at my fingers, I marveled as her calf muscles bunched against my palm. So delicate yet so powerful.

My alpha looked like a princess but fought like a warrior.

Even now, dark bruises covered her skin, remnants of the beatings she'd taken. The beatings she'd survived.

It only made her hotter.

Intoxicating cranberries filled my senses, and my vision crystalized with hyperfocused clarity as my mouth watered.

My need to taste fucking cranberries or die battled with my respect for Sadie. She deserved a gentleman, not a rabid animal.

A wave of blinding pain, the worst yet, made my dick jerk against my stomach and sticky precum smear my abs.

Fucking cranberries.

Feminine arousal spiked like an aphrodisiac, and every thought fled my brain as my hand wrapped tighter around Sadie's leg.

The choice was out of my hands. It was already made.

I yanked my alpha into my nest, and as I threw her onto the bed I'd been rutting against, I omega-whined with excitement.

Skin smoldering, I shredded my pants, desperate to show off my cock to my alpha.

Sadie's white hair fanned around her, gold skin glowing in the firelight, as my warrior princess lay on the bed. In my nest.

She purred.

My balls tightened.

Her ridiculously lush lips, stained red like the cranberries that wafted off her, mouthed something.

"No," I responded mindlessly.

My alpha warrior worried too much. As her omega, it was my job to calm her.

I needed to show her that I would take care of her. "Look, Sadie." I grabbed my cock and pushed it down, precum weeping from the tip at the proximity to my alpha.

There was a reason male omegas were priceless treasures, and it wasn't just because we calmed alphas and unified packs.

Females had locks inside their pussies that stroked alpha cocks.

But it was omega men who were called the masters of female flesh and the enslavers of pleasure and rumored to be blessed by the moon goddess herself.

Our cocks vibrated to a frequency that no enchanted sex toy had ever been able to match; our knots were attuned to a clitoris and instinctually ground against it.

We were sex gods.

Sadie snapped something about Clarissa, and rage unfurled through my chest. How dare she mention an inferior alpha in my nest.

A whine ripped from my throat.

I wanted to scream at Sadie, shove my teeth deep into her flesh, and ram my cock into her tight pussy.

It took every ounce of self-control to say, "No. Never. Only Sadie."

Sadie didn't say anything, and my stomach twisted.

She was going to reject me again because she recognized I wasn't good enough for her.

She disapproved.

"Please, Sadie." My heart was breaking.

Instead of her leaving like I expected, her purr rumbled louder, and the growing rage in my chest immediately extinguished.

I relaxed.

My alpha was pleased with me.

Sadie needed to see my cock. I had to show her that I was good enough for her, that I would only bring her pleasure.

I tried to show her, but my prideful alpha wouldn't look down, and a chuckle rumbled through my chest.

Such a little brat.

Sadie licked her luscious lips, like she knew exactly what she was doing to me.

I was barely cognizant that we were speaking.

Her golden skin flickered in the flames, catlike features mesmerizing me like no alpha had ever done before.

I saw her face in my daydreams and my nightmares.

I grabbed the silky skin of her sharp jaw—I couldn't help myself—and I traced my fingers across those berry lips.

Sadie purred louder but wouldn't look down.

I pressed my thumb into her sweet mouth and pushed on her warm tongue until her pretty head tilted, ruby eyes staring at my aching cock.

"Good girl," I praised her.

The scent of cranberries and arousal grew stronger.

More precum wept from my shaft.

I praised her again, "Good girl," and her pupils expanded until her eyes were black. My nose tingled, and I groaned at the scent of her wet pussy.

My knot vibrated.

Cranberries spiked sweeter. I licked my lips and shuddered. Her taste was an aphrodisiac.

But I didn't move.

As waves of agonizing need rolled through me, I dug my heels into the carpet and stood still.

Sadie deserved to be treated right, and I would not rut her like a mindless beast.

Sweat rolled down my spine as she gaped at my vibrating dick.

Abruptly, she fell off the bed.

Sprawled on the carpet, white hair tangled around her

golden skin, she smiled up at me like the perfect playful alpha she was.

Before I could stop myself, I growled, "You're mine."

She agreed.

Every cell inside my body stilled with shock, and my inner voice that had been screaming at me to be a gentleman went silent.

She agreed.

Sadie agreed.

My alpha agreed.

She was mine.

I lunged forward and pulled at the sweatshirt that was covering her flesh, hiding her away from me, and I ripped the offending material to shreds.

Golden skin gleamed, and dark-cherry nipples puckered on teardrop tits.

Each of her tits was a little less than a handful, small enough that I could suck the entire thing into my mouth and sink my teeth around it. They were perfect.

Sadie covered her chest, and a flush stained the tops of her cheeks.

"Don't," I whispered as I fought the urge to pin her hands above her head and rut her.

Sadie was delicate and inexperienced; her first time should be special.

My knees gave out, and I crawled atop her.

Her pulse leaped against the delicate skin of her neck, and the fluttering of her tawny skin mesmerized me.

If I bit into it, if I pierced the skin, others would know she was mine.

I'd have to bite it every day, so she always wore my mark, but that was no problem.

I leaned forward to claim her.

Sadie shivered in the dim light, and memories of overbearing alphas stalking me through dark rooms had my muscles seizing.

I stilled.

Memories of overwhelming fear, as the alphas lost themselves to their urges and rutted me like beasts, made my stomach cramp.

The worst part hadn't been that I wasn't sexually attracted to them, that I hadn't wanted them to take me, that I'd begged them not to.

The worst part was that I'd liked the violence.

When they'd stalked me, my dick had always been hard. And when they'd roughed me up, bitten me as they took what wasn't theirs to take, I'd come repeatedly.

It was part of why I'd fled.

Cruel faces had laughed as they'd dragged knives down my flesh, and I'd moaned with pleasure.

As a crazed alpha had rutted me, he'd slapped me with his impossible strength until my head snapped to the side.

At the force of his blow, I'd always come.

They'd spat in my face. "You're the most twisted omega in this whole fucked-up realm. Omegas are supposed to be soft. You're lucky we bought you, because you could never handle a woman. You'd break them." He'd slapped me again, and my body had jerked with pleasure. "I've never even heard of an omega liking it rough. Such a waste. You'd scare any woman away."

That night, I'd run.

The worst part: I liked my sex violent, and I'd never been in heat before.

In the present, arms trembling with Sadie splayed beneath me, I choked out desperately, "If you don't want this. The heat is overwhelming. I'll stop. Sadie. Tell me. Please."

I hated myself.

Of course she didn't want me; I was acting like a rabid beast.

Pulling away, I fought the urge to slam my fist against my head. I would lock myself in the bathroom. Pull the marble vanity off the wall and blockade the door so I couldn't get to her.

Delicate fingers grabbed my shoulder. "Yes, I want this."

I stopped breathing.

"Please, I want all of you. Don't hold back," she rasped.

All semblance of control snapped.

CHAPTER 29
SADIE
AGAINST THE WALL, VIOLENTLY

A TIDAL WAVE of cinnamon crashed into me and dragged me under. It was overwhelming and breathtaking.

It was everything.

Logs crackled and popped as fresh snow piled higher.

Xerxes's lush lips trailed down the sensitive part of my neck. He left soft, featherlight kisses. Reverently, he kissed across my clavicle and down my chest until his lips whispered across my belly.

I moaned softly, "Xerxes." His name was a plea.

"Alpha," he growled back.

Long, callused fingers gripped my waist.

His kisses trailed lower.

"Xerxes," I repeated mindlessly.

He sat up, and there was a loud rip as he tore off my sweatpants and they joined the pile of ruined clothes.

Shivering, I grasped his shoulder and tugged his warm body back against me. The soft carpet tickled my back as I panted.

Desperate for him.

Xerxes dragged his tongue slowly across my stomach. "Sweet fucking cranberries."

He moaned loudly and nipped at my lower belly with his teeth.

I moaned as the pinch bloomed into pleasure.

He dragged his teeth across my flesh, nipping harder and harder until I was a writhing mess.

Suddenly, he bit even harder, and his teeth broke my skin.

I yelped with surprise, the sound turning into a moan as euphoria sparked in its wake.

Xerxes went still.

After what felt like forever, Xerxes finally moved.

He whispered, "Sorry," and softly kissed my stomach.

His lips gently trailed across my torso, but he never nipped or bit like he had before. The inferno between us dulled, and I squirmed, unsatisfied.

His light touches weren't what I wanted.

I chewed on the side of my mouth.

Xerxes kept kissing me, like I was so delicate I would break, but it wasn't what I wanted.

Maybe he likes to be gentle. Don't scare him.

His tender ministrations continued, and my agitation spiked until I finally begged, "Please."

Again, he stopped moving and pulled away from me. His face shattered with concern. "I hurt you."

"No, I meant…" I trailed off, unable to verbalize what I wanted, and turned my head to the side.

Sun god, this was awkward.

Xerxes sighed roughly.

Arms trembling, he pulled himself back, so we weren't touching and said, "So sorry."

Fuck, I was blowing it.

I reached for him. He shuddered as I grabbed his shoulders and tugged his body back toward mine.

Don't be a little bitch, Sadie. As fast as I could, I said, "Please-bite-me-again. I-liked-it."

Xerxes inhaled.

The energy in the room shifted.

Snowy wind howled louder, as if the nest was sentient and picked up on its omega's mood.

Delicate touches were forgotten as his fingers dug into my hip bones and his nails raked across my delicate flesh.

Xerxes lowered his mouth to my shoulder and bit down.

Copper tanged the air as his teeth broke my flesh and drew blood.

In another lifetime, if I was more delicate, I might have cared that his fingernails were gouging my flesh as he attacked my neck with his mouth.

His teeth bit my skin, but his tongue soothed the wounds.

Hot fire bloomed, then cool relief.

Xerxes groaned against my neck and dragged his stubble down across my chest.

His scruff scraped across my sensitive nipples, and I gasped loudly, core aching as my hips arched off the ground.

"My alpha likes it rough," he moaned as his teeth and tongue bit and soothed marks he left all over my small breasts.

"Mm-hmm." I nodded in agreement and pulled his hair with all my might.

In another life, I might have been offended that hands were squeezing my already bruised flesh so tightly that new bruises were blossoming.

The more Xerxes nipped, sucked, and bit my skin, the more his agitation grew.

He growled loudly, "Say you're my alpha."

Flames sparked higher in the fire.

His cool, silky hair trailed across my chest and stomach in a soft caress. A soft contrast to his bites.

He shoved his knee against my core and ground against me.

Xerxes growled, "Say it."

In another life, I would be outraged by how he ordered me about and staked his claim across my flesh like a conquering pirate.

I tipped my head back and arched my chest up into his bites.

My fingers scored across his back as I tore at his skin, desperate for him to touch me harder, claim me deeper.

The fingers gripping my hips lifted me, then slammed me down against the carpet.

Xerxes dragged his stubble across my nipple, then closed his teeth around my overly stimulated flesh.

"SAY IT!" He bit down.

I screamed.

His knee shoved harder against my core, and it spasmed with flutters. My wetness slicked his knee, and I slid against it and clawed at his back desperately.

My hips slammed upward as he pressed me down harder.

Purple eyes glowed like beacons, and he dragged himself up to snarl in my face. "Say the fucking words."

I leaned forward until my lips rested softly against his, and he stilled and opened slightly, an invitation for a gentle kiss.

So close, I could see the glowing ruby of my eyes reflected in his.

I inhaled cinnamon, the tangy, spicy fire on my breath, and I exhaled into his mouth. "No."

There was a split second where Xerxes processed that I'd thrown down a challenge.

The moment he understood, the snow became a blizzard, the soft fire an overwhelming heat.

"Good girl," Xerxes praised as he grabbed underneath my arms and, in one smooth move, stood up and slammed my body hard against the wall.

I alpha-purred.

He pinned me with his size while he arched forward.

The low ceiling barely cleared his head.

In another life, I would have been outraged by how he tossed my body around.

I wrapped my legs around his hips and bucked my core against him. In this position, the movement of his knot made his thick dick vibrate against me.

Need gushed from me.

I ground against the delicious friction.

Reaching forward, I bit Xerxes's pec with all my might. Spicy copper exploded across my tongue, and I moved my head to bite beside it.

His hips snapped forward, and the wall shook as my back slapped against it.

My eyes watered at the vibrations against my core. My thighs shook with the beginnings of ecstasy.

White flakes fell around us, and the enchantment coupled with the chill against my back gave the sensation that I was being ravaged in a snowstorm.

I dragged my mouth across his other pec and bit down until my teeth punctured flesh.

Then I did it again until I marked every square inch of his skin.

Claimed him.

Blood dripped down my chin, and I rasped, "My omega."

Xerxes paused and stared at me.

"Good, baby girl," he said reverently as his hips threw me harder against the wall, then he leaned down and dragged his stubble across my sensitive neck.

Need pulsed between my chest and core as his chest rubbed against my overly stimulated nipples.

With his hips pinning me to the wall, he brought both hands up to my boobs and palmed them.

I arched my back harder, desperate for more friction.

The cinnamon on my lips, vibrations between my legs, stubble against my neck, and palms against my chest had me writhing, untethered to reality.

He overwhelmed me with need.

I slammed my fists against his muscled back, begging him for something I didn't completely understand.

Desperately, I hit him and moaned.

There was no warning.

Xerxes's teeth bit into my neck, his fingers pinched both my nipples, and he slammed his hips forward.

The wall shook.

I screamed.

Xerxes groaned with his teeth still buried in my neck. "My alpha."

Warm blood poured down my neck and across my chest.

Xerxes's palms dragged through the warm liquid as he mercilessly pinched and pulled at my nipples. Hot need dripped down my legs and across his pulsating dick.

It was too much.

It wasn't enough.

I spoke mindlessly between moans. "You're my omega. No one else's."

My nails raked across his back, and I was barely cognizant of the chunks of flesh I took with me.

Xerxes slowly scraped his teeth across my jaw.

I tangled my fingers in his glossy hair and yanked with all my might, desperate to push him over the edge.

He took a step back, grabbed my ass.

I wrapped my arms around his neck to steady myself, disappointed as he stepped away from the hard wall.

As I panted loudly, need gushed down my leg, and I pouted. Annoyed, I bit his massive bicep. "Don't want the bed."

Spice tingled across my tongue like an aphrodisiac, and my legs slipped off from around his waist.

"You're so perfect. You're everything, baby girl."

Xerxes wrapped his hand around my throat and slammed me back against the wall.

Then, he sucked on both my nipples.

Hard.

He bucked, and the leather from the knives strapped around his powerful thighs slammed into my lower belly with such ferocity that I knew they left imprints.

I rolled my hips against him.

Once again, my legs wrapped around his hips. Digging my heels into his hard ass, I ground against him with each ragged breath.

The blizzard roared.

"Fucking do it," I begged as the room shook.

Xerxes grabbed beneath my arms and lifted me higher against the wall. He leaned his head forward so our eyes were inches apart.

With one hand holding me up, he reached down and grabbed himself.

With impossible slowness, he dragged his vibrating dick across my slick entrance. His thick head teased my heat, and tremors shook my core.

I gushed.

Xerxes whispered reverently, "My baby girl," as he slowly rolled his hips forward.

He removed his hand from his pulsating cock and wrapped it back around my throat as he pushed inside me.

My sex clenched around him.

Slowly, he filled me.

His impossibly wide dick split me open.

The flutters became an earthquake as the vibrations overstimulated my delicate flesh.

I gasped, tears pouring down my face, and could barely articulate, "Stop."

Xerxes stilled, dick spearing my entrance as he took me against the wall.

He didn't breathe.

Instead, his fingers tightened around my throat, stealing my breath from my lungs as his cock split my entrance.

The tip hurt as he held still for long seconds.

It vibrated inside me, and I trembled.

I liked pain.

Xerxes pressed his lips against mine and breathed into my mouth, "Poor little alpha. You're going to take it, and you're going to like it."

It was already too much.

His fingers tightened around my neck until I saw stars.

Xerxes gently pulled my neck forward, then banged my head against the wall.

He shoved his vibrating cock a little deeper, leaned down, and sucked my small tit into his entire mouth.

Then the bastard bit down.

I screamed as I came.

I was barely conscious, and his fingers were unrelenting as he choked me harder.

"It's too much," I moaned as euphoria blinded me. "I can't come again."

Flecks of cinnamon sparkled in the air around us.

I burned alive.

Xerxes chuckled against my neck.

"I haven't even begun."

In another life, I would have shuddered at the fact that I was losing my virginity against a wall, to a massive warrior who was once my enemy, as he choked me out, bit me till I bled, pulled my nipples raw, and told me I was his possession.

Dick still spearing my entrance, Xerxes whispered in my ear, "Tell me you're my alpha, baby girl. Tell me your omega owns your fucking soul."

I snarled, "Then fucking begin."

Xerxes released my entire boob with a pop and dragged his tongue wantonly across my lower lip.

The hand choking me lessened its pressure, and I opened my mouth to gasp for air.

He used the opening to angle his head and press his tongue deep into my mouth.

It wasn't a kiss.

Xerxes mercilessly battled my tongue, shoving cinnamon down my throat. It was a claiming.

With his mouth still consuming mine, he growled into me, "That's my baby girl."

The hand around my throat squeezed tightly until I saw stars.

Just before the world could go dark, his fingers released, and I gasped, choking on the cinnamon tongue still buried deep in my mouth.

I dragged my tongue along his and fought to claim him back as he buried himself deeper into my mouth.

Wrenching my head to the side, I snarled, "*You're* mine."

Purple eyes engulfed in fire, too-pretty omega features sneered. "Bet."

As the word crossed his lips, he rammed his vibrating cock through my virginity, slamming my body against the wall.

I screamed.

He bellowed.

The pain was excruciating—his knot ground against my clit with impossible speed—so was the pleasure.

I sobbed as once again I came.

"MY ALPHA!" he bellowed.

There was no air in the room, only cinnamon, sex, and aggression.

Xerxes pulled back and repeatedly slammed his dick into my cervix.

I'd been right; he was a dark prince.

Purple eyes glowed demonically, long hair billowed on a blizzard, and muscles rippled with impossible strength.

The hilts of his daggers jabbed into my thighs.

I'd always liked villains.

Xerxes quietly growled, "I own your cunt."

I screamed as another orgasm hurtled through me.

As shock waves pulsed through my core and ass, I brought my lips to his ear. "Fuck you, Xerxes."

My voice was awed, the words a prayer.

It sounded like, *I love you.*

The last semblance of any sanity snapped, and Xerxes succumbed to his snarling beast.

Xerxes growled, "No, fuck you, baby girl."

It sounded like, *I love you more.*

My omega ravaged me.

His hips were punishing as civility melted off his face. His mask fell.

No one would ever mistake what we were doing for lovemaking.

Xerxes took me aggressively against the wall. He fucked me. His knot ground against my clit and vibrated at a frequency that defied physics.

He used my body, and I used him back.

The omega took me until there was nothing left to take, and I could do nothing but scream in ecstasy as he pounded me into another dimension.

I sobbed.

He bit down.

I bled.

His dick vibrated faster.

I came with a scream.

He slammed me harder into the wall.

I whispered his name.

Xerxes spoke reverently as he rammed his pulsing dick inside me, his knot stimulating my clit until I screamed. "You're my alpha. I claim you. I own you. There will never be an omega who ever fucks an alpha like I fuck your cunt."

I came again.

He snarled, "You're mine, baby girl."

I bit down on his neck as hard as I could. "No, you're my omega."

Xerxes tangled one hand in my hair and one hand

around my throat, ripped his dick out of me, pulled my head back at an impossible angle, turned me around, and shoved my chest forward.

Suddenly, my core was uncomfortably empty.

His chest engulfed my back as he pinned me so my body was flush against the wall, my sensitive nipples scraping against wood as he pressed harder.

I couldn't see anything and growled with disappointment.

He sheathed his dick into me with one motion.

At this new angle, his tip slammed into my cervix, balls tight against my heat. His fingers rubbed against my clit.

I would have screamed as shock waves pulsed through my core, but I'd lost my voice.

The hand in my hair wrenched my face back further, and he shoved his tongue into my mouth as I strained at an awkward angle.

Xerxes slapped my ass and rammed against me at the same time.

His hands twisted my nipples painfully as my face banged against the wall. My core pulsed and wetness dripped down my legs.

Xerxes pistoned his hips faster and sent me hurling to new heights.

He dragged two fingers over my lips, then shoved them deep into my mouth until I choked on cinnamon and musk.

I moaned.

Xerxes gagged me with his fingers.

Suddenly, his other hand slapped my clit, and the sensation was so powerful my womb cramped as I came.

For a second, my omega stopped moving.

Again, Xerxes whispered, "That's a good baby girl."

Hot liquid pulsed inside me, and he resumed slamming

me against the wall as he pinched my chaffed nipples and rode out his release.

His legs trembled, and he jammed me tighter against him so I couldn't move.

Strong hands pulled my thighs wide so he hit new depths as he fell to his knees.

He rolled onto his back and held me with my back to his chest, keeping me atop him with his dick buried deep.

"Mine." He bit down hard on my neck, and my pussy spasmed with agreement.

In another life, I wouldn't have lain atop him, boneless, with his vibrating dick buried deep inside me.

But I hadn't fought in the barren wasteland of the shifter realm, in the hot sands of the fae colosseum, and in a Mafia fight club to not enjoy an omega taking my virginity with such violent abandon that I'd touched nirvana and transcended the boundary between mind-numbing pain and exquisite pleasure.

So when Xerxes finally pulled his dick out of my heat, wrapped his hand around my throat one last time, and pushed me onto the floor, I didn't fight it.

When he raked his fingers across the cum on my thigh and shoved his fingers into my entrance as he stabbed his tongue as deep as he could inside my mouth, I lay back and enjoyed it.

"You'll keep my cum inside your cunt," he growled, tongue still in my mouth, fingers still buried deep inside me.

I nodded sleepily and whispered, "Whatever you say, omega," as an alpha purr trembled through my chest.

Anyway, I was 99 percent sure that, as a female alpha, I couldn't get pregnant, but I wasn't about to bring that up. I let him do his thing.

"My omega," I murmured, my lips curled into a content smile.

Xerxes's voice cracked on a sob as he whispered, "I love you."

He trailed featherlight kisses across my face.

My heart froze in my chest. *Holy fuck.*

The warmth from the fire crackled deliciously and pulled my eyelids lower. Soft jazz music twined around us, fresh snow gathered in piles.

He wrapped his naked body around mine until I was completely cocooned. He shielded me from any harm.

I whispered back softly, "I love you too."

Because it was true: I didn't want to go a single day without the fierce omega at my side.

Wetness dripped across my cheek.

He was crying.

In this life, I was too tired to give a single shit.

At some point, a small, fluffy kitten curled up beside me, purring softly, and I pulled it against my chest to cuddle.

I purred back.

Love you so much.

I claimed him.

Smiling, I licked spice off my lips.

One thing flitted across my consciousness before I fell asleep: how had I ever thought that cinnamon was sweet?

It fucking burned.

CHAPTER 30
XERXES
HIS NEW RELIGION

TWO HOURS earlier

I dragged my lips across her skin and moaned as cranberries exploded across my tongue. She was sweeter than I ever could have imagined.

"Xerxes," she moaned, and my dick jerked.

My alpha wanted me back. She wasn't mindlessly agreeing to fuck an omega in heat; she'd chosen *me*.

I kissed her reverently, trying to express with my mouth my awe.

She was too good for me.

"You'd scare any woman away."

I needed to be gentle.

The scent of her need became overwhelming, and I ripped her sweatpants off before I could stop myself.

My mouth watered, and I immediately went back to tasting her skin. I could die happy with my face buried against her flesh.

Mindlessly, I moaned words about how sweet she was.

Nothing had ever tasted so good.

I nipped at her lower belly and just barely stopped myself from hurting her.

She moaned loudly, and the sound went straight to my aching cock. My balls tightened impossibly.

Intoxicated, I dragged my teeth over every inch of her tummy and delicate lines of muscles.

Bruises and contusions from her fights were scattered across her golden skin, and I nipped atop them.

Sudden rage blinded me—other alphas had left their marks on her.

She would wear *my* marks, not theirs.

Before I could stop myself, I slammed my teeth through her skin and moaned with satisfaction as cranberry blood filled my mouth.

She yelped and jerked beneath me.

My cock wept at the sound, but my stomach plummeted. I forced myself to stop moving, ignoring the waves of pain that burned my dick with increasing ferocity.

"You'd scare any woman away."

If I lost Sadie, I'd die.

When I'd gathered my self-control, I whispered, "Sorry," and kissed her gently. Trying to show her what she meant to me through softness.

For her, I could do this.

I continued to kiss her stomach and chest softly, peppering her with gentle kisses. My molars ached with each gentle motion, and the fire in my belly cooled as the waves of heat burning my dick grew more painful.

It didn't matter what I wanted; I'd be a proper omega for her.

"Please," she begged.

Bile burned my throat as I pulled myself back off her. "I hurt you."

Fuck, I wanted to scream with desperation. The most perfect alpha I'd ever met, and I'd already scared her away.

Why did I have to be so fucked up?

"No, I meant…" she trailed off, too disgusted to even look at me.

I was a monster. "So sorry."

If I ran into the bathroom and locked the door, she'd have a chance to get away. I just needed to break the counter and sink and jam the door to stop myself from chasing after her. Walter would protect her until the men came back.

Suddenly, callused fingers grabbed my shoulders and tugged me forward. "Please-bite-me-again. I-liked-it."

Sadie spoke so quickly that it took a few seconds for my brain to process what she'd said.

When I did, I inhaled slowly.

Sadie hadn't been begging me not to hurt her and to be gentler. She'd been begging at me to bite her.

To take her harder.

She wanted it rough.

The walls I kept locked around myself fell away, and like a second skin, I shed any semblance of pretending to be normal.

I grabbed her narrow hips and squeezed as hard as I could, knowing my fingers would leave bruises across her flesh.

My handprints would stand out.

Sadie moaned, and the scent of feminine arousal spiked.

My little alpha warrior was fucked—she had no idea what she'd done, but she was about to learn.

I bit her shoulder as hard as I could until cranberry wine dripped down my chin.

The four concrete walls of control that surrounded my

heart began to crumble, and the chains of my past that fortified the walls rattled as they loosened.

The bruises from the other alphas still covered her flesh, and that was unacceptable. She was *my* alpha.

Not theirs.

I bit down, as hard as I could, across every glorious inch of her sensitive neck until she writhed and begged beneath me.

The more she trembled beneath me, the more I needed to show her just how high I'd take her.

It was my turn to teach her that no one would *ever* fuck her like I fucked her.

I dragged my stubble across her perfect breasts, shoving my face against her cherry nipples until her golden skin was bright red with agitation.

She arched her hips up, body jackknifing as she moaned.

"My alpha likes it rough," I whispered across her skin like a prayer.

She was a blessing from the fucking moon goddess, and I'd spend the rest of my immortal life worshipping her.

She agreed. And my scalp stung as she pulled my hair painfully.

I nearly came.

The lock around my chains broke off, and it disintegrated into nothingness. Never to be seen again.

My hands held her tighter, my mouth became rougher, and Sadie bucked harder against me as she moaned louder.

Pleasure sparked like lightning between us.

I ordered her to say that she was my alpha as I feasted on cranberries.

As I ravished my alpha, her fingernails broke the skin on my back and dragged slowly across my flesh.

Pain and pleasure mixed until everything was a hazy blur.

My chains fell away, disappearing into thin air.

Never had a woman been so perfect.

I slammed Sadie's hips down against the carpet, grabbed the cherry nipple with my mouth, which had been taunting me since I'd ripped off her sweatshirt, and bit down as I commanded her to be mine. "SAY IT."

She screamed, and her wetness gushed against my knee.

I commanded her to say it as I tasted, bit, and owned every inch of her sweet fucking skin.

Suddenly, Sadie leaned forward and rested her lips against mine in a tentative, gentle kiss.

The walls of control around my heart stopped breaking as I desperately tried to rein myself back in and find control.

Had I been wrong? Does she want me to be softer?

"No," she exhaled into my mouth.

Sadie was taunting me.

She was goading me to take her rougher, challenging me to let myself go and give us both what we wanted.

One of my walls broke off and crumbled to the ground.

Who was I to deny my alpha anything?

"Good girl," I praised as I easily lifted her and slammed my warrior alpha against the wall so the room shook around us.

Sadie purred, and my dick wept.

I silently muttered a prayer to the moon goddess.

I'd found my religion.

She was pinned beneath me.

Sadie wrapped her legs around my waist, and the most exquisite wetness dripped across my burning dick as she rubbed herself wantonly.

Then she leaned forward and bit down savagely on my chest.

Painful pleasure exploded across my flesh as my alpha claimed me back. Her lush lips smirked as she moved her head to another unblemished inch of skin and bit down again.

My second wall crashed to the ground.

My hips snapped as I slammed my dick against her core, giving us both the delicious friction we craved.

She bit me harder.

I pounded against her harder.

My blood dripped down Sadie's chin, and she grinned at me. "My omega."

I nearly came.

The third wall poofed out of existence.

I'm never letting her go, so sweet and violent. So fucking perfect.

"Good, baby girl."

I threw her against the wall with all my might, both of us groaning as her slick heat gushed at the friction.

As a reward, I dragged my stubble against her sensitive neck until I smelled her blood.

She slammed her fists against my back with surprising strength, pounding against the open wounds from her nails.

My eyes rolled back in my head.

As a reward, I bit down on her neck, pinched her cherry nipples as hard as I could, and slammed my hips forward so my vibrating dick pounded against her clit.

Sadie screamed deliciously. The warm blood from where I'd savaged her neck was slippery across her chest and slicked my fingers as I tortured her nipples.

Her head was flung back in pleasure, my bite mark stark on her neck, as my fingers coated her pert nipples in gore, and I played with her like she was my toy.

I would never recover from this.

From her.

My baby girl was perfect, and I'd die for her.

Everything became a hazy blur as we tortured each other.

My only cognizant thought was that she was still a virgin and I should take her on the bed.

I pulled back to bring us over, but my warrior alpha bit my bicep savagely.

"Don't want the bed," she mumbled.

Fuck.

There had never been a more perfect woman. I was going to build a shrine dedicated to her.

"You're so perfect. You're everything, baby girl," I praised my little beauty.

Once again, her pupils expanded at my words, and she trembled. Did the other men know she had a praise kink?

Fucking idiots. We should have been praising her all day, every day.

I wrapped my hand around her delicate neck and slammed her against the wall. Her head lolled and I mercilessly bit down and sucked on her nipples till.

Sadie wrapped her heels around me and snarled, "Fucking do it."

So cute—my alpha thought she was in control.

I lifted her easily and positioned my vibrating cock at her narrow entrance. She writhed and gushed as I slowly dragged it across her entrance, taunting her.

"My baby girl," I promised her as I choked her with one hand and slowly pushed inside her.

She was tighter than I could have ever imagined possible. No omega lock could ever grip my dick harder than my little alpha's cunt.

"Stop," she begged, tears streaming down her face as her pussy fluttered around my vibrating cock.

I choked her harder.

For a split second, I blacked out at the vise grip of Sadie's cunt.

I came back to consciousness, to Sadie, still trembling with pleasure on the tip of my dick.

Like she'd taunted me earlier, I pressed my mouth to hers in a mockery of a gentle kiss. "Poor little alpha. You're going to take it, and you're going to like it."

Her pussy spasmed around me.

I choked her harder.

It spasmed again.

I slammed her head back against the wall.

Again, her pussy clenched.

I shoved myself into her insane tightness a little deeper, sucking her entire tit inside my mouth.

"It's too much. I can't come again," she cried with ecstasy as her pussy spasmed, and I saw stars.

My poor little alpha was about to get everything she didn't even know she wanted.

I couldn't hold back my chuckle, my teeth against her neck. "I haven't even begun."

There was a long moment where doubt burned my chest and I wondered if perhaps I was hurting her.

I pulled back.

She snarled. "Then fucking begin."

My last wall exploded into smithereens, and there was no barrier left to protect me from myself.

There was no pretending.

The haze overtook me.

Before I knew what I was doing, I had her mouth spread wide beneath me, dick spearing her to the wall, as I shoved my tongue so deep into her that there was no doubt who she belonged to. Who was claiming both her holes.

"That's my baby girl," I praised deep into her throat.

I'm going to fuck her like this every day for the rest of my life. Take her so deep that she remembers she belongs to her omega.

Her sweet cunt spasmed again, and I rewarded her by choking her harder.

But my alpha had the audacity to pull away from my mouth and say, "*You're* mine."

Poor baby girl was delusional.

"Bet." I rammed my hips forward and slammed my thick cock through her impossibly tight channel.

Sadie screamed.

I bit down on her nipples mercilessly and rammed into her until she was sobbing and coming on my vibrating dick.

The flutters pulsating around my cock were bursts of euphoria, like nothing I'd felt before.

I laughed as my alpha warrior sobbed as she came.

Everything about her was perfect.

I fucked her violently, snapping my hips with all my might as she trembled beneath me.

For the first time, I understood why Cobra always claimed she was his possession. Not that she could ever be truly owned.

You couldn't own perfection.

"I own your cunt," I taunted my warrior.

She came again.

Spasming on my dick, gushing cream across my lower abs, she gasped, "Fuck you, Xerxes."

No alpha had ever been sweeter. Her words sounded like, *I love you*, and my heart hurt in my chest as it squeezed.

"No, fuck you, baby girl." *I love you too.*

I stopped pretending I wasn't a monster, and I tortured her sensitive flesh until she came again, and again.

I pressed my face to her temple and muttered reverently, "You're my alpha. I claim you. I own you. There will never be an omega who ever fucks an alpha like I fuck your cunt."

We both knew that I was really saying, *I love you. I love you. I love you. I love you.*

My balls tingled, and I knew my release was close.

But I wanted more.

I snarled at her, "You're mine, baby girl." *I fucking love you so much.*

Little teeth bit down on my neck, and I barely felt the pinch as Sadie moaned, "No, you're my omega."

She was everything I'd ever wanted, everything I'd never thought I deserved.

Chest burning with a foreign sensation, I lost all control.

I ripped Sadie off my dick, turned her around so I could see her perfect heart-shaped ass, then rammed my cock back into her heat. Burying my hands in her silky strands, I wrenched her head back so I could take her mouth as I took her cunt.

Sadie's eyes fluttered as she moaned.

I chuckled at my sensitive little alpha.

Ruthlessly, I pounded into her harder, tweaked her nipples, and rubbed her clit with my fingers.

Such a sweet little cunt. There would never be a woman as maddeningly exquisite as my baby girl.

As the tingling in my balls intensified, my dick throbbed.

I held back with all my strength because I wasn't coming unless she did too.

Shoving my fingers into her throat, I gagged her and pounded her as hard as I could.

The scent of her cream filled the air as she clenched and fluttered around my dick one more time.

"That's a good baby girl," I praised as I let my seed erupt, and I rode it out by ramming us both against the wall, pulling her cherry nipples till she cried.

Vision blurring with aftershocks of nirvana, I collapsed onto my knees, pulling her thighs wide so I could remain buried inside her.

I rolled over, relishing the feel of my alpha sprawled across me. It was an honor to hold her, to cushion her with my body.

To serve her.

"Mine." I bit down on her neck one last time. Needing to establish my mark so no male would question who she belonged to.

The heat was no longer making my dick hurt with agony, but it crashed over me in a wave of instincts.

There was still something I needed to do.

I pulled myself out of the exquisite heat, rolled Sadie onto her back, took my sticky cum off her golden thighs, and shoved it back up inside her. "You'll keep my cum inside your cunt," I ordered.

Panic tightened my chest at the mere thought that the heat hadn't worked, an irrational urge to impregnate my alpha blinding my thoughts.

I kept my fingers buried deep inside until the instinct died down and I could relax.

"Whatever you say, omega." Sadie chuckled and curled into me as my cheeks burned with embarrassment over my absurd actions.

Alpha females couldn't get pregnant.

But my alpha didn't mock me. She just purred and snuggled against me. "My omega."

My past was no more, and my eyes burned as I whispered, "I love you," and peppered Sadie with gentle kisses.

I pulled her tight against me and wrapped my body around her, protecting her from any threat.

"I love you too," Sadie whispered so quietly I barely heard it.

I would die for her.

Tears leaked down my face and dripped across the woman in my arms who had accepted everything I'd spent so long hating about myself.

After an hour of holding her, I unconsciously shifted into my kitten form and padded over to the warm spot between her arms.

I wanted to be held by my alpha.

Sadie tightened her arms around me and pulled me flush against her chest.

The first alpha to accept my kitten form. *My alpha.*

Cranberries had never been so sweet.

A realization flitted across my consciousness before I fell asleep: the heat had spurned me on, but I'd been fully aware and conscious.

I'd desperately wanted everything that had happened.

I prayed to the moon goddess that Sadie was okay with that.

CHAPTER 31

SADIE

OH SHIT

I MOANED as I stretched out my aching limbs. Apparently, I'd been run over by a car, then tortured while I slept.

Every single cell throbbed with pain.

Also, why was my bed so hard?

Pulling open crusted eyes, it took me a long moment to realize I wasn't in pain because Aran had snapped and beaten me in my sleep.

Nope.

Fire crackled and snow swirled in a dark room, but it was the stench of cinnamon and sex that had my eyes widening and memories crashing into me.

A fluffy white kitten was curled in the nook of my arm.

I remembered Xerxes saying that he was ashamed of his kitten form, and that alphas taunted him for it.

The little fluff purred against me, and my heart broke into a million pieces.

My chest twisted as I drowned in the waves of foreign emotions.

For the longest moment, I closed my eyes and pretended the footsteps crunching through snow were Lucinda's and we were exploring through the forest of the shifter realm. Life wasn't easy, but we were young and filled with children's naïveté that everything would be okay.

Instead of crisp forest air, musky sweat and coppery blood hung heavy.

I sighed heavily as the mirage broke. Buck naked in an omega's nest, I debated my options.

1. I could start screaming and cause a scene (extremely gratifying but emotionally exhausting).
2. I could play it cool and pretend I was a sexual goddess who regularly fucked men violently (appealing but hard to pull off).
3. I could find Walter and ask if he knew a therapist, because my mental issues extended to sexual issues (boring and predictable; no one was surprised).
4. I could go brag to Aran that I'd lost my virginity before her, so she was officially the crusty prude between the two of us (very enticing, but Aran would probably attack me, and my body was on its last leg).
5. I could just act normal (like a loser).

Evidently, having my hymen brutally removed had shifted something inside me, because I wanted to choose the fifth option.

I was turning into a proper lady.

Just kidding. My aches throbbed in tune to my heartbeat, and I was in too much pain to do anything other than kiss Xerxes's kitten head.

Denial was my bestie.

"You're so cute," I cooed and ran my fingers gingerly across his fluffy white ears.

Kitten Xerxes rolled over and showed off his tiny belly.

I reached forward and gave his fur a gentle kiss. His miniature paws clawed at the strands of my hair that fell around him.

My heart melted, and I held my hair in front of his paws like a string. "Little kitty wants to play?"

Xerxes batted at the strands and kicked his back legs adorably.

After ten minutes of play time, Xerxes sat up and ignored my attempts to throw my hair into his face. His purple cat eyes went from sleepy and playful to unamused.

He haughtily sniffed the air and licked a paw.

My omega had regained control, and he was over my antics.

Too bad for him, because I was still amused. "Wittle itty bitty cute kitty." I scratched under his chin until he trembled and closed his eyes. I peppered his head with kisses as I scratched. "Sadie's wittle baby."

Xerxes bit my finger with his incisors. Poor thing put his whole body into it, but he was so small he didn't even break the skin.

I giggled. "Who knew you had such a biting problem?"

Suddenly, as if my words had shaken him out of a trance, the kitten scrambled backward off my lap.

Before I could toss my hair at him again, a very naked six-foot-five male was crouched on the rug.

His olive skin shone in the firelight, but it wasn't smooth and unblemished with its usual shine.

The air left my lungs, and I choked in shock.

Xerxes's neck, and both pecs, were covered in bruises and welts with hundreds of small, round indents.

I'd bitten every square inch of his skin.

With his lean muscles, long hair, deep *V* lines, and daggers glowing with enchantment as they returned, strapped to his thighs, he looked like a wild warrior of lore.

As I appreciated my work, Xerxes scrambled backward.

His face contorted with horror.

I grumbled and covered my naked bits with my hands. "Well, that's comforting." What woman didn't want her love to scramble away from her in disgust after taking her virginity and telling her he loved her?

It was not good for my lady ego.

Xerxes spoke, and his voice was no longer the guttural growl from the day before. His honeyed accent was back. "Baby girl, I'm so fucking sorry. I can't believe..."

He covered his mouth with a shaking hand and moved further away from me.

I ignored the way my heart melted when he said "baby girl."

But now he was apologizing.

The romance books I'd loved to read growing up had made men sound way less dramatic than they really were.

Highly upsetting and unfortunate for women everywhere.

The beginning of a tension headache pounded through my skull. "Dude. Don't make it weird."

Xerxes opened and closed his cut jaw, dragging lean fingers across his stubble. "Weird?"

My core clenched at the scratchy noise as my nipples remembered the rough abrasion dragging across. *Was it too soon to bring up that we'd said, "I love you"?*

His nostrils flared, and his eyes began to glow.

I squeezed my legs together and debated trying to crawl toward him sexily.

From the ache pounding through my kneecaps, I'd probably collapse like I was geriatric.

Still, I squinted and debated it.

I wasn't a coward.

Before I could plot my path, Xerxes shoved his palms into his face and turned away. He muttered to himself, "What the fuck is wrong with you? Stop it."

Sun god, he had a nice ass.

I would have risked the kneecap pain and crawled toward him—his thick butt cheeks were beacons of light in a dark world—but I got distracted by the *gouge* marks that covered his back.

Dried blood streaked across his skin, and the marks were so deep it looked like he'd been whipped.

Suddenly, I felt like utter shit.

Nausea churned my stomach, and I scurried backward away from him. "I'm so sorry about your back."

He didn't turn around.

Just hunched his shoulders further downward and muttered expletives under his breath.

He seemed distraught.

I shoved my knuckles into my mouth as it dawned on me.

Holy sun god, I was a man-eater.

Fuck.

Before I could gain the confidence to report myself to the appropriate authorities, there was a loud banging on the door.

Cobra yelled, "Xerxes, what the fuck are you doing? We can feel your pain."

Oh great, now they were going to see what I'd done to him and I'd be carted off to the don for punishment.

My brain churned as I struggled to remember the consequences for abusing an omega.

Something about disembowelment, but I couldn't remember if I was also going to be set on fire or just shot with a bullet through the brain.

Xerxes hunched even lower until he was crouching with his arms around his legs. He didn't answer, but his entire body trembled.

I deserved the fire.

"Fuck, Xerxes. Are you okay, man?" Ascher's fist joined Cobra's.

Jax's voice was much calmer than the other two's. "Stop banging and shouting. That's not going to help him. You're making it worse. He's probably just having a nightmare. You know how it's been for him. He's okay."

"He's not okay," I responded instinctually, then slapped my hand over my mouth.

Xerxes hunched deeper into himself.

There was silence in the hall.

I grimaced as Xerxes's hairy crack was clearly on display. Not a pretty position.

After five minutes of nothing happening, I wondered if the alphas had gone somewhere else, and debated informing Xerxes that I could see his butthole and he should probably put on pants.

I opened my mouth to apologize again but was cut off by the metal door creaking.

Suddenly, it was pulled off its hinges and tossed into the hall by a snarling bear that let loose a bone-chilling roar.

In a blink, the bear retreated as Jax shifted back.

I opened my mouth to admonish him for breaking the no-shifting rule, although I didn't think the don knew what we did in our own house, but I stopped because of the intense expression on his face.

Ascher and Cobra flanked him on both sides as they stalked into the nest like avenging warriors.

Xerxes whimpered, and my instincts screamed at me to protect my omega.

I dragged myself off the floor, my joints creaking and popping, and I flung myself in front of his naked, crouched form.

"You're scaring him," I snarled at the alphas as I tried not to notice how pine, chestnuts, and frost mixed deliciously with cinnamon and sex.

They stopped moving, jaws falling open as they stared at us.

I covered my bits with my hands and tried to sound authoritative. "I'm sorry for what happened to him, but it was the heat, although I know that is no excuse for my actions. But you need to give him some space. He's clearly hurting."

My face burned with shame, and I looked away. "I hurt him."

Three pairs of alpha eyes glowed with fury.

I deserved it.

No one moved.

The violence and tension ratcheted up.

A callused hand gently touched the back of my shoulder, and I turned around in surprise.

Long, patrician fingers—that had choked me mercilessly as I screamed, sobbed, and came—gently traced across my neck.

I swallowed thickly.

Xerxes whispered, "I'm not upset because you hurt me. I'm fucking gutted because of what I did to you." The fingers on my neck trembled, and a lone tear trailed down his face.

My brow furrowed as I stared up at my dark prince. "But I loved it."

I love you, hung heavy in the silence between us.

Xerxes shuddered and whispered, "Are you sure?"

I stepped closer.

My head was level with his chest, so I gently kissed a pair of deep teeth marks that dragged downward from where I'd scraped across his flesh.

"Yes. But are *you* sure?"

Callused fingers gently traced my jaw, and I moaned at the memory of what those fingers had done to me.

We both knew what we were talking about.

Xerxes bent down so his lips traced softly over mine. "I've never been surer of anything in my life." He kissed me gently and pulled back with an arched brow. "Are you really okay, baby girl?"

I shivered and nodded.

Sure, there were a million issues we had to work through, and I still couldn't bond with him, but I understood what he was asking.

A smile split my face, and I nodded. "My omega."

Xerxes groaned and pulled me close, engulfing my lips in a proper kiss.

I melted against him, his fingers tangling in my hair as he kissed me reverently. With his lips, he told me what I meant to him, and I told him back.

It was bliss.

A low hissing noise interrupted the moment, and I pulled away from Xerxes, who apparently was not going to report me to the authorities.

Turning back around to the three alphas, I parted my legs in a power stance, protecting Xerxes with my body.

He was *my* omega, and I didn't like other alphas being hostile around him.

They were ruining our moment.

Classic men, making everything about themselves.

Xerxes pulled me behind him and shielded me with his larger body.

Up close, I stared at the strips of bloody flesh I'd left across his back. Sun god, it looked like I'd been trying to dig his skin off.

Abruptly, the low hiss became louder and mingled with a roar and loud bleat.

I peeked around Xerxes's arm.

The three alphas' faces were contorted in fury, eyes glowing brighter than I'd ever seen as they looked at Xerxes's waist.

Looked like I wasn't the only alpha stunned by his unique penis.

It really was revolutionary. I couldn't wait to see Aran's face when I told her. She was going to be *so* jealous.

Ascher's hand visibly shook as he dragged it roughly over his horns.

Jax's golden chains tinkled as he looked away, like he was going to be sick.

Cobra's jewels turned into shadow snakes that roamed across his flesh. He stood still, like a statue.

Sun god, I knew Xerxes's knot was groundbreaking, but they were being a tad dramatic about it.

Not like they had clits to stimulate anyways.

Xerxes flexed his muscles like he was preparing to fight, and he shifted to block me completely.

The silence expanded.

Cobra was the first to break it, his words a deadly hiss. "Issss that what I think it issss?"

I peeked over Xerxes bicep. Cobra was still staring at his omega knot.

"Yeah, and it vibrates," I said tentatively, trying to diffuse the awkward tension that had paralyzed the men.

My tone was meant to be blasé, but I couldn't hide my excitement.

Jax roared to the ceiling. The sound vibrated through the small room, and I collapsed, my hands over my ears.

I rolled my eyes.

Ascher's horns lengthened on his head, and his tattoos jumped as he tensed and stepped forward.

He snarled at Xerxes, "How fucking dare you," hands fisted and shaking with rage.

Cobra hissed, "You took what wassss mine. I will sssss-lowly remove your sssskin from bonessss."

Jax growled softly, "Are you okay, my love?"

"Wait, are we not talking about his vibrating knot?" I was confused.

Jax looked away again, like he couldn't speak because he was desperately trying to stop himself from violence.

Ascher's hands shook harder as he clenched and unclenched his fingers. He opened his mouth and closed it, like he couldn't find the words.

It was Cobra who snarled back, "The fucker hassss your virgin blood coating hissss dick."

"Oh."

Suddenly, I got it.

CHAPTER 32
SADIE
WHY ARE MEN LIKE THIS?

Moon goddess, save me from dumbass men.

I sighed heavily as I realized what this little standoff was about, and pushed past Xerxes once again to stand in front of him and face the men.

You could run from male unwellness, but you couldn't hide.

My omega tried to fight me, but with a swift kick to the side of his knee and an elbow jabbed precariously near his balls, he let me have my way.

Hands on my hips in a power stance, I faced the alphas.

"Yeah, he took my virginity. Who gives a fuck? I wanted him, and he wanted me. Don't be babies. It's just a hymen."

I couldn't help but smile as I thought about just how my omega had taken me.

Ascher swore.

Cobra's pupils changed into snake ones.

It was Jax who bellowed, "She's still missing some of her teeth from the fights. How could you do that…" He trailed off, raking his hands through his long braids as he pointed at my body. "*Look what you did to her*!"

Xerxes put his hand on my shoulder to pull me back against him protectively, and I didn't miss the tremor that rolled through him.

He was more scared than anyone that he had hurt me, and the men were making it worse.

I sniffed haughtily. "Stop trying to ruin what happened. It was beautiful."

Xerxes choked, and I narrowed my eyes as I thought about it.

"Well, maybe 'beautiful' isn't the right word. It was profound. Exciting. Exhilarating. As the kids say these days, 'It was lit.'"

I grabbed Xerxes's hand and squeezed it reassuringly.

"Literally no one says that," Cobra snarled.

"I heard Jinx say it," I snapped back.

"She was talking about setting someone on fire. No one else says that." Cobra still had snake eyes, and his shadow snakes were going crazy on his flesh.

My own shadow snake gave me a small zip of love.

It was so cute.

Ascher finally regained his composure. "Beautiful my fucking ass. Is that why you're covered in bite marks and blood like an attack victim? Sorry to break it to you, Sadie, but whatever you two did was not fucking."

Agitation sparked through my chest. "How dare you? Just because you've clearly never experienced *true passion* doesn't mean you get to judge us."

I took a step forward, my voice rising as I saw red. "You've never made a woman orgasm dozens of times with a vibrating dick."

Ascher's horns expanded larger than I'd ever seen, and amber eyes exploded with fire.

"Oh, Princess, you think because you've had sex once,

with an omega in a mindless heat, that you could handle an alpha male?" He tipped his golden head back and laughed cruelly.

I snapped, "Well, I seem to remember you fucking my mouth and tits a few days ago. Also, why would I ever want an overrated alpha when I have an omega with a *vibrating cock, you closed-minded fuck*!"

Cobra's voice was cutting. "Kitten, you'll take an alpha, and you'll like it."

The shadow snake on my flesh sent more happy sparks as it twirled across my skin.

Jax growled.

Ascher grew taller and wider as he partially shifted, and his tone dripped with scorn. "You couldn't handle an alpha anyways. Who said we even wanted to fuck you?"

My heart twisted as he hit my insecurities.

Maybe they only wanted me for oral sex; they had never gone all the way.

There was a *shhhhk* behind me.

Xerxes brandished his twin blades. "How dare you insult her?"

Suddenly, he turned to me and spoke quietly like he needed to explain. "When omegas complete a bond, they go into heat every few months and their bodies burn until they have sex with their mates. It's a way of ensuring they procreate. But it's a super intense and intimate experience that they will only do with someone they trust and want."

He trailed a finger across my jaw. "Understand, even though we aren't mated, that's what you are to me, baby girl."

My heart thumped heavy in my chest as I nodded.

I love you hung in the air between us.

Behind us, Cobra made a choking sound and dragged me out of the spell of Xerxes's purple eyes.

I gnawed on my lower lip and looked at the other men.

Ascher's scoffing words lingered and I was afraid to see the rejection on their faces.

"Fuck, Princess, I didn't mean it." Ascher pleaded, "You're just covered in marks, and seem injured, and it's killing me inside."

I narrowed my eyes as I weighed the merits of wallowing in a pity party and holding his words against him for the rest of his life, or forgiving him.

It was a close one.

The former definitely won out.

Jax finally gained enough control to speak, and his voice was sharper than I'd ever heard it. "What could you have even done to leave such marks on her body?"

Burned chestnuts filled the space.

I looked up at Xerxes and rolled my eyes at the wide grin splitting his lips.

Men were so predictable.

Abruptly, the three alphas rubbed at their chests and staggered back.

Their eyes glowed with the same bright ring that had appeared when they'd formed a pack, and they stumbled like they were envisioning something.

I grimaced. If Xerxes was showing them what we'd done through their bond, there was no shot that was going to defuse the situation.

"Fuck, fuck, fuck, fuck," Ascher chanted under his breath as he staggered into the wall and hit his head.

Xerxes grinned down at me and dragged his fingers across the back of my neck like he knew exactly what had sparked my arousal.

Damn intoxicating omega.

"Sun god save us," Jax muttered in prayer.

Cobra's lips parted. "No." It was like he refused to believe what he was seeing.

His gorgeous features were carved granite as he stood unnaturally still.

"Yep." I popped the *p*, unable to help myself.

Good, I hoped they were watching me cream on Xerxes's vibrating dick, and I hoped they realized he was more of a man than they would ever be.

How dare they try to shame him and make him think what we'd done was wrong?

Cobra's head snapped up, and his emerald eyes, colder than the cut jewels they resembled, speared me where I stood.

"So Kitten has a praise kink."

I scowled. "It's not that big of a dea—"

Abruptly, Cobra lunged forward, and I sputtered with surprise.

He towered in front of me, shadow snakes in a frenzy across his porcelain skin.

Stepping back, I bumped against Xerxes, who protectively wrapped a bicep around my naked chest.

Still in his hand, the wicked knife glinted menacingly as it lay close to my flesh.

Cobra leaned forward.

Xerxes tightened his grip.

Biting frost mixed with spicy cinnamon, and my eyes watered as the harsh scents mingled.

Lucinda's assessment that Xerxes and Cobra were more bark than bite flitted through my mind.

Pressed between the two of them, I realized something profound.

My sister was a shit judge of character.

Cobra whispered, "Kitten wants to be choked."

He crowded my personal space until his gorgeous cheekbones and perfect lips were centimeters from my own.

I hummed in agreement.

"Kitten wants to be bitten." Cold fingers trailed across my sensitive neck, leaving a trail of ice in their wake.

Sarcasm dripped from my voice. "Obviously."

"Kitten wants to be thrown against a wall. Repeatedly." Fingers trailed lower, tickling my chest with frost and lazily running across Xerxes's tense forearm.

I rolled my eyes. "Groundbreaking observational skills."

"Kitten wants a cock rammed into her cunt until she blacks out. Kitten wants to come so hard she sobs." A slightly forked bright-red tongue ran along plush lips. "Isn't that right?"

Icy fingers slowly trailed across my lower belly.

Nails dragged along my inner thigh.

I studied my cuticles like I was bored. "A high-caliber lady like myself has certain needs. What can I say? Xerxes gets me. He doesn't just tease me like some people."

The forearm across my chest tightened until I could barely breathe.

Icy fingernails dug into my thighs.

Two very large, impossibly attractive males pressed their bodies into me, and since I had a pulse, my pussy cramped with need.

Cobra's nose flared, and his eyes rolled back in his head.

Frost burned my inner thigh as his fingers trailed delicately along the seam of my heat.

"Hmm." Cobra tapped his free hand across his lips like he was considering something as he said softly, "So you love Xerxes."

I froze at his words, heart pounding in my chest.

Two chilly fingers parted my folds and sheathed themselves in my heat, and Cobra chuckled as he pumped them inside me.

As I was still sore from Xerxes, Cobra's ice-cold fingers had me spasming from painful pleasure.

I gushed on his fingers.

"How do you feel about the rest of us?" Cobra hissed softly as he leaned closer, eyes like emerald chips.

He's jealous.

My legs gave out beneath me as his fingers raked across a particularly sensitive spot inside me, and Xerxes's arm across my chest was the only thing that held me up.

His warm cock began to vibrate across my lower back.

My omega enjoyed restraining me as his packmate finger-fucked me.

Cobra leaned closer. "What were the words?"

He added a third finger and bent them so they rubbed against a spot inside me, and I moaned at the exquisite pleasure.

Haze blurred my vision as he ruthlessly pumped his fingers, and Xerxes restrained me tighter.

"Oh, right." Cobra brought his other hand to my clit and pinched it. "Now I remember."

Frozen cinnamon burned my skin like frostbite.

Xerxes dragged the flat side of his dagger slowly across my chest. He adjusted his fingers on the hilt so his thumb and forefinger were free.

Cobra fucked me with his fingers faster.

Xerxes raked his thumbnail across my chest, then pinched my sensitive nipple.

At the same time, Cobra pinched my clit and tugged it as he slammed his fingers deep inside me.

I choked on a sob as my pussy clenched with euphoria, and my vision blurred.

Cobra sneered mockingly in my face. "Come for me, baby girl."

Xerxes tormented my overly sensitive nipples.

Cobra tortured my sore pussy, and two other alphas groaned loudly.

Frosty cinnamon, warm chestnuts, and rich pine wrapped around me in a luscious fog.

When my core finally stopped fluttering, Cobra dragged his fingers out of my heat and brought them to his mouth.

Xerxes gave my nipple one last pinch and kissed the back of my neck softly.

"Shit, that was hot," Ascher growled.

He gripped his tattooed dick in his hand, white cum dripping down his fingers.

Jax stood unnaturally still, nose flared, with a massive erection tenting his sweatpants.

The world had a dreamlike quality as Jax stalked across the room and grabbed Cobra's hand.

Slowly, Jax dragged Cobra's pale fingers into his dark-pink lips and wantonly licked my cream off them.

"Obviously," Jax drawled, his deep voice imitating what I'd said a few minutes ago.

"What?" I asked, legs shaking from my release as exhaustion from the sexual onslaught of the past hours made me want to curl up and sleep for days.

Jax slowly dragged his tongue across Cobra's jeweled fingers, gathering up every drop.

"Obviously Sadie has a praise kink. Little alpha likes to be bossed around." Jax arched an eyebrow, reminding me of his large body kneeling over me as he shoved his pierced dick down my throat. "Don't you, love?"

Xerxes chuckled, and Ascher began to pump his cock again in his fist.

My skin erupted in goose bumps, and I looked away from the men as my face burned with embarrassment.

An uncharacteristic wave of self-consciousness twisted my gut, and I pushed myself out of Xerxes's hold.

Were the men making fun of me?

On shaky legs, I stumbled around the room with my head down, looking for my sweatpants.

The aftermath of my orgasm left me feeling raw and vulnerable.

All the men were still in a pack without me and were able to communicate with each other.

It hadn't mattered before, but now it seemed vitally important.

Were they just using me for sex?

I found a pile of ripped clothes and awkwardly flung the tatters over my frame.

"I'm gonna go talk to Aran," I mumbled under my breath as I moved to the door.

Jax blocked my path, and he gripped my arms. "You misunderstood, little alpha."

Warm chestnuts saturated the air with musky sweetness. "It was an honor to have you beneath me, and you have nothing to be ashamed of."

He dragged his thumb over my lips and pressed a soft kiss to my forehead. "You're perfect for us, and we're going to make you ours. We just need to sit down as a group and clear the air. It's a lot to expect you to handle all of us at once." He pressed featherlight kisses across my closed eyelids. "We don't want to overwhelm you. Is that okay with you, sweetheart?"

I nodded, warmth infusing my chest as my anxiety drained from me.

Jax wrapped me in a bear hug and held me tight, pressing gentle kisses to the top of my head. "I love you," he breathed quietly in my ear.

"Love you too," I whispered as I relaxed into his warmth. "You're right," I sighed. Chestnuts really were a superior nut.

He said quietly against my hair, "You're our sweet alpha. We'll figure everything out, love. We just need to trust one another."

Cuddled against his chest, I said, "Trust has to be earned."

Jax smoothed a hand across my forehead and pressed another soft kiss there like I was a delicate flower that might break. "It will be. We're not giving you up, Sadie."

Frost nipped at my skin as Cobra stepped close to us and whispered in my ear, "Oh, and Kitten. I will tease you until I decide you're ready." He smirked down at me. "Perfection takes time."

I couldn't help the shiver that trembled through me, and I mumbled, "Don't press your luck, you psycho."

Cobra's tongue traced the shell of my ear. "You will tell me you love me too, Kitten. Or I will do things to your body that will make your time with Xerxes seem tame."

I gulped and leaned forward, cold air nipping at my exposed chest as I whispered back to Cobra, "Is that a threat or a promise?"

Cobra hissed. "Oh, Kitten, it's a fucking threat."

I squeezed my legs tighter together and tried to ignore the emerald gaze that was slowly trailing over my exposed body.

Xerxes groaned, "We need to get her proper clothes."

Ascher snapped back at him, "I still don't get why you had to bite her so many times. Sun god's tits, your fucking handprints are wrapped around her throat."

"Jealous much?" Xerxes's honeyed accent was a smooth drawl.

Cobra snarled, "She was *my* fucking kitten first. I don't care what happened here. I want to make it clear to everyone that she is *mine*."

I rolled my eyes at his petulant tone. "I'm not anyone's."

"YOU'RE MINE!" Cobra screamed and whirled around, slamming his fist against the wall.

"Don't be rude to her," Xerxes growled.

"Well, violently fucking Sadie against a wall as you took her virginity was *rude*," Ascher snarled back.

"My kitten. Give me her. Now." Cobra tugged at my arm and tried to pull me out of Jax's arms. He'd lost whatever pretenses of civility he'd pretended to have.

Jax and I sighed heavily at the same time.

I pushed out of his grip. "Moment's over, you're all drama queens, and Cobra, you're joining Aran and me in therapy."

Cobra snarled, "I'm not talking to some quack doctor about the fact that I own *my* kitten."

I clapped my hands in his face. "I'm choosing to ignore that, so I don't stab you. Also, I'm going to find Aran right now so I can talk shit about you."

"Well, I'm going to talk shit about you with Jax," Cobra taunted back.

I rolled my eyes.

"Remember that I fucking owned you first, Kitten. If you forget, you *will* pay."

What. The. Sun. God. Was wrong with him?

I curled my hands into fists and counted to ten.

It didn't work.

I roared as I shifted into a saber-toothed tiger and stalked across the room.

Cobra hissed back a laugh, jewels transforming into shadow snakes as I cornered him against the wall with my massive furry body.

Before I knew it, I wrapped my mouth around his neck, arm-long fangs grazing his flesh as I shook him back and forth like a doll.

"PUT HIM DOWN, SADIE! SHIFT BACK NOW!" Jax alpha-roared.

I dropped my prey and instinctually shifted back into my smaller form.

Suddenly, Cobra's hands were wrapped around my throat, and he choked me. He lifted me up by the neck and threw us both against the wall.

"You like this, Kitten? You want it rough?"

I kicked him in the knees and body slammed *him* into the wall.

Cobra whispered in my ear, "Don't pretend to play rough, little Kitten, because you won't be able to handle what I give you."

There was a loud smack as Jax ripped Cobra back by his hair and threw him across the room as he roared, "You better not be threatening her!"

I marched and grabbed my ridiculously tattered clothes, pulling them around me like a regal cloak.

"Please, we both know that *I* threaten *him*."

With as much dignity as a woman who had just shifted into a tiger and shaken a man in her mouth like a doll could muster—which was terrifyingly little—I marched out the door.

There was a loud crash and yells behind me, and it sounded like all four men had started to fight one another.

I rolled my eyes.

They could work through their issues without me.

Still, as I walked down the hall, happiness bubbled in my chest as I thought about Xerxes telling me he loved me, and how amazing the sex had been.

The grand window at the end of the hall showed that it was nighttime, and a storm raged outside.

I opened my bedroom door.

The room was empty and dark.

"So," a deep voice said from the dark.

I screamed with surprise.

"The slut has returned."

CHAPTER 33
SADIE
DINNER PARTIES

Aran sat in the dark, smoking a pipe.

"Um…" I trailed off, confused why she was sitting in a chair with no lights on.

She flourished the long stick between her fingers, and I wondered how much drug use warranted an intervention.

We stared at each other for a long moment.

I ruined the intensity of the moment by giggling. "It's hard work being a ho, but someone's gotta do it."

Aran bowed her head low, just like everyone did to the don. "Thank you for your service, oh impressive skanky one."

"I prefer the term *sexual deviant* or *twat*."

"Wow, it was that good?"

I let the tatters of my clothes fall to the floor and showcased the teeth marks and handprints that littered my body. The wounds were much fainter because shifting into a tiger had healed most of them, but the outlines of the bruises still lingered.

They still got the point across.

Aran choked on smoke. "Mother of the moon goddess."

"That's not even the best part." I couldn't help but brag.

"What else could there be? Were you hit by a car? Run over by a vampyre? Did a skyscraper crush your clit?"

I couldn't hold it in. "Omegas have pulsating knots on the tops of their cocks that are like the world's fastest vibrators."

Aran's jaw dropped. "No."

"Yes."

"Fuuuuuuuck, I should have gone for Xerxes."

A low alpha growl rattled in my chest. "I'll kill you."

Aran put her hands up in the air and laughed. "Joking, joking. Your men are too sweet for me."

It was my turn to gape at her. "What?"

They were all overly possessive, unhinged terrors who were the opposite of sweet.

Case in point, I'd just been violently fucked against a wall.

Aran sighed heavily and sucked in smoke, like this was something that had been troubling her for a while.

She shook her head. "I need darker men that can handle my more aggressive side."

Images of Aran trying to smother people in their sleep flashed before me.

No one could argue that she wasn't self-aware.

I nodded as I thought about it. "Oddly, I see that for you. But what man does that leave? The rumored devil himself?"

Aran waved her pipe dismissively. "Nah, I'll probably just be a spinster my whole life. Since I was raised to be a breeding tool, it's very empowering to choose celibacy."

Her mouth turned downward, and she slumped dejectedly.

I flopped onto the bed. "Hey, don't be like that. It's also

empowering to be a raging slut. Take back the power from the men, and all that good stuff. What happened to the bad bitch at the sex clinic?"

Aran flinched like I'd struck her.

Her bottom lip trembled.

Throughout everything we'd been through, I'd never seen her look so dejected as she did right now.

She dragged a shaking hand across her short hair.

It was growing out in a tumble of curls, different from her straight hair in the fae realm.

Aran saw the question in my eyes and fingered the locks. "Mother gave me an enchanted toe ring as a kid that kept my hair straight. Said my naturally unruly curls were ugly."

Aran shrugged like it was no big deal. "I took it off the other day, since it helps keep me disguised."

Such a small thing seemed so sinister.

"Aran, what happened after the sex clinic?" I asked softly, afraid of her answer.

She scoffed.

"Fucked-up stuff happened," she whispered as she inhaled smoke and the pipe trembled between her lips.

"Shit," I responded eloquently, afraid to push her too far but also to let her stew silently.

Abruptly, as if she'd made a decision, Aran stood up and threw her pipe to the ground. "I'm being a little bitch. If anyone would understand, it's you. I need to stop wallowing. Gah, it's killing me."

She stomped her foot and heaved with aggression.

I nodded slowly, unsure what was happening.

Aran grabbed the bottom of her black T-shirt, but her hands shook so hard she couldn't lift the fabric.

The room was still dark, and the shadows cast a nightmare-type quality around us.

Lightning flashed outside in the inky night, and rain battered the window.

Aran stomped her foot again and muttered expletives under her breath, then as if she was acting before she could talk herself out of it, she tugged off her shirt in one jerky movement and turned around.

The manor creaked as thunder crashed, and another bolt of lightning illuminated Aran's pale body.

It was my turn to tremble.

Enchanted blue letters glowed in the dark.

They were carved sideways into Aran's back.

Deep, jagged wounds that took up the surface of her entire back and left no doubt that some had dragged a blade roughly through her flesh.

"WHORE" was carved into her skin.

"Mother said she was inspired by your scars." Aran's voice was completely devoid of emotion.

Lightning flashed and thunder cracked in quick succession.

The manor shook.

"But she said your scars lacked finesse because any enchantment could cover them up. According to her, that 'defeated the purpose of the lesson.'"

I bit down on my tongue to stop the scream that bubbled in my throat.

"The first day she met you, she had her palace aide create a blade that would permanently mar flesh and be impervious to other enchantments."

My teeth gouged into my tongue, and I tasted blood. I whispered, "I'm so sorry. If we hadn't gone to that clinic, this—"

"No." Aran turned around and pulled her T-shirt back over her head. "Don't play the 'if only' game. That's what

Mother wants us to do. She would have always found a way to use it against me, to punish me for running away. It was just a matter of time."

Aran shrugged like it didn't matter, and smiled.

But her mouth wobbled, and her shoulders slumped.

"Still." My eyes burned, and I couldn't stop the tears that spilled over.

To have a word carved into your skin with such a hateful connotation.

It was one thing to jokingly call each other whores in an attempt to overcome the latent prejudice; it was another thing to have it carved into your skin, never to fade or be enchanted away.

I'd been so happy when the enchantment had removed the scars from my body. I'd felt so free.

Aran would never have that.

I gasped in air shakily. "I'm so sorry."

There was nothing else to say.

My best friend didn't cry, but her lip continued to tremble, and she sat down next to me.

She wrapped her arms around my shaking shoulders, and I hugged her back as tight as I could.

"I hate her so much," she muttered, her voice monotone and eyes dry as I held her and cried for both of us. "She made sure it was enchanted to burn whenever my body got the least bit turned on."

A sob wrenched from my throat.

I bunched my fingers into the cover as I fought the urge to scream.

My chest tightened with rage. "The half warriors did this. They sold you out to that monster."

Aran shrugged. "It doesn't really matter who is to blame. It's already done."

I hated how desensitized she sounded.

Aran was the brightest spirit I'd ever met. Her personality was as vibrant as her shockingly blue hair and eyes.

As she held on to me, I realized this was what she'd been silently battling these last few weeks.

It explained the constant hardness in her eyes and the homicidal impulses in her sleep.

How many times had I seen her compulsively itching at her back and dismissed it as something mundane, like a bugbite or a rash?

I'd been so ignorant.

This whole time, she'd been suffering.

We held each other as lightning cast eerie shadows across the room, and rain slammed against the side of the mansion.

"It will be all right," I lied.

"It always is," she lied back.

For the next few hours, neither of us spoke, slept, or moved. We just held each other desperately because the world wasn't a nice place.

Hours passed, and I watched Aran withdraw deeper into herself, as if sharing her trauma had made it real.

No drug was powerful enough to shield her from herself.

We all sat together at the long dining table for the first time since we'd arrived at Xerxes's mansion.

Aran sat next to me but was silent as she pushed her food around the plate.

Something had broken inside her, and I wondered if she'd ever be the same.

My stomach wouldn't stop hurting for her.

The massive chandelier twinkled above us, its expensive crystals a sharp contrast to our sweatsuits, haggard appearances, and overall shitty lots in life.

The only person who looked at home sat at the helm of the table.

Slowly cutting his steak, back ramrod straight, suit impeccably tailored, the don was the picture of refinement.

He'd sent a letter in the morning, announcing he would be joining us for dinner.

Like some high-society maiden.

I'd voted that we send a letter back saying he wasn't invited, but Jax had pointed out that he would probably still arrive and slaughter us violently.

I couldn't make myself care.

Apparently, when Hunter had slammed his foot into my ribs until I'd prayed for death, something had shifted inside me.

Maybe it was the violence.

Maybe it was the pain.

Maybe it was the postapocalyptic landscape and the voice in my head.

Maybe it was the heinous word carved into my best friend's back.

Maybe it was the sex.

Maybe it was the endless monotony of a stressful existence.

But I just couldn't make myself care.

I wasn't hungry, but I shoved three bread rolls into my mouth at once, cut a chunk of butter with my knife, then crammed it past my lips.

I chewed aggressively in the don's direction, mouth open, daring him to make a comment.

The don arched his dark eyebrow at me and smiled like he had a secret as he took a sip of his wine.

He didn't say anything.

I chewed harder.

If Walter noticed the awkward tension at the table, it didn't affect him in the slightest, and he twitted about, filling glasses and helping the maids serve our five-course meal.

His bushy mustache quivered with excitement at his getting to host a formal dinner.

None of the girls seemed to have reservations about the don—their lack of survival instincts was highly concerning—and they talked animatedly about their first day of school.

They occasionally cast worried looks in Aran's direction, but had stopped trying to talk to her when it was clear she had nothing to say.

Lucinda and Jala whispered to each other.

Since they were both more reserved and only two years apart in age, it wasn't surprising that they'd grown so close.

Jess was animatedly telling a story around the food in her mouth. "Yeah, and then the teacher asked us what the square root of three thousand was—" She took a massive bite. "—and—" She took another bite. "—answered wrong and cried."

Jess and Cobra went to grab the last bread roll, but Jess snatched it first.

Cobra hissed at her, but she just shoved it in her mouth, grinning at him, and continued her story. "Teacher did nothing. Such a bully."

"Wait, did someone bully you girls at school?" Jax put down his silverware, gray eyes flashing like slate.

Cobra's jewels transformed into shadow snakes, and he looked over at Lucinda and Jala with concern.

Xerxes brandished his knives.

An irrational response if you asked me—what was he going to do, stab schoolchildren?

"Who are we beating up?" Ascher cracked his tattooed knuckles.

Ignoring the men, I turned to my sister. "Lucinda, did the kids say or do anything to you or Jala?"

She and Jala had an air of sweet innocence about them that was honestly terrifying.

They were too trusting.

"Why do you assume we'd be the ones bullied?" Lucinda furrowed her brows. "You don't know what we can do."

"Yeah, we're not weak," Jala said with conviction, but ruined the moment by reaching over to squeeze Lucinda's hand for support.

They shifted closer together as everyone at the table stared at them.

We really needed to toughen them up.

"Hm-hmm," Jess said around the massive bite she'd been struggling to chew. She chugged water, waving her hands, and swallowed.

"You misunderstood. The teacher asked what the square root of three thousand was, and a guy said fifty-three. Jinx burst into laughter and asked him if he was 'mentally stunted and had been dropped on his head as a baby'"—she lowered her voice in a mimicry of Jinx—"'because it is obviously 54.7722557505 and only a single-celled troglodyte would think otherwise.'"

Jinx rolled her eyes and petted Noodle, who was belly-up in her arms, but didn't deny it.

"The entire class laughed, and the dude's eyes filled with tears. Then Jinx asked him if he wanted a nappy and bottle to go with his blubbering." Jess sighed heavily. "He was eighteen, and because of his bloodline, is expected to be an alpha."

"Good work." Cobra reached his hand across the table and gave Jinx a high five.

The don nodded as he cut his steak, like he agreed with Cobra's assessment.

Jax raked his hands tiredly through his braids. "Jinx, we talked about this. You can't bully your classmates."

"Don't be so dramatic. I was simply educating him on his shortcomings," Jinx said with the biting scorn that only a twelve-year-old girl could muster.

"See what I have to deal with?" Jess gestured to her small sister petting Noodle, who now had his mouth open and a blissed-out expression on his furry face.

He still had fake eyelashes on.

Jess continued, "At least this realm holds classes based on what you test, not age. We all tested into the highest classes, so I can keep an eye on her. We don't want the chemistry lab repeating itself."

"Wow, Lucinda. I didn't know you did that well in school?" I smiled at my little sister with pride.

Lucinda blushed like I was embarrassing her and said, "I can do a lot, sis."

Jala giggled.

Apparently, I was the only one at the table who struggled in an academic setting, because my answer to the square root of three thousand would have been thirty.

A sick realization hit me.

Was Jinx right?

Am I an idiot?

Jinx took a delicate bite of asparagus. "If a person can't defuse a small chemical explosion, then they shouldn't be allowed in a chemistry lab. I stand by that."

"You blew up the room, and one student *died*," Jess said with rising frustration.

"Wrong. The blast didn't kill him. He died from third-degree burns," Jinx said in a "duh" tone. "That was his own fault. He wouldn't have survived the cold shifter realm anyway. I did him a favor."

Jess scowled down at her much smaller sister, her copper-toned skin flushing as she gripped her fork like a weapon. "Wait, Jinx, someone died? You never told me that."

A low rumble escaped from Jax's throat as he also glared at his sister.

Jinx gritted her teeth. "I didn't need to, because he died from the burns. Not the blast."

Cobra nodded. "You can't fault her. If the blast didn't kill him, it clearly wasn't her fault. Lay off. How old were you when it happened?"

"Eight," Jinx said.

Cobra pointed his knife like he'd proven a point. "See, she was just a child. Give her a break. When I was that age, my snake accidentally ate a family of four."

"What?" Jax, Ascher, and I said at the same time.

Xerxes didn't even blink, just kept eating like Cobra's statement didn't surprise or concern him.

Aran was silent, pushing her steak back and forth like nothing anyone said mattered.

Ascher looked down at her with a frown.

"Exactly. It happens," Jinx said to Cobra, and the corner of her mouth pulled up into what almost appeared to be a slight grin.

For her, that was the equivalent of a beaming smile.

I took it back; the don was not the only person who looked at home in the elegant mansion.

Jinx's posture was perfect, long black hair lying in a silky sheath down to her waist. With too-pale skin and massive dark eyes, she looked more like a caricature of a doll than a flesh-and-blood person.

Jinx arched her dark eyebrow as she caught me staring.

I quickly looked away.

Actually, maybe I wasn't completely dead inside, because she terrified me.

"I'm sorry, son, that I wasn't there to help you." The don spoke for the first time, and his perfect posture broke as his shoulders hunched with something that resembled despair.

He stared across the table at Cobra with tired eyes. At that moment, the terrifying Mafia leader looked almost...weak.

Cobra shrugged and said nothing.

The table fell silent as everyone processed that both Jinx and Cobra had committed *murder* at eight years old, and that they thought they were in the right.

"My visit is not purely of the social nature," the don broke the silence as he cut his steak.

If he told us we were getting tortured again, I was shoving a bread roll up his ass.

"The third trial begins now," the don said casually.

CHAPTER 34
SADIE
DON'S ORDERS

Before anyone could blink, I shoved my chair over, hit the ground, and rolled under the table for protection with my steak knife between my teeth.

I crouched low, waiting for the gunfire to erupt.

"Um, Sadie," Lucinda called, and I ignored her.

She was so innocent.

I waited.

The danger came, but it wasn't in the form I suspected. Cobra's jeweled fingers reached under the table and grabbed the bulge in Jax's sweatpants.

Jax jerked with surprise and slammed his booted foot upward, right into my face.

I yelped in surprise, slamming my head on the underside of the table.

Moaning in agony, I was too stunned to fight the tattooed fingers that grabbed my shoulders and hauled me back into my seat.

Ascher patted my head condescendingly. "Poor princess."

"Sorry. Are you okay?" Jax asked as he reached across the table.

I smacked his hand away.

Cobra smirked knowingly, a satisfied expression on his gorgeous face.

"Pervert." I scowled at him.

Cobra's shoulders shook as he chuckled. "Very impressive hiding spot, my kitten. Please, tell me, what was your plan? Just crouch under there as we were all slaughtered in a hail of bullets?"

My face burned, but I refused to be ashamed. "Every man for himself."

"How positively bloodthirsty." He tsked. "I'm hurt."

From the way his shoulders still shook with laughter, it was clear he was *not* hurt.

He pointed at Lucinda and gasped for air like it was hilarious. "You even abandoned the girls."

"I knew he wouldn't hurt them," I snapped, rolling my eyes at his dramatics.

He kept laughing.

"Whatever." I dabbed my napkin demurely on my lips like a proper lady and addressed the don. "So I take it you're not going to kill me in a hail of gunfire?"

The don said dryly, "I hadn't planned to. At least, not yet."

I narrowed my eyes, trying to figure out if he was making a joke or threatening me.

Cobra hissed, his entire demeanor changing in a blink. "Hurt her, Father, and it will be the last thing you do."

The don arched his brow at his son.

"Need I remind you that she is not, and cannot, be a member of your pack? Or have you forgotten?" His "Loyalty" tattoo rippled on his neck as he spoke.

"Oh, I don't need reminding." Cobra had snake eyes, and his shadow snakes writhed across his pale flesh.

The don waved his hand and kept speaking like he hadn't just caused the entire table to seize with tension at the reminder of their pack status and my lack of inclusion.

"To complete the third trial, you must each capture someone on the city's most-wanted list and present them at the Equinox Ball."

"Dead or alive?" Xerxes asked.

The don's voice hardened. "They must be brought in alive."

The white snake that had been wrapped casually around his neck began to hiss and slither in a circle.

Any softness disappeared.

"But, after your impressive performances in the second trial, I thought I'd offer an olive branch of sorts. I know you are new to this realm and are not as familiar with the city. So I have come here to recommend that you focus on bringing in the independent Ortega brothers. There are five of them, one for each of you."

He pulled an envelope with a red wax seal out of his suit pocket and placed it on the table.

"All the information about their illicit activities, and coordinates for their suspected locations, are in here."

No one reached for the letter.

"A reminder that alphas are not given weapons or allowed to shift until after the trials. So you must use your other skills."

He looked at me when he said "other skills," and my chest clenched.

Did he know about my blood powers? Why was he looking at me?

Under the table, Aran grabbed my hand and squeezed it.

Both our hands trembled.

Shit. If Aran had also picked up on the don's look, then maybe he did know?

A tension headache began to throb in the front of my skull.

The don dabbed his napkin across his lips and stood gracefully. "Thank you for hosting me. I am always here for you, if you need me."

The don walked away but turned around as if he remembered something. "I will have formal wear sent to the house for the ball." He paused.

My stomach dropped at his expression; it was the one every person made before they delivered awful news.

"The Equinox Ball is in two days. You only have tomorrow night to complete the trial. Do not fail."

We had one day to complete the trial.

My stomach dropped.

Ascher swore.

Everyone at the table shifted uncomfortably as they realized how fucked we were.

The don paused as if he was struggling to find words.

Finally, he said quietly, "Be careful, my son. This realm is crueler than you can even imagine."

With those uplifting words of encouragement, he left.

There was a long moment, then Jax warily picked up the envelope. He broke the seal and read the cursive script.

"What does it say?" Ascher asked impatiently, as Jax stayed silent.

Cobra leaned over Jax's shoulder and paled.

Slowly, Jax smoothed out the paper. "The Ortega pack

are wolf shifters and are suspected to have ties to the Black Wolves."

Xerxes's silverware clattered against his fine china plate.

Alpha scents thickened with warning.

Cobra hissed and looked over at the omega, who was sitting still as a statue. Ascher banged his tattooed fists against the table, and glasses sloshed.

Clarissa's warning rang through my head.

Xerxes must have told the men about the Black Wolves, or maybe they'd figured it out because of the bond.

None of the girls said anything, but they sank lower in their chairs like they could feel the shift in the energy and knew something bad was happening.

"He knew," Jax said. "The Ortega pack is a front that will allow us to handle the wolves."

"Why not just tell us to bring them in for our third trial?" I asked.

"Because you have to bring the captures to the ball alive," Cobra said, "and we won't be leaving them alive."

Jax nodded in agreement. "There's more. It says the Ortega brothers run something called a black ribbon club and that we will have to blend in to infiltrate it."

Xerxes swore at the name.

Everyone turned to him expectantly; he was the only one familiar with the realm.

He blew out air and glanced at the girls. "It's a—" He sputtered like he couldn't find the right words. "—dark club."

"What do you mean?" I asked.

Xerxes's cheeks tinged pink. He rubbed at the bite marks I'd left across his neck, and he whispered, "I believe you'd know it as a BDSM club."

Ascher choked on his wine.

Xerxes didn't look anyone in the eyes as he spoke. "They're very popular in Serpentine City. Most are Mafia controlled, but there are a few seedier, illegal establishments."

Jax glanced at his sisters and tried to deflect. "Well, the letter says it's believed to be a front for the real underground club where the Ortega brothers can be found. We should check it out tomorrow."

"We'll need to go shopping first for appropriate clothes. The club will only be open at night, and we have to pull all this off tomorrow night." Xerxes didn't look at anyone.

"What does BDSM stand for?" Lucinda asked.

Ascher choked again and sputtered wine everywhere.

I debated crawling under the table, and my face burned as I said, "Well, it's hard to explain. But when two people are in a trusting relationship, and love each other very muc—"

"Bondage, discipline, dominance, submission, sadism, and masochism," Jinx said. "Technically, the proper acronym is BDDSSM."

"What are you binding?" Jala asked as Lucinda scrunched her face in confusion.

"Jinx," Jax growled threateningly.

Cobra put his fist in his mouth as his shoulders shook with silent laughter.

"Another person, usually a naked one, during rough penetrative sex," Jinx said casually as she cut her steak into tiny pieces.

Cobra lost his silent battle and burst out laughing.

"You learn something new each day," Jess said with amazement.

Lucinda brought her hand to her mouth in shock, and Jala's pink eyes were large as saucers.

Jax pressed his palms into his eyes and muttered something about sisters being the death of him and sending Jinx off to an intensive military school.

I shuddered at the thought of Jinx with combat skills.

"Where did you learn that?" Ascher asked the twelve-year-old, while Xerxes looked at his blades like he was debating stabbing himself through his skull.

Jinx shrugged. "I've been places."

"Excuse me." Jax growled, "What *places* have you been, when you're twelve years old?"

"You know. Places." Jinx took a delicate bite and sipped from her crystal glass.

Aran was still silent beside me, pushing her uneaten food back and forth, not reacting at all to the wild twelve-year-old spouting sex facts.

Her shoulders hunched lower as she itched mindlessly at her back.

Fuck.

Her itching made me nauseous because it was a reminder that she could never have sex without pain.

I gripped my steak knife tighter and wished I'd tortured the queen longer with my blood and made her hurt herself like she'd hurt Aran.

A loud banging noise and the sounds of Walter talking to someone in the foyer interrupted my dark thoughts.

Everyone fell silent at the butler's uncharacteristically agitated voice.

It felt like my bleak mood had summoned danger.

"I'm going to check it out. Stay here," Xerxes ordered as he stalked out of the room.

Xerxes's voice was muffled, and a few minutes later, he returned to the dining room, with Walter trailing.

His olive skin was unnaturally pale, and he raked his fingers across his stubble like he was frustrated.

In his hand, he clenched a bright-red piece of paper with words on it.

Xerxes looked at Aran, and the nausea in my stomach turned into razor blades.

I tapped my foot with concern as my intuition screamed at me that what he was about to say wasn't good.

Everyone stared at him expectantly.

"The High Court has delivered flyers to every residence in Serpentine City," Xerxes said as he held the paper up.

My heart pounded so hard that my chest hurt.

He read, "A ruler from another realm is being held hostage in this city. They must be returned to the High Court's embassy on Fifth Street. Emergency summons have been put in place in the city. Summon us by speaking the number of our street in Latin."

Xerxes took a deep breath.

My stomach dropped out from beneath me, as I knew what he was going to say before he did.

"It is the rightful Queen of the Fae Realm." He paused and said quietly, "Arabella Alis Egan."

Aran didn't flinch, just calmly piled her mashed potatoes into a small mountain.

Xerxes kept reading, "A woman covered in scars who is suspected of being a half-breed is expected to have kidnapped her. Contact the High Court if you have information."

Tension was a tangible weight, and my head spun with relief that my enchanted ring concealed my scars, and terror for my friend.

Everyone waited for Aran to break down or say something.

When she finally spoke, it was just to say, “I don’t have a middle name. They should fix that.”

She was too beat down to even care.

Once again, we were fucked.

CHAPTER 35
SADIE
SHOPPING

"UM, THERE'S BEEN A MISTAKE," I said as I peeked my head out of the dressing room.

Xerxes had taken us to the "shopping district" of the city, which was one massive skyscraper.

The central part of the building was hollowed out, and a glass elevator went up and down continuously.

On all sides, going 120 floors into the sky, were shops for clothes, the home, and everything else a person could think of.

It was a far cry from the small businesses in the shifter realm.

I didn't even know it was possible for so much stuff to exist.

"No, there hasn't," Aran said tiredly as she tapped her foot outside the changing room.

After the flyer got delivered yesterday, she'd sat in the corner of the room, in the dark, with a pipe in her mouth.

She wouldn't come to bed or talk to me.

I'd forced her to come along on the trip, knowing she loved shopping.

She'd pointed out that I was risking getting executed and she was risking being forced to rule a bloodthirsty realm, all so we could pick out clothes for a BDSM club.

I'd told her it was worth the risk.

I was pretty sure she'd only agreed to the trip because she was low-key hoping we'd be attacked and she'd have a reason to fight people.

Sadly for her, she was still enchanted as a boy and the High Court had released a picture of her looking very girly and different with pin-straight hair.

But she still wore a baseball cap and sunglasses to hide her curly blue hair and bright-blue eyes.

Odds were basically zero that she'd be recognized.

As long as her disguise held, we were safe.

I called out from the changing room, "No, there definitely has been a mistake. I don't understand how they made it so the straps cover everything but my boobs and vagina. How does that make any sense?"

I quickly pulled back the curtain to flash her my outfit.

The black material crisscrossed in straps starting at my ankles and climbing up to cover my throat.

Aran was in the throes of a deep depression, but my getup still made her jolt with surprise.

Cobra, who was walking past at that exact moment, tripped and slammed his face into the wall.

"Buy that. Immediately," he croaked.

Aran rolled her eyes and pulled her other choices off the hanger. "Try this." It was a gossamer white fabric that had fluffy feathers and sparkles across the boobs and sleeves.

I pulled it on and gasped.

The white contrasted with my gold skin and made my hair shine like pearls.

The feathers were fluffy and feminine, and the fabric

showed my body when I moved, but I didn't feel completely naked like in the other outfit.

"You're a genius," I said to Aran as I opened up the curtain.

"I know, I'm a great shopper," Aran said, but her voice was strained and her smile didn't reach her eyes.

What was a surprise was that all four of the men, who were supposed to be finding their own clothes, stood behind Aran.

"Princess." Ascher groaned and shoved his tattooed fist into his mouth.

"Oh fuck, baby girl," Xerxes muttered.

"Love," Jax breathed out roughly, eyes wide as he admired me.

"I told you guys," Cobra said to the men as his eyes darkened. "Although, Kitten, I personally prefer the last one."

"Noted." I tapped my mouth like I was considering it. "Don't care."

I shut the curtain with a snap.

When I'd settled on getting the nightie in white, I walked to check out.

However, I glanced at the tag and nearly passed out.

It was ten thousand credits, and the symbol next to it was the same money symbol used in the shifter realm.

Ten thousand credits was the cost of a large house, and about what Jax said they had paid us for each battle in the shifter realm.

"Aran, did you see the price?" I showed her the tag.

She shrugged. "So?"

"Wow, very royal of you."

The despondent expression was still pasted on her face as she explained, "Sadie, the mannequins in the store are all covered in jewels, and there are real crystals in those feathers. The material is butterfly silk, which is the most expensive fabric in the realms. What did you expect?"

"I'd set my budget at fifty credits," I said sadly as the butterfly silk sparkled in between my fingers.

"I don't know if you want me to act like I relate to you right now, but I don't speak poor-unfashionable-person language. Sorry."

My spirits lifted. If Aran was feeling well enough to joke, then maybe she was back to her old self.

I chuckled, but Aran's face didn't twitch.

"Oh my sun god, you're not joking."

She grabbed a leather strip off the wall that was covered in skulls and started to wrap it aggressively around her throat.

It dawned on me what she was doing, and I slapped her hands, pulling it off her. "Really, in a public store?"

"Better than being queen of the *fucking fae*," she snarled and pouted as I held the leather strap away from her.

"Shut up," I whispered furiously. "Someone will hear you and take you back."

"Kinky, Sadie." Ascher walked by and grabbed the strap. "Didn't know you were into props."

Before I could explain the situation, Aran chimed in, "She also wanted that ball gag," and pointed to the most terrifying-looking device I'd ever seen in my life.

Ascher smirked and added it to his pile of toys. "I like the way you think."

"I'm going to stab you," I whispered aggressively at Aran as two very tall beta women, with hair down to the floor, sashayed by.

They had black whips in their hands and an assortment of revealing clothes.

"Why haven't you come up to check out?" Xerxes asked as he walked over.

He must have found clothes, because he had a sparkly black bag on his arm.

Xerxes wore a baseball cap and had sprayed some type of enchanted mist that temporarily masked his cinnamon scent.

"I need to find new clothes. Can you believe this?" I shook my head and showed him the price tags.

His purple eyes crinkled with confusion. "Do you need a different size? I can ask."

"Yeah, it's not gonna fit her muscles," Aran said sarcastically.

"Now you're just being mean. See if I stop you from strangling yourself next time."

Xerxes looked back and forth between us with confusion.

Aran rolled her eyes like she didn't care and chewed at her fingernails.

"No, the price, Xerxes. Can you believe this? It's robbery!" I showed him again.

Xerxes shifted back and forth awkwardly. "I don't get it."

"See, Sadie, you're just being dramatic. Stop being poor," Aran said as she looked around warily, like she'd just noticed that she was exposed in a public place.

I had a sick realization. "If you ever rule, you're going to be a bloody dictator, aren't you."

"One could fucking hope." Aran itched at her back and walked away like she was bored with the conversation.

Xerxes cleared his throat and said softly, "Baby girl, you're not buying this." He took the hanger out of my hand

and gave me an intense expression that made my stomach flip.

"I know. I just need to find a different store."

He stared at me for a long moment.

Ever since the "heat incident," where I'd accidentally come on his vibrating dick a dozen times, Xerxes had been looking at me with a dark expression.

I love you hung in the air between us like a tangible weight.

I breathed shakily, unsure how he could make me feel so on edge just by staring at me.

Xerxes turned around, but instead of handing the items back to the lady who worked for the store—she was modeling one of outfits that had cutouts around the boobs and lady bits, which was truly inspirational—he walked to the counter.

"You're back, Sir Xerxes. Did you find everything you wanted today?" the beta sales lady asked sweetly, leaning forward to showcase her exposed boobs.

"No," I said quickly and lunged for the overly expensive nightie in his hand.

Xerxes shoved me aside with one hand and sent me sprawling across the floor.

"What she meant is I'd also like to buy this in the emerald-green color," Xerxes said.

Why would he get two of them?

We only had one day to complete the third trial.

"Of course, sir. You have great taste." She giggled, completely ignoring the fact that he'd just manhandled me. "Do you want to pay again by fingerprint?"

I launched myself at him, but he expected my move and grabbed me by my ponytail.

Xerxes yanked my head back till I yelped.

"Be good, baby girl," he murmured into my ear as he restrained me.

Then he turned back to the worker and nodded casually, like he wasn't manhandling me, and pressed his hand on the shimmering black stone.

Apparently, the payment system worked throughout all the realms and was enchanted to connect a person to the amount of credits to their name.

Jax had explained that money in the shifter realm worked in the beast realm through this credit system.

My mind was still blown.

Seemed suspect.

"Oh, look, sir, since you've spent seventy thousand credits today, you qualify for a free toy."

I choked. "Wow, what a bargain."

"I'll take the sex knife." Xerxes smirked and picked up a small, glittering blade that was encrusted in rhinestones and glowing with a blue enchantment.

My mind had stalled at the words *sex knife*, so I almost didn't process that the cashier was writing down her address on the receipt.

"I'd love to play with you, sir." She gave him a coy look and walked around the counter.

She swiveled her hips suggestively, showcasing her crotchless panties.

My stomach twisted with an unnamed emotion, and I suddenly had the urge to shift into a saber-toothed tiger and pop her head like a grape.

Xerxes arched his brow down at me, and I realized I'd been making a low growling noise.

He didn't stop staring at me as he said, "No, I'm taken. I already have an alpha."

Then he took his bags and dragged me by the ponytail

out of the store as I glared back at the lady and told her with my narrowed eyes that I would destroy her if she ever came near Xerxes again.

We all piled into the massive glass elevator, and it dropped with a whiz. Our feet lifted off the floor.

"So, are you going to visit her?" I asked casually, knowing he'd said no, but still needing to be reassured.

Xerxes, with his hand wrapped around my ponytail, gave it another yank. "Hm, maybe."

A growl ripped from my throat. "Do it and it will be the last thing you do."

We came to a stop, everyone's feet slamming back onto the ground, and Xerxes released my ponytail only to grab my throat in a choke hold.

Cobra chuckled. "Oooh, Kitten pissed off the omega."

Xerxes pushed me forward aggressively, so I had to walk backward not to fall over.

Shifters walked around us and didn't pay us any attention.

What kind of sick place was this realm, where a woman being yanked around by her hair didn't even merit a second glance?

Xerxes walked me backward until I slammed against a pillar.

"Stop shoving me against things." I kicked at his shins as hard as I could.

"I thought you didn't want to commit to our pack?" Xerxes arched his eyebrows, purple eyes blazing. "Was I wrong?"

"That's not exactly what happened." I kicked harder, but he didn't release me. His muscles didn't budge, so I turned to the other men. "You're seriously going to just stand there as he chokes me in public?"

I made my lower lip tremble and widened my eyes like I was sad.

Cobra sniffed the air and smirked down at me. "I'm tempted to touch your cunt to see if you're as wet as you smell."

Ugh. I rolled my eyes. "Why're you actually a pervert?"

"Kitten, I'd fuck you right here in front of everyone, and I wouldn't even blink. I'd take you so hard you screamed my name."

I ignored the way my core heated at his words.

Cobra was a lost cause, so I turned away from him and focused on looking pitifully at Ascher and Jax.

Xerxes's fingers tightened like he couldn't help himself.

Ascher ran his tattooed fingers across his horns and sighed. "I'm sorry, Princess, but I have to agree with him. You were the one who said you wouldn't join the pack. What's your answer? Either you want us or you don't."

Of all the times for the men to decide for us to have this conversation.

Cobra inched closer and flicked his finger over my nipple, and I jackknifed my foot into his balls as hard as I could.

He smiled like I'd kissed him.

My breath caught as worry flashed through me when he leaned into my personal space. Was he really going to touch me in a public place?

Hundreds of shifters milled around us.

Jax pulled Cobra back and put him in a headlock. "Not in public." He growled at him.

"Why not?" Cobra stared at me and licked his lips.

Xerxes's fingers tightened until I could barely breathe. Was he trying to kill me or turn me on?

I couldn't tell. And weirdly, I didn't want to know.

"Jax, save me," I said desperately as I clawed at Xerxes's hand.

"Xerxes, let her go." Jax reached forward and used his massive size to constrain both Ascher and Xerxes.

I sighed with relief as oxygen flooded back into my brain.

Ascher wrapped his arm around me in support, and I slapped him away.

He was still a traitor.

"Well, that was exhilarating." Aran stood to the side, hunched over as she itched aggressively at her back.

"You didn't do anything to help me!" I said.

"First, you act all embarrassing and poor, and now this. Don't be a drama queen," she mumbled but didn't look at me. She was too busy itching at her back.

Her obvious distress freaked me out.

"We're not leaving until we find some type of healing ointment for…" I trailed off because Aran was miming stabbing me in my peripheral vision. "For me. Sometimes my bruises itch."

"Kitten is hurt." Cobra's eyes blazed.

"Baby girl, why didn't you say something?" Xerxes growled.

Thus began a small excursion, where the men panicked that I was falling apart and they hadn't noticed.

Which was highly ironic because they'd just been publicly choking me.

Their irrational concern over my well-being had its benefits.

Case in point, we finally left the mall with five different creams for itchiness.

One of which was labeled a miracle cure, with a price tag that I was pretty sure was over one hundred thousand credits, but Xerxes had taken it out of my hand and bought it before I could say anything.

Ascher was the only one who wasn't completely brain-dead.

He kept looking between Aran and me like he knew exactly what we were doing.

At one point, he pulled Aran aside and asked if she was okay, his handsome face twisted with guilt and concern.

Since Aran had responded by hunching lower and biting her nails more aggressively, the worry hadn't left his face.

It made me feel better to know I wasn't the only one concerned about her.

When we finally returned to the mansion, we still had a few hours until nightfall.

I followed Aran up the stairs, looking forward to a long nap.

But stopped with surprise.

The girls had made a makeshift track out of toilet paper down the length of the hall and were screaming as Noodle raced against a hamster.

I decided it was not my business where the hamster had come from.

When Lucinda yelled something about Jinx owing her ten credits because Noodle ran off the course and the hamster won, I ignored it.

Frankly, the girls developing a gambling problem was the least of my concerns.

However, my nap plans were interrupted by the scent of warm chestnuts, and a sheepish-looking Jax tapping me on my shoulder. "We need to come up with a plan."

Aran took her ridiculously expensive creams out of my hand and closed the door.

I opened the door and pulled her back out. "This is a

battle, and we only have one day to get it right. You're a battle strategizer. You're coming with me."

Aran bit harder at her nails but allowed me to pull her along as she said, "If you're too scared to face the men alone, just say that."

"Really?" I said with conviction, "I thought you knew me better than that. I'm not a coward."

She rolled her eyes but didn't comment. She didn't need to.

We both knew I was full of shit.

CHAPTER 36
SADIE
PUPPETS ON A STRING

We sat around the roaring fireplace in the great room.

Well, everyone faced the fire except for Aran, who sat with her back to the fire and a hoodie pulled over her head.

I'd asked Walter to turn it off, but Aran had snapped at me that she didn't need to be babied and was fine.

Her face was pale, and her blue curls stuck out of her hood in every direction.

She wasn't fine.

None of us were.

The fact that we had only tonight to capture the Ortega brothers and eliminate the Black Wolves was a tangible noose above our necks.

Now, after an hour of fruitless brainstorming—while the girls screamed upstairs like they were participating in their own fight club—we were no closer to a plan that sounded effective and feasible.

The whole not being able to shift in this realm, not having weapons, and having to get the attention of what sounded like masochist BDSM-prone alphas with a sex problem seemed impossible.

Cobra said for the millionth time, “I don’t understand why I can’t just use my snake venom to take them out.”

Jax snapped, “We’ve been over this. We’re not risking you getting killed because you shifted in front of people.”

“Technically, it’s not shifting,” Cobra argued back.

“Stop with the semantics.” Jax’s chest rattled with a roar. “No one’s going to care about the technicalities when there’s an enchanted bullet in your brain.”

“Jax’s right,” I said as Xerxes and Ascher nodded in agreement.

I sipped the hot coffee from my cup, which glowed blue with an enchantment that kept the liquid warm.

A sudden thought struck me. “Wait, how is everything in this realm enchanted? I thought it was a fae thing.”

Aran waved her hands dismissively. “Common misconception. A person ‘pure of soul’ who is particularly powerful burns a part of their flesh as a sacrifice to the sun god or moon goddess, and then the gods allow them to channel their will into an object. So any species can create an enchantment.”

I had the sudden urge to fling my coffee cup out of my hand. “That’s fucked up.”

Xerxes shrugged. “In this realm, the entire industry is run by one reclusive family. No one knows how they keep themselves pure, but it’s an extremely difficult endeavor.”

“Yeah, Mother had a man trapped in a palace room. He gave the flesh sacrifice. There was a separate palace department that came up with the uses.” Aran shuddered like she’d been overcome by a phantom chill.

I opened my mouth to ask a million more questions, but I remembered Aran saying she’d helped create enchantments.

From the sadness in her eyes, it hadn’t just been for fun.

"Back to the problem at hand," Ascher said. "How the fuck are we supposed to catch the attention of the Ortega brothers, somehow get information on the Black Wolves, destroy the latter, and capture the former? All tonight at a BDSM club?"

He raked his hands through his horns and slumped back in his chair.

We were doomed.

Jax dragged his hands over his face tiredly.

"*Kill him*!" Jinx screamed from the floor above, and then there was a loud crashing noise that sounded like a chandelier had shattered.

Walter was a blur of gray as he sprinted past the room.

None of us moved, but the anxiety in the room increased in intensity at the reminder that it wasn't just our lives at risk if we failed at the third initiation task.

The girls would be alone in an unfamiliar world.

I dug my palms into my eyes. "Well, there's only one option for the first part of the plan. We get the Ortega brothers' attention by standing out in the club."

Everyone stared at me.

"Sexually." I grimaced.

Jax asked tiredly, "Sadie, how are we supposed to stand out in a club full of experienced BDSM players?"

"We could figure it out," Xerxes said slowly as he thought about it. "It really is our only option."

Cobra smirked, "I'm down."

Ascher ran his hands roughly over his horns. "So you're all fine with wax play? Whips? Floggings? Knife play? While a room full of strangers watches us? It's fucking not that simple."

I glanced over at Xerxes, who had a smirk on his lips. "I may have some experience with knife play."

The men turned to him in shock.

Memories of his savagery in the bedroom made me shiver. I was not surprised.

Xerxes said with conviction, "It's the only thing that makes sense. We have one night to pull this off. We don't really have any other choice."

"He's right. We can do this," I agreed.

Jax arched his brow like he didn't believe me, but no one refuted the plan.

No one had a better idea.

"Say we catch the Ortega brothers' attention," Jax replied. "Then what are we supposed to do? They'll have weapons and aren't just going to give up the Black Wolves."

Aran sat up straighter and waved her hand. "Oh, that part's easy. It's pretty obvious what you need to do."

Everyone stared at her.

She narrowed her eyes when she realized it wasn't obvious to everyone else, then sighed heavily.

"You'll have to pretend to be disappointed with Xerxes. And tell the Ortega brothers you want to give him back to the Black Wolves. Then once they lead you to them, Sadie infects the brothers with her blood and holds them hostage. To take out the wolves, Xerxes will have the element of surprise and he has the best chance of slitting their throats with the sex knife before they realize it's a trap."

There was a long pause as her plan sank in.

"Fuck, that might work." Ascher smiled down at Aran, who avoided eye contact and bit harder on her nails.

"I like it." Cobra's jewels flashed to snakes like he was imagining the carnage.

Jax shrugged. "I don't have a better idea. I say we go for it."

The three alphas nodded, clearly relieved that we had

some type of game plan and there was some hope we would survive this.

"We can't," I said as my stomach hurt thinking about it. "We can't do that to Xerxes."

Xerxes had been sitting as still as a statue the entire time.

But I knew him enough to notice that his fingers gripped the hilts of his knives too tightly.

I remembered the horror on his face when he was worried he'd bitten me too hard.

How he'd trembled to hold himself back, terrified of driving me away with his intensity.

The shame etched onto his face.

Rage bubbled in my throat.

The fucking Black Wolves hadn't just hurt him physically. Emotional scars went deep.

With flames casting shadows across his almost too-pretty features, long blond hair flowing around his waist, Xerxes's purple eyes hardened into chips of amethyst. "I can do it."

I said quietly, "You shouldn't have to. It's not fair to you."

He clenched his jaw. "Life isn't fair."

Cobra hissed, "We will do thissss to destroy the cowardssss that hurt him. We will tear them limb from limb and sssshow them what happenssss when you hurt our pack."

Xerxes looked over at Cobra, his lips parting slightly, like he hadn't expected him to care so much about his well-being.

Xerxes looked away. "You don't need to do this for my sake. We can just take out the Ortega brothers and ignore the wolves. I don't expect everyone to put themselves in danger for me. I know the circumstances of our pack were forced."

Cobra hissed, and Ascher's horns expanded.

It was Jax who laid a hand on Xerxes's shoulder. "It doesn't matter how it came to be. We are a pack, and you are one of us now. We look out for each other."

Ascher shifted uncomfortably. "Besides my idiocy in the past, what Jax says is true. We're a pack, and you're our omega. I wouldn't want to stand beside anyone else."

Cobra nodded. "From what we've learned, omegas are usually weak, simpering fools who can't defend themselves from harm." He shivered, like the thought disgusted him. "You're the only omega I'd want in our pack."

Panic bubbled in my throat at the reminder that the don still expected them to find a female omega.

Xerxes stared at the alphas, a sheen across his eyes, and when he spoke, his smooth voice was uncharacteristically rough. "I wouldn't want any other alphas." He paused. "Besides Sadie, of course."

I waved my hand dismissively. "Don't let me ruin the moment. And seriously, Xerxes, you belong with us—them, I mean. Anyone can see it."

"Kitten's right," Cobra confirmed as he leaned over and slammed his fist into Xerxes's arm.

From anyone else, it would have looked like Cobra was attacking Xerxes.

At the contact, a massive grin split Xerxes's face, and he slammed his fist back into Cobra's bicep. "You're not so bad, for an alpha."

Ascher chuckled. "Just give it a year. You'll want to kill him."

Jax wrapped his arm around Cobra's neck and ruffled his dark hair. "He's an acquired taste. Like whiskey."

Cobra's canines lengthened, and he bit down on Jax's forearm.

Jax didn't flinch.

"He's definitely vodka," I said, thinking about how Cobra's alpha scent resembled frostbite.

"How very touching," Aran said dryly as she chewed her nails. "The only problem with the plan is the Black Wolves themselves. We don't know what they know, and they could have a contingency plan, or be expecting us."

I looked at her in confusion. "How would they have a plan when we just decided to try to get to them? We weren't even going to go after them until the don gave us a hint."

Ascher shook his head. "I think your plan is sound, Aran. You don't need to worry."

Jax and Cobra nodded in agreement.

Xerxes stayed silent. He seemed to be reeling from the alphas' admission that they viewed him as their omega.

Aran stood and said she was going to bed.

As she walked by, she muttered something under her breath about attending our funerals.

In her absence, the flames in the fireplace cracked and popped louder, reaching new heights.

Like her presence had been stifling them.

My gut twisted as, once again, a sense of déjà vu washed over me.

Like something was so obvious, but it was just outside my fingertips.

The men formulated the specifics of the plan, how we would treat Xerxes, and what toys we should use.

How we should interact with the people in the club to convince them we belonged there.

Xerxes warned about how dark the beast realm could be and how people expected violence.

Ascher gave tips. Apparently, he had his own experience with BDSM.

Cobra and Jax strategized the quickest way to kill the wolves.

The room spun around me.

"I'm scared," I blurted out before I could stop myself.

My face burned with embarrassment as I picked at the threads of the blanket draped across my lap.

No one laughed.

Callused, tattooed fingers twined around mine.

Ascher leaned over the edge of the couch and held my hand, his amber eyes burning with sincerity. "Me too, Princess."

His openness made me want to be honest.

My voice cracked. "It still scares me, but I wish I would have been allowed to form a pack with you guys."

The only sound was the cracking of logs in the fire.

The silence was heavy.

Ascher's hand tightened around mine. "Every day, I feel like shit for turning everyone over to the fae queen. Everything is my fault. Now Aran's falling apart, and we can't be with you without risking your life. I ruin everything."

I squeezed his hand back as I struggled to find the appropriate words.

"But then I wouldn't be your omega," Xerxes said quietly from across the room, "and I'd still be hiding from myself and following the orders of a madwoman."

Ascher stared across the room at Xerxes, like he'd just taken a weight off his shoulders.

Intensity swirled among us.

Secrets begetting more secrets, as if they longed for company.

Jax spoke quietly, "I'm scared every day that I'm going

to fail my sisters and all of you. I've been alone for so many years, and now I have so much to lose. It feels like I'm just waiting for everything to be taken from me. Now that there're so many reasons to fight, I don't think I'm as strong as I thought I was."

A log popped in the fire.

The crystal chandelier above our head tinkled as the girls sprinted down the hall. It swayed back and forth.

Their laughter was far away.

"I know I can be an unhinged bastard most of the time, and I don't handle things well," Cobra said softly as he looked over at me.

Memories of him being so sweet sometimes and so cruel other times drifted between us like a live wire.

I gave him a sad smile and a small shrug.

With my eyes, I told him—*I understand you don't shift into a beast form, that you're always a beast.*

I get it.

His behavior wasn't always appropriate, but who was I to judge anyone, when half the time I was a hot mess?

Did I wish Cobra was an easy, nice man like the ones in the romance books I'd grown up reading? Yes.

Did I understand Cobra would never be like everyone else and would probably drive me up a wall with his mood swings for the rest of his life? Also, yes.

Emerald eyes darkened as he understood what I was saying.

There was a long pause as Cobra breathed shakily, like my silent acceptance had given him courage.

"I wasn't always covered in jewels," he said quietly. "I don't remember anything before the fae queen took me, but as a child, I always had a black snake around my neck. Like how the don wears his."

The chandelier rocked quicker, crystals clacking.

Cobra gripped the arm of the couch. "The fae queen never hid that I'd been kidnapped. She told me that her informants had taken me because they had it on good authority that I would be an alpha shifter, and since the half warriors were such a hit, she wanted to try a beast gladiator." He breathed deeply.

"She thought my snake was a pet, so she would set it on fire, cut it, and hurt it to get me to obey her. Not knowing she was really just torturing me."

Coffee burned my tongue.

"She wouldn't stop hurting it, and I was so young and scared. One day, she wanted me to stab another child during training, but I refused because at the time, I hated violence. I'd lost control of my snake a few times, and it was awful. I was terrified of hurting others."

He shuddered.

"She cut the tail off the end of my snake to make me obey." Cobra's voice changed, like he'd lost himself in the past. "I was only eight, and I thought I was going to die. It hurt so bad."

Logs cracked.

"Barely conscious, I stabbed the other child through the heart. They died as I vomited and lay limp on the ground, feeling my snake bleed out as my life slowly drained from my body."

My fingers shook, and liquid scalded my hand.

"The queen left. She'd gotten what she wanted and didn't care about my fate. But a soldier picked me up and carried me into an empty room. He laid the bloody snake on my chest and tipped a glowing liquid down my throat, and he told me this was the only thing he could think of that would protect me from harm."

He shivered.

"I begged him to take me away from the queen, but he said that I had to stay in this realm and learn to survive. That bigger things were at stake."

I bit down on my tongue until I tasted blood.

"When I woke up, jewels covered my body, and when I thought about my snake, the jewels changed into shadows. Melded into my flesh, where no one could touch them. The queen was ecstatic when she saw me, convinced that the jewels were a rare beast trait and that she'd killed my snake." Cobra's voice deepened.

"She had me fight other children, then adults for sport, all with the end goal being the gladiator games. But they don't have a sacred lake in the fae realm, and when I never shifted forms, she assumed I was a beta and only good for small fighting rings, and…other things."

My stomach dropped.

"When I was in my twenties, the fae male I fought offered to pay for my services after the match. The queen saw my potential, and I slowly transitioned from full-time fighter and part-time prostitute to vice versa."

Cobra shrugged casually. "So that's why I have these." He held up his arms, and the jewels twinkled in the light. "A fucking curse."

Suddenly, he sat up straight and turned to Jax. "My snake never became tangible, no matter how hard I tried, until that day in the shifter realm. That's why it was so hard to transition it back to jewels. I was so scared I'd never see it again."

Cobra turned to me, a sheepish look on his face. "Also, I never severed the connection to your snake, just made it feel like it was dying, because I wanted to hurt you back."

His pale cheeks became tinged pink as he mumbled, "I'd never actually leave you."

My heart pounded harder in my chest as I thought about how much comfort the shadow snake had still given me.

Even when Cobra had been furious.

"I think a part of me knew you didn't. It was always way too happy around you."

I smiled at him and shook my head, the shadow snake twining around my fingers, offering images of support.

Cobra smiled back, and the expression made his gorgeous features unimaginably perfect.

I forgot how to breathe.

Jax wrapped his arm around Cobra and pulled him close, and Xerxes was staring at the man in awe.

"Fucking hell, that was bleak. How did you escape?" Ascher asked.

Cobra shrugged. "The soldier returned one day and told me to tell the queen I didn't have a shifted form, but I always had control over my snakes. That I should threaten to tell the whole realm unless she released me. I thought he was crazy, but weirdly it worked. She must have known it would get back to the don and was scared."

Cobra rubbed his eyes tiredly. "Now that I think about it, it's weird that the soldier escorted me to the shifter realm and not the beast realm. He had me immediately tested at the sacred lake."

My vision blurred.

I tipped forward out of my chair.

The coffee mug slammed into the hardwood floor and shattered into a million pieces.

Voices shouted from far away.

"What the fuck, Sadie?" Ascher slapped my face lightly

as Cobra shook my shoulders, and Jax and Xerxes crowded beside them.

All four men stared down at me in concern.

Aran had escaped the fae realm with the help of a strange man.

A similar man had randomly shown up and brought me to get tested at the sacred lake.

My voice cracked as I asked, "Did the soldier have bright-blue eyes and wear a long black cloak?"

Cobra took a step back. "Yes."

"Fuck us." I groaned.

The truth crashed over me, and my limbs went weak.

At that moment, the massive clock on the wall chimed, signaling midnight.

We had one night to pass this test—one night to survive.

Time kept mercilessly moving forward, and we were running out of it.

I didn't have the luxury of wallowing.

Everything was a blur as Ascher pushed me forward up the stairs, and Jax reminded me to get dressed for the club.

They said we'd talk about it later, and I nodded like everything wasn't crumbling around me.

My mind was elsewhere.

In the room, I told Aran what Cobra had said.

The truth. That the same cloaked man had forced all of us to get tested. Positioned all of us so we would meet in the training compound in the shifter realm.

I watched Aran pale and hunch lower, like if she made herself small enough, the truth couldn't hurt her.

I barely remembered walking down the stairs, the men complimenting me on my outfit.

Barely noticed the rain soaking me on the way to the car.

Was barely cognizant of the neon skyscrapers and the way Cobra clenched my hand in the back seat.

How Jax looked at me with worry. Ascher smoothing his hands across my head. Xerxes giving me a soft kiss on the cheek.

The world was nebulous and indistinct.

In the future, I'd come to think of this day as the dividing line in my life.

The distinction between the before and the after.

The after characterized by a singular realization that changed the fundamental nature of existence.

It had been everywhere, in small signs we'd all become experts at avoiding.

Averting our eyes when it was right before our faces.

But there was no more running from the truth.

We were pawns.

And always had been.

CHAPTER 37

SADIE

THE BLACK RIBBON CLUB

NEON LIGHTS GLOWED HIGH into the night as misty rain spattered around us.

Unlike what we'd seen after the first trial, this part of the city wasn't dead at night.

It was alive.

Shifters crowded the sidewalks in small glittering clothes that revealed more skin than they covered.

Club signs flashed, and high-heel-clad legs waited in long lines.

The car stopped, and Xerxes pushed us through the crowds, leading us around the side of a purple skyscraper.

As we walked further down the narrow, dark alley, open faces were replaced with dark masks, boisterous laughter turning into whispers.

Cigarette smoke was a hazy cloud.

The glittering fabrics on the main streets, as people jostled to get into the ritzy clubs, were so very different from the heavy eye makeup and leather-clad bodies that slithered through the alley.

I looked out of place in my sheer nightie, with white feathers and crystals glowing against my golden skin.

The men, however, fit in.

They wore matching black leather pants, and their torsos were bare except for black leather straps that crisscrossed over their biceps and pecs.

Black kohl was smudged around their eyes.

Jax's nipple piercings and golden chains glinted against his glistening dark skin. Ascher's colorful flame-and-rose tattoos glowed underneath the neon lights. Cobra's jewels refracted specks of light across the dingy alley walls.

I shivered as Ascher pressed his hand against my lower back and led me forward.

His warm skin burned through the sheer material.

Xerxes glanced down at me, purple eyes flickering with heat. "Are you okay, baby girl?"

I nodded.

Xerxes hardened his jaw and looked away, like he could see the lie on my face and it physically pained him.

He'd purposefully left himself unconcealed, spicy cinnamon wafting off him. His long hair was pulled back into a high ponytail, highlighting the spiked leather collar wrapped around his neck.

Cobra held the silver chain attached to it, wrapped tightly around his hand, a scowl darkening his handsome face as he roughly yanked Xerxes forward.

A reminder of what we were here to do.

Muscles rippling, faces tight with tension, the men looked like demons of lore, and people stared as they stumbled out of the way.

Violence clung to them.

I breathed in dirty rain and exhaled calm.

I pushed all the messed-up things back into the deep recess of my brain. Where they couldn't touch me.

Rain drizzled harder, and black kohl streaked down their faces like war paint.

Through the rainy haze, a symbol on a neon sign flickered—it was a black ribbon.

A long line wrapped against the wall, but unlike those in the static lines on the main street, bodies pressed against one another.

Hips gyrated in sync.

The line thrashed with pleasure.

Xerxes shook his head and pointed us forward. Then Cobra tugged him along, like he was in the lead.

Under the flickering sign, a seven-foot-tall bouncer with thick leathery skin blocked the door. The alpha scent of wet grass wafted off him.

His nostrils flared as he leaned closer to Xerxes, and he said, "No weapons allowed."

The bouncer patted us down and narrowed his eyes at the metal in Xerxes's pocket.

"Sex knife." Xerxes shrugged.

The bouncer leaned closer to him, and recognition sparked in his eyes. He hurried to unhook the velvet rope and let us through.

Cobra led, roughly yanking Xerxes forward as the rest of us followed.

The bouncer's eyes trailed across my naked body partially exposed in the sheer fabric, and bile burned the back of my throat.

I pushed my shoulders back and forced my face to harden.

Ascher's fingers, still pressed against my lower back, curled and dug into my skin.

Pine spiked muskier. His gait faltered slightly, like he was fighting a reaction, but he quickly masked it.

It took every ounce of my willpower not to gape as we entered.

High ceilings towered above the massive open space.

Metal stairs with chain railings climbed stories into the sky and filled the middle of the room in a massive maze.

Colored lights flashed.

Darkness, then neon red; darkness, then neon orange.

Bodies filled the stairs, wrapped around one another, pumping into one another in endless positions.

Concealed in shadows, then exposed by flashing colors.

Bodies dangled off the railings from leather straps, hundreds of feet in the air, as people on other levels pushed into them, licked their bare skin, pushed into holes, and pulled at cocks.

Cigarette smoke wafted.

Lights flashed.

Techno music pumped.

Moans echoed.

Leather masks with holes over the mouths concealed faces, whips cracked against flesh, leashes tugged collars, knives dragged across skin, lighters were held over flesh, burning cigarettes pressed against partners, handcuffs constrained, and ropes tied.

Cum dripped off leather.

The burning scent of betas was overpowering, but rich alpha scents and a few hints of omega sweetness joined the crescendo of sensory overload.

In the very middle of the maze of stairs, floating by enchantment, was a round velvet platform.

White lights flickered above it, the centerpiece of the room. Everyone's eyes were on them.

Five women fucked one man.

He was blindfolded, on his hands and knees, as strap-ons slammed into his ass and mouth and he pumped into the woman lying beneath him.

Two stood above in full leather outfits and slammed long whips across his flesh.

There were thousands of people in this club, and we needed to catch the Ortega brothers' attention and get access to their backroom club.

The instructions had said it was invite only.

Xerxes pointed at the platform, and I nodded in agreement.

Jax's and Ascher's faces tightened with worry, and the fingers resting on my lower back curled until nails dug into my skin. Cobra arched his eyebrows at Xerxes and me.

"For the girls!" I yelled at Jax and Ascher.

Faces scowled.

No one said anything.

Cobra yanked Xerxes's chain and led us forward through the writhing masses.

Climbing up the network of stairs, I bit down on the side of my mouth to distract myself from the sheer depravity.

Cocks pumped into holes.

Women and men were tied to the railings so they were completely exposed. Women with strap-ons, men with dicks, people with wild-looking toys casually walked up to the constrained bodies and entered their orifices.

Touched them like they knew them.

As we walked up the maze of narrow paths, hands roamed.

Grabbing at us, like they had the right to touch.

Jax's hand joined Ascher's on my lower back as they led

me forward. Cobra and Xerxes walked in front of me, never more than a few inches away.

The four men surrounded me in a blockade.

A beta man grabbed Ascher's horn. Tattooed fingers moved impossibly fast, and Ascher turned the man's wrist until it snapped.

We walked forward.

A beta woman tugged on Jax's gold-twined braids. He whipped his head around and roared at her. She stumbled back in fear.

Noses lifted, lips were licked, and mouths dropped as Xerxes walked past.

Men and women trailed after him, running their fingers across his olive skin, then bringing their fingers to their mouths.

I growled.

Xerxes kept his head down and did nothing as his leash tugged him forward.

"Mine," Cobra sneered at the people touching Xerxes.

He stopped to grab the omega's face and dragged his tongue slowly across his cheeks, like he'd done to me in the mansion.

Staking his ownership.

Xerxes arched his eyebrow at Cobra and smirked, but quickly schooled his expression.

We plowed forward.

Two men wearing nothing but leather thongs stood in the middle of the stairway and blocked our path.

Ascher and Jax pressed against me tighter, and Xerxes and Cobra bent their knees as they prepared to fight.

"Sadie, is that you?" the one man yelled with a big smile, and I recognized the green scales across his face.

It was the alpha from the ring that had introduced

himself. Beside him stood the blond man that had talked to me after our fight.

We needed any advantage we could take.

I shook my head slightly and shoved past Cobra and Xerxes, ignoring the hiss behind me as I walked toward the two men.

The white feathers and diamonds of my sheer dress glowed underneath the flashing lights, contrasting wildly with the leather all around.

People stared at me.

"Dean and Logan, isn't it? What are you guys doing here?" I asked casually and forced my arms to my side like I was comfortable standing half-naked in front of random men.

Their eyes slowly traced my body.

I stayed relaxed.

"We got an invite from our packmate. Said things would be going down here tonight, and looks like he was right." Dean grinned, showcasing his dimples.

I leaned forward into their personal space, angling my head up so they could hear me.

Dean closed his eyes as he breathed in deep. Logan reached forward and trailed his hands down my long white hair.

They were both handsome and fit, but they seemed boyish and young compared to the men standing behind me. Too eager.

Their alpha scents were slightly sweet.

I preferred when they burned.

"I heard there was a secret club here," I said coyly and licked my lips as I stood on tiptoe to yell. "Have you heard anything about that?"

Dean tipped his head back and laughed, green scales flashing in the shadows. "Aren't you a wild one."

Logan shook his head. "Everyone knows you have to be pretty depraved to get an invite. At the very least, you have to put on a show." He gestured to the floating platform a few stories above us.

"Hm, interesting," I said coyly and smiled up at them. Our instincts had been right.

They moved closer, licking their lips, clearly expecting a reward for the information.

I shied away from their roaming hands but leaned higher on my tiptoes and puckered my lips, aiming for Logan's cheek.

A hand grabbed my hair and pulled me back before I could make contact. Cobra slammed his mouth into mine with such ferocity, my knees gave out.

I would have fallen if not for his other hand curling around to grab my ass.

Frost burned my lips.

Finally, he released me with a hiss and pushed me into Jax's arm.

The big man held me still against him while Ascher trailed kisses down my jaw, his hands pushing underneath the gossamer fabric to trail across my naked body.

"Oops, sorry about that," Cobra snarled at the two men, who were scowling at Jax and Ascher touching me. "Sometimes Kitten forgets herself."

Snake eyes glowed in the dark.

I shivered.

Jax leaned forward to claim my mouth as Ascher slowly licked across my neck. Xerxes stared at the three of us, purple eyes on fire.

Cobra yanked Xerxes's chain and dragged him past

Logan and Dean, who were still standing in the middle of the stairs.

Jax released my mouth, but his callused hand tightened across my ass as he pushed me forward.

Ascher kept sucking on my neck.

"Sorry about that," I mumbled to Logan as we pressed past them and followed Cobra.

Jax's gold chains tickled my skin as he leaned forward and growled into my ear. "Oh, you're going to be sorry."

I rolled my eyes but couldn't mask my tremble as Ascher's teeth nipped my neck.

"It's all about the plan," I said through gritted teeth.

Jax tweaked my nipple through the sheer fabric, his gray eyes hard as slate as I licked warm chestnuts off my lips. "You're playing with fire, little alpha."

Ascher bit my neck harder. Jax's other hand cupped both my ass cheeks as he pushed me forward through the crowd.

There was a line of bodies waiting alongside the small staircase that led to the floating platform.

Cobra pushed past them all.

People growled and yelled but stopped speaking when Cobra turned and hissed at them, eyes glowing and shadow snakes churning across his pale skin.

"Give it up for these ladies," a man in a suit spoke into a golden microphone as he gestured to the five women holding up the limp, naked men in their arms.

Strobe lights stopped flashing, and bright light shone on them.

Music pulsed.

They bowed, and two of them cracked their whips in the air.

There was a roar as the crowd went wild.

The announcer turned to the entrance. "Who's the next group going to perform for all of us tonight?"

Cobra punched the men who were walking forward and shoved them aside.

Cobra walked out onto the platform under the spotlight. He dragged Xerxes behind him, who tilted his head down and made a show of stumbling.

We followed behind.

Cobra spoke into the announcer's ear, and the man's face split into a grin.

"It's the Black Ribbon's lucky night. We have three alpha males, one alpha female, and an omega ready to put on a show."

The platform rattled from the wave of cheers.

"And they're all new to the city, so this will be particularly exciting." The announcer paused for dramatic effect. "Except for the omega."

The crowd hushed, and the music bounced. "Does anyone remember Cinnamon?" He paused. "Xerxes is back in Serpentine City!"

Cheers erupted, and the platform rocked from the force.

"The floor is yours." The announcer winked and left the platform.

The white lights shut off, and everything was pitch black.

The music switched, and the beat picked up and was faster, more frenzied.

Red strobe lights pulsed overhead.

Four men turned to me, eyes glowing in the dark.

Cobra wore a cruel smile. "You think you can kiss other men, Kitten?" His eyes flashed to snake eyes.

Xerxes's demure expression disappeared. He stared at me, his face hardening with anger.

"I warned you, little love," Jax whispered in my ear.

"It's just us, Princess. Ignore everyone else. They don't matter," Ascher whispered in my other ear.

Apparently, he was the only one concerned about my mental state.

"I was just doing it to play the part. We need all the help we can get tonight!" I said with annoyance.

This was not the time or place for one of their possessive alpha bullshit meltdowns.

Ascher dragged his teeth down my neck, tattoos jumping as his hands gripped my waist.

He bit down. Hard. "You will never touch another man, ever again." Ascher's amber eyes glowed as he glared up at me.

"Don't tell me what to do," I snapped.

Cobra took another menacing step closer. "Kitten, this isn't a negotiation."

I was surrounded.

Cobra licked his lips. Xerxes flicked open his sex knife. Jax growled. Ascher glared.

I tried to take a step back, but Jax boxed me in.

I'd made a grave miscalculation.

CHAPTER 38

SADIE

SHADES OF BLOOD RED

THE RED STROBE lights flickered faster and highlighted the harsh planes of three angry alphas and one collared omega.

I swallowed thickly.

Saying I would do whatever needed to be done felt vastly different from actually doing it.

Also, I hadn't factored in the men being mad at me.

The platform beneath our feet spun in a slow circle, and it reminded me of a screaming coliseum and fighting against bloodthirsty gladiators.

The music pounded.

It was a different battle, but a war all the same.

I didn't like the malicious sneer on Cobra's face, or the way his lips curled up at the corners. Strobe lights and shadows danced across his face.

The shadow snake on my skin gave a zip and sent me images of happiness and love.

Damned bastard thought he was smooth.

I sent back images of me strangling him while he begged for mercy.

He tipped his gorgeous head back and laughed, shoulders shaking as the snake sent more zips across my flesh.

Abruptly, the laughter left his face, and the darkest scowl I'd ever seen contorted his expression.

The shadow snake sent me another zip of warmth and support, and I realized what he was doing. He was preparing me, reminding me that this was acting.

It wasn't real.

Cobra grabbed Xerxes's ponytail and shoved him to the floor. Playing along, he sprawled across it like he was scared.

Cobra's cheekbones could cut glass as red shadows painted his glittering jewels and the wicked *V* that framed his abdominals.

An otherworldly god.

He dug his fingers into his belt buckle and pulled out a whip that I hadn't noticed coiled against his thigh.

With a dramatic movement, he snapped his wrist, and the long tail cracked through the air. His arm swung forward, and it slashed across Xerxes's chest, leaving a long trail of red.

Xerxes moaned with pleasure but quickly concealed his expression with a wince.

Cobra cracked it again.

The crowd roared with excitement, loving the violence.

For a second, it was a belt that cracked through the air; my flesh that was split in two; my blood that ran down my chest after a merciless beating.

I gasped shallowly.

There wasn't enough oxygen in the room.

Jax's warm hands grabbed my throat and tipped my head back.

He kissed me roughly but pulled back to whisper in my

ear, "You're okay. We got you. No one is going to hurt you. It's all a show."

I kissed him back, gasping, "Please don't let him whip me."

A roar rumbled through his chest as his hands cradled me softly while his mouth pillaged aggressively. When he pulled back for air, he whispered, "Never. We planned to do this to Xerxes, remember?"

I nodded, but it was a lie.

I'd been so worried about Aran that I'd made a serious mistake by not paying attention to what the men had planned.

Fuck me and my horrible attention span.

Breathing deeply, I reminded myself that they would never hurt me.

Even while Cobra sneered, cracking the whip across Xerxes's flesh, the shadow snake sent me images of cuddling and warmth.

This was Cobra, Jax, Ascher, and Xerxes. I trusted them, and our lives were at stake.

"I can do this," I whispered back to Jax.

He kissed me once more, then nodded at the other men.

Cobra threw his hands in the air and bellowed to the crowd, "*Who wants to see an omega fuck an alpha*?"

Screams sounded, and the platform shook from the roar of response.

Cobra cracked the whip loudly.

Cobra was a show master in his element.

Shifters screamed as his gorgeous face sneered; he oozed sex, depravity, and violence.

Jewels shimmering under the lights. He was demonic.

He slammed the whip across the omega's chest, red welts blossoming, blood spraying.

Xerxes flinched dramatically, like it hurt, but his eyes smoldered.

The violence turned him on.

Cobra stalked toward him, then leaned down and slammed his palm across his face.

The roar of the crowd covered Xerxes's moan of pleasure.

Cobra sent me more images of love through the shadow snake on his skin as he leaned down and pulled out Xerxes's massive cock.

His knot was vibrating.

Need gushed between my legs as I remembered just how Xerxes had taken me. What that knot had done to me.

The omega tilted his head down and curled his shoulders like he was ashamed, but he looked at me with his purple eyes, and he licked his lips.

Faster than my eyes could track, his eyebrow arched mockingly at me. He quickly masked his expression.

Fuck.

I clenched my thighs together.

Sprawling across the platform, olive skin stretched over endless muscles glistening with sweat, blood dripping across his chest, hard cock standing stark across his leather pants, black kohl smeared down his face, collar around his neck.

Xerxes had never looked so tempting.

It was wrong.

But I was painfully turned on.

The roar of the crowd was far away. The moving platform, strobe lights, and cigarette smoke cast a dreamlike quality around the moment.

"*Bad omegas get fucked by alphas*!" Cobra bellowed for show as he cracked his whip in the air, face contorted in rage.

From the hard bulge in his leather, he was enjoying the

role-play. Of course he would thrive as a psychotic BDSM master.

I was so busy watching what was happening between Xerxes and Cobra, that I was taken by surprise when Jax and Ascher grabbed my arms and dragged me forward.

They brought me to Cobra like I was some virgin sacrifice for the taking.

I fought the urge to roll my eyes at the dramatics and instead tried to look meek and scared, which was excessively difficult.

An inappropriate giggle bubbled in my throat.

Cobra leaned forward and whispered just for me, "You've been a bad girl. And bad girls get punished." His tongue flicked out and snaked down the side of my face.

I swallowed another chuckle.

Cobra sounded ridiculous.

He moved impossibly quick and latched his mouth around my breast, teeth and tongue scraping through the sheer material that barely covered me.

The giggle died in my throat as a burning fire replaced my mirth.

I drowned in frost.

Cobra sucked each of my nipples, then pushed two fingers roughly inside me.

We both knew he could feel how wet I was as I gushed on his fingers, turned on by his little show.

Cobra's face contorted into an evil grin as he pumped his fingers faster, then leaned forward and bit down on my nipple.

I yelped with surprise and clenched my thighs together as wetness dripped.

Cobra pulled his fingers out of my sopping heat and dragged them slowly across my lips. "You're going to take all of us, my kitten. You're going to take our cocks until you understand what it means to be owned by us."

For the sake of feminists everywhere, I ignored the way my core fluttered when he said they owned me.

I'd worry about it later.

For now, my knees were weak, Ascher's and Jax's arms the only things keeping me upright.

Rearing my head back, I spat on Cobra's face.

The crowd roared.

I sent the shadow snake images of love and support and gave Cobra a wink. "Do it. You won't," I mouthed with a taunting sneer.

It was a show, after all.

If I'd been in danger before, now I was dead.

Snake eyes flickered, and Cobra lunged forward, shoving four fingers deep into my pussy while his thumb pressed at my back entrance.

His forearm bunched, face contorted in a sneer, as he pistoned into my heat until I gasped and moaned unintelligibly. "You're going to take all of us," he growled.

This time, it was a threat.

He tilted his head back and roared to the crowd, "*Take her to the omega*!"

Jax and Ascher grabbed me and dragged me over to where Xerxes was still sprawled across the ground, cock out, with bleeding whip wounds dripping down his chest.

His face was a stormy mask, and I sneered back, matching his energy.

From the way his purple eyes glowed brighter, he was also enjoying the drama.

We all were.

Ascher and Jax grabbed my thighs and pulled them apart roughly, holding me atop Xerxes.

I shivered.

Jax's hand tangled in my hair as he whispered in my ear, "You'll take him deep."

"*Lie down, omega*!"

Xerxes sprawled backward as Cobra slammed the whip across his chest, his knot vibrating faster with each hit.

Ascher's callused fingers parted my sopping folds as he and Jax lowered me downward. They positioned me, spasming cunt nestled on top of the vibrating tip of Xerxes's dick.

Jax pulled my hair back roughly, and I moaned.

He stared down at me.

"Do it," I whispered, showing him with my eyes that it was okay.

That I wanted it.

Ascher and Jax slammed me down on Xerxes's throbbing cock, and I didn't have to pretend.

I screamed with shock and pleasure as his dick slammed into my womb.

Knot vibrating against my clit until I couldn't tell where the pain ended and pleasure began.

He was so much bigger than I remembered.

The sensation was overwhelming.

I didn't move as tears streamed down my face. I could do nothing but sit atop the omega and shudder as he vibrated inside of me, knot strumming my clit higher and higher.

"*Ever seen an alpha fuck another alpha*?"

The platform shook from the force of the cheers as shifters stomped on the stairs and chains rattled.

This was my second time ever having sex, and it was in the middle of a rowdy BDSM club under strobe lights.

I hadn't even had sex in a bed yet.

I would have laughed if the pleasure weren't slowly blurring my mind, making everything hazy and far away.

"Stay relaxed, my princess," Ascher whispered in my ear as his warmth burned my back.

He leaned down, so he knelt on the ground behind me, legs spread wide and low.

Warm, callused fingers lifted up the sheer material of my short dress.

Fingers shoved into my mouth, and I tasted intoxicating pine as he whispered, "Get them nice and wet, Princess."

Suddenly, those same fingers trailed against my back entrance.

Cobra stalked across the platform, a circus master in his element, and made a show of adding his own spit onto Ascher's fingers. Then he slammed the whip across Xerxes's chest.

His cock jerked inside me, and we both moaned.

Ever so slowly, Ascher worked fingers into me.

Still squirming with Xerxes's dick spearing me, knot vibrating against my clit, the sensation was incredibly overwhelming.

Cobra's fingers grabbed my chin, and he whispered, "Good girl."

Ascher's finger pressed inside me, and he stretched my tight hole back and forth.

I creamed on Xerxes's dick.

The knot vibrated faster, and I tipped my head back, tears gathering in my eyes. It was so much.

Ascher added a second finger.

Cobra released my chin, then slowly stepped over Xerxes's body, so he stood with his crotch in my face.

Slowly, he unzipped his leather pants and pulled out his jeweled cock.

Xerxes's hips jerked, and his knot slammed against my clit, the shock wave making me spasm around him.

The tension built higher in my body.

Ascher spat on his fingers, then added a third into my tight hole.

Cobra pulled out his pale alpha cock. It was longer than Xerxes's and had emeralds embedded along the shaft in a swirling pattern. His alpha knot was swollen at the shaft, impossibly thick.

I licked my lips.

Cobra smirked down at me, traced his fingers across my lips. "I own you. Do you understand what I'm saying?"

He paused.

"You're *mine*, Sadie."

I narrowed my eyes up at the handsome bastard that drove me crazy.

Cobra spoke so only I could hear him. "I don't care what you tell other men."

He glanced down at Xerxes, whose vibrating dick was buried deep within me.

"I don't care if you tell them you love them. That doesn't change that you were *mine* first."

He dug his thumbnail into my bottom lip as he pressed my mouth open wider until my jaw ached.

Cobra snarled, "Because, Kitten, what I feel for you is beyond love. Do you understand?"

My eyes widened, his words piercing through my haze of lust.

He leaned closer.

"I fucking own your mind, body, and soul. Absolute ownership. You are my possession. My fucking everything."

There was a long pause as emerald eyes speared me.

"Do you understand what I am saying?"

Nodding slowly, I let him see the truth in my eyes.

I mouthed silently; *I love you too, Cobra.*

His perfect face transformed into an intense expression, as if something had snapped inside him.

Suddenly, he shoved his throbbing jeweled cock through my lips.

His hands were buried in my hair, and he slammed into my face like he was saying, *I. Love. You.* With every thrust.

I kept my eyes on his emerald gaze, even as I choked around his dick.

I love you too.

My core gushed across Xerxes's dick.

Suddenly, Ascher's fingers were replaced by a warm, slick cock.

My eyes widened as he pushed forward with painful slowness.

The smallest pressure, stretching me impossibly wide as Xerxes's cock still twitched deep inside me and Cobra used my mouth.

Abruptly, Cobra pulled back, and dark fingers unbuckled his leathers and dragged them down his thighs.

Jax stepped over Xerxes and positioned himself behind Cobra.

Cobra's dick leaped against his stomach as Jax spat on his pierced cock and slowly worked it into the snake shifter.

Cobra buried his hands in my hair as he resumed fucking my mouth. But this time, Jax set the pace.

He was merciless.

Abruptly, Ascher shoved forward, and I screamed around Cobra's dick as he filled my narrow shaft.

Cobra fucked my mouth so fast that I couldn't breathe.

My eyes fluttered shut from lack of oxygen.

Cobra yanked back and whispered praises down at me as he caressed my chin.

"You're mine Sadie. Mine. Mine. Mine," he repeated endlessly.

It sounded like—*I love you so, so, so, so much.*

Ascher didn't move, just stayed impossibly still as his dick speared my ass. He leaned forward and bit my neck, whispering endearments against my sensitive skin.

His hands tugged at my nipples.

Everything was too much.

Jax fucked Cobra violently, slamming Cobra's cock deep down my throat till I gagged. Ascher speared my ass while Xerxes filled my core, his knot still punishing my clit and driving my ecstasy higher.

It was so much.

The music pumped, strobe lights flashed, and cigarette smoke filled my nose.

I drowned in sensations.

I was light-headed, like I'd taken a hit of a powerful drug, so the world had a nightmarish quality about it.

I didn't even know if it was pleasure.

It was just *a lot.*

As if he could read my mind, suddenly, Xerxes's hands grabbed my hips roughly, and his hips jerked upward.

I screamed around Cobra's cock.

Xerxes moved his hips and fucked me from the floor. I was on top, but no one would ever mistake who was in charge.

His hips slammed his knot hard against my clit, and Ascher moved in tandem behind me.

I sobbed.

The pleasure-pain blurred and contorted until reality

became far, far, far away as my body was strummed to the highest possible euphoria.

Cobra cracked the whip in the air.

Xerxes slammed his hips faster, Ascher pulled my nips harder and joined his rougher movements. Jax's hips became more frenzied, and I couldn't breathe as I gagged and choked on Cobra's dick.

The strobe lights flashed faster.

Shadows contoured and twisted over our writhing mass.

I bawled as I came.

Pussy and ass spasming in such powerful waves, I barely noticed Cobra pulling out and coming all over my face.

Or the way he dragged his fingers through his cum and pressed them into my mouth.

Jax tipped his head back and roared as he filled Cobra.

Ascher bit my neck as he came in my ass.

Xerxes's cum filled my womb as his fingers dug into my hips.

I barely noticed when the men pulled themselves painfully slowly out of me, hot liquid filling my orifices.

I didn't hear the loving words Cobra said as he wiped at the sticky cum that coated my face.

Didn't know what Jax said when he whispered softly in my ear.

The lights turned on above us, and the announcer said something.

I stumbled on shaky legs off the platform.

The men's faces were contorted in concern, but I was too overwhelmed to care. Panic made my head spin, and with each step, my body ached, reminding me of what had just happened.

Pushing through the flailing limbs, naked flesh, and

leather, I sprinted down the stairs toward the glowing signs of the restrooms.

When I was finally inside, I threw myself into a stall and shut the door.

Face pressed against the cold door, I struggled to orient myself.

The hard truth of what had happened was unavoidable.

Not the act itself, but how I'd felt during it, the overwhelming feeling that had clogged my throat and burned my brain.

I'd just been used.

Fucked by four men in front of thousands of people.

Eyes closed, I slammed my head against the stall, relishing the pain that sent stars shooting before my eyes.

I was well and truly screwed.

Because I'd loved every second.

And, somehow, it had felt like the sweetest declaration of love.

CHAPTER 39
SADIE
VIOLENCE SPILLS OVER

After banging my head against the bathroom door like a lunatic, I finally calmed down enough to recognize what was happening.

I'd made the transition from prude to slut, and I was struggling with the lifestyle change.

Breathing deeply, I pressed my cheeks against the cold stall and calmed my heart.

I might be dumb, but I wasn't a dumb bitch.

"It's just a dick. It's not that deep," I whispered to myself as I dry-heaved into the toilet, farted out a concerning amount of white substance, slapped my face, then spread my arms and legs wide for confidence.

My panic attack waned, and I was able to see my new slutty reality for what it was: a blessing.

"They're basically *your* bitches. You aren't their bitch," I whispered while shadowboxing against an invisible opponent.

Memories flashed through my mind.

I'd told Cobra I loved him after he told me I was his possession and he owned me.

Oh my god, I'm their bitch.

I proceeded to learn a very important lesson: it's impossible to strangle yourself with toilet paper.

I yelled with frustration when the damn paper ripped for the tenth time right when I was starting to get some good pressure, and a woman's voice called out, "Are you okay in there?"

I groaned, "Why is it so soft and pliable but so easily broken?"

"What?"

"By the holy sun god, just let me die in slutty shame."

My toilet lady got angry. "Oh please, we both know there's no such thing as a slut."

I wailed, aware that I was being melodramatic but unable to stop myself.

"But what do you call a woman who gets violently fucked by four men and enjoys it?" I shuddered. "Like really violently, and like really enjoyed it. I can't emphasize enough how much enjoyment." I paused. "And how much violence." I coughed. "Whatever you're picturing, make it twenty times worse." I coughed harder. "As concerning as possible."

My toilet savior sighed. "I'd say she was one lucky woman."

I breathed deeply and composed myself. "You have no idea how much I needed to hear that right now."

I pushed open the stall, and my savior stared back at me.

Turned out female empowerment came in the form of a four-foot-tall woman wearing a leather suit with holes cut out around the nipples.

"You're so wise," I said gravely.

"Oh my god, you're the girl who was just on the platform!" She slapped my arm with surprising strength. "Bitch,

I've never seen four more attractive men in my entire life. If you don't want them, I'll take them."

I laughed.

She didn't.

"My name is Jenny, and I live in the financial district around Third Street. Tell them I'm here every weekend."

"Um." I pursed my lips, unsure what was happening.

"Thank you so much. You're the best." Jenny gave me a hug. "Tell them they can find me by the back exit sign. I'll be waiting for them." She smiled and pranced out of the bathroom.

I narrowed my bloodshot eyes in the mirror as I splashed cold water on my face.

What had just happened?

Had I just set the men up with another woman?

I scrubbed my face, wondering how things had gotten so confusing.

On one hand, I wanted to attack Jenny for even looking at the men, but on the other hand, I felt bad because she was looking forward to them and she'd helped me out of a dark place.

It was a pickle.

"That's the women's restrooms!" Dean's voice yelled outside, and I jumped in surprise.

"I know. Just go back to the stairs. I'll meet you there later. Don't interrupt me," a voice snarled back. I recognized it, but I couldn't place it.

That was the only warning I got.

A familiar bald alpha with a cigarette in his lips charged into the restroom with his gun pointed at my face.

I stilled in shock as I tried to process what the fuck was going on.

Apparently, Dean and Logan's third pack member was Hunter.

The alpha who'd beaten me until I'd chosen death, who I'd also happened to infect with my blood.

Fuck.

I'd been hoping he'd just forget about it.

An enchanted gun hovered inches from my forehead.

I stated the obvious. "This bathroom does not have good energy."

The safety clicked off as Hunter pressed the barrel into my forehead.

I pursed my lips. It seemed like he was holding a grudge.

"Listen, it really wasn't personal."

Hunter stepped closer until his caustic alpha scent overwhelmed my senses. "I'm making it fucking personal. I found out from Z you'd be completing your third initiation here and wanted to make sure I didn't miss the fun."

He pressed the barrel harder against my forehead.

I'd already had my mental breakdown, so I couldn't panic appropriately.

"This is how it's gonna go." His cigarette hung from his lips, and he leaned forward so the burning end was precariously close to my face.

"You and I are going to enter into an agreement. I won't tell everyone that you're part witch, making you a wanted half-breed, and in return, you're going to do something for me." He pulled down his zipper, making it clear what he was referencing.

I glared at him with disgust.

I took it all back; what had happened with the men was beautiful and, frankly, inspirational.

This was violence.

He smirked, and bile burned my throat as I mentally reviewed my options.

I bit down on my cheek until I tasted coppery blood.

"You so much as begin to shift, or I see a glimpse of whatever that shit was that flew at me before, I'm pulling this trigger." Hunter's eyes were manic and wide. He licked his lips, and he shoved the butt harder into my head.

He wanted to do it.

Fuck.

Hunter smirked, thinking he had won, as he pushed my head down.

I fell to my knees and sent images of what was happening to my shadow snake, praying to the moon goddess that the connection worked like I thought it did.

Everything was happening so fast.

I couldn't think.

The gun was cold against my forehead, and I mentally screamed at the snake, begging Cobra to understand.

To help.

"They thought they could threaten me and get away with it." He laughed. "That's not how this city works."

Blood filled my throat as I bit down on my tongue. He didn't make any sense, but it didn't matter.

Hunter pulled his dick out of his pants.

He stepped closer.

Could I spit my blood at him? Could I shift? Could I do it faster than a bullet to the brain?

I had a half second to decide.

"Open your mouth," Hunter demanded, and I gnashed my teeth together as hard as I could.

Terror paralyzed my chest.

From the corner of my eye, the flashing lights outside made shadows contort on the walls.

No, wait, the shadow was moving across the wall.

Relief made my head spin.

Cobra's shadow snakes slithered in one long black snake against the wall.

"Open your mouth," Hunter growled.

I leaned my head back, hyperaware of the gun that leaned with me, as I squeezed my eyes shut and begged the snake to take him out before he shot me.

Abruptly, the gun stopped pressing into my forehead.

I opened my eyes, and the gun clattered against the floor, Hunter's arm limp at his side.

Large snake's fangs sank venom into Hunter's neck as he stumbled in confusion.

I didn't hesitate.

Rearing back, I slammed my fist into his face as hard as I could.

Cartilage snapped beneath my knuckles, and I relished the feel of his face breaking my fist.

I'm going to fucking destroy you.

He grunted with confusion and pain as the venom coursed through him, and I beat him with my fist as hard as I could.

Blood splattered as I threw his body against the wall and stalked forward, slamming my knuckles at him until he was an unidentifiable, bloody lump beneath me.

"Open your mouth," I snarled at him like he'd threatened me.

I yanked down his jaw and punched out his teeth.

My knuckles burned in the best way.

His jaw broke with a satisfying crack, teeth falling to the floor.

"What, you don't enjoy being on the other side of it?" I taunted as I broke his skull, shattered his cheekbones, and made sure he would remember just who the fuck he had threatened.

Suddenly, the door slammed opened, and angry alphas stalked in.

Their eyes swept over Hunter's exposed dick, the gun on the floor, his busted face, and my bloodstained knuckles.

Faces hardened.

I'd thought I'd seen them angry before, but now I knew what true rage looked like.

They didn't hiss or roar; they were dead silent.

They stalked past me, chestnuts, cinnamon, and frost spiking like they were on fire.

Ascher stopped beside me and wrapped his tattooed arm around my shoulders. He pulled me tight against him, alpha-purring as he held me close and tried to offer comfort.

"Princess, step away from the fucker," Ascher whispered roughly as he dragged me away from Hunter.

I leaned against him, grateful for the support.

His tattooed hands trembled as they ran over every inch of my body, like he was desperate to make sure I was okay.

When he got to my busted knuckles, he hissed in air through his teeth.

"It's fine," I whispered. "I handled it."

"No, Princess, it's not fucking fine," Ascher growled as he wrapped his arms tighter around me and held me.

I melted into him as we watched the other men.

Jax pulled Hunter's hands behind his back.

The shadow snake slithered off his neck and back onto Cobra's skin, and Hunter stopped convulsing with pain.

With Hunter missing half his teeth, with a busted face, his words were barely understandable. "How dare that whore touch me. How dare you put your hands on me again."

Cobra hissed, "You dare call her names." He slammed his fist into Hunter's gory face with such force I was surprised the fucker didn't lose his head.

"You touched my kitten." Cobra said quietly, "You hurt what's mine."

Xerxes flicked open the sex knife.

"You'll never get away with this." Hunter's skin rippled as he began to shift.

"*Stop shifting*!" Jax alpha-barked, the power in his voice stronger than anything I'd ever heard.

The walls rippled as he spoke.

For a split second, Hunter stilled.

Xerxes didn't hesitate. He slashed the knife down Hunter's torso, from neck to navel.

Cobra reached his hands inside the split skin and grabbed Hunter's organs. "You dared to try to force yourself upon her." He snarled.

"Pigs like you don't deserve to live," he unraveled his organs, pulling them out with impossible speed.

Hunter screamed.

Cobra disemboweled him.

Jax held the thrashing alpha immobile, his face ice-cold.

They were merciless.

Xerxes picked the gun off the floor and clicked off the safety.

Jax released Hunter, and he collapsed to his knees, gasping as he grabbed at the organs still being ripped from his body by Cobra.

The omega walked to stand beside his packmates. Rage radiated off all three of them in tangible waves.

There was a loud pop.

Xerxes lowered the smoking gun.

Hunter's body collapsed, a glowing blue hole in the center of his forehead.

Cobra kept pulling at the organs, blood staining his pale hands as he tore at the dead alpha's body. His eyes were wide with mania, and he worked in silence.

"He's dead," Jax whispered and wrapped his arms around Cobra. "He's dead."

Abruptly, Cobra stopped and turned his head around.

He stared at my bloody hands, watched as Ascher held me and whispered words of comfort.

Cobra stalked across the room and reached his hand for my face, but he pulled it back when he realized gore dripped from his fingers.

"Kitten," he whispered brokenly. "This is my fault."

I shook myself out of the stupor I'd fallen into. It was slightly traumatizing, and yet weirdly satisfying, watching your assaulter get his organs ripped out and a bullet to the brain after you beat his face into a bloody pulp.

Free therapy.

Jax growled and raked his hands down his face. "Fuck, this is our fault."

I didn't think I'd ever heard him swear before.

"How?" I asked with confusion.

Jax sighed heavily.

"After the second trial, when you and Xerxes—" He waved his hand as if he didn't know what to call our violent sexcapade. "We went to the club and cornered Hunter. We beat him up pretty good and threatened to kill him if he ever hurt you again."

Cobra snarled, "I didn't lie."

Ascher sighed heavily, like he was beyond exhausted by recent events. "We also talked to Clarissa and told her that it was our fault for misleading her, but that we'd never had any real interest. We were idiots who were trying to get a rise out of you after we thought you rejected us."

Cobra wiped gore off his hands onto his leather and said, "I wanted to beat her up for lying and touching you. I still think we should have."

"It was more our fault for leading her on, and you know it," Ascher snarled back.

If I weren't feeling extremely unwell, I might have marveled at the fact that Ascher, who had once referred to all women as sluts, had recognized that he was the problem and not Clarissa.

However, since I was still in a state of extreme duress, I decided not to be impressed by a man doing the bare minimum.

"So—" I clapped my hands and pointed to the dead alpha at our feet. "—what do we do now? Pretty sure there was a law against murdering other alphas."

Jax said, "Rule two hundred and three. Punishment by death."

"But rule ninety-four, punishment for sexually assaulting any shifter is death and disembowelment," Cobra argued back. "We were in the right."

I narrowed my eyes and stared down at the dead body. "That feels too easy. We should burn him and flush the ashes down the toilet."

Ascher laughed, the sound out of place among the death and gore. "You've clearly never gotten rid of a dead body before."

"And you have?"

Suddenly, Ascher looked uncomfortable as he rubbed at the back of his neck. He couldn't meet my eyes.

"Oh my sun god, how many people have you murdered, Ascher?"

He squinted and mumbled, "One for every tattoo."

I covered my mouth in shock because every inch of his golden skin was covered in tattoos.

I'd made love to a serial killer.

Another panic attack seized my lungs.

Before I could go back into my bathroom stall and resume falling apart, the door to the bathroom slammed open.

All of us jumped, and I spat out my blood, preflinging it across the room, not willing to be caught with a gun to my forehead like last time.

It was the bouncer from outside.

Thankfully, he didn't see the ball of blood hovering in the air beside him.

"You've caught the attention of the owners," the bouncer said as he gestured at an enchanted broadcast stone in the upper corner of the room.

I let my levitating blood fall to the ground, hoping the stone didn't see it.

The bouncer smiled as he looked at my busted knuckles and Cobra's gore covered hands. "They're impressed with your savagery and want to personally invite you to their private club. Follow me."

With that, he turned around and left.

I stepped over the dead body and grimaced at Cobra. "Good work, I guess. But, I had it handled."

"I killed him, baby girl," Xerxes whined like he was looking for praise.

Cobra grabbed his leash and dragged him forward. "No talking, omega, unless I say so."

He mumbled something about Kitten being his and him seeing me first under his breath, but I chose to ignore it.

I gagged as I walked into the club, because Hunter's blood made my steps squishy.

Technically, we'd accomplished our goal.

But for some reason, it didn't feel like a win.

CHAPTER 40

COBRA

THE PAIN OF POSSESSION

TWO HOURS earlier

I gripped Xerxes' leash tight as the music pulsed and flashing red lights cast ominous shadows across flailing bodies.

The shifters thought they were dangerous and exciting, with their ghastly leather clothes and whips.

Just another realm obsessed with sex.

But I'd already played this game in the fae realm.

It was nothing new.

Shifters pawed at us, mindless in their euphoria. The mob mentality of sex, a dark drug, as nulls and betas desperately tried to lose themselves in something more exhilarating than the mundane reality they existed in.

Tried to forget they were nothing more than sheep.

In a realm that didn't respect them.

If I were alone, maybe I would have lit a cigarette and touched them back.

Lost myself in the mind-numbing haze of sex and violence that was a little too easy to pretend to enjoy.

But I wasn't alone.

The red shadows and desperate faces took on a sinister light as I tugged Xerxes forward, cognizant with every step of the small woman in a sheer white dress that trailed behind us.

From the set of Xerxes's jaws, the way he looked over his shoulder constantly, he felt the same way I did.

She shouldn't be here.

I watched her in my peripheral vision.

Sadie's ruby eyes were wide, her lush lips parted on a silent gasp as she took in the frenzied people performing all manners of sex acts across the maze of stairs. She curled in on herself, shoulders hunched as hands grabbed and toys slapped against flesh.

But she forged forward, not looking back or missing a step as we pushed our way through.

My kitten had no idea.

She didn't see the man that grabbed at the back of her dress.

Didn't see Ascher gouge out the offender's eye with his fingernails in an efficient maneuver that left the man with a gaping cavity on his face.

Someone grabbed a strand of her snow-white hair with his fingers, and Jax quickly broke his arm in three different places before Sadie could even feel the tug.

Ascher's and Jax's eyes glowed brightly, bodies strumming with tension.

You could see in the way the bodies shifted that people were drawn to Sadie's stunning golden skin and shockingly unique features, but it was the edge of violence that radiated off her that made them claw at her desperately.

An ignorant fool might have said she was different and others recognized it.

But the truth was more complicated.

Sadie was out-of-place while simultaneously right at home in the dark club. If she were given enough time, she'd become the wickedest of them all.

I led us further into the frenzy.

The shifters crawled on hands and knees as we walked past, desperate to touch Sadie and to taste Xerxes.

An omega and a female alpha: two rare jewels in a cruel realm.

They were mine.

The golden string in my chest, the bond that connected me to my packmates, strummed with warning as Xerxes noticed an alpha charging behind Jax and Ascher, his eyes wide as he stared at Sadie.

The alpha's nostrils flared as he followed.

He'd smelled cranberry wine.

The string between us panged with warning as he lunged forward with a sharp knife, intent on fighting us for her. He could smell that she wasn't our packmate, and he thought she was up for grabs.

His mistake.

I yanked Xerxes's leash, giving my kitten a show. Distracting her.

Sadie might fight like a warrior and bathe in the blood of her enemies, but there was something so innocent about her violence.

The void beckoned me closer, and I schooled my expression at the terror that always gripped me when I thought of my kitten.

It was why I hadn't fucked her yet, the reason I held myself back from ravaging her.

The world was already too cruel, and I refused to be the one to break her.

Knife in his hand, the alpha made his fatal mistake as he tried to swipe at Ascher and grab Sadie from our protection.

Shadows danced.

I tugged Xerxes's handsome face closer and dragged my tongue across it, making sure Sadie's attention stayed fully on us.

Jax shifted to shield the violence happening behind her.

Ascher dislocated the alpha's shoulder and took his knife. In a flash of steel, he slit the man's throat, then kicked the body off the stairs.

Leather bodies gyrated and fucked, desensitized to violence.

It all happened in a split second.

The gold thread that had been screaming with tension between us instantly quieted with relief.

We eliminated the threat.

I pulled Xerxes's leash forward, both of us relieved that Sadie hadn't seen her attacker, as I led us further up the stairs into the masses.

The gold platform spun slowly high above, a beacon and a curse, taunting me with what we were here to do.

With each step toward it, the void screamed at me, bellowed at me to stop.

We couldn't do this to Sadie.

I sent images of love and support to my shadow snake that lived on her flesh—the favorite part of myself.

In my peripheral vision, the corners of Kitten's lips turned upward, and she sent me love back. My knees wobbled because she knew what she was doing. Knew that I was there and who she was technically talking to.

To me, no woman had ever been so perfect, so sweet, and so fucking vicious.

I straightened my shoulders and led us onward.

We would pass this third trial because my kitten's life depended on it.

Failure wasn't an option.

The void screamed.

Gold thread no longer offered the warmth and support they usually did; we all were out of our minds with stress over what we were having to do.

Fuck.

I almost stopped and demanded we go back, tell Sadie we weren't fucking doing this.

That we'd find another way.

We hadn't fucked her yet because we were afraid the intensity would scare her away. Terrified of hurting her, of dimming the spark in her red eyes.

And now we were going to do just that, in the worst way possible.

In public.

In front of thousands of depraved shifters.

I yanked harder on Xerxes's leash and kicked at shifters who got in my way.

Ahead, two alphas stood in the melee, staring at Sadie, waiting for her.

The bond screamed with warning as we recognized the two alphas who had hit on her after they'd fought her in the second trial.

I licked my lips with anticipation.

Oh, how I longed to hurt them for daring to smile at her after they'd marred her flesh.

As a child, I'd been horrified by my snake's bloodlust, by the wild temperament I'd housed inside myself. I didn't want to be a monster.

But you didn't get to be what you wanted to be in life.

You got to be what you were.

After years of torture, I'd stopped trying to pretend I was anything other than fucked up. A dark void of violence that yearned to exact retribution.

That loved to hurt others.

Except for the select few that were *mine*. Those I would protect until my dying breath.

It was the only code I lived by.

Sadie pushed forward. Xerxes and I hadn't been expecting it, so we didn't stop her when she walked up to the alphas.

She tilted her head back and curled her white hair around her finger coyly.

I read her lips. She was asking about how to get into the private club. Her stature wasn't her normal haughty stance. She was acting, playing the part like I was.

The gold string burned.

Erections strained the leather pants of the two alphas who stared at her with undisguised longing, sniffing her skin and shuddering when she wasn't looking at them.

My hands shook with the need to maim.

To kill.

A low hiss rattled from my chest. The sound grew stronger the closer she stood, the longer she talked to them.

My vision flickered, and the world plunged into darkness and glowing orange heat signatures.

The alphas raised their eyebrows at her expectantly.

Kitten's shoulders slumped slightly, and she rose on her tiptoes, leaning away from their hands as she aimed for their cheeks.

Gold thread exploded, and the void snapped.

With impossible speed, I flung myself forward and tangled my fist in her silky locks.

I dragged her head back before cranberry lips could touch alpha skin and kissed her as hard as I could.

Before I could do something I regretted—like gut the men with my bare hands and fuck Sadie atop their corpses to stake my claim—I flung her back into Jax's and Ascher's hands.

The gold thread calmed but didn't stop burning.

We were all pissed.

I taunted the fuckers who dared get too close to her, mollified by the way Jax and Ascher kissed her all over and covered her with our scent.

If she were our packmate, she would reek of us and we wouldn't need to threaten others.

But she wasn't, and it was driving us all mad.

The void still screamed at me.

My leathers were too tight as blood rushed to my dick, the urge to claim Sadie a constant ache I'd come to live with.

Yanking Xerxes, I marched forward to the platform.

Visions of Kitten's lips almost touching the cheeks of the other men replayed in my head like a nightmare.

The void was all I knew.

Instead of running from it, I fell into it. Allowed it to help gird me for what was inevitable. What we were all going to do.

What happened next was a hazy blur.

I snapped a beta's femur when he got in my way.

I told the announcer who we were, what we were, and watched the man's eyes light up with excitement at a show.

Kitten glared at me, legs wide on a spinning platform, as her sheer dress did nothing to conceal her cranberry-red nipples and sweet little cunt.

Lights flickered above her, making her gold skin glow like the little goddess she was.

"You think you can kiss other men, Kitten?" I taunted her, reminding her of what had plunged me into the void.

Reminding her of the hard truth she was too afraid to accept.

She was mine.

Kitten rolled her eyes.

My dick became painfully hard at her defiance. She was such a little brat. The predator inside me always reared up with excitement when she gave me sass.

The men told her the error of her ways, all of us enjoying the way she spat fire and was completely unrepentant.

Kitten didn't kowtow for any man.

I taunted her, loving the way sparks leaped in her eyes.

Xerxes lay down on the spinning platform.

I cracked the whip.

Slammed the leather across his flesh, watching with satisfaction as the crowd roared and the omega's eyes glazed with pleasure. The whole time, watching Sadie's face. Loving the way she gnawed on her lower lip and pressed her thighs together.

The crowd screamed as thousands stared at my kitten's perfect little body.

Her unique golden skin glowed like a beacon.

It was a nightmare.

She was *mine*, yet I pulled out Xerxes's cock and nodded to the men to bring her over like we'd planned.

I cracked the whip and roared, but sent images of love and warmth to my snake on her skin.

Begged her to know what she meant to me, that this wasn't at all how it seemed. Begged her to see the truth.

I touched her. Pleasured her.

Drowned in sweet cranberry wine as I screamed to the crowd and cracked the whip, still loath to do this to my kitten in front of all these people.

We'd waited so long to take her, wanting to make it special.

Do right by her.

This wasn't right.

Her eyes gleamed with something, and the void bellowed at me to stop. That she was being pushed too far, that she was breaking before my eyes.

But it wasn't tears.

Suddenly, Sadie spat on me.

Images of love and support flooded through my shadow snake.

She winked, "Do it. You won't." She mouthed as her lips curled in a devious smile, and her saliva dripped down my face.

Relief like nothing I'd ever felt flooded through me and continued down the golden string. Fucking sun god, she was so perfect. So fucking pure. So fucking rabid.

It wasn't a nightmare.

This was a dream.

CHAPTER 41
COBRA
RUBY EYED DELIVERANCE

I screamed to the crowd, cracked the whip, and brought the club to a fever pitch, aware my jewels gleamed under the shadows.

The otherworldly beauty that had plagued me my entire life was now a fucking boon. Because *my* kitten was obsessed with me.

I could taste it on my lips when she'd spat on me.

The crowd was enthralled by me.

But all I cared about was one woman.

I nodded at Jax as he smirked back, pushing Kitten down Xerxes's cock, her head flung back in ecstasy.

Ascher knelt, spreading his legs impossibly wide behind Sadie so he was kneeling in a split, in the perfect position to nudge himself into her tight hole.

Kitten's eyes glazed in euphoria as she trembled, speared atop Xerxes. He didn't move, content to just lie there and watch as she flung her head back and purred.

From the expression of rapture on his face as he stared at her, he was as far gone as I was.

She was his savior.

I cracked the whip across his chest, rewarding his patience with our kitten.

He shuddered with pleasure.

I dragged my hand across Jax's bicep as I stalked over to our woman.

He nodded at me, a smirk on his handsome lips as feelings of awe and gratitude flooded down a golden thread.

Emotions I'd never felt in my miserable life.

Standing in front of her luscious lips, I ignored the screams of the crowd as I focused on my redemption.

Tracing fingers across her lush ruby lips, I said, "I own you. Do you understand what I'm saying?"

I stared down at my kitten, begging her to comprehend what I meant.

It was impossible to put into words the all-consuming obsession I had with her. She was my everything, and I would raze the world for her.

I begged her to see that I was sorry for every time I lost my mind and made her angry, because no matter how much I wanted to be a gentleman for her and treat her right, I was still just a savage animal.

I wasn't civil like other men. But that didn't make what I felt any less real.

It only made it stronger.

More savage.

"You are *mine*, Sadie," I snarled as I stared down at my redemption. Anger ignited in my soul at the thought of her caring about another man more than me.

"I don't care what you tell other men." I glanced down at Xerxes, whose dick was buried inside *my* cunt.

In the omega's memories, I'd watched Sadie whisper, "I love you too," back to him. It had shifted something inside me.

I didn't want her to say those words to me.

No, I wanted her to say, *You own me, Cobra, and I am fucking yours for all of eternity.* That was what I wanted.

I whispered, "I don't care if you tell them you love them. That doesn't change that you were *mine* first."

I dug my thumbnail into her bottom lip and wrenched her mouth open so I could see her pretty pink tongue. *My tongue.*

"Because, Kitten, what I feel for you is beyond love. Do you understand?"

You. Are. Mine.

I leaned closer as I promised her, "I fucking own your mind, body, and soul. Absolute ownership. You are my possession. My fucking everything."

I. Am. Yours.

I begged her to see what I was saying with my eyes, as her pretty cunt and tight ass were fucked by my packmates.

"Do you understand what I am saying?"

Sadie's ruby eyes widened as she stared up at me. Slowly, she nodded her pretty little head.

She mouthed, *I love you too.*

I'd been lying to myself; that was exactly what I needed to hear.

Something snapped inside me as I realized the implications of what she had just said to me. *Kitten cares about me as much as I care for her.*

It shattered me.

I plunged my cock deep down her throat and told her with each thrust of my hips that I loved her back. Tenderly holding her chin still, I fucked her throat.

Worshipped her.

Jax took me from behind, his warmth and impressive size a familiar weight that grounded me.

Endless pleasure burned through my senses as I was surrounded by those I cared about. Those I would do anything to protect.

They were the reason the void no longer tried to break me, the reason it welcomed me with open arms.

When Xerxes finally moved and Ascher wrapped his arms around Kitten and matched the pace, her eyes glazed over with pleasure.

Euphoria sparked across the gold thread.

We were complete.

When she screamed as she came, when I pulled back and coated my seed across her golden skin, the void whispered what I'd been unable to face all along.

I didn't own my kitten.

My kitten owned me.

And it was everything.

When we'd all stop trembling from releases that brought us to an ungodly high, the lights switched on above us, and the announcer walked back out.

He yelled things to the crowd, and the entire club roared in response, but I didn't hear what they said. I was too busy staring at Sadie. Her eyes widened with fear, and her breath caught.

Fuck. I screamed across the bond as we all realized at once that Sadie wasn't okay.

It had been too much.

Too fast.

Just what we'd been so scared of.

I drowned in the void. I'd lost myself in my anger and allowed it to fuel me forward. Fuel my performance.

What woman would be okay after what we'd just done?

I was a monster.

Before I could do anything, Sadie turned and bolted, running away from us, down the stairs in the masses.

I shoved past the announcer and sprinted after her, breaking beta limbs as I followed the growing-fainter scent of cranberry wine.

This was our fault.

My fault.

I had to make it right.

The gold thread screamed with tension, fraying at the edges as desolation and anxiety streamed through it.

The highest highs had the lowest fucking lows.

Kitten deserved to be coddled after we'd all taken her for the first time. She deserved to be pampered and given soft kisses.

Gentle cuddles and warm sentiments.

I sent endless waves of love and warmth to my shadow snake, desperate to help calm her. But she sent nothing back.

Like she was too anxious to notice.

An orgy of nulls and betas fucking moved from one stairway to another, the flailing limbs blocking the scent of cranberry wine.

I whirred around, my nose overwhelmed by the stench of sex.

Unable to track where my kitten had gone.

I hissed and kicked a beta that blocked my way, stomped on fingers.

The fucking club was a massive maze of stairs.

My vision changed to heat signatures, but it didn't make it any easier to find Sadie.

Jax growled behind me and Ascher swore as we realized we didn't know where she'd gone.

I focused on my snake on her skin, which allowed me to

get a general direction. She wasn't on the stairs and was on the floor somewhere to the right.

Choosing a random stairway, I hurried down it. We needed to find her and reassure her, make sure she was okay.

Fuck. I snapped the arm of a beta that got in my way, slowing me down as I tried to get to my kitten.

Suddenly, my shadow snake screamed with terror as Sadie sent me images of her on the floor of a bathroom with a gun to her head.

Everything went silent.

The men stilled with terror as my emotions flooded through the gold thread that connected us.

I didn't hesitate.

Grabbing the chain railing, I threw myself off the stairway, falling four stories to the ground and landing with a crunch as the floor broke beneath me.

My three mates followed.

Sadie screamed at me through the shadow snake.

The bathroom was across the club.

My jewels left my skin as I sent all my shadows streaming impossibly fast toward her.

Coalescing into one massive snake, they reached the bathroom in record time.

My shadow snakes tasted the air, sensing the world differently. But I could make out an unfamiliar alpha holding Sadie.

With a lunge, my fangs slammed into his neck, and I pumped him with my most potent toxins.

The distance to the bathroom was about a hundred yards, but it felt like forever. I sprinted with the other men, slamming open the door and stalking inside.

I wasn't expecting what we walked in to.

Sadie had the much larger man pressed against the wall, and she was driving her fist into his face with so much force that blood sprayed across her.

Hunter was unrecognizable.

For a moment, my chest warmed with pride as my little kitten beat the fucker.

She shifted to the side and revealed his exposed dick.

He tried to rape her.

My mind blanked, and I saw red.

A few days ago, we'd visited Hunter and beaten him until he was mangled and begging on the ground. I'd promised him death if he ever hurt her again.

He hadn't listened.

He tried to rape her repeated in my mind.

There were red marks on Sadie's knees from where he'd made her kneel.

The void swallowed me whole.

He would die.

Ascher grabbed our snarling Sadie and pulled her away from Hunter. He whispered softly to her, tattooed body shaking as he held her.

The bond among us screamed with rage and fear.

We picked off where kitten had left off.

Jax held the fucker's arms behind his back and ordered him not to shift, which made him stop convulsing.

The fucker said things, and I snarled back, but I wasn't aware of anything other than the bloodlust blinding me.

Xerxes didn't hesitate, his rage tantamount to mine.

He sliced the sex knife into the alpha from neck to navel.

The void welcomed me as I dug my hand into the fucker's abdomen and unraveled his organs.

He screamed, but it wasn't enough.

For what he'd done to Sadie, it would never be enough.

Everything was dark as I focused on hurting him. Breaking him. Pulling him apart at the seams till he understood what it truly meant to try to hurt what was *mine*. To fuck with one of my own.

He'd never make the mistake again.

Xerxes put a bullet through his head, but I couldn't stop pulling. Couldn't stop trying to hurt him.

He'd died too quickly.

It wasn't enough.

But I'd threatened him, and he'd hurt her.

I dropped the organs and turned to where Ascher was comforting our kitten.

I reached for her but stopped when I realized I'd mark her with the horrors of what I'd just done.

FUCK! I screamed into my head.

She'd just seen me unravel; seen the violence I'd tried desperately to keep from her.

But Sadie didn't look at me with horror. Instead, she gave me a small smile as she shook off the blood that was dripping down her knuckles.

Fuck, she's magnificent. She would have handled him even if we hadn't shown up.

I loved her.

The knowledge settled around me like a slow song, warm blanket, and toasty fire.

Jax explained how we'd threatened the alpha, although clearly we hadn't done a good enough job, and I snarled about killing the fucker.

But my reactions felt detached from myself as all my attention was on my kitten.

The realization of what she truly meant to me brought the possessive need to own her to a newfound intensity.

She was my everything.

A combination of ferocity and softness that made me want to kneel at her feet.

Suddenly, the bouncer showed up and told us we'd been invited to the private room. But I could barely bring myself to care.

My attention was still enraptured.

Kitten leaned close and praised me for killing the fucker.

I saw it in her eyes, in the way she smiled up at me, not at all scared by the fact that I'd disemboweled Hunter in front of her.

She said she loves me.

Another piece of me shattered away, irrevocably gone, as I remade myself in her image, for the task I didn't know I was born to provide.

I would be Sadie's protector for the rest of my life.

Xerxes commented that he'd technically killed the fucker, and I swallowed down a hiss as I yanked on his leash.

The omega might also be mine, and Sadie might tolerate his masochist ass, but *I* was her main protector.

She loves me.

I would prove myself better than him.

Because even though I pretended to be civil, I was still nothing more than a beast, and Sadie was my possession to protect.

Just as I was hers to own.

CHAPTER 42

SADIE

BLACK WOLVES AND KIDNAPPINGS

THE BOUNCER LED us to the back of the club, then used an enchanted key to unlock a red velvet door.

He pushed it open, and it took my eyes a second to comprehend what I was seeing. I'd expected a similar scene with flashing lights and pounding music.

It was pitch black.

Dead silent.

Ascher's and Jax's hands rested on my lower back, and I was grateful for the contact.

Something clacked to my right, and I swiveled my head.

A flash of scales.

Glowing eyes.

All light dissipated into pitch darkness. Had I imagined it?

Slurping noises and grunts.

My breaths were too loud, my heartbeat a tangible noise that pounded through me, and my steps echoed.

Skin crawling as darkness swallowed us, I could barely discern the outlines of Cobra and Xerxes in front of us, following the bouncer deeper into the abyss.

Biting down on my lower lip until blood dripped down my face, I levitated five droplets in front of my head.

I was ready to throw them at the Ortega brothers as soon as we found them, before they could draw their guns.

I wouldn't make the same mistake again.

Grunts echoed, and I whipped my head to the left.

Chains rattled.

We walked deeper into the belly of the beast.

My skin pebbled with goose bumps.

Eyes glowed, and I turned my head to the right. They were gone.

Ascher and Jax moved their hands from my lower back and instead gripped my biceps, like they were prepared to throw me out of harm's way.

My blood droplets vibrated in the air, annoyance coursing through me.

They should hide behind me.

A loud roar.

Hacking noises.

Abruptly, we came to a stop. Metal rattled, and the bouncer pulled out a glowing blue key.

He yanked open another door.

Smoke spilled out, and hazy light illuminated a small section of where we'd been walking.

Holy fuck.

To the left was a massive metal cage, and inside, a horned beast I'd never seen before growled softly.

"Through here," the bouncer said, his voice mixing with the sultry music that crooned from the room.

He gestured for us to walk into the hazy smoke but didn't enter himself.

The door slammed shut behind us.

Through the smoke, shapes took form.

Five men with dark hair and wicked scars across their faces lounged on a massive green velvet couch, cigarettes hanging from their lips, dicks out while at least a dozen women lay at their feet, fondling them and sucking.

A naked woman hung from straps on the ceiling, a microphone in her hands, head hanging back, eyes closed, as she sang a sad, sultry song.

Enchanted machine guns in each of the man's hands pointed directly at us.

This was no private club; it was a trap.

But it was the same men sketched in the don's letter—the Ortega brothers.

They smirked, cigarettes bobbing as they straightened their forearms and waved the machine guns back and forth.

Red dots traveled across each of us.

"Gotcha," one of the men drawled, eyes half-closed as three women pleasured him.

They thought they had us.

But I'd already infected them with my blood.

I flung it across the room as soon as we'd entered.

Sweat dripped down my temple as five droplets slowly traveled through layers of muscle and tissue, seeking their sources of power.

But we had a plan.

Instead of slamming my blood through their bones, attacking them with my power, and commanding them to obey, I focused on control.

If the plan was to work, they couldn't know they were infected.

We needed them acting normal to get the Black Wolves. Then I could take them over.

It was the hardest thing I'd ever done, holding myself

back when bloodlust demanded I take them over, control them, make them drop to their knees, obey me.

But this wasn't a battle.

This was espionage.

Sweat dripped down my spine as I clenched my hands into fists, my cells screaming at me as I held my blood back.

It was like trying to control a rabid bear on a leash.

My vision blurred as I concentrated.

We said nothing.

The brothers were silent, content to take their pleasure, confident that their guns had us pinned.

"We'd like to give this omega back to the Black Wolves." Cobra's face contorted with malice, and he yanked on the chain around Xerxes's neck. "He's fucking defective."

Anger radiated off him, and if I hadn't known any better, I would have believed him.

They said nothing about his request.

My gut twisted with rage for the women who were lying at their feet, black collars around their necks their only clothes, as they pleasured the men who fondled them like they were objects.

I almost lost control of my blood and screamed at them to let the women go.

Anyone could see what the fuck was happening here.

They were being used.

Sweat dripped down my brow, blurring my vision as I searched desperately for control.

My blood slipped, burrowing deeper into the men, inches from the points of no return, where I'd completely take over their free will, but we needed them unaware.

There was only one option.

I flipped on the numb.

The world went cold.

Black and white.

Hold your power back. Concentrate.

I obeyed.

It had been like holding a rabid animal on a chain that was bucking further out of my grip, but now my arm was steel, my fingers paralyzed on the numb's invisible leash.

It didn't give.

Pay attention. This is a trap. One wrong move and you're all dead.

I didn't wonder what the numb meant or how we were at risk when I had control of the brothers, just held still and waited because I could taste the danger on my tongue.

A brother grunted as he found his pleasure and gestured lazily with his machine gun across the room.

The room had a false wall, and it slowly lifted up.

It revealed eight people.

Four girls and four men holding guns to their heads.

Even numb, I felt something close to fear.

Stay still. Don't move.

Four ridiculously muscular men had darkness in their eyes and pressed the barrels to the heads of four teenage girls, who were sitting unconstrained in chairs.

Jinx, Lucinda, Jala, and Jess sat wide-eyed with fear.

Molly's warning about the dangers of the beast realm echoed through my head: *"Mind games and cunning are commonplace."*

The don had set us up.

Was this even the third trial?

Was it all a trap?

How were the girls being held in the backroom of a BDSM club? Nothing made sense.

Concentrate.

"We heard you were looking for us. How about a trade? Xerxes for these girls," one of the wolves said, his voice a rough growl, green eyes glowing bright as he stared at my omega.

Guns cocked.

I took a step forward.

STAY STILL! the numb screamed at me, and I stopped.

Infect the men. Turn their guns.

I slammed my power into them with so much force that I was left with the unexplainable knowledge that they were now brain-dead.

My fear for the girls drove me. I didn't have to speak.

Five Ortega brothers sat up straight and turned toward the girls. Arms in front of them, they aimed their machine guns at the Black Wolves.

Pull off the safety valves.

Clicks echoed.

The wolf who'd spoken before, who had his gun pressed to Jinx's head, tipped his head back and laughed. "Yes, we'd heard rumors about your abilities. But it's truly more impressive in person."

His face hardened.

"They pull the triggers and we pull ours. We've ruled the shadows of this city for five hundred years. Want to test our reflexes?"

The barrel of his gun stabbed harder into Jinx's temple.

"It was all too easy to follow you. The butler and boy didn't even put up a fight. Don't worry, it was a quick death for both of them. Little anyone can do against a hail of bullets."

Aran was dead.

They. Killed. Aran.

My knees wobbled.

CONCENTRATE.

Jinx looked unconcerned as she slowly stroked her ferret.

Jax shook with rage. Cobra, Ascher, and Xerxes stood still as statues, calculating and assessing.

"You want a trade," Xerxes said slowly. "Then let's trade. I'll go with you willingly."

The wolf chuckled. "Of course you'll go with us willingly. Only problem is you'll shoot us as soon as we release the girls. Can't have that."

I inched closer.

DON'T MOVE.

The wolf tapped his lips like he was thinking. "Yes, I do believe we'll have to kill one of the girls to ensure that you understand the circumstances." He smiled, and all four men shoved the barrels harder against the girl's temples. "But which one?"

Look at Lucinda. Focus on her.

Lucinda dragged her fingernails across her forearm, gouging herself with her fingernails repeatedly.

To anyone else, it would have looked like a sixteen-year-old harming herself from anxiety.

She's your sister.

Memories of her reassuring me she could handle herself, that she was stronger than I realized, flashed before me.

I understood.

Suddenly, the unspoken words that had hung around us when she'd told me I didn't need to worry about her seemed so loud.

So obvious.

Her fingernails dragged violently until her entire arm was a cut-up mess of flesh. Blood oozed across her arm from hundreds of cuts.

Steady. Get ready to shoot.

No one paid Lucinda any attention, just a young girl hurting herself in a stressful situation.

Her blood didn't float in the air like mine did.

Like a snake, it gathered into a small stream and trickled up her arm.

Distract them.

"We'll never let you out of this room alive," I snarled.

The wolves focused their attention on me, mouths curling into smirks and gazes glaring. "You know nothing about how this city works," said the man with his gun pointed at Jess's head.

He had a black eye, and Jess's face was covered in bruises. She'd put up a fight.

Get ready. She can't hold him long.

Lucinda's thin trail of blood crawled across the barrel of the gun and disappeared into the man's hand.

She whispered something under her breath.

Everything happened at once.

Lucinda's eyes glowed bright red, and the Black Wolf she'd infected swung his arm to the left and fired.

He blinked with awareness as his bullet traveled through the brains of his two packmates, who held Jala and Jess at gunpoint.

FIRE AT THE OTHER TWO.

I took the opening.

Pop. Pop. Two Ortega brothers fired their guns, controlled by my blood.

A smoking blue hole appeared in a forehead.

Three wolves crumpled to the ground.

The wolf Lucinda had taken over, had just killed his two packmates.

And I'd killed him.

Jess grabbed Jala and Lucinda and shoved them behind her as they scurried away from the dead bodies.

One wolf still stood.

The leader.

The bullet that I'd made one of the brothers shoot at him was embedded in a glowing wall of blue that shimmered in a circle around him and Jinx.

Enchanted shield device.

Extremely expensive and rare.

Behind it, he held the barrel to Jinx's head as he stepped backward; the shield traveling with him.

She's his only bargaining chip. He won't kill her.

Fire.

The Ortega brothers opened fire, hundreds of bullets plowing into the blue shield. None penetrated.

You won't be able to get through the shield.

"Xerxes will follow me outside this door," the wolf said as he backed up to a door against the wall. "Anyone else follows, and I kill her immediately. My shield will hold, and you won't be able to get to me. I have nothing left to lose."

He kept the barrel pressed into Jinx's head.

Don't let him leave the room. You'll never get her back.

"*Stop*!" Jax alpha-barked, and the wolf stilled for a moment.

However, he was strong, because he quickly shook it off, turning the handle of the door.

Xerxes took a step forward to follow.

DON'T LET HIM LEAVE THE ROOM WITH HER.

Bullets sprayed against the shield uselessly.

The woman hanging from the ceiling kept singing.

Jax roared and shifted into a bear. He tore at the shield, but nothing happened.

Ascher shifted into a ram and barreled headfirst, but it didn't break.

Cobra's shadow snakes slammed against the shimmering blue enchantment, unable to penetrate just like the bullets.

The wolf smirked as he twisted the doorknob. "You can't penetrate the shield. She's stuck in here with me. There's no getting in."

Jinx smirked up at the much larger man. "No," she said calmly.

The look in her dark eyes was terrifying.

Jinx smiled and said, "There's no getting out."

Jinx's jaw unhinged, and she screamed like she had the first day we'd met the don, "*Freeze*!"

Everyone froze.

Behind the shield, the wolf's gun barrel hovered where Jinx had stood moments ago.

"Do it now," Jinx said with a smile to the ferret as she crouched down and placed it gently on the ground.

The ferret shifted.

Into a man.

Suddenly, a massive naked warrior with shimmering skin stood taller than the wolf shifter.

Jinx's command wore off, and the leader swung the gun at the new intruder while he himself started to shift into his wolf form.

But the naked warrior took up the space inside the shield with his impressive muscles.

Even partially shifted, the wolf didn't stand a chance.

The warrior broke the wolf's arm, slammed his fist into his throat, and kicked out his knees.

Then, with a sharp twist of his biceps, he broke the wolf's neck before picking up the gun and shooting him repeatedly through the head and chest.

It all happened in half a second.

Finally, the warrior stomped on a silver device that hung off the wolf's belt.

The glowing blue shield disappeared.

The warrior heaved with rage, dark eyes glowing, black hair disheveled, blood splattered across his naked body. His knot and the sweet scent of licorice identified him.

He was another omega in disguise.

"Loyalty" was tattooed across his right thigh.

The ferret was a man.

I'd been right: the don had planted a spy.

Jinx gave the warrior a high five.

Across the room, Lucinda stared up at me with big eyes, tears streaming down her face.

The threat is eliminated.

I clicked off the numb.

CHAPTER 43
SADIE
DEATH

Grief washed over me in endless waves as we sat in the car driving back to the mansion.

Everyone was silent.

The omega had introduced himself as Warren after Jax had beaten him bloody for being a perverted ferret.

Now Warren sat next to Cobra, who had his jeweled hand around the back of the omega's neck in a death grip.

Warren looked repentant and had Lucinda's sweatshirt wrapped around his waist to preserve his modesty.

"I knew what he was as soon as the don gave him to me, and he was always respectful. He left the room when we changed. It wasn't weird," Jinx had argued as the men slammed their fists into Warren's stomach.

No one had listened to her.

Now we rode in silence.

The truth was a noose around our necks.

Aran and Walter were dead.

My stomach and chest burned like I'd been gutted, and I struggled to breathe. We were going back to the mansion.

Back to their bodies.

The only thing that stopped me from losing all semblance of sanity was the five brothers crammed painfully on top of one another in the back seat.

I still controlled them.

We'd decided it was the safest way to keep them constrained, because who knew what enchanted devices they had on them like the wolves.

We couldn't risk it.

Sweat poured down my face as every muscle in my body burned.

The ball was in the afternoon, and the night was just fading into a gray morning. Who even knew if we'd passed the third trial. Had there even been one to begin with?

Everything reeked of betrayal and sabotage.

Just one big setup.

I breathed through the pain.

Lucinda gripped my hand in hers, her savaged arm still dripping blood, her eyes wide with shock.

The don had warned us this world was cruel.

But it was so much worse than I could ever have imagined.

When the car came to a stop, I dragged the Ortega brothers behind me through the rain, but stopped at the entrance.

Bullet holes speckled the front door, and the ornate glass on either side had been shot out. Shards lay at our feet.

I couldn't lose Aran.

I couldn't face any of this without her.

I refused.

My hands shook so hard I couldn't twist the doorknob. No one stepped up to open it, and all of us stood on the stoop, unable to face the truth.

Eventually, Xerxes walked up and shoved it open.

Blood was everywhere.

The foyer stank of death.

Aran lay on top of Walter like she'd tried to shield him with her body, and both were riddled with bullet holes.

No one could survive that.

I keeled over and heaved bile across the gore-splattered marble.

Lucinda and Jala joined me. Jess collapsed.

Xerxes backed away.

Warren stood in the doorway, staring at the scene in horror.

The alphas didn't move.

My legs gave out, and I fell to my knees. The Ortega brothers mimicked my motion, my power still wrapped around them.

I screamed.

They bellowed.

Jinx was the only one that walked up to the bodies.

I fell forward onto my forearms, so much pain coursing through me that I couldn't cry, could do nothing, as the world fell apart around me.

The little girl knelt in front of Aran's body and prodded it.

Her head snapped up, dark eyes wide. "She's—" she whispered so quietly I couldn't hear the rest of what she said.

I heaved up bile.

Jinx stumbled backward, eyes frantic. "She's alive."

Her words penetrated.

I crawled forward through the broken glass and blood, the Ortega brothers following mindlessly.

"*Aran!*" I screamed as I collapsed atop my best friend.

Bullet holes covered her body, and every inch of pale skin was stained red. Her skin was icy, colder than snow.

She was dead. It was a cruel joke.

I shook.

"Look at her chest." Jinx's voice was far away.

Aran's chest was a mess of bullet holes.

I stared at it with single-minded intensity, refusing to blink, forcing myself to stare at the carnage that was my best friend.

Ever so slightly…

It rose.

My eyes widened, and I grabbed her shoulders, shaking her as hard as I could. "*Wake up*!" I screamed as I clawed at her gore-covered skin.

All rationality fled my body.

Ascher fell to his knees beside me. "How?"

I didn't care how, or why. I didn't give a flying fuck. All that mattered was she was still breathing.

"HELP HER!" I screamed frantically at everyone, unsure of what I was asking for, just knowing that we needed to do something.

Anything.

Sweat poured off my body, the strain of using my blood powers mixed with the acidic hope that burned me from the inside out, and I collapsed onto my back beside Aran, choking on manic screams.

Xerxes yelled something about a medical kit.

Maids ran around us.

I prayed to every god—promised myself, anything they wanted—if they would just let her live.

The Ortega brothers sprawled on the ground beside me, mindless puppets connected to my will.

Xerxes poured vials of liquid down Aran's throat, and

Ascher used tweezers to pull out the enchanted bullets that were buried in her flesh, the ones that hadn't gone straight through to Walter.

The butler's chest didn't move.

Tears streaked down Xerxes's cheeks as he worked, glancing over at Walter every few seconds.

I mourned for him.

The girls scrubbed the blood off Aran's skin, and Jax wrapped belts around her limbs to stop the blood flow.

Her chest kept moving, but she was glacier cold.

Xerxes stopped pouring liquid down her throat and started stabbing her with various needles.

Jinx helped Ascher pull out bullets.

Glass from the window breaking had left long gashes across her body. Jala, Cobra, and Jess stitched them up.

Warren handed over supplies, wet rags, and drugs as Xerxes shouted at him to grab things.

Exhausted from using my powers, I could do nothing but lie among the carnage, praying that my friend would be okay.

Hours passed.

Aran's condition didn't change.

I stared down at her face, willing her to wake up.

I swore at her. Called her every dirty word I could think of. Promised to hunt her down in the valley of the sun god if she dared leave me.

Warren said something about the ball coming up.

I screamed expletives at him until he paled and said nothing of it again.

Xerxes kept working, injecting and stabbing her, ordering maids to get different drugs from the store. They came back with bags full, and he mindlessly stabbed her with needles.

Ascher pulled out bullet after bullet, working at an exhausting pace, refusing to stop until the hundreds of shards had been removed from her flesh.

Aran didn't wake.

Time ticked by faster.

I got light-headed, sweat pouring off my face and blurring my vision, as I used my blood powers for far longer than I should have.

Everything cramped, and the world spun around me.

If there was any truth to the third trial, we needed the brothers.

I didn't release them.

There was a long, ragged breath, and someone hacked aggressively.

I turned my head to the side in slow motion, body like a starfish across the bloody foyer, toward my best friend.

Aran's blue eyes were open, and she was coughing.

For the first time, tears leaked out of my eyes, and I choked on a shallow sob. I'd never known such relief.

There were no words for the sensation slamming through me.

I crawled toward her, sobbing.

The girls cried with me.

Tears streamed down Ascher's face.

Xerxes helped Aran sit up, all of us wincing at her mangled state, the holes that still were gaping across her body.

She shouldn't be alive.

After aggressively hacking, Aran choked out, "Ow."

Everyone chuckled.

"You stupid fucking cunt," I snarled, perspiration still half blinding me as my muscles burned.

Aran held up her arms and inspected the bullet holes

covering them. "Shit." Frost radiated off her, a cold mist that crackled in the air in a white fog.

"How dare you get yourself shot like this." My voice trembled with anger as I glared at her.

"Shit," Aran repeated as she looked around with wide eyes.

Her face fell as she took in my haggard appearance.

We both knew she was powerful; even if she avoided it, there was darkness inside her.

There was no way she'd been taken by surprise by a hail of bullets. No way she couldn't have done something in that split second of gunfire to avoid them.

She looked down guiltily.

We both knew it.

I grabbed her by the tattered collar of her sweatshirt and pulled her close to my sweat-stained face. "You don't get to leave me."

Crystal-blue eyes sparked with fire as she stared back at me.

Hands tried to pull me off her, but my fingers didn't release.

"*Promise me*!" I screamed into her face, shaking her with desperation. "Please," my voice cracked with another sob.

Ever so slowly, she nodded, her mangled arms resting gingerly around my shoulders as she pulled me close.

"I'm a coward," she whispered. "My back, my mother, the fae realm. It was all too much."

I squeezed her back, and she trembled beneath me.

"But I promise. For you and the girls. I promise."

"Um, Sadie." Lucinda tugged at my arm, and I realized the pressure on my back was the five Ortega brothers hugging us.

I gagged, ordering them to get off. My mindless puppets stumbled away.

"The ball is in less than one hour. You have to go or you'll fail the third trial. Your lives are still at risk," Warren said frantically.

"Who's that?" Aran asked.

"That's Noodle, the ferret," I spat in his direction and glared at him.

I still remembered him running around with underwear on his head.

It didn't matter if the don gave him to Jinx to protect the girls like he'd claimed. The man was a pervert.

Aran swore vehemently, summing up the situation. "Why is he still alive?"

I shrugged. "He saved Jinx's life. But I think Jax is just waiting to kill him."

Warren paled.

"Do you feel alive?" I asked tentatively, unsure how my best friend seemed to be okay even though physically she clearly wasn't.

"Not really, but I don't feel dead." Aran shrugged, then winced at the movement.

Everyone stood up and looked around, taking in the fact that all of us were covered in Aran's blood and shards of glass.

We had less than an hour till the ball.

A maid, who stood next to Xerxes, holding supplies, gestured up the stairs and said, "The don delivered lots of formal wear yesterday so you could choose what you liked best. It's in your closets."

Xerxes stared down at the sheet he'd had the maids place over Walter's dead body.

I could read the question on his face. It was the same one I was asking myself.

How were we supposed to go to a ball after everything that had happened? How were we supposed to act normal after all this?

Jax cracked his neck. "Everyone is attending. The girls and Aran. We're sticking together."

We all nodded in agreement, although I grimaced down at Aran's gaping wounds.

Ascher gestured at Aran. "We need to get her a hover-chair. She can't walk."

Xerxes said something to the maids, and they scurried off.

"Sit here and stay," I ordered the Ortega brothers, my limbs shaking from the strain of commanding them.

The world wobbled around me, but I forced myself to act normal as I turned to Ascher. "Please carry Aran to our bedroom. I need to clean her up."

He nodded and picked her up gingerly.

Lucinda went to hold my hand, but Cobra picked me up before she could grab it.

"You're almost done, Kitten. You can do this," he whispered down at me. "Deep breaths," he coached.

Annoyance sparked.

"Don't tell me what to do," I said weakly.

Cobra chuckled even though his eyes were tight with concern as he carried me to the bedroom.

The shadow snake on my back sent me images of support, like I was a weakling who needed his help.

"Fuck you," I growled and sent back violent images. "I don't need your help."

"No, Kitten," Cobra whispered as the snake sent me images of love and warmth. "I fuck you."

He winked as he turned on the shower and set me down on the toilet next to it. Ascher gingerly set Aran on the floor next to the tub.

Cobra left the room, but Ascher lingered.

"Are you sure you don't need help?" Ascher asked as he narrowed his eyes at my sweat-stained face and trembling muscles.

I would never forget how he'd dug the bullets out of Aran for hours, working tirelessly to save my best friend.

"Thank you," I whispered, my voice catching.

Ascher's tattoos rippled across his torso as he dragged his fingers along my hairline and leaned over me.

"Princess, you understand I would do anything for you?" His amber eyes were dark with intensity as he stared down at me.

"Anything," he repeated.

I swallowed thickly. He'd thrown himself face first off a platform in the fae realm to cushion my fall with his body.

"I know, Ascher. You've shown me."

The big man fell to his knees in front of me, his tattooed biceps lying on either side of the toilet as he caged me in.

Intoxicating pine filled my nose.

Ascher said, "I know I've fucked up in the past, and I have some anger issues, but I would go to the ends of the earth for you, Sadie."

He swallowed thickly, flames leaping across his throat. "You're my everything," he said as he dragged a colorful knuckle across my lips.

The man who was closest to my age, who'd already killed hundreds of people, trembled before me.

"I love you, Princess," Ascher whispered as he leaned his head forward so our foreheads touched.

He inhaled deeply, and his voice broke. "I love you so

fucking much it terrifies me. I don't know how to fucking take care of someone. Don't know how to be something for anybody. But I want to be someone for you."

I held my breath as a buzzing sensation spread across my chest.

"Princess, I want to take care of you. I want to love you."

I exhaled shakily. "I love you too, Ascher. I want to take care of you too."

Ascher grabbed my face and slammed his warm lips against mine, consuming me with his mouth until all I knew was the heady scent of pine.

He pulled back. "Even if you have crazy fucking friends."

I chuckled and punched him in the arm weakly. His hands on my face were the only things keeping me sitting upright as exhaustion pummeled through me.

"Please, don't mind me," Aran drawled. "Should we all do celebratory anal now that we've established we all love each other?"

Ascher chuckled as I groaned with embarrassment.

Why was she like this?

"No, please continue," Aran said. "I only puked in my mouth six times." She lowered her voice in a mockery of Ascher's. "*Oh, baby, I love you so much I just wanna protect you and have your babies and be a little bitch for you.*"

"Oh, fuck off. You're just jealous," Ascher said as he rolled his eyes at her.

Aran continued, "Is he always this sappy? I've literally never been so embarrassed for someone in my entire life. Did you plan that speech beforehand, because if so, I'm *ashamed* for you, man. You should have come to me first."

"All right, I'm leaving," Ascher said as he stood up and looked down at me. "Are you sure you're okay, Princess?"

The corners of his mouth pulled up in the cutest little smile, like he was still buzzing from telling me he loved me.

Sun god, he was adorable.

Six feet, five inches of tattoos, muscles, and sweetness.

I grinned back at him, then rolled my eyes dramatically. "We're fine. I'm not some weak woman that's going to collapse as soon as the men leave." I pushed my shoulders back and projected competence. "Go get ready. We don't have time."

With furrowed brows, Ascher backed out of the bathroom, eyes on my face as he waited for me to ask for help.

"Love you," he said softly, a red tint staining the tops of his golden cheeks, before he turned around and hurried away.

My heart soared as my body gave out on me at the same time. I slumped forward, exhaustion hammering through me.

"So we both agree that was cringy and embarrassing?"

"Oh, shut it," I groaned at Aran as I collapsed onto my knees in front of her. "No, it was sweet," I mumbled under my breath defensively.

"So how are we going to do this?" Aran asked, changing the subject with a weak chuckle, her face a bloodstained mess.

Her gore covered my skin.

"The only way we can," I said with conviction, then awkwardly shoved her body over the lip of the tub into the shower.

Immediately, I collapsed beside her.

We lay together under the hot spray, fully clothed,

unable to move, limbs tangled, as I handed her a bar of soap and we both scrubbed weakly at our skin.

The water ran red around us.

"I think we're cursed," I said through gritted teeth as I picked shards of glass out of my skin, the water stinging unbearably.

Aran haphazardly rubbed soap across the holes still dotting her flesh.

Bloody limbs entangled in the tub. It was a morbid scene.

"You know, they banned guns in the fae realm because enchanted bullets don't just kill shifters."

Aran paused.

"They also kill fae."

Droplets slammed against the tub and hammered our sensitive flesh.

Aran turned her head and pulled her hair back to expose her neck and ears. "My hair wasn't the only thing that changed when I took off my mother's toe ring."

It took me a second to process what she was showing me.

Then it hit me. "Well, fuck."

Aran slumped against me, and I patted her head as we lay dejectedly under the warm spray.

Thinking about how everything was messed up, thinking about how nothing was what it seemed.

Because Arabella Alis Egan, fae princess, rightful ruler of the fae realm, heir to the seat of death, daughter of the fae queen, wanted fae monarch, didn't have fae ears.

Aran wasn't fae.

CHAPTER 44
SADIE
THE BALL

THE DON SENT A LIMO.

Lights flashed, reporters yelled questions about our trials, and betas screamed and reached out as we walked down a gold silk carpet that spanned three city blocks.

The entire financial district was blocked off for the celebration.

To the casual onlookers, we were glamorous starlets walking into a large domed glass structure.

An ultraexclusive event held by the don every equinox.

The birthplace of the new alphas who would rule Serpentine City.

My knuckles were white as I pushed Aran's floating hoverchair. It was the only thing keeping me upright.

Sweat dripped down my forehead as my vision wavered, the five brothers trailing behind me mindlessly.

It was the reason I'd forgone makeup.

But I wasn't completely giving the middle finger to ostentatious demands of authority.

My shimmery gold dress had an open back, and it

contrasted nicely with the dark circles under my eyes and the strain on my face.

Aran wore a black suit that covered her body, but the gashes across the side of her head from the bullets were bloody and uncovered.

Betas standing along the roped-off carpet winced when Aran levitated by.

She grinned and flipped them off, unruly blue hair a wild mass of curls that were stained red with blood.

Déjà vu hit me as I remembered a fancy carpet in the shifter realm.

Back then, Aran had preened and smiled at the attention, and I'd stood beside her all dolled up and pretty.

An outsider would remark how far we'd fallen.

Aran flipped off a reporter and rolled her eyes when the woman gagged at the jagged cuts across her face.

It felt like we'd risen.

We both were buzzing with the accomplishment of staring pain, fear, and endless odds in the face.

We'd survived certain death.

Adrenaline, exhaustion, and confusion warred inside me, and I felt slightly euphoric as I rode the forbidden high.

Aran sucked on her enchanted pipe, blowing electric-blue smoke into the face of the outraged reporter.

I giggled as I "accidentally" slammed the hover chair into her legs.

Aran laughed and held the pipe up to my lips so I could take another drag.

Sucking on the stick, my vision smudged from smoke and fatigue, I pushed us forward in a wobbly line.

"Sun god save us," Cobra grumbled as he tried to take the floating chair from my hands.

"Don't you fucking dare," I snarled as I held on to the handles like they were a lifeline.

Aran cussed him out with an impressive vocabulary, and Cobra gave up, realizing we were mentally unwell and dead serious.

"Has she always been like this?" Cobra asked Lucinda.

My sister sighed heavily. "One time after Dick beat her super bad, she suddenly had the urge to take up carpentry. She cut down an entire tree and was convinced she was going to build herself a chair."

Cobra gaped. "No shit."

Lucinda sparkled in her strappy white gown. She smiled sadly, clearly thinking about our awful childhood, as she rubbed at her cut-up forearm. "She didn't make anything, just dragged the tree through the forest, shouting to the moon goddess."

Aran pressed the pipe to my lips, and I took another long drag.

Cobra stared at me like he'd never seen me before, and I shrugged.

The closest solution I'd found to dealing with trauma was the pure elation of starting a new hobby project and not completing it.

Aran's hoverchair slammed under the rope, into an unsuspecting beta.

Lights flashed, and people screamed as Aran launched out of her chair and tried to strangle the man.

"Shhhhh, shhhh," I giggled as I shoved the pipe into her mouth and dragged her back into her chair. "It's okay, sweetie. He didn't mean to get in our way." I patted her head as she settled back down.

The beta we'd just plowed over, and attempted to assassinate, gaped at us in outrage.

"Don't be such a man about it." I huffed over my shoulder as I pushed past him back onto the endless golden carpet.

Aran rolled her eyes. "Everyone is so sensitive these days. I only choked him a little. You just can't do anything anymore. It's ridiculous."

I nodded in agreement. "I'm worried for the next generation. They're too soft."

Said generation (four girls ranging from twelve to eighteen years old) stared at us with concern as we attempted to race them down the carpet.

"You're just afraid to lose to a woman in a hover chair!" Aran screamed as we sprinted past them in a blur of speed and agility.

Of course we won.

We were the best.

"Pussies!" I flipped them off as I came to a screeching halt in front of the golden doors of the venue.

Two Mafia betas stood in tailored suits and sunglasses, blocking the door with their muscles and glowing guns.

"Loyalty" was scrawled across both their foreheads.

I stated the obvious. "Tacky tattoo placement."

The corner of one of their mouths twitched, and I took that as my signal to unload my grievances.

"What is with the endless carpet? Are you trying to kill us all from cardiac arrest before we arrive? Is that secretly the third trial?"

They didn't respond, and Aran generously handed me the pipe for another long drag.

After a deep inhale, I got up into the face of one of the betas and blew out smoke slowly, enjoying how he tried not to cough.

It really was a very powerful show of dominance.

"Have you ever used that gun, buddy?"

His eyebrow twitched.

We both lunged for it at the same time, but before I could disarm him and shoot him in the face for refusing to answer me, large hands that smelled like chestnuts wrapped around my neck and dragged me away.

"Jax, Sadie, Cobra, Ascher, and Xerxes. We're on the list. Also, we brought our family with us." Jax growled.

The betas didn't argue, just opened the doors for us.

"You better open that door for me, buddy," I snarled at the beta I'd wrestled with.

"All right, you've officially lost your privileges," Jax said as he pushed me into the venue. "You need to release the brothers now. You're not acting well."

Ascher grabbed the hoverchair.

Aran screamed, "I'm being kidnapped!"

Ascher rolled his eyes.

Cobra and Xerxes pulled the brothers forward (for show, we'd put handcuffs and chains on them), and I narrowed my eyes at Jax. "Is this your way of saying I'm not pretty?"

Jax narrowed his eyes back. "What?"

"Don't answer that," Jess said as she walked up beside him. Her green-black hair was plated in a braid and matched her velvet dress.

"I think they should stop smoking that pipe," Jala said with wide pink eyes, her hand clutched in Lucinda's.

Jinx rolled her eyes. "What, you don't enjoy two women acting like complete lunatics?"

"Don't test me," I hissed at her.

Jax closed his eyes and tilted his head back like he was praying to the sun god.

A full-blown smile transformed Cobra's face. "Kitten, did you just hiss?"

"Sadie, release your control of the brothers," Xerxes snapped as he tugged at my hair and omega-whined with displeasure. "Do it now."

Alpha instincts reared inside of me, and I obeyed.

Instantly, the crushing weight that had been driving me into a mindless state dissipated.

My legs buckled with relief, and Jax caught me.

I gasped slowly, suddenly aware that we were standing on the edge of a massive dance floor, and that I'd been acting crazy.

A few dozen shifters were present, and they twirled expertly as a live band played a classical tune.

The entire ceiling was glass, and the gray skies above were bleeding into the darkness of night.

It was like walking into a storybook.

Elegance, refinement, and decadence were the words that popped into my mind.

Aran's hoverchair wobbled as she lunged at Ascher.

Behind me, the Ortega brothers were face-planted onto the floor—I'd been right about leaving them brain-dead.

Xerxes and Cobra looked unconcerned, dragging them by chains across the floor.

"Aran," I hissed as my friend weakly mimicked stabbing Ascher in the kidney with a knife, as I wrestled her back into her chair. "Just pretend to be okay for a few hours," I whispered as I held her.

Aran's body was sweaty, her crystal eyes clouded with pain.

She wasn't present, lost in a pain-and drug-induced delirium.

Xerxes had stabbed her with at least thirty different needles.

"We can kill them all later," I promised, and she stopped

struggling against me. "You just have to be a spy for tonight. You have to be discreet."

Aran's blue eyes twinkled, and she grinned like a maniac. "We'll take them out later?"

I nodded conspiratorially. "On my cue. Just wait for it."

Mollified, Aran relaxed back in her seat and promptly started snoring.

"Should we be worried?" Ascher stared down at her with concern.

"Probably," I said.

Suddenly, the doors opened behind us, and Warren entered. "You need to bring the brothers to the don immediately. He's at the high table directly across the dance floor."

"Don't tell us what to do," Cobra snapped at him, and Jax growled with agreement.

"Why did you have to come with us?" I asked as I glared at him. "I thought your role was to be a perverted ferret."

Warren sighed heavily and dragged his hands through his hair. "I told you, I was assigned by the don to protect the girls. It's my first mission." His annoyingly sparkly skin glistened as he sent a boyishly pitiful glance at the girls.

"How old did you say you were?" I asked.

"Eighteen," he mumbled as he focused on his shoes. "I just shifted."

"Oh cool, I'm also eighteen. I'm going to get tested soon." Jess beamed at him like she'd just made a friend.

"And I'm sixteen, Jala's fourteen, and Jinx is twelve," Lucinda supplied helpfully as she also smiled at the boy like she was smitten.

I shared a glance with the men. None of us liked how much the girls were fawning over him.

We had to kill him.

Warren had the decency to look embarrassed as he said, "I know. The don was worried about your safety."

Lucinda had the audacity to giggle and bat her eyelashes at him.

I opened my mouth to give my sister the sex talk, and the all-men-are-trash talk, when a beta with a gun in his waistband and sunglasses cleared his throat. "The don will see you now."

Cobra and Xerxes charged ahead, dragging the brothers across the dance floor as shifters continued to twirl around us, completely unconcerned by the violence.

My skin prickled.

The beast realm was a terrifying place.

We came to a stop in front of a raised dais, where the don lounged casually in a golden chair.

He had a cigarette in his lips, betas with guns surrounding him for protection, and a bored expression on his face.

'The Ortega brothers," Cobra sneered as he kicked one of the limp bodies on the ground. "They're still alive. Mostly."

The don kept smoking his cigarette but didn't say anything.

Clarissa walked up to stand beside us, a bloodied man limping behind her in cuffs.

She fluttered her eyes coyly at the men and gave me a death glare before turning to the don. "Here's Carle Fruya, the beta weapons dealer from the wanted list."

The don said nothing.

Suddenly, six betas walked forward from seemingly out of nowhere.

"Please, I have contacts. I have an entire network I can give you," Carle begged the don, his dark eyes frantic.

The betas pointed their guns at our prisoners.

Six pops rang out in synchrony.

They killed them all.

The music kept playing; the shifters kept twirling in their sparkly dresses, and the don didn't even blink as he slowly smoked his cigarette.

Blood splattered across the glistening white floor.

The now-familiar stench of gunpowder and burning steel filled my senses.

A shiver rolled up my spine.

The shifter realm had been terrifyingly cold and the fae realm savagely bloodthirsty, but the guns in the beast realm were downright sinister.

Everyone stood in front of the dais, waiting.

Finally, the don waved his hand, and five stunning women in blush-colored dresses floated in front of us.

Divine sugary scents wafted off them, and their features were doll-like in their perfection.

They were omegas.

The girls blushed prettily and smiled up at my alphas as innocence radiated around them, their scents and demeanors begging an alpha to wrap them up and protect them.

Indescribable pain twisted in my chest.

I took a step back.

My heartbeat was loud in my ears, and I knew what the don was going to say before he said it.

"You will pick a female omega to complete your pack and bear the next heir. You will choose tonight or—" the don arched his eyebrow, not needing to finish his sentence.

The threat was apparent.

I didn't wait to see what they said, just discreetly grabbed Aran's floating chair and dragged us away.

Aran passed me the pipe, and I took it with shaking fingers.

It was amazing how when you'd thought you'd hit rock bottom, there was still farther to fall.

CHAPTER 45
SADIE
GHOSTS RETURN

I SAT in the corner of the room.

Yes, stealing a plate full of hors d'oeuvres and devouring them while facing the wall was not a healthy coping mechanism, but I was too exhausted to care.

Instead of wallowing in depression because the men were falling in love with a pretty omega female, I'd chosen the classier path.

Eating and staring at the wall while I planned their deaths.

Sure, they'd all said they loved me, but that meant nothing at the end of the day.

I loved bread, or a good book, but I wouldn't die for it.

Love didn't mean the men were going to choose certain death at the hands of the don.

I wasn't irrational; I understood they had lives and responsibilities they couldn't forsake.

It just sucked for them because it would be the last choice they ever made.

I wasn't going to graciously let them go, or some annoying weak woman bullshit.

I'd made a plan.

It was simple—if the men chose an omega after telling me they loved me, I would shoot them in the face.

They were dead.

If they really loved me, technically, they'd want me to kill them for betraying me.

It made perfect sense.

I sighed heavily. It sucked that I was going to have to kill all four of my lovers later tonight, but someone had to do it.

What was the alternative? Let them be with another woman? I scoffed aloud.

The only thing more depressing than my upcoming very tragic quadruple homicide was my best friend's erratic behavior.

Aran had promised to "hunt down our prey" and had hovered off, which was concerning if I bothered to think about it.

Which I didn't.

Last time I'd seen her, Aran was spinning around the dance floor with a small circle of beta females who were taken by her manly charms.

I hoped she found true love.

Cause all I'd found was pain, heartbreak, and a small case of acid reflux that I thought was stress induced. It was likely from the four pieces of food I was trying to swallow at once.

I'd also faced the wall because I'd spotted Warren twirling Jess across the dance floor, and it had filled me with an un-sun-godly level of rage.

Everything about the boy pissed me off: (1) he was a ferret, (2) he had manipulated the girls, (3) he ate underwear, (4) he had sparkly skin that I was definitely not jealous of, and (5) once again, the underwear.

It was obvious he sucked.

I shoved another piece of food that was labeled "mini meat delicacy" but was 100 percent a small hot dog into my mouth. I wondered if Cobra was hissing at the omega girls and showing off his pretty jewels.

I'd kill him first.

He'd want that.

Emotions screamed across my shadow snake, but if I imagined the snake being smothered, I was able to tune it out.

I needed time alone to eat hot dogs and plan their deaths without them interfering.

What else did the universe want from me?

I'd had group sex in a BDSM club in front of thousands of screaming shifters.

Been assaulted in a bathroom at gunpoint, enslaved five men with my blood, and had to watch the girls almost get murdered.

I thought I'd lost my best friend, and now *my* men were being wooed by perfect omega girls.

They hadn't even followed me.

Sure, I'd slipped away before they'd realized, smothered my connection to the shadow snake, and hid behind a massive house plant in the corner of the room. Yes, I hid behind a buffet of food that concealed my scent, but it was still the *principle* of it all.

Wasn't love always supposed to find a way?

No one had found me.

Therefore, they were all dead.

I curled in on myself and debated having a nice, long cry, but something about a meltdown seemed so gauche.

Either I was *that* bitch, or I wasn't.

And *that* bitch didn't cry over men; she enslaved them

with her blood powers, laughed as they cried, and killed them for betraying her.

I ate another hot dog.

A horrifying realization hit me: Was I becoming a villain?

I do look good in black.

"Are you okay, sugar?" Molly asked, and I screamed with surprise, choking on a hot dog at her sudden appearance.

"No," I answered honestly after I'd spent five awkward minutes trying to swallow.

Her impressive muscles bunched as she looked down at me with a sad smile. "This realm will do that to you."

I opened my mouth to explain how actually the pain had started a decade ago, back when my "master" had beaten me bloody for sport. I snapped my jaw shut at the tension on her face.

While it was hard to remember sometimes, everything wasn't all about me.

"Are you okay?" I asked.

Molly's eyes were bloodshot, like she'd been crying, and her tanned skin was sickly pale.

She ran her trembling fingers down her face. "No, I'm really not."

A long minute passed as we both stood in silence, the weight of our mutual grief wrapping around each other.

Finally, Molly asked quietly, "Will you come with me? I need to…" she trailed off, her hand shaking harder. "Never mind, forget I was here."

She backed away.

"No, wait." I jumped to my feet and followed after her.

"What do you need? Is someone hurting you?" I asked with confusion, glancing down at her boulder shoulders and wondering what terrifying creature could scare Molly.

"I can't. No, don't," Molly sputtered as she walked quickly away from me, zigzagging through dancing couples as the string instruments played a fast tune.

I hurried to catch her.

Something was very wrong.

At the corner of the dais, Molly spun around and whispered furiously, "Sadie, you need to leave. You need to get out of—"

"Molly, you made it," Z said with a smile as he walked up to us, going right into her personal space.

As I turned my head to the newcomer, I made eye contact with the don, who sat above us on his throne.

He stared at me with burning emerald eyes, his expression intense.

I turned back to Molly and didn't miss the way she flinched at Z's appearance.

"Stay away from her," I growled and shoved at Z weakly.

Just following Molly across the room had left me gasping for air. My vision kaleidoscoped as sweat poured down my face, and I tried to look tough.

Z grabbed my wrists easily and smiled down at me.

Staring into his dark eyes, the memory of Hunter saying Z had told him about our third trial whispered through my brain.

Oh shit.

Before I could do anything, a knife flashed through the air.

Burning pain.

Z shoved me away, and I stumbled, unsure of what had just happened.

What hurt so fucking bad?

In slow motion, I looked down.

Gore.

It lay on the floor, a small ring glowing blue on it.

Blood dripped.

My finger lay severed on the white marble ground, severed cleanly off by one swipe of a blade.

Shock set in, and I turned in horror to stare at Z, who was sneering down at me with a knife in his hand.

Molly's shoulders slumped, but she didn't look surprised.

I couldn't think.

Couldn't move.

Just stared in horror at my finger on the ground, the gaping cavity on my hand spurting blood, and the instructors who had betrayed me.

But Molly had tried to warn me.

I shivered as sweat burned my eyes, and I went to wipe it away. Warm blood spurted across my face as I accidentally brought up my mangled hand.

Everything shook as I shivered uncontrollably.

This was my limit.

What. The. Fuck.

I would have collapsed, but my knees had locked, the world spinning around me as the shock overwhelmed me.

I wasn't coming back from this.

Did I even want to?

The don's words ran through me—*"Be careful, my son. This realm is crueler than you can even imagine."*

Blood dripped from my hand as I stood there and waited.

Waited for the punch line.

The purpose of the savagery.

Waited for the fucking point to be made.

"You bastard," I whispered at Z as shock slowly wore off and unadulterated rage burned me from the inside out.

"Quinque," Molly said, her voice cracking like she regretted the words the minute they left her lips.

It hit me.

A flyer had said to speak the Latin number of the street, Fifth Street, and the High Court would appear.

Slowly, the pieces fell together.

A scarred woman kidnapped the fae queen and is wanted.

I glanced down at the low scoop neck of my dress, felt cold air kissing my skin from the open back.

My scars were stark and hideous against my golden skin.

An inappropriate chuckle bubbled in my throat. Was this why villains laughed maniacally?

I got it.

Because somehow, I was back where I'd started, covered in scars.

The enchanted ring that had disguised them lay on my severed finger on the floor.

They played me.

There was a loud bang as two figures appeared before us in a cloud of smoke, their silhouettes concealed by the rolling fog.

The music stopped.

Z smiled at Molly in anticipation, and she mouthed "sorry" at me while simultaneously looking at Z like he hung the moon, like they were deeply in love and this was a grand romantic gesture.

They'd been playing me all along.

More inappropriate laughter bubbled in my throat.

My finger lay on the ground.

It mocked me.

It didn't escape my notice that I stood alone, far apart from everyone else in the room.

The don stared coldly down from the dais.

Across the floor there was a loud hiss, a deep roar, and screamed expletives. My men and the girls were surrounded in a circle by Mafia members pointing guns at them. Z had planned it all out.

I would face this alone.

The fog cleared.

For a long second, shock settled through my bones, and my brain refused to process what it was seeing.

My neurons screamed at me that there had been an error, that it wasn't real.

It couldn't be.

Adrenaline and shock had pulsed through me so many times in the last twenty-four hours that there was nothing left for my body to give.

No emotion left to feel.

For the first time in my life, without having to flip a mental switch, I was numb.

"Hello, Sadie," Dick said casually. "Long time, no see." It was the same man who'd beaten me my entire life.

The same evil man, except massive blue crystal wings arched off his back.

Wings.

Next to him stood a man in a black cloak, and unforgettable blue eyes glowed underneath his hood. The scent of ice wafted off both of them.

It was the man who'd taken me, Aran, and Cobra to the sacred lake.

I took a step back.

The throbbing pain in my left hand was the only thing I could feel.

Z grabbed my shoulder and stopped my retreat. He flung me forward.

I slipped on my blood and collapsed to my knees.

My vision closing in on all sides, I stared blankly up at the two men.

"For what reason did you call the High Court?" Dick asked Z in the same voice that haunted my nightmares.

Z bowed his head, a smile still plastered across his face. "We have found the half-breed, the scarred woman that captured the fae queen."

Another round of inappropriate mirth burst inside me.

I was so dead it wasn't even funny. My fate lay in the hands of Dick, my tormentor, and the main antagonist in my story.

It was hilarious.

I didn't have an ounce of hope.

Dick's face reddened like it always did when he was enraged. "And what evidence do you have that this is the woman who took her?"

I nodded, accepting my fate.

But his words penetrated, and I stopped moving, gaping up at him in shock. He'd seen me in the fae realm; he didn't need evidence.

What the flying fuck was going on?

Z immediately explained, like he'd been expecting this. He pulled out a familiar syringe from his pocket and held it up.

"We'd heard rumors about a girl with red eyes from the fae realm and suspected her immediately. Molly injected her with this drug that reveals half-breed traits, and it caused her to fight extremely fast, and she had an episode where she muttered about hearing a woman's voice. It wouldn't have had any reaction if she weren't a half-breed."

Holy moon goddess. Cobra was right: my muscles hadn't looked bigger.

Disappointing.

Dick's face didn't change, and Z waved his hands more dramatically as he tried to get his point across.

"Plus, an alpha, Hunter, fought her in the second trial, and he said she threw something at him and it overtook his free will. She only survived because she commanded him to stop fighting her."

Dick's expression darkened, and Z smirked.

He knew he'd won.

"She didn't have any scars, but we noticed the enchanted ring on her finger. Heard they were commonly used for bodily concealments in the fae realm. I chopped off her finger, and look at her body."

Z spat with disgust.

He sneered at my abused form while pointing to my finger proudly.

I couldn't stop myself from rolling my eyes as I glared up at Dick.

Oh, he knew about my scars all right.

Dick and the cloaked man, apparently High Court members, stared at Z for a long time.

Nobody spoke.

The silence stretched, and I shifted at the awkwardness.

My head was spinning from blood loss, but I couldn't gather the courage to touch my gaping finger hole.

Just let the blood slowly drip out of me.

I was tired, but maybe I could still use it. *Should I fling it at Z or Dick first?*

Definitely Dick.

I couldn't take my eyes off the man that tormented me, standing next to the man who'd somehow positioned all of us in the shifter realm.

"Why did you do it?" Dick asked Z.

Molly sighed, and Z's smile fell. "Molly and I lost our

packmates last year. Without a pack, we've lost our resources and have been relegated to training new recruits." He spat when he said recruits, like it was the most heinous job possible.

"With this reward, we can afford to attract new packmates and can go back to policing the city like we should be."

Dick's eyebrows furled, his signature expression before he lost his temper and beat the shit out of a person. Or at least beat the shit out of me.

"I believe the flyer said there would be no reward."

Z's mouth dropped with confusion.

The cloaked man pulled out a familiar flyer and handed it over.

Dick read, "A woman covered in scars who is suspected of being a half-breed is expected to have kidnapped her. Contact the High Court."

He dropped the flyer onto the ground.

Dick's voice dripped with scorn. "It says nothing about a reward. It says to contact us, which you did. That is all that was needed."

He looked away from Z, eyes dark with fury, and his massive blue wings unfurled impressively as he turned to me.

I stared up at my monster.

He glared back.

CHAPTER 46
SADIE
THE THIRD TRIAL

"Fuck you."

I spat at Dick.

My saliva dripped down his leg and filled me with satisfaction.

Dick's complexion was ruddy with anger. "I see you're as incompetent as ever. Really, you got your fucking finger cut off by an idiotic alpha?"

"I see you're as homicidal as ever. Where's the belt? I know you're just dying to beat me," I mocked.

"Also, didn't that dude"—I pointed at the cloaked man who still stood beside him with his hood up—"take me from the sacred lake while you chased after him like a crazy man? Now you're working together? Must be awkward."

Dick's face reddened another shade.

He was so easy to wind up.

Dick's lips puckered like he tasted something sour. "We had a minor disagreement on the best way to raise you. I wanted to give you more time to come into your powers. He wanted to throw you into training. I was trying to protect you."

I burned with anger.

"You did a great job of protecting me." I gestured at the scars littering my body. "Parent of the fucking year."

Dick's spittle rained down, like it always did when he lost control of his rage.

"Do you not have fucking *blood powers*? Did I not beat you with a belt till you *bled*? Can you still not *see* that everything I did was for your benefit? Or are you still the same ignorant little girl?"

I blinked.

Then I blinked again.

Grabbing my head in my bloody hand, I scrambled to my feet until I was face-to-face with Dick.

"You're telling me you TORTURED ME EVERY DAY OF MY FUCKING LIFE BECAUSE YOU WERE TRYING TO HELP ME UNCOVER MY BLOOD POWERS?"

My voice was rough and ragged, a result of his handiwork.

"YES!" he screamed back.

We stood chest to chest, snarling in each other's faces.

Under the glass ceiling of an opulent ballroom, in a cruel realm filled with guns and monsters, the evils of my past slanted and twisted into something different.

Still nightmares, but maybe less evil?

I'd always thought it was weird how Dick had beaten me like it was a routine.

A chore he had to do.

He'd always get so mad at me, like he wanted me to do something but I wasn't doing it.

I'd always thought it was strange how he didn't have a motive.

He'd just given me a motive.

I covered my mouth in horror, and I took a step away from him.

"Why?" I rasped out, my blood splattering both of us as I gestured at him with my bleeding wound. "Wings?" I added weakly, not even sure what I was asking.

He understood.

Dick spoke quietly so only I could hear. "War has come to the realms as it does every eon."

He paused.

The soft splat of my blood dripping onto the ground echoed between us.

A familiar sound.

Dick sighed heavily, and for the first time, he looked down at me like he didn't hate me.

Something close to pity flashed across his face.

When Dick spoke, each word smashed across my consciousness, breaking down my psyche into smithereens.

"A champion is needed to lead the shifters and fae into battle. They are some of the strongest warriors in the realm, but they struggle to obey the gods. This champion is created using rare technology from the god realm. They are made for the singular purpose of defense, and they have to embrace their birthright and learn to lead. But first, they have to learn to survive."

I took a step away from him.

His voice rose. "She births her champions, and every eon, they have no choice but to rise."

I took another step.

"It was my job to hurt you." Dick's eyes softened, like he had feelings and wasn't a soulless monster. "It was my job to break you and build you into something stronger."

I backed away.

"I'm what you would know as an angel. We are her

soldiers. I had no choice but to serve her and to help you. She gives a piece of herself to form her champion. To save the realms."

My knees shook.

Dick stepped forward, walking toward me, not letting me get away, demanding I hear the truth.

"When you were young, you didn't hear her. You weren't showing any signs of your birthright."

"No," I whispered as my back bumped into the dais.

There was nowhere left to run.

Dick came closer. "I was desperate—I sacrificed so much for you, more than you can know. Only when I beat you, did your eyes glow red. Only then did you *finally* hear her."

A silent scream burned my throat.

"They always make more female half-breeds," Dick whispered. "A backup plan if the expected champion does not come into their power. They've failed before."

I froze.

My lungs stopped dead as I realized what he was saying.

Suddenly, Dick looked tired and older than I remembered. "If you didn't hear her—if you didn't come into your blood powers—I was told to exterminate you and try the next one. If that one failed, there were three others."

We both turned our heads at the same time.

We stared across the ballroom at the four girls: Lucinda, Jala, Jinx, and Jess, who I'd always thought of as so sheltered.

Dick's words were so quiet I almost didn't hear them. "I know how much Lucinda meant to you. It was you or her. Even though you didn't know why, I knew what you would have chosen. You would have demanded I do it to you."

I turned back to Dick.

Up close, he smelled like the ice of the shifter realm.

Coldness wafted off him in a burning wave.

And as I stared up into the eyes of my antagonist, saw the truth shining in them, my bottom lip trembled.

It wasn't fair.

Dick was supposed to be the bad guy.

I wasn't supposed to understand what he was saying. I wasn't supposed to feel a swell of relief that he'd beaten me bloody to spare my sister.

I wasn't supposed to feel gratitude.

It took a couple of tries—my mouth was paper dry—but I finally croaked out six words.

"Who is this she that you serve?"

The second the question left my lips, I wished I'd swallowed it down. Wanted so desperately to take it back.

Dick tilted his head up, and I followed his gaze.

The glass ceiling of the ballroom, which had earlier showcased dreary gray clouds, was now a midnight-black sky.

It was clear why the ball was on the equinox.

For the first time since I'd been in this realm, clouds didn't cover the night sky.

Six full moons were massive, gleaming and pale in a straight line.

So large in the sky it seemed as if you could reach up and touch them. Like they were going to crash through the clear ceiling of the glass ballroom.

"The moon goddess," Dick said.

His voice was a quiet rasp, but he might as well have shouted. Screamed the words at me. Bellowed in my face.

The voice.

The woman who ordered me when I fought.

The feeling of endless strength, emotionless precision.

The thing that made me a killing machine.

The numb.

It was the moon goddess, the woman I'd always felt an overwhelming compulsion to worship.

Endless seconds trickled by as I stared up at the luminous moons and realized it had all gone wrong at birth.

I'd never had a choice in any of it.

"What about the poems reading themselves to us?" I asked.

Dick narrowed his eyes, "What poems?"

My intuition screamed with warning, and I gnawed on my lower lip, not wanting to think too deeply about the masculine voice that bellowed riddles at us.

What could be a secret from the High Court.

Not good.

I deflected and asked, "Why did you put my description on the flyer? What does the High Court want with me?"

Dick breathed deeply. "War is coming sooner than we ever expected, and we needed a way to contact you. To help train you."

Dick reached into his pocket and pulled out a circle.

It appeared to be some type of thin golden wire, about the size of a hand. "It's a halo, a way of communicating. Just tap the air in the middle, and it will connect you to me."

The monster from my childhood held it out to me.

My fingers trembled, but I reached forward and grabbed it from him. The metal was cold against my fingers.

We stared at each other.

Not knowing how to go forward, while knowing we'd never go back.

"Stay in touch, Sadie." Dick's ruddy complexion didn't seem so menacing as he backed away.

He stopped beside the cloaked man, who hadn't spoken a word, just stood still, eyes roaming across the ballroom.

There was a loud bang, smoke, and both of them disappeared.

I stared down at the halo in my hands and slipped the gold circle over my wrist.

I'd have loved to say I'd always known, that I'd felt the truth in my bones and had a sense of the bigger picture.

But that would be a lie.

Then the reality that my finger was still lying on the floor, the High Court was gone, and Z and Molly had betrayed me crashed over me.

Across the ballroom, a circle of guns surrounded the people I cared about.

Blood loss hit me hard, and I grabbed onto the dais to stop myself from face-planting onto the floor.

As the absence of the High Court sank in, the room buzzed with tension and energy.

Molly had the grace to look at me with regret, while Z narrowed his eyes like he couldn't fathom where his plan had gone wrong.

"Ahem," the don cleared his throat.

The buzz stopped, and the room fell dead silent.

"I don't believe I gave orders to draw guns?" the don said slowly, and instantly weapons were put away.

Cobra hissed loudly.

Three alphas and one cinnamon-spiced omega flew across the floor, falling around me.

Jax roared when he saw my finger on the ground, and Cobra's skin turned black with snakes.

Xerxes omega-whined, and Ascher fell to his knees, swearing.

I couldn't do anything other than grab the dais as I tried not to pass out.

Slowly, the men turned away from me with glowing eyes and stared down Z. Their intent was clear.

"Nobody moves," the don ordered, and the command in his voice was as potent as an alpha bark but much more terrifying.

The whole ballroom froze—every shifter paralyzed by the command.

Everyone except one person.

"HOW DARE YOU!" Aran screamed, careening around the corner as she headed directly at Molly and Z.

Paralyzed from the don's words, I could do nothing but watch as my friend lifted her arms in front of her.

Two ice daggers crystalized in her palm and flew across the room, directly into the heart of the two alphas.

Crack.

Crackkkkkkk.

There was a loud crunching noise, then suddenly Molly and Z shattered into a million pieces and dissipated like frost.

Like they'd never even existed.

Aran's eyes were pitch black, her face burning with fury as she trembled with rage.

"Harness your rage, escape your cage," a man's voice said from somewhere behind her.

Aran whipped her head around, like she was searching for the voice, but there was nobody there.

The don sighed heavily, and the room buzzed with the sounds of motion and mumbles as he released all the shifters from his compulsion.

"Well, that solved that problem," the don said casually, staring down at Aran with something close to respect. "You said you were a water fae?"

Aran nodded her curly head, eyes unfocused as she stared at the frost where two alphas had stood.

There was nothing left of them.

"Everyone who assisted Molly and Z, please present yourself at the dais."

The twelve betas who had drawn their guns on the men walked forward and stood in a straight line.

The room was silent.

Then, the Don pulled out a handgun and walked down the line. Pops rang out as he shot each one in the forehead.

Their bodies tumbled off the dais.

The "Loyalty" tattoo on the don's neck twitched as he clenched his jaw with rage. "Well, even though we've had a little show this equinox, we are still here for one reason."

The don turned to his son and gestured to the pretty omegas who sat on the stage with him.

"Which one will you be bonding with tonight?"

He'd just casually shot twelve men in the head without explanation.

He'd shown us the sheer power in his voice.

There was no disobeying him.

I backed away toward Aran, wanting the comfort of my best friend as my men chose a different woman and undoubtedly broke my heart.

The gold halo was heavy around my wrist, a reminder that I was birthed for a purpose.

It's fine, you have a different life path, I tried to reassure myself, but it wasn't comforting.

I grabbed Aran's hand and turned away.

We gripped each other like we were the only lifelines we'd ever had.

She was the only person who could understand what I

was going through, what it was like for your life to crumble beneath you, over and over again.

"No," Cobra hissed. "We're not taking an omega."

My eyes widened. The blood loss was making me delusional.

"I choose Sadie, and if you can't accept that, then you'll have to fight me to the death."

Cobra's voice echoed.

Jax growled, "We all chose her a long time ago."

"You'll have to kill me before you take her from me," Xerxes snarled, and there was a sharp sound that signaled he pulled out his knives.

"We'll kill you all if you try to stop us," Ascher promised.

Suddenly, there was a pressure on my scarred shoulder, and icy fingers tugged me, so I turned around.

"Look at me when I say this to you," Cobra snarled roughly.

I blinked as I stared up at him.

Suddenly, four men fell to their knees in front of me and bowed their heads low.

They defied the don.

They chose certain death for me.

"You can't," I whispered as my eyes burned and moisture streaked across my cheeks, as blood loss made my head spin. "He'll kill you."

Cobra's eyes glowed as he grabbed my hand and snarled, "Shut the fuck up, Kitten. I told you I loved you. What did you think that meant?"

"Actually, you told me you owned me," I pointed out with narrowed eyes. I was still slightly salty about it.

"Don't be fucking dumb," he growled. "What I feel for

you is more than love. You're my everything, and if that means I must die to be by your side. Then so be it."

My face crumpled, and my throat burned.

"But you can't. He'll hurt you."

This time, it was Xerxes who growled, "Baby girl, we're already fucking dead if we're not with you."

For a moment, I paused with horror. *Did they know about my plan to kill them if they chose an omega?*

Jax's chest rumbled, the chains on his golden braids tinkling as he shook his head. "We've told you, little alpha, that we love you. Do you think we lied?"

"Yeah, but he's threatening to *kill* you!" I snapped back, my hands shaking with fear even as their devoted words made my heart sing.

Had everyone lost their fucking minds?

I just found out my entire life was a lie and now *this*.

There was only so much a person could take.

Just because I was planning on killing them didn't mean I wanted the don to do it. That was different.

Ascher had the audacity to laugh, neck tattoos rippling as he knelt before me.

Suddenly, his amber eyes hard and voice harsh, he said, "Princess, they can try to kill us. But they won't succeed."

Great.

They were dumb.

I pinched my working fingers at the top of my nose as I prayed for patience.

Shaking my hand, I waved my hand that was missing a finger at them; blood splattered across the ground, and if that didn't sum up the vibes of the night, then nothing did.

It reminded me of what was at stake.

I yelled at them "No! Stand the fuck up right now. You

don't get to just *choose* to die for me. It doesn't work that way."

Cobra's perfect face transformed into a cruel smile.

That was my only warning.

Suddenly, he stood up, wrapped his jeweled hand around my throat, and dragged my face toward his.

Cobra whispered menacingly, "You're going to accept our love and bond with us right now, Kitten. You think you can stand here hurt and *bleeding* and tell me I can't bond with you? That I don't get to care for you?"

I rolled my eyes and 'accidentally' flung some blood on him. "Yes. That's exactly what I'm saying."

Cobra's face darkened. "I'm going to punish you later for your little act of disobedience. Understood?"

I choked on my scoff.

The. Fucking. Audacity. Of. This. Man.

"Or are you too chickenshit to accept us?" Cobra bent his massive body low so he could snarl in my face, "Are you too much of a little bitch?"

I saw red.

It took every ounce of control I had not to shift into a saber-toothed tiger and bite his cocky ass.

"Fine." I leaned forward and snarled back, "I was going to kill you anyways."

A purring hiss rattled in his chest.

"Oh, Kitten, don't talk dirty to me in front of all these people," he whispered huskily.

He really was a psycho.

"Fine, what the fuck," I growled as the anger coursing through my body allowed me to make a massively stupid decision.

Cobra gloated, a smile splitting his too-perfect face as he once again fell to his knees in front of me.

Xerxes pulled his knife out of his pocket and quickly slashed all the men's hands, and asked, "Will you bond with us, baby girl? Will you allow us to be yours forever?"

Under six full moons above a glittering ballroom where dark secrets had been revealed, in the cruelest realm, with all my scars on display, four men knelt and offered me the world.

"Just do it," Aran whispered her voice cutting through the thousands of reasons not to that echoed in my mind.

Xerxes lifted his head. "We refuse to live without you."

Ascher's voice broke. "We need you, Princess."

A low rumble echoed through Jax's chest. "Please, let us be yours."

Cobra hissed, "I refuse to go another fucking moment without you as my mate. If this is an ownership issue, I understand that I might be a tad…possessive sometimes. But I won't fucking apologize for it."

I rolled my eyes at him. "Why are you so obsessed with me?" Clearly, the blood loss was getting to me.

"Stop being so scared. It's pathetic and weak." Cobra snapped back.

He did not just call me weak.

My chest twisted with anger at the insult, and the emotion propelled me to grab the knife with my good hand.

Cobra wanted to be crazy.

I'd show him crazy.

I slashed my already bloody palm, because why not? At this point there was more blood outside my body than there was inside.

Before I could think about it, I slammed my mutilated hand against each of their outstretched palms.

A golden thread exploded through my chest.

The world remade itself in shades of shimmering jewels and an unfathomable depth of devotion.

Suddenly, the men stood up and enveloped me in a massive hug.

Of course, Cobra got to me first, and there was a brief scuffle as he snarled "mine" and tried to keep me away from the other men.

Jax growled and wrestled me out of his grip so everyone else could hold me.

Meanwhile, Cobra whispered that he was going to kill me if I ever got a finger chopped off again, and then went on about all the sordid things he was going to do to my body.

I ignored him.

Because gold was exploding in my chest and surrounding me with the endless warmth of love and devotion.

Far away, Aran and the girls cheered.

The don cleared his throat, and I sighed as I tried to push away, but the men held me tighter.

Refused to let me go.

Together, we turned to him.

Great, you acted rashly, and now you're all dead.

Instead of pulling out his gun and shooting us in the foreheads—which I was 99 percent sure was about to happen, but had decided I didn't want to live anyways without the men—the don did something even more shocking.

For the first time since I'd met him, a smile split across the don's face.

His voice boomed, "Congratulations, you passed your third trial."

I blinked.

The men were still beside me as confusion and hope strummed across the gold thread connecting all of us.

"The third trial is a loyalty test, and Sadie proved her loyalty to you in her first initiation trial. She refused to give up any information on you, even under extreme duress. Your test was to see if you'd earned her loyalty back."

We all stood in shock.

"What about the Ortega brothers?" Jax recovered first. "And the Black Wolves?"

The don shrugged. "Decades ago, the brothers worked with the wolves to steal Xerxes from the omega center. You needed a red herring, and I gave you revenge as a boon. I knew you'd handle them."

He waved his hand casually like he hadn't almost killed us, had just sent us on an easy quest.

My jaw gaped.

The don shook his head like we were hopeless. "I even gave you Warren to protect the girls. He is extremely talented."

The young boy blushed under the don's praise, and we all glared at him.

We weren't impressed.

"Clarissa, you were told in the beginning of your trial to befriend Sadie to help her adjust to this realm, since you're both female alphas. That was your loyalty test. You failed."

The don aimed his gun at the dance floor, and Clarissa dropped dead.

I grimaced.

A lot of people had been dropping dead recently, and I was starting to feel sick.

The don beamed like a proud father and gestured to Cobra.

He yelled, "Well, this is the best time to announce my

son has returned to the beast realm. Cobra is the crown prince!"

The room gasped.

Then the orchestra came alive, champagne was handed out, and everyone began to twirl around.

Missing a finger, scars on display, with a goddess inside me, I spun with each of *my* men across the glittering dance floor.

Love was more than a sentiment.

It was unwavering loyalty, even in the darkest place.

The Don

I smiled as my beloved son twirled his mate across the dance floor.

Physically, she was nothing special, but there was a fire that burned within her that I hadn't seen in centuries. A similar fire burned within the Aran boy.

I glanced across the room, smiling when I saw Jinx was glaring down at a beta soldier who was wiping at his face like he was crying.

She glanced up at me, and I tipped my hat to her. I'd been don long enough to know a soldier when I saw one.

She was going to grow into a magnificent killer.

Cobra twirled Sadie close to the dais, and I smiled fondly down at my long-lost son, who'd grown into an impressive man.

I smirked as Sadie narrowed her eyes at me over his shoulder.

I'd always known this would be their outcome.

Known since my beloved son's eyes had glowed when he'd bonded with the other men.

Known since she'd worn his shadow on her skin.

Snake's are possessive creatures. Our venom can't harm our mates, nor can we stand to be apart from them.

When Cobra bonded with Sadie–his eyes had shone white as the moon. All of theirs had.

They were fated mates.

And fate always found a way.

SADIE

HAPPILY EVER AFTER

"So, Sadie, how are you coping without your finger? How have you been feeling lately? I know this was a traumatic experience for you," Dr. Palmer said, her harsh face puckered like she'd tasted something sour.

It was her usual expression.

She was Serpentine City's preeminent therapist, and she'd been seeing Aran and me for the last couple of weeks.

Her services were compliments of the don.

"Honestly, it's been great. Xerxes and Ascher designed this special glove. Here, I'll show you."

I pulled out the fabric I always kept on me for emergencies.

"Wait for it, you're gonna love it."

After putting the black glove on my hand, I flexed my knuckles and pressed down on the button on the palm.

A wicked sharp knife sprang up where my left ring finger had once been.

"I'm actually better now in hand-to-hand combat. Makes stabbing people easier."

Dr. Palmer narrowed her eyes, and the stark lines around

her mouth became more severe. "You can admit to yourself that you miss having your finger."

I slashed the air dramatically.

"Are you not seeing this weapon? I'm honestly glad it's gone."

Aran, who was sitting next to me on the uncomfortable couch, nodded in agreement.

"Do you see how sharp that knife is? Why would she want a finger?"

Aran tapped her lip as she watched me withdraw and conceal my blade. "I've actually been debating cutting off one of my fingers so I can have one. No one sees the blade coming, and it makes a punch wickedly effective."

I beamed at her.

"Aw, I didn't know you were considering that. I could cut yours off for you."

Aran smiled back. "I'll let you know. Maybe we could do it next we—"

"No one is cutting off their finger," Dr. Palmer interjected, her usual monotone voice dripping with scorn.

The therapist closed her eyes like she was counting to ten.

When she opened them, she gestured to my tank-top-clad torso and tried a new line of questioning.

"And I see that you are still choosing not to wear the enchanted ring. How does seeing your scars each day make you feel?"

"Really great," I smiled. "I've established quite a reputation in the city. Shifters are terrified of the girl covered in scars. Makes the Mafia work easier."

Aran high-fived me.

"Yeah, you should see her on the street. Shifters turn and run when they see her. Everyone's terrified of the girl in league with the High Court and who's rumored to have a goddess inside her."

I punched Aran lightly on the shoulder with my nonknife hand. "Not as scared as they are of the fae guy who shoots icicles of death."

Red stained the tops of Aran's cheeks at the praise.

She was still disguised as a boy and had garnered quite a fan club in the city. Mostly beta women, and a few men, who were taken with her "fae" charms.

Dr. Palmer took a long sip of water and mumbled something about needing a raise.

"Fine," the therapist snapped and turned away from me.

She raised her hand. "Now, Aran, have you stopped sleeping in bed with Sadie now that she's in a pack relationship with four men? Since you're just her friend?"

The therapist narrowed her eyes at us.

She thought we were secretly in a relationship and couldn't understand our dynamic (she didn't know Aran was secretly a girl; that was confidential information above her clearance).

"No," Aran said as she looked at me and grinned. "I can't fall asleep if I'm not in the bed with her. I tried once, and it was awful."

Dr. Palmer scowled. "You are aware that is not healthy, and you're avoiding your personal problems by relying on Sadie. Which is unsustainable. Also, you're hindering her romantic relationships as well as your own."

"What possible relationships could I have?"

Aran laughed at such a ridiculous idea.

The one-hundred-thousand-credit cream had worked wonders for her itching, but her back still burned when she was turned on.

Plus, it didn't help that she was a wanted monarch on the run and disguised as a boy.

"Actually—" I pursed my lips. "—it's nicer sleeping with her. Don't worry, I have sex in Xerxes's nest with the men, like, constantly. But the men are all big and have a tendency to lie on top of me and crush me. I prefer to go to sleep with Aran after. It's calmer."

Aran gagged.

The therapist's wrinkles pulled tighter.

She closed her eyes while breathing deeply.

When she spoke, it was through gritted teeth.

"Isn't it true, Aran, that you're still trying to strangle Sadie in her sleep? I'm not sure how that is a calm experience."

"Hey," I said in defense of my friend. "A little smothering never hurt anyone. I'm a big girl and can fight her off."

Dr. Palmer dragged her hands across her face like she was at her wits' end.

"The point is you shouldn't have to fight for your life every night. That's not healthy."

I scoffed. "Sometimes we snuggle. Don't make it weird."

Aran nodded. "Sadie's cool like that."

The therapist's voice rose, which was highly unprofessional. "Have you at least stopped smoking, Aran? I know you were using the enchanted drug as a crutch."

"I've actually quit completely."

Dr. Palmer's eyes widened with surprise, and her face softened for the first time during our appointment. "Wow, that is actually very impressive, Aran. I'm proud of you for facing your—"

She stopped talking as Aran pulled out her pipe and took a long draw.

"Just kidding. I can't go ten minutes without it."

Dr. Palmer's eyebrow twitched.

A few minutes later, we were walking back into the mansion.

"I don't understand why she kicked us out. That was so rude," Aran said with annoyance as we entered the foyer.

I threw my hands up in agreement. "I get it—we're not perfect—but she doesn't have to be such a bitch about it? Like what does she want me to do, cry all day because I have terrifying scars and a cool knife? Sorry I'm not lame."

Aran nodded aggressively in agreement. "Exactly. Like okay, I'm not perfect. Sometimes I smother people in my sleep. It happens."

"And what bugs me is she gets so mad about you doing enchanted drugs. Meanwhile, she's always drinking coffee. Make it make sense."

Suddenly, Jinx appeared at the top of the grand staircase. "You guys are back. Would you like me to collect your coats?" Jinx asked with a soft smile as she bowed her head low.

For a split second, we stared at the girl.

"*Lucinda*, young lady!" I bellowed. "Stop infecting Jinx with your blood and making her play butler."

"She wanted to do it! Don't be such a mom!" Lucinda yelled back from somewhere upstairs.

Still, Jinx's entire body relaxed, like she'd been released from a mental persuasion.

She glared at us. "I'm trying to practice breaking free of her hold. You two ruin everything."

With that, the young girl whirled and marched away.

"Where is Jinx? We were going to practice breaking Lucinda's hold," Cobra said as he appeared from the hall.

"That is not appropriate." I glared at him.

"Aran, Sadie, look!" Jess and Jala said with excitement as they ran around the corner with knives in their hands.

"Ascher and Xerxes were teaching us hand-to-hand combat, and we learned how to roll and stab someone in their kidney!"

"Aren't you all supposed to be in school?" I asked with confusion.

"Nah, Jax said we could take the day off to work on self-defense. He says we need private lessons if we're going to keep living in this realm." Jala grinned.

Jax appeared around the corner with the stack of paperwork in his hands that we had to complete after each Mafia assignment.

From the other door, Xerxes and Ascher appeared with a bruised and bloody Warren trailing them.

"They're having us practice on Warren," Jess said as she grinned at the bloody boy.

Warren smiled back, and Xerxes slammed the hilt of a knife into his stomach so he doubled over.

"We're helping train all of them," Ascher said as an explanation, but we all knew they were just torturing the perverted ferret.

The don had demanded Warren stay with the family and accompany the girls to school in ferret form.

Now that Cobra had been revealed as the prince of the city, there were more threats on their heads.

"Why are you guys already back from therapy?" Jax asked. "I thought you still had another hour."

I waved my hand at him dismissively. "She let us out early."

Aran nodded. "We think Dr. Palmer's intimidated by our prowess. Which we get."

Jax looked at us in disbelief. "I feel like that's not it."

"Anyway, I'm going to go take a nap," Aran said with a yawn as she trudged up the stairs.

I followed after her and said casually to the men, "I think I'm just going to hang out in the nest. Come see me when you're done with training."

The sudden silence in the room was loud as all the men understood what I was saying.

A few hours later, I rode on top of Xerxes on the fluffy bed while Cobra took me from behind, Jax filled my mouth, and Ascher watched from the corner while stroking himself and yelling instructions.

Soft snow fell around us, and a warm fire crackled.

When we were all sated, we cuddled under the fluffy blankets, basking in the scents of cinnamon, frost, chestnuts, pine, and cranberries that filled our nest.

Alphas rumbled with contentment, and Xerxes shifted into his kitten form so he could lie on top of all of us and also purr.

The gold string strummed with love as we snuggled, and I marveled at how lucky I'd gotten.

The gold halo still hung around my wrist. The other day, a mirage of Dick had appeared in the center, informing me he would contact me in a few weeks.

I hadn't discussed the revelation with anyone, and if they mentioned it, I played it off. Only Lucinda recognized the polished, winged version of Dick.

But she hadn't pried.

I'd assured everyone that I would explain when it was time, and they respected my decision.

We'd had enough trauma to last a lifetime.

For now, we had time to just enjoy each other, to just enjoy the present, before we looked to the future.

Suddenly, the doorbell rang, and Cobra stirred.

Aran hollered that she would get it.

I closed my eyes as I hugged my men tighter, and I pushed my concerns down into the abyss at the back of my mind because, for now, life was perfect. We fell asleep in a cocoon of love and support.

I woke up in the middle of the night to fingers around my neck.

"What the fuck are you doing?" I grumbled and slapped at icy hands.

Cobra snarled quietly. "You're mine now. You *will* wear my collar."

My eyes snapped open at his words, and I looked down. It took a moment for my eyes to adjust because only the soft glow from the fire lit the nest.

When they did, I gasped.

A leather choker was wrapped around my throat. Attached to it was a long silver pendant that hung between my scarred breasts, all the way to my waist.

I picked up the shiny gold heart at the end of the chain and brought it close so I could read the inscription. Two words were engraved on each side.

Cobra's Property.

I flipped it over.

My Kitten.

"Absolutely not."

"You're my mate," Cobra snarled back, like that made everything okay.

I raked my hands over my face tiredly. "Fuck you. Then why don't you put a collar on all the men?"

"Because it's different. They're not my kitten like you are," Cobra said in a "duh" voice like *I* was the one being dumb.

I growled and flung myself at him, not sure if my plan was to choke him or just beat him up.

Bodies groaned as we wrestled across them.

"Go back to sleep, you two," Xerxes rumbled tiredly.

I hissed with annoyance, "Cobra is trying to make me wear a collar."

Xerxes's eyes shot open.

A few moments later, Xerxes restrained me across Cobra's lap as the psycho spanked me.

Cobra whispered reverently as he massaged my backside, "I told you I would punish you for fighting me at the ball."

"He did tell you that," Xerxes said casually like they weren't both being completely irrational. He tugged at the long chain around my neck and whispered, "Baby girl, you're going to count for us or we're adding ten more."

Cobra's palm smacked my ass, and I groaned with pleasure.

Then he trailed his hands down the cursive letters I'd gotten tattooed down my spine. *L. O. Y. A. L. T. Y.*

It looked pretty badass, if you asked me.

Of course, all the men had gotten theirs tattooed across their necks for maximum effect, even Ascher, who'd just placed it over his existing flames.

I'd picked my back because it was covered in a patchwork of scars. My skin told my story, and I wasn't forgetting the past, because I was done hiding from it.

Instead, I was making something new.

Cobra spanked me harder, and I growled, "Fuck you both." But the bond strumming between us told a different story.

"We love you too," they chorused back as Xerxes yanked on the chain and Cobra spanked me.

Afterwards, when we all collapsed satiated, Jax pulled me against him.

The big man scooted me between his legs and whispered, "Are you okay love? Were they too rough with you?"

"Nah, it was fun," I said sleepily as chestnuts surrounded me.

Jax gathered my tangled hair in his hands and gently plaited it.

Ascher sat up with a cheeky grin. "I'm good Jax, thanks for asking." He rolled over, so he was pressed against me.

I giggled at his antics.

Jax's warm fingers traced across my neck and sent delicious tingles down my spine.

Since I lost my finger, he'd appointed himself in charge of doing my hair. I told him I could still do it, but he would hear nothing of it. As a result, I constantly found myself tugged against the big man as he braided my hair.

Now, I melted against Jax as he lay my hair down gently and and peppered soft kisses across my forehead.

In his arms, I was warm and loved.

"Aw, I want a kiss too," Ascher whined, his tattooed hands grabbing playfully at us.

The three of us laughed as we snuggled together.

Not wanting to be left out, Cobra and Xerxes pushed themselves close, so we lay in a giant pile.

In the shape of a star, a gold string connected our pack.

Love held us together.

Forever.

I wouldn't have it any other way.

ARAN
ELITE ACADEMY

THE DOORBELL RANG.

"I got it!" I yelled, not wanting to disturb Sadie and her men.

My best friend deserved some peace, especially after everything. Her missing ring finger was a constant reminder that those fuckers had hurt her.

The darkness in my soul rattled against its cage.

Pausing with my forehead pressed to the wall, I breathed in smoke from my enchanted pipe.

You killed them. They're gone.

I willed myself to remain blasé and to calm the monster—that I'd come to identify as myself.

As I descended the grand mahogany staircase, inhaling smoke with each step, I fingered my sweatshirt pocket.

Caressed the smaller finger-length pipe Ascher had gotten for me.

Again, the doorbell rang.

What rude fucker was calling at midnight?

I gritted my teeth as my monster snarled louder, banging against its steel cage.

Another pause, another long, deep drag. Any stimuli threatened the carefully desensitized state that I'd worked so hard to create.

The space between my shoulder blades itched.

Breathe in smoke for five seconds, hold five seconds, breathe out five seconds, pause five seconds.

Repeat.

A storm howled outside, and rain slammed against the brick structure.

Thunder cracked.

With a falsely constructed sense of ennui, I opened the door, and the night storm echoed throughout the dark foyer.

"What do you want?" I asked calmly.

Silhouetted in the dark was a massive figure. Taller than the door with layers of muscles that could only be used for one thing: war.

Sucking in smoke, I pushed the door shut in its face.

Step one to being cold and callous: You don't engage in basic impulses like fear. You react to nothing.

Survival of the unfeeling.

Crack.

The massive *thing* slammed a hand against the door and stepped past me into the mansion.

"Are you Aran?" a baritone voice growled as the man flung the door wide.

Wet shoes squeaked on polished marble. Pouring rain traveled on cold wind and slammed against the both of us.

I focused on my cage, fortified steel bars, until the slightest rattle of emotion was silenced by a prison. I assessed in a hazy inhale of smoke that if the creature was asking for me, it wasn't a threat to the others.

I relaxed my shoulders. "Who's asking?"

Lightning flashed.

And illuminated a towering male with a brutal scar slashed across his eye.

Long hair dragged in a wet braid against the marble floor, and a tailored suit stretched across an impossibly muscled figure.

Twin opal fangs protruded from red lips.

"I'm asking," Lothaire growled, voice dripping with anger.

He wasn't used to being questioned.

"Ah, Lothaire, the vampyre. I've heard of you." I nodded and sucked in smoke, presenting a lazy, uncaring figure.

I'd done more than hear.

I'd watched him bow to my mother under the dual suns of the fae realm.

Watched him attack Sadie on the hot sand of a gladiator stadium. Watched him proclaim her unworthy as he attempted to drain her blood.

He'd stood witness to my atrocities.

Said nothing, just observed, as I'd ripped out my mother's beating heart and consumed it.

The cage rattled.

My back burned as the slur "WHORE" festered on my flesh, an enchanted penance for a wrong I hadn't even gotten to commit.

Lothaire had bowed to my mother.

Smiled at her.

Breathe in smoke for five seconds, hold, breathe out, rest. Repeat.

Why is he here?

Lothaire's singular eye flashed like the storm that raged against us.

He spoke as if he read my mind. "A power anomaly was

detected in this realm on the equinox, and rumors are that a man named Aran was responsible."

Lothaire took another menacing step forward. "Are you Aran? I won't ask again." His voice dripped with warning.

Thunder boomed.

The mansion shook.

I took a long drag of my pipe and focused on feeling nothing and expressing nothing. Being nothing.

After all, Lothaire had planned this visit for that very purpose, to unnerve me.

But the one class I'd succeeded in above all else, beyond what I should have, was battle analysis.

Lothaire had come at midnight, in the height of a storm. Entered without invitation. Stepped into my personal space. Said nothing of why he was here, just cryptically demanded my name. Demanded I answer him.

I took another long drag and sighed heavily.

Somehow, everything was war.

Small skirmishes, allies, foes—all with changing allegiances—and every player possessed an agenda uniquely their own.

Game theory at its finest.

But how could I respond and best him when I didn't know his motive?

The facts I knew: He called me Aran, he referred to me only as a man, he was referencing the event three weeks ago when I'd killed Sadie's attackers, and he'd come at night with the purpose of unsettling me.

Plausible deduction: He wasn't here for the fae queen, and he wanted something of me that I wouldn't want to give.

Exhale smoke, inhale calm.

I shrugged. “I’m not the person you seek. Don’t know anything about a power anomaly. Why are you here?”

First rule of game theory: You don’t give away information.

A threatening rumble filled the foyer.

He stalked forward.

Fuck.

I’d miscalculated. Game theory assumes all actors are rational.

Without warning, Lothaire slammed his fangs into my neck.

Stabbing pain, then exquisite pleasure blinded through me, and the enchanted wound on my back burned like I’d been set on fire.

I bit down on my lip to stop from screaming.

Lothaire stumbled away from me, wiping blood off his mouth. His voice was raspy with surprise. “Who are you? What are you? Why are you so powerful?”

Shit. I’m a few wrong moves from him figuring out I’m not even Aran, that I’m Arabella.

I rolled out my shoulders slowly, like I was stretching. Like the wound on my back wasn’t filleting me with agony.

Nonchalantly, I said, “Water fae. I’m a cousin of the monarchy. Aran Egan.”

In a battle, the best lies were those closest to the truth.

Lightning cracked, and highlighted Lothaire’s harsh features.

His lips pulled into a smile, and his scar puckered tight across his missing eye. He stared down at me with unnatural stillness as he crowded my personal space. “Are you sure you’re fae, Aran Egan? You have quite the power in your blood.”

My face was a blank mask, eyes dead, muscles permanently relaxed with boredom.

With haughty male arrogance, I rolled my eyes. "Obviously I know who I am. I'm Aran, cousin of the royal family, and water fae."

My body language screamed that his question was preposterous.

Lothaire smiled like he'd won the war.

"Perfect. Congratulations, Aran Egan, water fae, you've officially been enrolled at Elite Academy."

My mask fell. "Excuse me?"

"This is a highly coveted institution and I expect you to perform rigorously." Lothaire's smile transformed into an outright snarl.

Thunder boomed.

"Classes start tomorrow."

Before I could protest, reanalyze the situation, and decide the best path forward, Lothaire grabbed my arm. "We leave now."

Flames exploded. And we disappeared.

To be continued

Read the beginning of Psycho Academy at blog.jasminemasbooks.com.

Also, please leave a review on Amazon! It allows me to keep writing books.

See you at Elite Academy!

Sadie & Aran's stories will overlap and continue together in the next books ;)

ABOUT THE AUTHOR

Jasmine Mas loves writing about Alphaholes and kick ass girls that bring them to their knees.

She attended Georgetown University and the University of Miami School of Law. She is a lawyer who loves hanging out with her readers, drinking 5 iced coffees a day, and trying to convince her husband that ancient aliens exist.

Sign up for updates and bonus content on the Cruel Shifterverse straight to your inbox at

blog.jasminemasbooks.com

Hang out with her on Social Media
TikTok: @jasminemasbooks
Facebook: @JasmineMasBooks
Instagram: @jasminemasbooks

THANK YOU

Special thank you to all my beta and ARC readers! Also, thank you to Lyss Em, you are an amazing editor.

Also, thank you SO MUCH to everyone who decided to give the Cruel Shifterverse a chance. ❤

Finally, thank you to my mother, who prefers happy cowboy romance books, but has spent hours doing the final proofread of each book with me. Every time I brought up a sex knife, or had them do drugs, I laughed thinking about how you'd get mad at me. And then, (*chefs kiss*) you did. You are my biggest inspiration ;).